1482

T3-AKD-788

D

HARRY
GOLD

LEE COUNTY LIBRARY
107 Hawkins Ave.
Sanford, NC 27330

ALSO BY MILLICENT DILLON

FICTION

Baby Perpetua and Other Stories

The One in the Back Is Medea

The Dance of the Mothers

NON-FICTION

A Little Original Sin:
The Life and Work of Jane Bowles

After Egypt:
Isadora Duncan and Mary Cassatt

You Are Not I:
A Portrait of Paul Bowles

Out in the World:
The Selected Letters of Jane Bowles (editor)

The Viking Portable Paul and Jane Bowles (editor)

HARRY GOLD

A NOVEL

MILLICENT DILLON

THE OVERLOOK PRESS
WOODSTOCK · NEW YORK

First published in the United States in 2000 by
The Overlook Press, Peter Mayer Publishers, Inc.
Lewis Hollow Road
Woodstock, New York 12498
www.overlookpress.com

Copyright © 2000 by Millicent Dillon

All Rights Reserved. No part of this publication may be reproduced or
transmitted in any form or by any means, electronic or mechanical,
including photocopy, recording, or any information storage and
retrieval system now known or to be invented without permission in
writing from the publisher, except by a reviewer who wishes to quote
brief passages in connection with a review written for
inclusion in a magazine, newspaper, or broadcast.

Library of Congress Cataloging-in-Publication Data

Dillon, Millicent.
Harry Gold : Harry Gold, a novel / Millicent Dillon.
p.   cm.
1. Gold, Harry—Fiction. 2. Espionage Soviet—United States—Fiction.
3. Manhattan Project (U.S.)—Fiction. 4. Spies—United States—Fiction.   I. Title.
PS3554.I43 H37   2000   813'.54—dc21   99-086844

Manufactured in the United States of America
First Edition
1 3 5 7 9 8 6 4 2
ISBN 1-58567-012-X

To my brothers, George and Robert

HARRY
GOLD

WHENEVER I THINK of Harry—which I do less and less often these days—I see him on a subway train from Queens to Manhattan, approaching the mid-point under the East River.

I see the lights blinking, and in the dimness he seems to be in the process of switching. Before the mid-point, he is in one life. After the mid-point, in another. And in the moment in between, there is a strange sound, a hum, a mild roaring, like the reversal of a tide, a change of pressure in the air, in the ears.

At Thirty-Fourth Street, Penn Station, he exits from the train, carrying his little black bag. He plods up and down stairways and through tunnels until he finally emerges in the great central hall. Taking his place on the long line at the ticket booth, he waits patiently. He requests a one-way ticket to Philadelphia. When his train is announced, he goes to the gate and gets on line. At last an official appears. When his turn comes, he shows the official his ticket and is allowed through. He climbs aboard the train with some effort, as the steps are high for his short legs. He walks through the aisle crowded with soldiers sitting on packs, with civilians sitting on suitcases. He walks through that car into the next car, and then the next, almost to the end of the train. Just as the signal is given for the departure, he swings down from the high steps onto the platform, and walks into the waiting darkness.

Hiding in the shadow of a pillar, he listens to the sound of the engine overcoming momentum. He sees the acceleration of the figures in the windows, passing him by, faster and faster. He waits until he sees the lights of the end car blinking in the distance. Then he makes his way to the gate. The official is gone. He slips under the chain.

In the great central hall he takes his place on line at the ticket booth. It is the same booth he has been to before. He knows he could come back and back again and still not be noticed. He buys a ticket to Boston. He goes to the gate. He gets on the train to Boston.

N OW THAT THE switch has been thrown, now that Harry's daily life is in abeyance, he doesn't feel as if something has been taken away from him, but rather that everything has been restored to its rightful place.

He has watched the others fill up the seats in the car, and in the process has made sure that no one has followed him. Even though he knows that no one sees him, he is a stickler about being cautious. It is a little like taking out double insurance. He has examined each passenger in turn, noting how they chose their seat, whether they looked around first, if they averted their eyes, if they appeared like someone trying not to be noticed. He has paid particular attention to how each passenger stowed his luggage. There are, he is certain, many things to be learned from luggage. Reassured, he has settled into his journey to Boston.

Through the dirty window glass he sees another train on the next track overtaking his train. The two trains have synchronized in time. Passengers are reading on the other train, passengers are falling asleep, passengers are talking, just as on this one. The inhabitants of the two trains are mirror images of each other, leading parallel lives in adjacent traveling rooms. Suddenly, the other train pulls ahead. In an instant the faces, the bodies, are gone. Vanished, just as Klaus has vanished.

When he gets to Boston, he hurries out with the other passengers, leaves the station, walks three blocks, and doubles back. It is not yet time to make his visit.

9

In the waiting room he has coffee and a doughnut and then another doughnut. He purchases a Boston paper. He glances briefly at the news, before turning to the sports pages. It looks as though it's going to be a St. Louis series, the Cardinals against the Browns. He follows the Phillies, of course, no matter that much of the time they are in the cellar. They are his hometown team. He also follows the Yankees, hoping they will lose. He hates the Yankees, who won the Series last year. They are like bullies to him.

Again he checks his watch. It is not an action of impatience, only of precision. It would never occur to him to think "I could be doing something else instead of this," or "I could be somewhere else instead of here." Each moment is simply in transition to the next, a part of a necessary sequence.

After he has read the comics, he gets up and goes over to the wire trash can. He is always careful not to leave remnants of his presence out in the world. He has trained himself to do this through long years of practice. As he is about to drop the paper into the can, he sees, half-hidden by other papers and candy wrappers, the cover of a *Life* magazine. He makes an exchange, his paper for the *Life*. Then he goes back and seats himself on the bench where he has been waiting.

He doesn't know why he took the *Life*. He doesn't even like *Life*. The editors and writers are always exaggerating in one way or another, presenting what they call the "larger picture." And indeed, once he begins to leaf through the magazine, there comes to him a familiar rumble in his stomach, a tremor of dissatisfaction. Nothing in his life measures up to what is pictured in these pages.

Take this ad showing a woman standing before a white cottage with blue trim, surrounded by a white picket fence. Inside the picket fence, on a plot of grass edged with pink and yellow and orange flowers, are a dog and a young child playing. The woman is smiling. The child is smiling. Even the dog is smiling. "Women want homes like this," the ad says, "not just a house but a home where you have time to relax and enjoy life."

Not mine, the thought comes. No dog, no white picket fence. In the face of such absolute certainty as to what women want out of life, the home of Louisa and Doris and Dan has been deemed inadequate. He closes the *Life*. He checks his watch. He gets up and leaves the waiting room and boards the bus, still clutching the *Life* in his hand.

He has been given orders to appear at the house of Klaus's sister, Lottie.

There he is to assert himself. He, who always disappears so easily into the woodwork of daily life, must make his presence known boldly, must demand, must insist upon attention. Where is Klaus? Why did he suddenly drop out of touch without notice? He has not shown up at their scheduled meeting, nor did he appear at their alternate meeting. Y has said that he is concerned that Klaus is having second thoughts. It must be made clear to Klaus, Y has emphasized, that there are to be no second thoughts.

When he gets off the bus, he searches for house number 363. He walks past it; he goes around the block; he comes to it again. It occurs to him that this street is a little like the street in Philadelphia where he might have gone, the twin of this journey, the one not taken. Here, like there, each house has its own tiny front yard. Pots with plants, the bicycle of a child, a child of six or seven. (Just the age of Doris and Dan.) He walks up the path to 363, mounts the two steps, and is on the landing. He has chosen the appropriate moment, not too early, not too late for his mission.

As he waits for an answer to his ring, he anticipates that he will see in the sister the shining red-blond hair, the intense blue eyes of the brother. But it is a woman of another description entirely who opens the door. She has brown curly hair, shoulder length. Her eyes are a deep, dark brown.

"He's not here, I'm sorry," she responds to his inquiry in her accented English. Everything about her is soft, her voice, the way she stands, so receptive, waiting.

"Are you expecting him?"

"No." She hesitates. "He usually comes once a month, around this time, but I doubt that he's coming this month."

"He might come, though."

"No, I don't think so."

"He might call you."

"It's possible, but I don't think so."

"Just in case, I'll come in and wait a little bit, if you don't mind." He sees the startled look on her face as he brushes past her. It is not like him to push past a person, especially such a soft person, to enter into her home uninvited. Yet this is what he has done.

From her eyes he can tell that she cannot decide if she should be afraid. He may have pushed his way in, but anyone looking at him could never judge him as threatening. But then it is not Lottie that he is supposed to threaten. Does she know about Klaus? No, it is not possible. He would never endanger his sister by letting her know what he is doing.

"I'm almost sure he's not going to call." Her deep-set eyes are even darker than before, so dark they could pull you right in, if you were inclined to be pulled in. "He said something about having to go out west—"

"So then I will have waited for nothing. I'll take the chance, with your permission," he says and smiles a soft reassuring smile. "I'll just wait here quietly. I assure you I won't be a bother."

Soon he is in the living room, sitting on the couch, and she is serving him coffee. She looks distracted, even nervous, but clearly she is not in a panic. Perhaps she is thinking, In this country such things happen. A man comes to your door and pushes his way in for news of your brother. Maybe this is the way people behave in America. After all, she has not lived here that long; she could think that way.

"I know Klaus is very anxious to see me," Harry offers. "Our lab has just found the solution to a technical problem that would be of great interest to him. I understood that he might be here today." He does not elaborate on how he came to this understanding.

"But as I told you, I'm sure he's gone out west somewhere—"

At the sound of a child crying, she jumps up and hurries out. He can hear her comforting the child in the next room, saying over and over again in her soft voice, "Poor baby." Minutes pass and the crying has subsided. He hears her footsteps in the hallway, but then almost at once the screaming starts up again.

Shortly, she reappears with the child in her arms, flushed and whimpering. She offers the child a bottle but he pushes it away. She lifts him to her shoulder and pats him on the back, but he breaks out in a loud cry. She gets up and walks around, trying to soothe him. She sits and offers him a bottle. Again he refuses it, stretching out his legs stiffly, screaming even louder. Harry is unnerved by the sound, and at the same time oddly irritated. To him the crying has an element in it of being forced, of being willed.

Frantically, Lottie offers the bottle and this time the child accepts it. Sucking on it, he lolls upon her lap, his legs rolled out in a kind of abandon. She is looking down at him with a tender smile, as if he were a prince, Harry thinks, and she a servant, grateful to accede to his every whim. He cannot rid himself of the thought that the child has used the crying to demand attention. And what if that is so? he rebukes himself. What concern is it of yours?

He is about to ask whether she has any idea where out west Klaus might have gone, but Lottie puts her forefinger to her lips, picks the child up and carries him out, her hips swaying softly. Harry gets up and goes to the window, pulls back the white lace curtain, and looks out into the street. No, there is no one standing there, watching.

He looks around the room. On the mantel are several photos. One is of Klaus and Lottie. It must have been taken some years ago. He looks so young, untouched, as if he had no sense of what his life would become. She looks even younger and softer. But the long curly hair is the same, the tender smile is the same.

"I hope he can sleep for a little while," Lottie says as she returns. "He's been waking up at night, and he's just over-tired." She asks Harry if he has children. Two, he says, twins, age six.

"That must have been hard when they were little. What did you do when they both cried at the same time?"

He has not thought of this before. "It was difficult," he says.

She nods and they sit in silence. "I think if he hasn't called by now, he's certainly not going to, so—"

There is a knock on the door, and she jumps nervously. At a second knock, she gets up and hurries into the entryway. Harry rises slowly. He never likes to move fast, especially not now when he is preparing to confront Klaus. But it is not Klaus. It is another man. Watching her from the living room, as she stands close to this man, almost touching, Harry knows it is not her husband either. He has been told that she and her husband are separated, that the husband is in California. But he would have known in any case that it was not her husband, by the way she stammers and then whispers, by the way she smiles and then looks down.

She leads the man, who is tall and dark, into the living room, and introduces him as Norman Sly. Harry gives his name as Raymond, the name Klaus knows him by. Lottie offers them coffee; the two men decline. The three sit in silence, a silence that Harry refuses to break. He sees Sly looking at her, she trying not to look at him.

"Cool today," Norman Sly says.

"Yes," she says.

"It's supposed to get warmer."

"I hope it does."

Harry can hear the longing in her voice, a longing to be alone with this man. What does she see in him? That he's tall, dark, and sly. But what do I give a damn if he is sly or not sly? I have come here for one thing only, to reestablish contact with Klaus.

Lottie looks at her watch. "If he hasn't called now, I'm sure he won't be calling."

"I'll wait a little longer, just in case." Just in case she is lying.

Harry can feel the pull between her and the man, palpable as a magnet pulling upon iron filings. She jumps up and says, "I should go in and check on the baby." After she leaves, Norman Sly crosses his legs; he shakes his dangling foot. Then he gets up and follows her. Harry can hear them whispering in the adjacent room.

He picks up the *Life* magazine and opens it to a photo essay, "*Life* Goes Back to Penn Station" by Alfred Eisenstadt. The photos are of couples, soldiers and their girls, sailors and their girls, kissing goodbye in front of the gates leading to the trains. I have been at those very gates, Harry says to himself.

Leafing through the pages, he comes again to the ad showing the woman in the white cottage with the white picket fence and the dog and the child. "Women want homes like this, not just a house but a home where you have time to relax and enjoy life. And in these days of tired bodies and disturbed minds, it's good for one to think now and then about the new kind of house *you* will have after victory . . ."

As Lottie and Norman Sly come back into the room, Harry gets up slowly. He has seen on her face an expression of need so naked, it is like a cry. "I can't wait any longer. Please see that Klaus gets this," he says, handing her an envelope. It has been given to him, if all else failed.

"I'll be glad to give it to him, when I see him, but I have no idea when I'll see him."

He is outside on the pathway to the street, when he hears her call after him. "Your magazine. You forgot your *Life*." He sees, by the expression in her eyes, that she is already in the process of forgetting him.

O NCE AGAIN HE is on the subway, going under the East River. He gets off at Thirty-Fourth Street, enters Penn Station, purchases a ticket to Philadelphia, gets on the train to Philadelphia, and gets off the train to Philadelphia, just as it is departing.

He returns to the long line at the ticket booth.

"Where to?" asks the clerk, as he reaches the front of the line.

Harry hesitates.

"Hurry up," the man behind him complains. "We don't have all night. Don't you know there's a war on?"

He turns and looks at the huge board, high up at the center of the vast room, with the list of arrivals and departures. McKeesport, he sees. "Round trip to McKeesport," he says.

"The nine-thirty is a local," the ticket clerk volunteers. "If you wait another hour you can get the express and it'll get you there two hours earlier."

"I'll take the local," Harry says, picking up the ticket.

"Finally," the man behind him mutters.

Once the train is well on its way south, once the tenements have been left behind—each lit window, so close, you can be a witness, briefly, to the life inside—once the suburbs give way to the dense darkness of open fields, he finds himself wondering. At work, that is to say, at his lab work, he is capable of absolute concentration on the matter at hand. Stray thoughts simply do not intervene. But now, in the full easiness, even slackness of his self-chosen mission, he allows himself to speculate as to why Y hasn't contacted him since he reported on his trip to Boston weeks ago. Of course, he would never ask Y, Why? Still, slumped in the green plush seat, elbow on the grimy windowsill, listening to the rhythm of the wheels on the track, he cannot help wondering.

Looking out the window, he sees a light in a house, then more darkness, then after an interval another light in another house, then more darkness. He turns away from the window to observe the life around him, the train life, a community of beings whose population keeps changing. At each stop he watches those getting off and those getting on. He examines their physical characteristics, the way they move, their hurrying and their delaying, their eagerness and their boredom. He also makes note of the number of beings in the car at any given point and stores the information in his brain. He has room for an infinite amount of numbers there, retrievable at will.

At the next stop an old woman with thick ankles, wearing a shabby grey coat and worn brown oxfords, falls heavily into the seat opposite him. She sets two shopping bags on the floor, one on either side of her. She closes her eyes and leans back against the seat, but after a minute sits bolt upright and begins to search in the shopping bag to her right. She pulls out a porcelain figurine of a cat, examines it, then puts it in the shopping bag on her left. She sits back, sighs, shuts her eyes, opens her eyes, and then leans over and begins to rummage in the shopping bag on her left. She pulls out an object wrapped in brown paper, unwraps it partway, and examines it. From where Harry is sitting, it looks like another figurine, but not of a cat. Then she wraps the object up and puts it into the shopping bag on her right. So she goes on, minute after minute, fussing with the contents of the two bags, redistributing them, as if she were attempting to create an exact equilibrium between the two, of weight or of value, Harry cannot tell.

A harsher grinding of the wheels is signaling that the train has come to a worn section of track. There is something lulling in this rough rhythm to Harry. He feels the forward thrust of the train and the retarding force of friction being transmitted through the wheels, up through the carriage, up through the worn plush seat, up through his spine, his neck, to the very top of his head.

His head lolls back, then snaps forward. He can hardly keep his eyes open. The woman across from him is still fussing with her packages, moving objects from one sack to the other. This repetitive motion too is contributing to his sleepiness. At this moment, he does what he has never done before on any mission. He lies down. The seat next to him is unoccupied so he spreads himself across that seat as well as his own. He scrunches his knees; he curls his back. This is one of those rare occasions when it is an advantage to be small.

As he succumbs to sleep, he becomes aware of a sharp yet musty odor stinging his nostrils. He forces himself to ignore it. Waking once, briefly, he realizes he has turned in his sleep and is on his back. In this position he feels awkward, exposed. He turns again, so he is lying half on his side, half on his stomach, his face pressed into the malodorous green plush.

At the first rays of light coming in through the grimy window, he is startled awake. His first thought is that he has neglected his duty, gone AWOL in some terrible moment of forgetting. He sits up hastily, searching for his little black bag. It is right where he placed it, next to the window. He has not been derelict in his duty. On this mission he has no duty, so how could he be derelict? Outside he sees telegraph poles, a road, fields, shrouded in morning mist.

Not surprisingly, considering the hours spent in his curled up position, he is stiff. He shakes his head, he rolls his shoulders, he stretches out his legs, careful not to disturb the old woman who is still sleeping. But she must have heard him moving around, for she opens her eyes and sits up. It occurs to him, with a shock of recognition that is almost electrical, that she is looking at him, no, not simply looking; she is staring. Moreover, she is laughing.

As if shot out of his seat, he jumps up and hurries to the end of the car, opens the door, steps onto the swaying platform, opens the second door, and stumbles into the next car. He falls into an empty seat, his heart pounding. Luckily, despite his terror at being seen, he has not lost his sense of the necessary. He has brought his black bag with him. He grasps it with both arms, holding it tenderly, like a child. This bag has contained so much information over the years, as well as his toothbrush, pajamas, etc. But this time it will carry no information. Today he is a courier to no one, from no one.

The craziness of his current enterprise suddenly appalls him. He can hardly believe what he has chosen to do. Why McKeesport? He doesn't know anything about McKeesport. He had to take a trip somewhere; he saw the name McKeesport; it seemed a good place to go. He has the strangest sense of having fallen into a dream, except that most of his dreams have to do with being late for an appointment. On this trip he doesn't have an appointment with anybody, so how can he be late?

Maybe, the thought suddenly comes to him, the old woman wasn't really looking at me. Maybe she was half asleep and confused me with someone in her dreams. That could explain the staring, and the laughing, he tells himself. It was nothing but an aberration.

He settles back in his seat, still cradling his black bag in his arms. Opposite him is a grey-haired man, reading a newspaper. His clothes are rumpled and worn; his shoes are badly scuffed. The man puts down his paper, takes off his glasses, and looks at him. Harry cannot believe his eyes. *This man, too, is staring at him.* So it was not an aberration. Facts are accumulating, are being generalized to a principle. A laugh is about to erupt from him, too. Harry sees the open mouth, the coated grey-pink of his tongue.

He jumps up and rushes out of this car into the next. He makes his way down the swaying aisle. He caves his chest in, he hunches his shoulders, to be even smaller. On either side of him, as he passes—he does not look but he is sure this is so—still others are staring at him, grinning, winking, nudging their seatmates. In a prelude to judgment, he has been made visible.

The train slows to yet another stop. In the morning light he sees no station, only the smallest of structures, a half-open shed at the edge of a field. It stands there as an invitation, a promise of a break in a cycle gone wildly awry. He clambers down the steps. Almost immediately the train moves again. He watches it, waiting to be sure that no one else has gotten off the train. No one has.

This town—and a very small town it is—has become his destination. He knows nothing about how life is lived in such a place. Indeed, it seems to him, without subways, without high buildings, without the constant background of noise and bustle so familiar to him, to be a desolate place, stripped of vitality. He passes a wooden house, then a small store, then two other wooden houses, then another store, then more houses. The stores are shut. There is silence everywhere. It is seven A.M. on a Sunday.

In one shop a yellow cat sleeps on a ledge in the front window. Inside are a few tables and chairs and a counter. Above the counter is a sign advertising Coca-Cola. To the left of that is a hand-written menu on a chalkboard: "Burger, 35 cents. Shake, vanilla or chocolate, 15 cents." It is reassuring to know that at least here they eat, they sleep, they go about their business as elsewhere. He wonders what time they will open, if indeed they will open at all on Sunday. He is incredibly hungry.

A large tan dog is sleeping on the sidewalk. Now and then it shivers in the morning cold. Warily Harry walks out on the street, going the long way round him. He has a longstanding fear of dogs, stemming from an occasion when one snapped at his heels, yapping and barking, threatening to betray his presence. It is their acute sense of smell that makes them so dangerous, as far as detection goes.

Detection—the word rings like a bell in his brain. He has not forgotten what has happened on the train. If he thinks about it—No, he will not think about it. He looks behind him. Nothing has altered. The cafe is still closed. The tan dog still shivers. He, himself, is feeling a chill. He hopes he is not coming down with a cold.

Just ahead of him is a small white church with a green roof and a tiny steeple. He wouldn't mind sitting indoors for a few minutes until the town awakens. The front door is locked but he sees that a side door is open. Inside is a plain room with wooden benches arrayed before a raised platform. He takes off his black fedora and sits on a back bench. He finds the silence and plainness comforting. These bare wooden walls evoke a long-lost stillness in him, the stillness stretching out in time and he being stretched out with it, as if he were being pried open. (None of this has anything to do with belief as belief, he reminds himself. After all, this is a Christian church, and he is a Jew, though by no means a practicing Jew.)

There comes to him the thought that Y has not contacted him because of what happened in Boston, because of something that he did or did not do on that mission. He recalls each instant of his visit: his knocking on Lottie's door, asking for Klaus, the entering, the brushing past her, sitting in the living room drinking coffee, hearing the sound of the little boy screaming, her getting up and going out, his getting up and seeing the photo and going to the window—No, there was no one watching outside—her bringing the child in, comforting him, giving him a bottle, his own aversion to the way the child's legs lolled with such self-satisfaction, her going out, carrying the sleeping child, her hips swaying, her coming back in, the knock on the door, the appearance of Norman Sly, his detection of their secret life, his waiting, his getting up and leaving her the letter.

He did just what he was supposed to do on the mission: He waited for Klaus and finally, when he didn't come, he gave Lottie the envelope for him.

But here in this silent room where people pray to be forgiven for their sins, his justification sounds false. He is forced to confess that when Lottie and the Sly man came back into the room, he allowed extraneous things, things meant for daily life, for ordinary life, to intrude on his secret life. Moreover, he did this in the home of the sister of Klaus, a man who above all people keeps his secret life intact. Indeed, Harry sometimes thinks Klaus is a being without a personal life. If he could be like him, so impersonal, so precise, he would be. But in Klaus's sister's house, he was nothing like him. He let in her need, as if it were a cry he was hearing. He saw her longing; he could not refuse it. That is why he left, that is why he did not stay on, and perhaps, in so doing, he missed Klaus.

It didn't make any difference that I left, he tries to reassure himself as he gets up from the bench. He probably wasn't coming, just as she said. Besides, there is no way that Y could know any of this, so it can't be why he hasn't been in touch with me. All I told him was that I went there and I waited, and Klaus didn't come, so I left the envelope with his sister. (And if Klaus didn't come, will he never come? Is it possible that he has seen him for the last time?)

Out in the street he puts his hat squarely on his head. Though the sun has risen higher, there is still no sign of anyone stirring. He passes a house with a white picket fence. From within he hears voices—a man, a woman, children. In a moment they will come out on the street. Will they look and

laugh as he goes by, as those others did on the train? He cannot stand the
thought of such raw exposure.

Soon—only a short distance further on—he has left the town
behind. On either side of him are mounds of red clay. The road is no
longer macadam, but a reddish-grey hard-packed dirt, its surface barely
softened by the melting frost. He feels the warmth of the sun on his back.
He is sweating in his heavy overcoat. He hears a bird singing. Otherwise
there is only silence.

At the top of a rise, he looks south. Before him is a broad plain
stretching out to the horizon. It is an unsettling experience for him to be
a solitary figure in a landscape. In the city he is surrounded by people, by
noise. Everyone rushes past, singly, in twos, in threes. In their rapidity, he
becomes rapid. In their business, he becomes busy. It is like a wonderful
ether through which he moves, unrecognized but vitalized.

Far in the distance he can make out a train moving toward him. It
looks like a toy, laboring through the fields. It is going north, just as he
will go north on his return journey. As he follows its progress, he has the
sensation that space here is not the space he is accustomed to. It has lost
its sense of enclosure and its clear definition—so many feet from here to
there, rigid and unyielding. It has become malleable, responsive to any
impulse of the eye and mind. If he wanted to, he could leap out into it at
any point, be here, there, at the horizon. He could, in an instant, be alongside that train, looking in through a window upon a man, not sleeping, as
he slept earlier on that faded green plush seat, but bolt upright, chatting
amicably, with others.

The train is approaching a trestle, harsh black in the morning light, its
iron members crossing and recrossing ominously. As it goes over the trestle, a shroud descends upon it, shutting out what has been and what will be,
what hasn't been and what won't be, mixing up the street in Philadelphia
where Doris and Dan and Louisa spend their days with that street in Boston
and the house of Klaus's sister. Barriers are no longer impermeable. There
is osmosis. Things, thoughts, are seeping through membranes.

Behind him is the east. Klaus is out west. Go west, young man, he
says to himself, smiling at his little joke, Horatio Alger's advice to those
who wish to make their fortune. He knows his fortune, if he is going to
have one, will have nothing to do with money. (If they find Klaus out west,
he will be sent to threaten him there. And if he refuses to threaten him?

Then what will he do? Hide? Change his name? Put on a disguise? He has never needed a disguise. Until today, he has been his own disguise.)

With a sense of fear and at the same time a sense of excitement that he is about to be loosed from all that he has been—in his daily life, in his secret life—he hurries downhill. Ahead of him, in the middle of the dirt road, lies what appears to be a large animal, dead or wounded. Harry hates the thought of blood but he is drawn forward to see if something needs to be done, though what help can he be to a large animal? When he gets up close, he sees it is not an animal but a man, curled up, not dead, but sleeping.

Clearly, a man sleeping in the middle of the road must be either mad or drunk. Or is there something in the air that is seizing people, as he was seized on the train, with a sudden and irresistible urge to sleep? He leans over the man, who gives off a terrible odor, and says, "You'd better get up. You're lying in the middle of the road." When there is no answer, he shouts a warning. "Get up! You're in the middle of the road."

"Leave me alone," the man mutters.

"You have to get up," Harry persists. "If a car comes, you could get hurt."

"Nobody's coming."

"Not now, but maybe one will."

"Who cares?" In a moment, he is snoring again.

Harry starts to walk away but then he turns and looks at the pathetic heap in the road. He goes back to him and shakes him by the shoulder. "Why don't you just move to the edge of the road? You could sleep there."

"I told you, let me be," the man mutters and lashes out with his arm, hitting Harry on the nose so hard it stings. "I want to sleep here, and I'm going to sleep here, and you're not going to stop me."

At that moment Harry hears a grinding of gears. Looking back up the hill, he sees a small truck just coming over the rise, moving rapidly. With an effort he did not know he was capable of he half-drags, half-rolls the man into the shallow ditch beside the road. The truck careens by, its brakes squealing as it veers from one edge of the road to the other.

"You son of a bitch," the man in the ditch yells.

Harry does not know if the man is yelling at him or at the driver of the truck, which is leaving a trail of dust behind it. "My hat, where's my hat?" Harry says, suddenly aware that his head is bare. In his struggle to get the man off the road his hat must have fallen off. Spying it wedged beneath the man's shoulder, he stoops and gingerly pulls it out from under him. What a mess it is, dirty and out of shape. The hat, like his hands, reeks of vomit and dirt. He must find someplace to wash the smell off.

"Hey! Where you going?" the man yells, as Harry turns and starts back up the hill toward town. "Come back and help me. I need help. Don't leave me here. You pushed me in here and I can't get up."

It's true, Harry has to admit, I am responsible for his being in the ditch. He retraces his step down the hill reluctantly, and, holding his breath, gets into the ditch beside the man and tries to hoist him out. "What the hell happened to your face?" the man says, peering closely at him. "You look like some fucking man from Mars. Green, you're green."

Harry lets go of him and stands up. Slowly and deliberately, he takes his white handkerchief out of the breast pocket of his suit jacket. As he lifts it to his face, the stench of his hand makes him want to retch. He rubs the handkerchief across his cheek and examines it. Yes, it is green. So that's why they were looking at him, those people on the train. That's why they were laughing. It's simply that the green plush seat rubbed off on his face when he slept on it, face down. It is not that he suddenly, irrevocably, became visible.

"Don't stand there like an idiot. Help me. I need help."

With a prodigious effort, accompanied by groans of "Not so fast, you're hurting me," from the man, Harry manages to get him out of the ditch and onto the road, though once he is upright, he sways dangerously. He grasps Harry's arm and belches. "Help me home."

"I don't know where you live."

"That way, down the road, that way," he gestures with his head.

Half-carrying, half-dragging him, Harry staggers forward. The man is a dead weight upon him, for all that he seems a bag of bones.

"Wait! Stop! I have to catch my breath. Goddam, I need a drink. You don't happen to have a bottle on you?"

"No, I don't."

"I didn't think so. What are you doing around here, anyhow?"

"Walking."

"I can see that. You don't have to be a genius to see that. You some spy or something?"

"What makes you say that?" he asks, shaken.

"Slinking around in your dark coat and hat—"

"There's nothing to spy on here."

"You never can tell what spies are looking for." Before Harry can say anything, he yells, "Oh, God, get me to my house. Hurry!"

Once more they go forward, lurching then stumbling, then lurching again. By now Harry is sweating profusely but he doesn't want to stop even to wipe his brow. He has achieved some measure of forward momentum with this man, erratic though it is. Together they are a two-headed, four-legged being, making limited but definite progress, up a rise, down a rise, up a rise. They reach a bend in the road. "Don't stop. There's my house. Right there."

He is pointing at a shack set back from the road, as grey and as miserable as its owner. The door, the front steps, the roof are all askew. Nothing is straight; nothing is level.

"Don't put me down here!" the man yells, just as Harry is about to deposit him on the crooked front step. "Get me there! Back there! This cramp is about to kill me."

In a feverish haste, as if he himself were about to explode, Harry drags him to the sagging door of the outhouse behind the shack, opens it and propels him in. The man fumbles with his trousers. "I can't get my goddam fly open. Help me!" Once he is unbuttoned, his trousers drop to his ankles, and he falls onto the seat. At once there is an explosion of gas, of solid, and of liquid. Harry cannot believe there can be that much excrement in one being. He smells the terrible smell. He turns away in revulsion. So this is what happens when one makes up one's own mission instead of being assigned one.

The man sighs in relief. "What's the matter, never seen no one shit before?"

Harry shakes his head, up, down, sideways. He doesn't know what to say.

"Hand me that newspaper," the man orders him. "Okay, now I'm done."

Harry drags him back to the front of the shack. "In there, inside," he groans. Harry hauls him up the one step into the room and, pushing aside two torn blankets, lays him on top of the dirty mattress of an iron cot. On his back, breathing heavily, the man holds up his hand as if he is about to make a pronouncement. "There's nothing so overrated as a fuck and so underrated as a good shit," he says. In an instant he is asleep.

Everything about this man offends Harry. His language is filthy, his clothes are filthy, he is filthy. Harry feels contaminated just being in the same room with him. If only he could clean himself up a little, but of course there is no running water in this shack, though he does find a piece of yellow soap on a splintered wooden counter. Outside, near a pile of tin cans, is a rusty pump. He takes off his coat and washes his hands with the soap under the stream of water. He wets his handkerchief, soaps it, then wrings it out, and uses it to mop his face. When he rinses the cloth out, a shadow of the green dye still clings to the fabric. He takes his crumpled fedora out of the coat pocket and wipes it with the wet cloth. It still smells terrible. He hopes he hasn't ruined it.

"No! No!" a terrible cry comes from the shack. "No! No!" it comes again.

Harry runs back into the shack to the man on the cot. He cannot believe that so powerful a lament could have come from the shrivelled being curled up before him. "No! No! Oh, God, help me," the man cries out again. His whole body is shaking. He is shivering either with cold or with fear, Harry cannot tell which. "It's okay," Harry tries to soothe him. "You're going to be okay." For an instant, he considers trying to remove some of the man's clothes, which are muddied with grime and vomit. Recoiling at the thought of such close contact, he simply places the two torn blankets on top of him. "You're going to be okay," he says again.

"Okay?" the man says feebly. As he huddles under the covers, his body is shaken by spasms. Each breath ends in a desperate kind of gasping. Then, slowly, the gasping subsides and bit by bit his breathing becomes shallower. Soon he is snoring, his mouth open, displaying the black and rotted stumps of his teeth.

Harry looks around the room taking in the detail of loose boards, rusted tools, torn curtains, and broken crockery. He walks over to the wooden counter and picks up a heel of bread lying there. It looks old but he hasn't eaten in so long he doesn't care. When he starts to chew on it, it tastes moldy, and he spits it out. He takes off his suit jacket and rolls up his shirt sleeves. In the corner he sees a rusty pail; he goes out to the pump and fills it with water. Using a brush with broken bristles, he scrubs the counter until the water has turned dark. He goes outside and throws out the dirty water, brings in clean water, and washes the chipped dishes.

When he has finished—it is not good, but it is better than it was—he rolls down his sleeves, and puts on his jacket. He is about to go out to get his coat and hat when he notices the man is sitting up, watching him. "Are you Lester?"

"Who's Lester?"

"Lester's my son."

"I'm not Lester."

"Who are you?"

"Raymond. My name is Raymond," Harry says.

"What are you doing here?"

"I brought you here. You were lying in the road."

"I'm beginning to remember now. You pushed me in the ditch."

"I pushed you into the ditch so you wouldn't get run over."

The man is silent for a moment. "So you're saying you were walking along that road and you saw me and just like that you pushed me in the ditch?"

"I told you. I didn't want you to get run over."

"I wouldn't get run over."

"Well, maybe not. In any case," Harry says, "it's been nice making your acquaintance but I have to go now."

"Where? Where you going?"

"Back to New York."

"You live there?"

Harry nods.

"All that noise. All those people. How can anybody stand it? Why don't you stay here with me?"

"Here?"

"Sure. You'd have a place to live, I wouldn't charge you nothing. You could help me with this place." He gestures with a bony hand. "I see you already did some fixing up."

"Only a little," Harry mumbles. "I'm sorry, but I can't stay. I have to go."

"Is it money you want? I have money. I carry it right here on me," he pats his chest, "under my clothes. I'll give you some of my money."

"I don't want any money."

"Sure you do. Everybody wants money."

"I have to get back—"

"To what? Anybody looking at you can tell you got no life there. What would you be doing walking around here, if you had a life there?"

"I—I—"

"Are you going to go and leave me alone, the way they all did, the way Lester did?" He begins to weep. "Are you going to leave me to die like a dog?"

Harry is filled with terror at seeing that the more the man weeps, the older, the more frail he seems. He is in a vise—he wants to go, he needs to go, but he can't go. It's as if a judgment is about to be pronounced on him, a lifelong sentence, to attend to this man, a man whose need is becoming more insistent every second. To stay with him would be like lying down with a leper. It would be living a single life of revulsion and pity, pity and revulsion, never knowing where the one begins and the other ends.

"Stay! Stay!" the man cries out and in his agitation kicks off the blanket, displaying his withered shanks under the torn and muddied trousers.

Although Harry is almost never angry—in his secret life or his daily life—at this moment rage rises in him. He recalls the little boy lolling on Lottie's lap, his legs turned out in sensual abandon.

"Come back, come back, Jew-boy!" he hears the man yell after him as he tears himself out of the shack, stumbling on the crooked step.

He grabs his coat and his hat, and puts them on as he runs. He keeps running on the dirt road, going east now, to the town, to the train station. However long it takes, he will wait for the train. He will stay on the train to Penn Station. He will get on the subway. He will go under the East River . . .

Just ahead, at the edge of the road, he spies a black object, his little black bag. He must have put it down when he pushed that man into the ditch. Leaving it there, forgetting it, he has violated yet one more essential rule of his secret life. Without breaking his pace, he snatches up the black bag and hurries on.

If someone were watching him now, he would simply see a little man in a black overcoat, with a ruined black fedora on his head, carrying a black bag, running uphill and downhill on a dusty road. But of course, no one is watching.

I SAW HARRY ONCE. I think it was 1947. I recall coming down a narrow hallway, passing on my left a dark wood breakfront. On top of each end of the breakfront was a tall thin lamp in the shape of a candle. I came to a door and opened it automatically, as one does when going through an action one has repeated many times. The door banged shut behind me, and there, before me, was a small man in a dark overcoat, on his head a dark fedora. He was leaning against the scuffed white wall of the vestibule. I noticed his half-lidded eyes.

Sometimes it happens in life that you are going along, doing whatever you are doing and then, somehow, there's a stopping, not an ordinary stopping, but a stopping like a hole in time. It was like that, looking at Harry. It was like being in the presence of an absence. I couldn't tell if I wanted to look—or needed to look—or if I didn't want to look. I solved the problem by turning away. I went to the vestibule door, opened it, and closed it behind me.

I was glad to be outside.

Some time later, months, even years later, I thought back to that moment and accused myself of having turned away from him because I was afraid. Afraid of what? What danger could there have been in continuing to look at him? No danger. He certainly didn't look the least bit menacing. And besides, it wasn't exactly as if I turned away; it was more as if my gaze was forcibly wrenched away. Or was it only that my gaze slid away? Was it not simply that there was in him a quality of such acute ordinariness that one couldn't keep looking at him?

But, of course, what was ordinary more than fifty years ago would not be ordinary today.

A T FIVE O'CLOCK on a Friday evening in December 1932, Harry stopped in front of the house on Phillip Street. The old snow on the sidewalk was melting and his feet were getting wet. Yet he was unable to go to the door. Once he was in, he would have to say why he was home early. Of course, he could say that he was not the only one who'd been laid off; his whole department was being closed down. But in fact, he was the first one who was let go. Like Abu Ben Adam, in that poem he had had to memorize in the eighth grade, his name "led all the rest," only in this case there was no angel, no "deep dream of peace."

He put his hand up inside his jacket pocket and felt the envelope with his pay, its contents already shrinking in the face of weeks ahead without a salary. When Pop lost his job last month, Mom said, At least Harry is still working, so we can get by. But now he too had been laid off. How would they pay the rent? How would they eat? Others might apply for charity but his mother always said, We will never do that. She also said, If anyone needs help, you help, you do not wait to be asked. This was the law of the house, set down as if it were the Law itself.

"Why so early?" Cecilia asked him, when he came in the door. He could have said then but he did not. He wanted her to be able to get through dinner in peace. He mumbled something about a problem, a delay in receiving supplies. He gave her the envelope. She took out three dollars and handed them back to him—for his carfare, for his lunches, for his clothes. She looked at him in surprise when he offered to help her by setting the table but then shrugged, "If you want to."

In the small room that served as both living and dining room, there was barely space to move. The dining table and the six chairs, pushed close to the wall, took up one half of the room. A parlor set—a couch, an overstuffed chair, and two end tables—almost filled the other half. Mom had picked out the set two months ago, before Pop lost his job. They'd never had a living room set before and she guarded it jealously. Once Pop sat in the chair and put his cup of tea on the arm. "No food on the chair, Sam," she said sternly.

"This isn't food, it's drink," he told her.

"It still could stain," she said, and Pop took his cup of tea back into the kitchen.

Carrying the utensils in both hands, Harry bumped into an end table and it rocked on its thin legs and fell to the floor with a crash. "What was that?" Mom called from the kitchen. She came in and shook her head as she righted the table. "You're so clumsy, Harry. Don't bother setting the table. I'm better off doing it myself."

"I'll be careful," he said.

She wasn't satisfied. She kept looking at him. She went out into the kitchen and she came back in again. She narrowed her eyes and put her hands on her hips. "What's the matter?"

"Nothing's the matter."

Pop came in and carefully edged his way to the overstuffed chairs and sat down and opened up the *Inquirer*. "Hi, Harry," he said. "You're home early."

"I asked you, Harry, what's the matter?"

"Nothing. I told you, nothing."

"Why does there have to be anything the matter with him?" Pop asked, turning to the comics. "If he says nothing's the matter, nothing's the matter."

Mom was silent but Harry knew she would be after him again later. He was no good at lying to her. It was as if he were transparent to her, and yet, she was so opaque to him.

When dinner was over, she called him into the kitchen. "I know you're hiding something. I can tell by the way you're acting." Telling her was an agony, like confessing a crime. Her response made it even worse.

She didn't yell or cry. She simply turned back to the dishes, as if this had been only one more blow after many others.

First thing Monday morning Harry was dressed and out the door, looking for work. He went to six places that day but the answer was always the same: Nothing. Tuesday, Wednesday, all that week he scoured the city for an opening in a lab where he could use his experience as a low-level technician and clean-up man. Everywhere, they were laying off.

Weeks went by, with the same rushing out in the morning, the same trudging back at night, on through December, then January, then into February. The payments couldn't be made on the living room set, so the store van came to take it away. By this time Harry was looking for any job; it didn't have to be in a lab.

At home Mom dusted and mopped and washed the floor and did the laundry with fierce energy. She shopped even more frugally than before, walking half a mile to save five cents. Sometimes in the late afternoon, when she had a blinding headache, she allowed herself to lie down in the bedroom with the shades drawn, but she always got up after a few minutes to prepare dinner. Pop hung around the house all day, working in the basement, making little cars out of discarded pieces of wood. He tried to sell them to the neighbors. Since they couldn't pay, he ended up giving the cars away, but he still kept making new cars. He said he had to keep busy with his hands.

Stan, Harry's younger brother, went to high school as usual. He knew times were hard but he didn't know how hard. In that family they didn't discuss such things. At dinner they might talk about a neighbor who needed help, or about what President Roosevelt might or might not do now that he was in office, or about *One Man's Family* on the radio. But there wasn't all that much talk about what you were doing. You had gotten through today. Today was over.

As for the distant past, that was never, or almost never, referred to. Harry knew Mom and Pop had come from Russia, with a brief stop in Switzerland, like a way station, where he was born. He had a vague memory from when he was a little kid about Pop saying something about Russia, something about Tolstoy. But early on he came to know that he wasn't supposed to ask about their past, and besides he really didn't want to know.

Once, a couple of years ago, for no reason, Stan suddenly asked Mom, "What was it like there?"

"Where?"

"In Russia."

"It was cold."

"But—"

"That's enough," Mom said.

It was enough of an answer for Harry. What was important was that they had their life here, in Philadelphia, where they rented a house of four rooms—a living room that also served as dining room, a kitchen, and two bedrooms—on a street of other houses that were just the same, that on this street there were many Jewish families and on the corner the butcher and the grocer who both gave credit, that two blocks over the Irish section, "The Neck," began and you didn't cross over into their territory, that Pop worked ten hours a day six days a week—when he had a job—and working at the level of dumb (that is to say, silent) necessity, he never complained, that some nights he came home with his fingers bleeding, and Mom spent hours bathing them with a boric acid solution, that Mom took care of them all, that she fed them and fixed their clothes and urged them on, that she pronounced the injunctions, the laws, the Law.

If in that family there was little or no talk of the past, there was a willed hope for the future, fueled by Cecilia with a fierce intensity. It was more a hope of holding on or holding off, than of getting. But now even that hope was being endangered.

One evening in February, around nine o'clock, a late hour for that neighborhood, they heard a knocking on the front door. It was Bernie Siegel, the next door neighbor, saying there was a call for Harry on his phone. Since Harry's family didn't have a phone, Bernie let them use his number for emergencies. When Harry picked up the receiver, he recognized the voice of Bob Silver from the lab. Bob worked in another department, which hadn't been closed, so he still had his job but he kept worrying about Harry. Each week he had another suggestion as to what Harry should do. Last week, when Harry's search for work seemed hopeless, Bob had suggested that Harry take his family to Russia, to Birobijan, where the Soviets had set up a place for Jews to live. We'd never do that, Harry said. We'd never leave Philadelphia. This is where we belong. He was astonished at the idea of going back to a place Mom and Pop had come from, a place that had been erased from history—from their histories—for all intents and purposes.

This time Bob had a different and more immediate suggestion. He had just received a call from his friend Dave White. "He's leaving his job at a lab in Jersey City, and I told him about you. He said if you get up there tonight, he'll go over what you have to know and you can go in and apply for the job first thing in the morning."

At once Harry ran home and packed his tan cardboard suitcase, the one he'd used when he'd been sent to camp as a kid because he was so skinny and wouldn't eat. As it wasn't a charity camp but part of the school system, Mom hadn't objected to his going. It was there that Harry had learned to eat anything and everything that was placed in front of him, so that at twenty-one he already had a slight paunch.

He rushed around the corner to his friend Si Schaefer, and borrowed six dollars from him. On the bus ride to Jersey City, he could not contain his elation. He had rarely been out of the city, and going to Jersey City was an adventure to him. I'll get the job, I've got to get it, he kept saying to himself. At the terminal he got off and took a local bus, as Bob had instructed him. It was after midnight when he got off the second bus.

At first he couldn't find Dave White's street. He was in a fever, rushing this way and that, as if it was a matter of life and death, which it was to him. He stopped a man coming toward him, and asked for directions. The man looked at Harry and then at the cardboard suitcase and then at Harry again. "Go left at the corner, then go two streets and turn right and you'll be there." The words were slow and begrudging.

In the dimly spreading cone of the streetlight, Harry could see that the man was regarding him suspiciously. He felt he had to explain. "I've got to see a man about a job."

"We got a lot of people out of work here. We don't need no strangers taking our jobs," the man said sourly.

"I wouldn't take a job away from anybody," Harry said and hurried to the corner.

The door to apartment 2B, second floor back, was opened by a big bear of a man with red hair and freckles. Dave White put his huge hand out and engulfed Harry's. "Glad you're here, Harry. Come in and have something to eat. You'll need to fortify yourself because we're going to be up all night getting you ready for your interview."

They ate spaghetti and they drank red wine and then they got down to serious business. Dave White went over the lab procedures in great detail. The company was involved in the manufacture of soap and was also doing research on detergents. Harry listened carefully and tried to remember everything so that when questioned, he could repeat it back letter perfect.

"Good, good," Dave encouraged him. "You're going to do fine. Only one thing—I have to tell you this—the lab supervisor doesn't hire Jews, so don't tell him you're a Jew. If he asks you, say No. I don't believe in lying but sometimes you have to. I hope your religious beliefs won't stop you from doing this."

"I'm not religious," Harry said.

Dave said he was Irish Catholic, "lapsed Catholic, not lapsed Irish. Once I was a choirboy, if you can believe it. Then one day, I was thirteen or so, I started looking around, and I saw how things really are. I realized that Marxism is right. Religion is the opiate of the masses."

"Well—," said Harry, not wanting to be impolite.

"Look around you, at the desperate state people are in. And yet, if you talk to them, you see how innocent they are. Religion tells them that things will get better, and if they don't get better, that it's God's will that they should suffer for their sins. What sin have they committed by being poor?"

Harry squirmed a little at Dave's words about innocence, as if they were an accusation against Mom and all she taught. As for God, he'd never come to any definite conclusions. He merely felt that speculating about God or even the idea of God was not in his nature. Still, given Dave's extreme kindness, it did not seem appropriate to challenge what he was saying, even though his tacit agreement made Harry feel oddly conspiratorial.

"Religion doesn't tell them that it's the system that's at fault, because you're supposed to obey the system in this world. It doesn't tell them that capitalism is the root problem, that it's rotten to the core. Do you think the fat cats, the Wall Street men, are going to allow it to change?"

Before Harry could think of a suitable answer, Dave went on, "Not likely. The only way the system's going to change is when the people—the workers—take things into their own hands. The day will come and it's not far off, I assure you."

Though much of what Dave was saying could be taken as harsh condemnation, he didn't seem bitter to Harry. In fact, everything about him, as he said these words, expressed exhilaration and hope, even a kind of exaltation. Harry had never met anyone like Dave before. He remembered how he'd been afraid of going into the Neck as a kid of twelve, and how he'd once been beaten up by a gang of Irish kids when he wandered through their territory on his way to the library. After that, Pop had insisted on walking Harry to the library until, finally, Harry had asked him not to; he said he'd go the long way around and wouldn't go into the Neck.

But here was Dave White, changing the way he looked at the Irish, erasing his old fears, rewriting his history in a way. He couldn't believe that anyone could be so generous, staying up all night to help him out, to make sure he'd get the job.

Now that Harry was working in Jersey City, he took a room close to where Dave lived. It wasn't much of a room: It was dark and cluttered and had a moldy smell, but it didn't matter since he just slept there. He was earning thirty dollars a week, out of which he kept eleven for himself—three for the room rent, four for food, and four for a round trip ticket on the Pennsy, so he could go home on weekends. That left nineteen for Mom and Pop and Stanley, which certainly wasn't a lot but at least they could get by for the moment.

He liked the work at the lab, as he would have liked the work at any lab. He loved the idea of experimenting, of starting out with a particular set of conditions, and then seeing what would happen if you changed some of those conditions. First you'd change one thing and see what the results were, and you'd go on from there, eliminating any cause for error. He thought of the whole process as making a mistake and correcting that mistake and then going on and making another mistake and correcting that until you finally came to the right answer. You just went on, slow and steady, and finally you solved the problem. You didn't have to be a genius, you just had to have patience.

One day, by accident, he dropped a dessicator containing twenty-two crucibles, a week's work. The glass shattered and the contents spilled on the floor. He simply cleaned up the mess and then he started all over again right away, working through that day and the night and the next day, to get back to where he had been.

It was true that he had some trouble with the supervisor, who wasn't sure whether he was a Jew or not, and would make remarks like, "They should take all the Jews out in a boat to the middle of New York harbor and sink it." Harry told himself not to respond and he didn't.

Weekday evenings when he didn't work he spent with Dave and Dave's friend Rosa Gallo. They ate spaghetti and drank wine and talked and talked, especially about politics, how it was imperative that the terrible wrongs in the world be righted. Though Dave now had a good job in an oil company lab, his thoughts were still with those who were not doing well. When he talked about the poor and the oppressed and about the special favors for Wall Street men who thought only of profits and nothing about human beings, the whole room seemed to shake with the vibrations of his deep voice, with his passionate energy and intelligence.

Rosa was Italian, and she too had grown up as a Catholic. She agreed with Dave that, like all the other institutions of society, the Church was guilty of supporting the existing system, which had to be brought down. She was a tall woman with dark eyes and a Roman nose, and when she spoke about the inequities in the world, her nostrils flared, and her eyes shone, as if the words themselves were only a step away from the realization of the revolution to come. Though Harry didn't agree with a lot of what Dave and she were saying, he couldn't help admiring their decency and their fervor, and their obvious willingness to sacrifice themselves for a cause they believed in.

One evening, Dave announced straight out that he was a member of the Communist Party. Harry didn't think much of Communists, either from what he'd heard about them or the little he'd read in the papers. The very word *communist* upset him, but how could he be upset with Dave after all he had done for him and his family? Rosa said she, too, was a Communist. Then they both began to try to persuade him to join the Party. Harry kept shrugging and saying, "I'm not really much interested in politics."

"How can you say that," Dave wanted to know, "when everything is political?"

He went on to speak about the amazing experiment taking place in Russia, a country which only sixteen years ago was suffering under the tyrannical rule of the Czars. "The Soviet Union may not have all the answers yet, but they're heading in the right direction, the only direction possible in an industrialized society." It would be the one place in the world where there was going to be equal justice. No one was going try to be above anyone else or live off somebody else's sweat. It was the only hope for the future in a world where madmen like Hitler were taking over. "Do you know that the Soviet Union is the one country in the world that has a law outlawing anti-Semitism?" Dave asked.

No, Harry said, he didn't know that. He didn't say that he couldn't get it out of his head that, revolution or no revolution, Russia was a place that had once been and then had evaporated, as if it had dropped into the sea like the lost continent of Atlantis.

Dave asked Harry to go to a Party meeting with him and Rosa. "Just come and listen," he insisted. "Don't take my word for it. Hear what they have to say." How could Harry say No? Certainly he didn't want to offend Dave. And besides, maybe there was something there that he ought to know about. He shouldn't close his mind. So he went with Dave and Rosa to a meeting in downtown Jersey City.

The minute he got there he knew these people were not for him. They were attacking not only the capitalist system but each other. An argument broke out that almost ended in a fistfight. An old Greek barber got up and announced that he had been an anarchist all his life, and as an anarchist, he condemned the cowardice of everyone present. "We should take to the streets, not later but right now!" he yelled. A husky longshoreman jumped up and roared, "Who do you think you are, calling us cowards? What right do you have to say what's the right time for us to act?"

A third man got up and separated the two men who had almost come to blows. The speeches went on and on until two in the morning. By that time Harry had long since lost patience. He longed to be at the lab, checking the results of his latest run. He couldn't understand how Dave and Rosa, two such bright and wonderful people, could put up with this tedious talk.

As they walked to the bus, Dave asked Harry what he thought about the meeting. "Well," said Harry, "they seem well meaning enough but I got tired of all that talk."

"You have to understand that there were a lot of newcomers present tonight and everybody had to be given their say."

"But what they said wasn't very logical. As a scientific man, I can't go along with such sloppy thinking."

Dave laughed. "There's a vision at work here that's both very logical and very scientific, I assure you. But it's a long process building up a cohesive group. It takes time and patience. What we're trying to bring about is not going to happen in one night."

"I suppose," Harry said, but he couldn't imagine that he would ever see a reason for giving up logical thought, even as a temporary expedient.

"You should go to New York some evening to attend one of the Party study groups," Rosa suggested. "You'll find they're much more intellectual. They deal directly with theory and with first principles."

"Good idea," said Dave.

On a Wednesday night, some weeks later, Harry made his way to downtown Manhattan to a building near Union Square, where a new study group was meeting. The discussion was already in progress when he got there. A thin blond man in a shiny blue suit was standing in front of a blackboard, gesticulating. He had a stern, deeply lined face, and his hands were in constant motion. Harry took a seat at the back of the room, away from the others who were clustered in the first few rows taking notes.

The leader was speaking of the history of the class struggle, beginning with ancient Rome, progressing through the Middle Ages with its feudal lords and serfs, and arriving at the evolution of modern bourgeois society, with its opposition between the bourgeoisie and the proletariat.

Harry found himself sinking into a stupor. He hadn't slept for two nights because of an experiment that had required his continual attention. His eyes kept closing, no matter how hard he tried to keep awake. He awoke with a start and saw that the man in the blue suit was drawing a diagram on the blackboard, under the word "WORK" in capital letters. The first section of the diagram was labeled "Raw Materials," the second "Machinery and equipment—Wear and Tear," the third "Paid Labor Time—Wages" and the fourth "Unpaid Labor Time—Profits—The Work We Do for Nothing." Over the last two sections the leader wrote, "New

Value Added By Our Labor." He stood back and pronounced the words "by our labor" three times. Then he tapped the chalk at the center of the last section. "It is this—the unpaid labor time—that is at the core of our struggle. The employer wants the largest amount of unpaid labor time possible. He wants more profit. But our interests are not the same as his. Our interests are directly opposed to his."

Harry shook himself, desperately trying to stay awake, but the man's voice was so deep and sonorous, and the words and rhythms of his speech so repetitive, that he kept going in and out of the sound. He heard "the owner of the means of production . . . the absolute power . . . the absolute dictator . . . the worker must agree because the worker has no choice . . . an invisible chain that ties the workers to the machines."

The next thing Harry knew, he felt his head snap up and back. He must have been asleep again—he didn't know for how long. The speaker's voice had grown louder, as if what he said before was leading only to this. ". . . a future different from the present, not one of bread lines, of families suffering because men can't put food on the table, a future that is ours by right." There was a grave silence in the room, an acknowledgment that no matter how bad things were in the outside world, in here the passion of this man's belief was proof that change was possible, that a promise was about to be fulfilled. So Harry observed, even as he noted that unlike the others he could not warm himself in the glow of the speaker's belief—or of any belief.

"That's all for now," the leader said as he handed out the reading assignments for the next meeting. "I'll see you next Wednesday."

In silence the students got up and filed out of the room. The man in the blue suit erased the board and looked at Harry, who was still sitting at the back of the room. "Is there something you want to ask me?" Harry wondered if he should ask him about believing, about believing in general and about believing in particular, but that seemed foolish, so he just shook his head and said, "Thank you very much. It was very interesting," and got up and went out into the hallway.

Near the door he saw a table with literature. Feeling guilty about his failure to pay total attention in this place where everybody else was so intent, he edged up to the table and began to examine the pamphlets. He picked up *The Communist Manifesto* by Karl Marx and Friedrich Engels and opened to the first page. "A spectre is haunting Europe—the spectre of Communism. All the powers of old Europe have entered into a holy alliance to exorcise this spectre: Pope and Czar, Metternich and Guizot, French Radicals and German police-spies."

His reading was interrupted by a man saying, "These on this table are for sale, five cents each. The ones on that other table," the man pointed across the hall, "are free."

"Oh," said Harry, and went over to the second table and got some free literature but when he looked back the man at the first table was staring at him as if he were a police-spy.

Naturally, the next time Harry saw Dave, Dave asked him how the study group went.

"It was—" he hesitated—"okay."

"Only okay. Why? Wasn't it scientific enough for you?"

"It wasn't that." Harry didn't want to go into the detail of his own inattention. "I didn't like the way he talked about workers being chained to a machine by invisible chains. I'm not chained to anything."

"You think you're not."

"I'm not. In the lab I'm free to experiment and—"

"He was speaking metaphorically."

"Even metaphorically— And another thing," he stumbled on, "I was bothered by the way he talked about work. When he talked about it, the only things he mentioned were pay and working conditions and profits and—"

"What did you expect him to say?"

"I thought he could have said something about the pleasure in work—the pleasure in solving a problem, the pleasure in getting it right— in doing things and discovering things, in finding out—"

"Harry, Harry," Dave shook his head. "I don't know what kind of a dream world you're living in. Most people work because they have to work, because they need the money for food and shelter and clothing. Right now in this country there are millions of people who don't have the money for the basic essentials. You know yourself there are people starving, without roofs over their heads. Maybe some day, when the world is a better world, when people are guaranteed security, guaranteed that they have the necessities of life, maybe then we can start talking about work in a different way. But right now, at this moment in history, what people need is a decent job to be able to pay the bills."

"I guess you're right," said Harry, shamefacedly, recalling how desperate he had been before Dave had helped him to get his job.

After that, there wasn't a night when Harry was with Dave and Rosa that they didn't put pressure on him, trying to persuade him to join the Party. He couldn't say No, he wouldn't say Yes. Sometimes they talked about the enormous cracks in the system, how so many people were falling right through. Old people, for example, what were they expected to live on when they couldn't work any more? "The whole structure of the society is based on treating people as a commodity that can be discarded when they're no longer useful," Dave said.

"You're right about that," said Harry, visualizing Mom and Pop as old and frail; but he would not let them go under.

"And what about the Negroes and how they're treated? What about the terrible persecution in the South—and in the North too?" Dave asked. Yes, that was true, Harry admitted, and there flamed up in him an anger at the terrible injustice still existing in the country: Human beings had been forced into slavery, and then supposedly freed but never really freed.

And yet, despite feeling that so much of what Dave and Rosa said was right on the mark, he could not bring himself to the final judgment that the system had to be brought down entirely, that revolution was necessary to bring about a final good. It was a leap he could not take. He wanted change, but change that was peaceful, gradual. He brought up Roosevelt's proposals for the National Recovery Act, to create new jobs.

"Band-Aids," Dave roared. "The patient is hemorrhaging and they're using Band-Aids. It's just patchwork. It won't hold."

"Maybe it will work, given time."

"Not on your life," Dave said emphatically.

But a few months later Harry was proved right. Because of the NRA and its new work rules, his old department at his former lab in Phila-delphia opened up, and they asked him to come back. Now that he was wanted by two labs, he was pleased but at the same time he felt torn. He liked his new job and he was getting some really good results. But then there was the supervisor—he didn't trust that supervisor. Besides, if he took his old job back, the same thirty dollars a week would go much further. He wouldn't need to rent a room, he wouldn't need the carfare for the Pennsy, the whole family would have more money. But then, if he left Jersey City, he wouldn't be seeing Dave and Rosa often. On the other hand, he would be back home with Mom and Pop and Stan.

He decided to go back to his old job.

The last night before he left, Dave and Rosa took him out.

It was a warm September evening and they went to Manhattan, to an Italian restaurant. They lingered over dinner, talking and talking. Then they decided to take the ferry to Staten Island and come right back on the same boat, just for the ride. Standing with his two friends at the front of the boat on the return trip, Harry looked at the lights of the city and listened to the lapping of the water and knew he was happier than he had ever been.

By the time they got off the ferry, it was late enough, or rather early enough, to have breakfast, so they went to a place that Dave knew near the docks and they ordered scrambled eggs and oysters. Life seemed one pleasure piled upon another.

Once again Dave and Rosa made their pitch for joining the Party. Harry listened dutifully, though it was like being part of an old conversation, whose words you already knew. They spoke and he listened; that was as far as it went. There was no risk, no danger in hearing them out. But then, suddenly, Rosa brought up something new. She began talking about how the Soviets were working to create entirely new patterns of social organization, doing away with the old ones.

"Take the family, for instance," she said. "It's a worn out institution that works to keep the people enslaved to old ideas, to hatred of other groups. But in Russia, as the state becomes more flexible, more benevolent over time, there won't be a need to set one group against another. The institution of marriage will give way. The family, with its rigid definition of what is and what is not allowed sexually will be replaced—"

"Replaced by what? What could possibly replace the family?" Harry cried out. He was so excited that he tore off the white cloth napkin that was tied around his neck and jumped up from the table.

"Take it easy, Harry, and sit down," said Dave.

"No, I won't take it easy. I'll never take it easy about my family."

He turned to Rosa, sputtering. "Free love, I suppose that's what you're advocating."

"What's wrong with free love? You're against it because you think women should be protected, that they should be kept pure, for marriage? Is that what you think?"

"I don't think there's anything wrong with protection or with purity."

"Protection for the benefit of who? Purity for the benefit of who?"

"I don't know what you're talking about."

"Take it easy, Rosa," Dave said. "And you too, Harry. Calm down."

"But she—" Harry sat down. He was shaking, but not with cold.

"I'm sorry, Harry," Rosa said, and she got up from her chair and walked around to Harry's side of the table. "I keep forgetting how young you are, that you're just a boy, you're just an innocent boy." She put one hand on either side of his face and brought her own face close to his. Looking up at her, he saw the flared nostrils, the dark eyes, and before he knew what she was doing, she put her lips to his. The kiss was a gentle kiss at first—but then somehow it was becoming something else. She was opening her mouth and using her tongue to open his. He could taste the slightly sour taste of the wine in her mouth. He felt a horror at his own response, a fierce pulsing and rising which was checked almost instantaneously by his embarrassment at being seen responding.

"Don't," he yelled, pushing her away. It was the first time that any woman but his mother had kissed him, and she had never kissed him on the lips.

"Leave him alone," Dave said sharply.

She retreated to her side of the table but not before Harry caught a funny look that passed between her and Dave. He didn't know what it was and he didn't want to know. He only knew he hated her for having made him look like such a fool before Dave, of all people. "I'm not a boy, and I'm not innocent," he said sullenly.

"Of course, you're not a boy. Rosa was only teasing. The truth is, Harry, it is really wonderful to see the way you stand up for your family. Rosa and I both admire the way you're so loyal to them. Don't you, Rosa?"

She nodded.

"You do?" Harry felt his head, his heart, his stomach flip over. Still, he held on a little longer to his anger, nourishing it with the words, "But why did she—"

"She made a mistake. People make mistakes."

"I'm sorry. I didn't realize how sensitive you are."

Tears came to Harry's eyes at Rosa's words. "I guess I am oversensitive about some things—especially about my family."

"Will you forgive me, Harry?" It was the old Rosa. How could he not forgive her?

"Come on, let's all kiss and make up," said Dave, holding his huge arms outstretched.

Rosa got up on one side of Dave and Harry on the other and Dave embraced them both together. They all laughed, even Harry, though he didn't think it was particularly funny.

Once again Harry was back in Philadelphia, back in his old job, back in his life with his family. The food was the same, Mom's good home cooking. His room—that is, his and Stanley's room—was the same. But other things were changing. His job at the lab was even better. His new boss, Dr. Rink, was praising him a lot and giving him more responsibility. He was also going to night school at Drexel Institute, working on a technical certificate. He'd had to drop out of the day program in chemistry at the University of Pennsylvania three years before to help support the family. Someday, he hoped to go back and get a real degree.

As for his old friends in the neighborhood, they too were changing. Si Schaefer was engaged and didn't have the time anymore to sit around and gab, but then, what with work and school, Harry didn't have much time either. It was sad to see the old gang break up, but some things would never change; they would always be friends. Thinking of friends, he realized how much he missed seeing Dave—and Rosa.

To his surprise, one Sunday, several months after his return home, Dave dropped by to see him. He said he was in town to see Bob and he just thought he'd come over. How good it was to see that old bear of a fellow and how pleased Mom and Pop were to meet him. They acted like he was their savior, which he had been. Hadn't he made it possible for Harry and for them to go on? Of course, Mom insisted that Dave stay for dinner. At one point, just as the pot roast was being served, Dave said

something about the terrible conditions in the country, and about all the
people without work and without food. Mom and Pop agreed that it was
terrible. Harry hoped that Dave wouldn't go on to talk about the
Communist Party because he knew Mom and Pop were liberal, but
Norman Thomas was as far out as they would even consider. Luckily,
Dave dropped the subject and praised Mom's pot roast, and she beamed
with pleasure. After dinner, Harry and Dave spent hours talking, Dave
about his work at the oil company lab and Harry about his work for
Dr. Rink. There was an excitement for Harry in this exchange, just as if
he and Dave were colleagues, working together, each somehow able to
anticipate what the other was thinking.

The next time Dave dropped by, it was a Sunday evening in May.
After dinner, Dave suggested to Harry that they take a walk in the neighborhood. Strolling down Phillip Avenue, Harry was proud to have his big
friend beside him. To Harry's surprise Dave knew the names of the flowering plants in the small front yards, names like lilac and crocus and lily.
Harry didn't know one flower from another. It was funny to think of such
a big man as Dave knowing about such little things as flowers.

Harry showed Dave his old junior high and then they crossed over
into the Neck. What problem could that be now, with Dave alongside
him? After a while they came to a small park with some swings and a
couple of benches. "Let's sit for a minute," Dave said.

"Sure," Harry said, and started talking enthusiastically about his new
work at the lab. Dr. Rink had given him a roving assignment, working first
on one project, then on another. It gave him the chance to learn a lot rapidly.

Dave looked around; the park was empty. "I certainly like your
family."

"And they like you, too. They'll never forget what you did for me—
and them." Dave smiled and waved his hand, as if he were embarrassed.
"There's something I wanted to talk to you about," he said. He's going to
ask me to join the Party again, Harry knew, and he sighed loudly, remembering the last time they had talked about it, in that restaurant near the
docks, when there'd been that conversation about the family and free
love, and then Rosa— "No, Harry, it's not about the Party. That's not
what I want to talk to you about."

Harry felt a certain relief but Dave still didn't seem ready to say
what he had to say. Instead, he said, "Can you smell that?"

"Smell what?"

"That flower," he said, looking around.

"I don't have a very good sense of smell."

"It reminds me of a flowering tree that used to grow right outside the house when I was a kid." A group of kids walked by their bench, laughing and talking. He waited until they had left the park. "I've just met a man from Amtorg."

"I don't know where Amtorg is."

"It's not a place. It's the Soviet Trade Mission. This man told me that they've been trying to set up trade agreements with U.S. companies but they're running into a lot of trouble. He said they're getting nothing but rejections."

"Why?"

"Come on, Harry, you ought to know why. None of these companies want to do business with a Communist state. The Soviet government is trying to do what it can to make life better for its citizens, but, let's face it, they need help. They're way behind technically."

"I'm sure they are," said Harry.

"They're looking for help through other channels. What would be most helpful, he told me, would be if people here, working in industries and in laboratories, would be willing to supply them with information on basic industrial processes. I told him about the work your company is doing on filler materials for paper, and sulfonated oils for textiles, and Vitamin D concentrates from fish oils, and that research you mentioned last time on solvents—"

"You mean ethyl acetate and butyl alcohol and butyl propionate—"

"Yeah. And I also told him about the work on ethyl chloride as a local anesthetic and the use of absolute alcohol to extend motor fuels."

"But I don't see—"

"He said any information on these things would be very valuable to them. He asked me to talk to you about helping them, and I said I would."

"I don't understand. He wants me to steal information for them?"

"No, no, no. Not steal, share. You wouldn't be taking anything away from anybody. All you would be doing is copying some information, flow charts and blueprints and in-house reports, and giving it to them. Most of the stuff is published in technical journals but they can't even get access to technical journals."

"But it would have to be done secretly, without anybody knowing?"

"Well, yes." Suddenly Dave burst out, "You have to consider what's going on today with Hitler taking over in Germany, and Mussolini in Italy. There's going to be a war—"

"Do you think so?"

"Not this year or next year, but soon. The Germans are going to attack the Russians. Hitler makes that clear in *Mein Kampf.* He says he's going to take over their land, so he can have—what does he call it? Lebensraum—take it over for the Germans from what he calls the 'sub-human masses.' So whatever can be done to help them—"

Harry slumped on the bench, as some more kids ran past them, shouting and laughing. Here was Dave asking him to help. Had Dave hesitated when it was a question of helping Harry? Still Harry hesitated. "But what if Dr. Rink found out?"

"He's not going to find out. No one's going to find out. All you have to do is copy the information and then you can put it right back."

"Does this mean I'd have to join the Party?" Harry said glumly.

"No, no. Not at all. In fact, they wouldn't want you to join the Party if you did this."

Harry didn't ask why "they" would or wouldn't; he was just glad not to be pressured any more to join. "I'll think about it."

"Good. That's all I ask, Harry, is that you think about it. Think about what it would mean to all those people in a country where everything is starting all over again, where they're sacrificing everything to bring about a new way of life. They're the only hope for the world." Slowly Dave got up. "When you've made up your mind, you can send me a note. Just yes or no. If it's yes, the people at Amtorg can take it from there. And if it's no—whatever you decide, you know it's all right with me."

Harry thought about the question day and night. He thought about it in the lab, where he ordinarily never thought about anything but work. He thought about it when he was at home, even at dinner with Mom and Pop and Stan. The question was like a wall, a screen between him and them. He couldn't act natural. Mom kept looking at him. "Are you all right, Harry? Are you sick?" she asked.

"I'm fine," he muttered.

"You're not getting enough sleep," she said.

"I am, I am. Stop picking on me."

She backed away, surprised by his testiness.

He kept trying to look at all the different sides of the problem, trying to eliminate certain considerations, so as to get down to a single truth, yes or no. He thought of duty, he thought of betrayal. But it was no simple matter. There was betrayal of one against betrayal of another. There was what he owed to Dave. There was what he owed to Dr. Rink.

He trembled at the thought of doing this terrible thing against his boss who had been so helpful to him. But would it really hurt him in any way? How could it hurt him? And was it really betrayal if no one was hurt, but only some, many, helped? He felt the needs of others pressing in on him, people trying to start all over again, from scratch, not helped by anyone, only hindered. All he could think of was need. As if he were a vessel, a bowl, collecting need, as if all need penetrated into him, bypassing his skin as if he had no skin, as if need were a law unto itself.

One night, he was lying in his bed wide awake. He heard his brother snore in the other twin bed. "Stan," he hissed. Stan mumbled something and turned from his back to his side and stopped snoring. Still Harry could not sleep. He tossed and turned for hours. At one point, he had a weird feeling—it could have been a dream although he almost never dreamed—that he was flying over a land mass far below him, a landscape nothing like Philadelphia. It was a world at absolute zero. No plants, no animals, only cold, and yet there was a howling wind. Beneath the sound of the wind there was another sound that was barely audible . . . a voice crying out . . .

In mid-June he sent Dave a one-word note.

Later it would come to him that all the time he was trying to decide, he had known that he would say Yes.

SECRECY, ONE'S OWN secrecy, what one feels but doesn't know one feels, is, not to belabor the obvious, a puzzling thing for us all. It was particularly puzzling for Harry, who had never thought of himself as someone who could have a secret from anyone else, let alone a secret from himself. Before this, he had always taken for granted that you felt what you felt, you knew what you knew. But now there was that within him that didn't know what he felt, that didn't feel what he knew.

In his work life, faced with an unknown substance, Harry was relentless in his attempt to identify it. He experimented to see how it responded when it was heated to the boiling point or was frozen, what happened when it was combined with known reagents. The point was to keep pushing at the borders of the unknown, trying to get it to reveal itself. But in the case of these shadows at the edge of feeling and thought, he simply shied away from investigation. He circumvented them, gingerly at first, and then with vigor. He paid absolute attention to his work at the lab—six days a week, ten hours a day—to night school, to studying, to eating, to sleeping, and to getting up in the morning and going to work again.

After some months, in fact so many that Harry thought Amtorg might have forgotten him, a possibility that both relieved and distressed him, a note came in the mail. It was spare and vague in its wording, indicating that another note was soon to follow.

Two weeks later came the second note, instructing Harry to be on the steps of the Art Museum the following Saturday at two. He was to wear one pair of gloves and carry another. His contact would be carrying a book with a blue binding in his right hand and a tennis ball in his left.

In anticipation of the coming meeting, Harry felt something akin to excitement, though it quickly turned to apprehension. It came to him that he did not know how he was supposed to act in this meeting. Certainly, he had read a number of spy novels in his time, including the works of E. Phillips Oppenheim and of John Buchan. All of them spoke of the demeanor of spies, mostly menacing, as he recalled. Not only was he incapable of conscious imitation of any of those characters, but when you got right down to it, he wasn't exactly going to be a spy. He was merely going to provide information.

Saturday, precisely at two, Harry waited on the steps of the art museum, wearing his one pair of winter leather gloves, and carrying a pair of red mittens he'd used as a kid. He kept watching the people mount the steps and hurry into the large front doors but he saw no one with a book with a blue binding in one hand and a tennis ball in the other.

Harry had been to the museum only once before when he was in junior high school and his class had been taken there for a special outing. He didn't remember much about the museum itself, only that he kept staring at the painted surfaces, whose representation of life he deemed very poor in terms of accuracy, particularly when compared with a photograph. He hadn't been back.

A large man in a grey coat, wearing glasses with thick lenses, was suddenly at his elbow. Harry hadn't even seen him come up the steps. In the man's right hand was a blue book; in his left a tennis ball. Harry opened his mouth to ask, "Are you—," but the man in the grey coat shook his head in warning. Then he hurried down the steps and walked at a rapid pace for some distance, with Harry scurrying to keep up with him. He circled a block and went on to another, then circled back again. Finally, he slipped into a cafe, and, picking out a table in the corner with no one nearby, he settled his large frame onto a straight chair. Sitting opposite him, Harry noticed that he was panting from exertion, his mouth opening and closing at regular intervals. With his thick lenses, he looked a little like a huge fish with bulging eyes. A strange demeanor for someone who was trying not to be noticed, Harry thought, but then decided he knew little about such things.

Putting the tennis ball and the book with the blue binding on the table, the large man looked around to make sure they were not being heard, and introduced himself as Paul Smith. Harry knew that this was an alias and he wondered if he should have thought up an alias for himself. A waitress appeared and Paul Smith ordered coffee and doughnuts for two. After a moment, he exhaled with great vehemence and smiled. It was an attractive smile, even ingratiating, though it was accompanied by a good deal of blinking.

In a heavy foreign accent, he thanked Harry for his willingness to help the people of the Soviet Union. He spoke of their hopes of building a just society that would serve in the future as a model for all other nations. But for now, circumstances had so arranged it that they were in need of help. He gave examples of several areas in which help was needed, including the process for the production of industrial solvents used in the manufacture of lacquers and varnishes, the process for the production of ethyl alcohol for pharmaceutical and non-pharmaceutical purposes, and the process for the production of Vitamin D from fish oils, all technologies which, he understood, "your company has great expertise in."

Before Harry could say anything, Paul Smith was instructing him on how he was to deliver the desired information. Since there was undoubtedly a large amount of material to be examined, a number of missions would be required. On each mission, selected blueprints of equipment and plant operating records were to be wrapped in plain brown paper and brought to New York. He personally would be waiting for Harry at a pre-arranged place, Harry would hand the papers over to him, he would take the papers to be copied, and then several hours later he would return the papers to Harry. Finally, Harry would take the train back to Philadelphia and replace the materials where he had found them.

Behind his thick glasses his eyes became more piercing. "If at any time you think you are being followed, you are to abort the mission. You will always be given an alternate time and place, should you be unable to make the agreed upon appointment. We had hoped," Paul Smith went on, "that you could undertake your first mission this week, but there has been an unfortunate delay in the organization of the photographic facility. I will contact you as soon as everything is in readiness. Do you have any questions?"

"None that I can think of at the moment."

"Good. We will be in touch, shortly. Incidentally," he asked, "you have been in touch with Dave White recently?"

"Not for a while."

"Now that you are to be engaged in this work, it will be unwise from this point onward for you to have contact with him or—" and here his voice dropped— "any member of the Party. Do you understand?"

Yes, Harry nodded, though he felt terrible at the thought of not seeing Dave, for whose sake he had agreed to become involved in the first place.

Putting forty cents on the table, Paul Smith said, "You will, of course, be reimbursed for your expenses, so keep a careful accounting of them."

"I don't really want any money," Harry said awkwardly.

"We'll discuss that at a later time." Standing, the agent loomed over Harry. "Wait for five minutes after my departure before you leave." He picked up the tennis ball and the book with the blue binding and made his way, heavily, to the door.

Harry finished his coffee and doughnut. The five minutes were over. He decided to wait an extra five minutes, just in case. He looked over and saw the doughnut, which Paul Smith had left untouched on his plate; he ate that too. There seemed to be a yawning hole in his stomach that would never be filled. At the same time his mind was crammed to bursting. One moment what he had agreed to do seemed simple, and at the next moment it was impossibly complex. What if Dr. Rink found out? But then, how could he find out if Harry returned the papers the same night? And even if he should find out, he could always say he wanted to work on the material at home. That wasn't prohibited.

I could stop right now, came the next thought, just walk out of here and never respond to any call or note from Paul Smith again. But then came an equal and opposite thought, that he had already committed himself, already promised Dave. At the thought of his friend, Harry recalled what Paul Smith had said, that he was never to see him again. What kind of a friend would he be, if, just like that, he cut him off?

At the end of exactly ten minutes, Harry got up and went outside. He scanned the faces of the passersby, a young woman with dark curly hair, two old men arguing loudly, a young couple strolling arm in arm. No, they were not looking at him; they didn't even notice that he was looking at them. He blinked a little as if he had just come out of the dark. Something odd was happening to his eyes. He had the curious sense that for the first time in his life he was looking at a surface, and behind that surface something was hidden.

It was midwinter when the call from Paul Smith finally came, advising Harry that he should proceed as he had been instructed. On the following Friday night Harry borrowed the materials from the lab that he had chosen to take on this first mission, wrapped them meticulously in brown paper, took a bus to the train station, got on the train to New York, got off at Penn Station, and went to the corner of Thirty-Eighth Street and Lexington Avenue, where Paul Smith was waiting for him. Paul Smith took the package and said he'd return in three hours, exactly.

There was a movie theater down the block, so Harry bought a ticket and went inside. Some B movie was playing, about a girl and a man and another man. He hadn't even looked at the title of the movie. He didn't know any of the actors in it either. But even if he had known them, he couldn't have watched, he was so nervous. All the time he kept wondering what was happening to his bundle of material. Were they handling it properly? Would they lose any of it? If they lost it, what would he do?

At the end of the movie he got up with the other patrons and went outside. It was snowing. He still had an hour to wait and he didn't want to stand around in the cold. He entered the tavern on the corner and had a couple of drinks. Idly, he gazed into the mirror behind the bar. Before him was a simple glass surface; the ambient light was bouncing off of it, being reflected back into his own eyes, and he was seeing himself, in depth, drinking. He got up and, hurriedly, went outside.

By now, the snow was really coming down. On the spur of the moment, warmed by the whiskey, he walked toward the East River. In the elemental whiteness all about him, the streets and buildings and sky all merged into one. He liked the eerie quiet. Only now and then a figure emerged like a dark shadow and then slipped back into the whiteness. When he came to the river, he looked out over the dark water and saw how the falling snow disappeared, melting into the blackness. Hiddenness was here too. Hiddenness was all around him. Why hadn't he noticed it before? Secrecy was in the air, thick as snow, protective as well as exciting.

On the corner of Thirty-Eighth Paul Smith was waiting. He was coughing and stamping his feet. Harry took the package from him, now not so carefully wrapped, made his way to Penn Station, caught a train to Philly, went back to the lab, replaced the papers, and, since by now it was morning, decided to do a little work.

When he finally did get home late Saturday night, he had dinner and fell into bed almost in a torpor. Instead of finding sleep, however, he found the terror he'd been putting off since the night before: the terror that people on the train might see him and know what he was doing, the terror that someone at the lab might see him putting the materials back. He recalled the movie *The Invisible Man*, in which Claude Rains was a scientist who had discovered a potion that made him invisible. But once he was invisible, he couldn't get back to being seen. He must have been naked when he became invisible, because the invisibility didn't extend to the clothes he was wearing. So when he put on a suit, you could see the suit moving when he moved. The audience laughed at things moving through the air, unsupported. But no one laughed in the last scene when the Invisible Man was shot. Just before he died you saw the imprint of his body in the snow. Then, slowly, his body became visible and you realized he was dead.

Habit is an amazing thing. Or at least it was to Harry. He likened it to momentum, the force that keeps you going once you've started on a trajectory. (Of course, it also has to be overcome to get you started.) He was like a steel ball rolling down an inclined plane, encountering no friction. Soon, so soon, his journeys to New York and back had become habit. This is what he did every other Friday night: He took things and he put them back. And nobody noticed.

Now and then he did feel a twinge of fear at the possibility that he might be caught. This, he supposed, would never go away. But perhaps if you did something, anything, often enough you got used to it, like wearing tight shoes. It was amazing what could become ordinary in life, in two lives.

He had learned almost at once that when he was in one life he must not think of the other. You simply turned your back on the other life and concentrated on the one you were in. It wasn't that you didn't *know* about the other life. Of course you knew about it. It wasn't like the story of Dr. Jekyll and Mr. Hyde, in which Dr. Jekyll not only didn't know about the existence of Mr. Hyde, he didn't even look anything like him, whereas in his second life Harry looked just the same as the Harry of his first life.

Finally, after months and months of deliveries, he had given Amtorg everything they needed or wanted from his company. Still, despite his telling them this, he was summoned to New York on the following Friday night.

When he arrived at the usual place, at the usual hour, Paul Smith suggested that he and Harry adjourn to a nearby bar. Once inside, he ordered double Scotches for himself and Harry. To his surprise, Paul Smith began by congratulating him. He told him how pleased "they" were to have the information he had provided. There was no question but that it would be of great use to the well-being of the Russian people. Harry was gratified to hear this, as not once before this had the agent said anything complimentary to him. Looking at his ingratiating smile, Harry felt a certain remorse at the thought that he had once thought he looked like a fish.

After the waiter brought the drinks, Paul Smith leaned over and took a package wrapped in brown paper out of his briefcase. He put the package on the table and slid it across to Harry.

"What's this?"

"Open it," the agent said.

He tore off the brown paper and there inside was a new two volume edition of a chemical textbook he had been longing for but could never afford. "For me?"

"Yes. In appreciation. From the Soviet people." Paul Smith raised his glass and together they drank a silent toast.

Flushed with pleasure, Harry decided this was a good time to make his own suggestion as to what he could do to help Amtorg from now on. The most helpful thing, he was sure, would be to provide information on experimental work being done at the various company labs. In fact, Harry had some ideas of his own about a new process using thermal diffusion that he'd be glad to share with them.

"Experimental work?" The agent's benign smile suddenly turned sour. "We are not interested in anything smacking of experimentation. We only want what has already been proved in actual production."

"But this is new and exciting stuff I'm talking about, stuff with great possibilities for future development."

"We have many laboratories in the Soviet Union that are capable of working on new—," and here Paul Smith sneered, "stuff."

"Oh," said Harry, sorely disappointed. The agent was breathing heavily, mouth open. Perhaps, after all, he did look like a fish.

"Consideration has been given as to what further contribution you can make that will be most helpful." Paul Smith leaned forward in his chair. "We would like you to go to the Navy Yard and get a job there."

"But what about my present job?"

"Leave it."

"Leave it?" Harry was stunned by the suggestion. "I couldn't do that. They've got it set up so I can take classes at Drexel. I have to finish my schooling. I can't leave my job."

Well then, Paul Smith countered, maybe he knew someone who worked at the Navy Yard, and he could get information about what was being done there from him.

No, Harry said firmly, he knew nobody.

The agent shrugged and drank his Scotch in silence. Then, in a voice that brooked no refusal, he continued. "Surely, among your friends at school, there are likely candidates who would be willing to help us out. That is to be your next assignment, to recruit new people to help our cause. And," he emphasized, "I will require continuing reports on your progress in recruiting others."

I'm not going to be any good at that, Harry knew. But he merely nodded, glumly.

As they parted, he thanked Paul Smith profusely for the volumes. "I've always wanted these," he said. They shook hands and Harry walked downtown while the agent went uptown. Harry turned once and looked back but the agent was lost in the crowd. Clutching the two volume set in his hand, Harry was grateful, but disturbed. He was shocked that they weren't interested in experimental work. It showed an appalling lack of scientific vision. Obviously he was not dealing with true scientists, or they would have jumped at the chance of getting such material. That was the problem, he sighed, in dealing with bureaucrats anywhere. They have no true appreciation of what matters.

Shifting the volumes from one arm to the other, Harry allowed himself a small feeling of pride at this gift from the Russian people, who no doubt didn't even know he existed. Still, what mattered was that he knew it was a job well done. Fame didn't matter to him. It never had. Only once that he remembered had he felt jealousy at another being the focus of all eyes, and that was at a high school gathering when Morty Zahn got up and played the piano and everyone had laughed and cheered; but that wasn't fame, exactly.

At Drexel, Harry kept looking at his fellow students, trying to decide who would be a likely candidate for recruiting. Even if he found someone, how would he broach the subject? He certainly couldn't say straight out, Would you like to be a courier for the Russians? After weeks of mulling it over, he finally settled on Don Leach as the most likely of those he knew. Don was a fellow student in the same certificate program, and several times over the years Harry had heard him express dissatisfaction with the slow pace of reform in Washington.

One evening, seeing Don huddled over his lab notebook in the library, Harry sidled up to him. Nervous though he was, he tried to be casual. He began with what he thought were a few light-hearted remarks about the weather—how it was so hot, even for Indian summer in Philadelphia. From there he went on to baseball and to yesterday's game in which the Phillies lost, again. Then he proceeded with his approach to an approach, not too general, but not too specific either. "I was wondering what your feelings were or would be about—I mean to say—it is very hard to know—for anyone—under the present circumstances—things being as they are—"

"What did you say?" Don said, not even looking up.

"I was wondering—do you have any—I mean—what is the—I

mean—we're lucky to be able to have information available to us—when there are countries where people have no information available to them at all, where, no matter what they do, the people are forced to live in poverty—in terrible conditions and—and it's not their—"

"Yeah, Harry, you're right, things are tough all over," Don nodded, as he turned the pages of his lab notebook.

Harry desperately tried to think of what Dave had said to him, so he could repeat the same words to Don. "I kind of think there are things that must be done—things are certainly still terrible in this country—even if some people think they are better—it's a Band-Aid, nothing but a Band-Aid—while elsewhere, in some countries, it's even worse—people are—"

Don Leach threw up his hands. "These numbers are not coming out right," he exploded. "I may have to do the whole goddam experiment all over again."

"Can I look at it? Maybe your calculations are off. There's one equation where the substitutions are very tricky."

"Would you do that? That would be great."

"Sure. I'd be glad to help you."

That night Harry sat down and wrote out a number of pages about his recruiting efforts with a young scientist, whose name he gave as "Si Shapiro." He elaborated on his discussions, saying that although they were not initially fruitful, he thought it possible that over a period of time, something might be accomplished with this "likely candidate."

He followed this first report with a number of other reports, spaced strategically over time, all recounting his efforts at recruiting imaginary people, using the names of his boyhood friends to give them authenticity. He invariably ended up by saying that, though no definite commitment had been obtained from the "likely candidate," nevertheless he would maintain contact and continue to attempt to enlist his services. He diligently turned the reports over to Paul Smith and never heard anything further about them.

ONE FRIDAY NIGHT, on the spur of the moment, Harry decided to visit Dave White. To see Dave, despite Paul Smith's order not to, was a reassertion to himself that he need not obey orders unthinkingly, that he could also use his own judgment. Having already deceived those who were so expert at deception with his recruiting reports, he felt curiously liberated. Perhaps there had been chains binding him before, not chains forged by the bourgeoisie, by the capitalist system, but of a more elemental kind.

He did not call Dave ahead of time but chose to surprise him by appearing unannounced at the door of his apartment. In fact, it was Harry who was surprised when a stranger answered his knock. A thin man in pajamas opened the door a crack. "What do you want? Who are you?"

"Isn't Dave White here?"

"No, he's not."

"When do you expect him?"

"I'm not expecting him."

"Isn't this his apartment?"

"It's his apartment but he's not living here anymore." The stranger started to close the door.

"Wait! How can this be his apartment if he doesn't live here any more?"

"I'm subletting the apartment from him. I don't know why you're making such a big deal of this at this hour. Do you know it's eleven o'clock at night?"

"For how long? For how long are you subletting it?"

"He didn't say. He just said he was going away for a while."

"Going where? When did he leave?" But the thin man in his pajamas had already shut the door.

On Monday evening just before quitting time, Harry went to see Bob Silver in his lab. He found him in a storeroom, checking out supplies. Right away Harry told him that he'd been to Jersey City to see Dave and he wasn't there. "Do you know what happened to him? Do you know where he went?"

Bob shut the storeroom door. "Dave's gone to Spain."

"When?"

"Some time ago. To fight for the Loyalists."

Harry was stunned. He'd read a little about the Spanish Civil War in the paper but he was too busy, what with his work and school, and his reports on recruiting, to pay much attention to the world outside. "Why didn't he tell people?" Why didn't he tell me? Harry meant but he couldn't say that.

"It's illegal, that's why. He didn't want to take a chance on the government finding out and stopping him. Even the—" he looked around the storeroom—"Even the Party didn't want him to go, at first. He had a lot of trouble persuading them."

Harry still couldn't understand how Dave could do this, go across an ocean to risk death in a war in a country that wasn't even his. "What about his family?"

"He doesn't have a family except for two old maid aunts, and he's not close to them. No," he said in a burst of enthusiasm, "the workers, the proletariat everywhere, they are his real family. Those are his brothers and sisters that are suffering in Spain, his brothers and sisters who fought against the capitalist system and won the revolution and established the Republic. And now everything they fought for is being threatened by Franco and Hitler and Mussolini—while the Western democracies just sit back and let everything and everyone go down the drain," he ended bitterly.

"I can't believe it—that he went to Spain."

Bob shrugged. "Whether you believe it or not, that's what he did. If you ask me, I'd say it's a heroic action."

"I guess," Harry stammered. "But he could get himself killed."

"That's what heroes do." Bob sighed and, after a pause, added, "I don't know about you, but I'm going home."

"Me, too," Harry said, though after Bob left, he stayed in the storeroom. Looking at a centrifuge on the shelf, he kept thinking about all the things Dave had said in their conversations that could have led him to take this step. He had spoken about his belief that Marxism was the way for man to learn to control his destiny; he had said that through Marx's teachings one learned to live rationally, to take a scientific view of history. But what was scientific, what was rational, about going to a strange country and maybe getting yourself killed? It certainly wasn't a way to control one's own destiny.

It was odd how lost Harry felt, abandoned really. As long as Harry had known Dave was there, in Jersey City, in that apartment with the green couch and the table and chairs and the Murphy bed, even if he didn't see him, he was reassured. In his mind, Dave was like a rock, solid, somehow always there to be leaned on. Now that he wasn't there, Harry couldn't imagine him anywhere. He certainly couldn't imagine him in Spain, in battle.

Recalling the movie *All Quiet on the Western Front,* he remembered the scenes of shells bursting, of dirt spraying, of men crawling over No-Man's-Land, of men being killed. He tried to place Dave in those scenes but, no matter how he tried, he couldn't. Death was not part of life as he knew it. He had never known anyone who had died. In his family they did not talk of death. It—like past history—wasn't spoken of.

Closing the door behind him, he went back to his own lab. He concentrated on his work, shutting out all thoughts about Dave, as if he'd locked them in a storeroom in his brain and thrown away the key. Finally he went home, had a cold supper, which Mom had left in the icebox, and went to bed. Stan was already asleep, snoring lightly.

As he lay in bed, the storeroom door burst open and thoughts poured out, flooding his brain, trivial and consequential all mixed together: the thought that Dave was a hero, the thought of Frank Merriwell in the boy's series he'd read when he was a kid—Frank Merriwell who had fought against the odds, fair and square—the thought of sports heroes, including

Babe Ruth and Dizzy Dean and Hank Lusetti and Mose Grove, particularly that time when Grove came in as a relief pitcher in the ninth with the bases loaded and struck out three men on nine pitched balls and won the game. You admired these heroes, you wanted to be like them, you wished you could be like them, your wish and your admiration built and built, so at times you even felt you shared in the heroism, you were part of that bigness. But for all those heroes, death was not a risk. Dave had chosen to go to a war in which he might be killed. What did it mean to believe so fiercely that you were willing to give up your life for that belief?

It came to Harry that everything he was doing in his life was puny. He was a little man, destined for nothing more than smallness, while those few heroes, like Dave, vaulted into some special and hallowed atmosphere, from which he was forever barred. He felt himself going over the same tortured logic of tortured feeling, always ending up in the same place—with his own unheroic self. He began with anxiety about what could happen to Dave. It went on to a sense of his friend as being large, almost monumental. It ended, inevitably, with his own puniness. Then he started all over again with his anxiety about what could happen to Dave, that he could die.

He told himself he had to stop. He told himself he had to get some sleep. All he was doing was going round and round in his thinking as if his brain were a centrifuge, spinning thoughts around, trying to separate out heroes from non-heroes. But then, suddenly, it was he that was separated out, into an entirely different orbit where another determination—another judgment could be made, where other needs resided.

As a boy, Harry had had periods when he was driven to intense masturbation, though in recent years, when it happened, it was more likely to be mechanical than intense. Now in the darkness, in the room he shared with Stan, who was still snoring lightly, he was acted upon by an erotic undertow. There was the seduction of himself by himself, the swelling from steady effort, the succumbing to imagining. Above him was the image of a woman, a huge woman. She was mounted on top of him. He sucked at her pendulous breasts as she was riding, riding him. He raised his head, he looked into her eyes, she was seeing him seeing her. He came with a muffled groan that was covered by the sound of Stan's snoring.

Afterwards, he sat up and looked into the darkness. He wanted to jump out of his own skin. He tried to console himself with the thought that he had another, secret, life. He lay back in bed and masturbated again, and yet again. It was like a frenzy in him, coming to climax, repeatedly. Then, sweating and shaking, feeling almost blind with dullness, he tried to sleep. He could not sleep. He got up and went into the kitchen, opened a box of Jell-O and ate the powdered Jell-O from the box, uncooked.

THE MORNING WAS a morning like any other. Last night he'd been in a frenzy; today he was his usual self, with no residue left from the night before except the faintest taste of the too sweet Jell-O powder upon his tongue. He had set the alarm at five so he could tutor a student who was about to take an exam. In the past months three students who were having difficulty with their course work at Drexel had come to Harry for help. Naturally Harry had said Yes to all of them. They offered him money for his tutoring, but Harry refused it. No, No, he insisted, I don't want to be paid.

He spent two hours with the student, making sure that he got all the concepts clearly, and then went to work in the dye lab, where he had a temporary assignment. Sometime in the late morning, walking past the oven, he heard an odd hissing sound, but at the moment his mind was on the broken glass he had just spied under the sink opposite the oven. Obviously one of the technicians had swept the glass there to hide it so he wouldn't be charged for breakage. Getting down on his knees, Harry began to pick up the glass, piece by piece. Suddenly there was a loud noise and he felt a terrific blow to his back.

Later he found out that a new lab assistant, assigned to purify a dyestuff, had decided for some reason to use ether as the solvent. He had put the dyestuff on a watch glass in the oven so the ether would evaporate off. As the oven heated up, the unshielded contacts of the thermostat sparked, causing the residual ether to ignite, which, in turn, caused the oven door to fly off and sail through the air. Unfortunately for Harry, it landed on his back as he was crouching to pick up the glass. To make matters worse, the force of the flying door wedged him in under the sink so tightly he could not move. Someone shouted, someone laughed, someone rushed to extricate him. He wasn't badly burned but his back was severely bruised and his hands were bleeding from being forced down into the glass fragments.

Dr. Rink came running when he heard about the accident. He asked Harry if he wanted to go to a doctor but Harry shook his head. He insisted that he wanted to go right back to work. Dr. Rink said No, absolutely not, and he ordered a company car to take Harry home.

Of course, Cecilia had a fit when the company car drove up to the house and Harry hobbled up the path in broad daylight. "I'm all right, Mom," he said, when she came rushing out. "It's just a few little bruises. It's nothing."

"You call this nothing?" she shouted when she saw his hands. She made him get into bed and bathed his wounds just as she had bathed Pop's torn and bleeding fingers. She had some pain pills which a doctor had once given her for her headaches and she gave these to Harry. He fell asleep and slept for hours, on his stomach. Several times he woke himself up, trying to roll over on his back, but he forced himself to stay on his stomach with his face turned to the wall.

The next day he felt even worse. When Cecilia brought him his food on a tray, he wasn't hungry but he made himself eat. "Finally you're getting some rest," she observed. "All it takes is a knock on the back from a flying oven door to put some sense into you."

Harry tried to force a grin but he was too miserable. He'd been going over in his mind that moment when he had heard that hissing sound as he passed the ovens. He had to have known or at least suspected that it indicated some kind of trouble, and yet he had gone right on to pick up the glass. His failure to pay attention suggested that he was not someone who could be relied on. Or was his lapse a form of punishment for his activities in this very bed last night? That's crazy, he told himself. Punished by an oven door that's become a projectile?

He turned to more pressing matters, to the mid-term examinations scheduled for next week at Drexel. He was in his last year at the Institute and he didn't want to spoil his straight A average. He called out to Mom to bring him his books. At first she refused but then, seeing how miserable he was, she relented. He lay on his stomach and worked diligently, focusing so intently he became oblivious to the pain.

The third morning of his involuntary vacation, the telephone rang. They'd gotten a telephone soon after Pop got his old job back, and it was still an exciting event to hear the ring. At first Harry thought it might be someone from the lab inquiring about his progress but then he heard Mom saying that he wasn't well and was in bed. She stopped talking and then he heard her say it again. Finally she came in and said, "Some man is insisting that he has to talk to you now. He won't give me his name. I told him you were sick but he won't take no for an answer."

Harry got up out of bed, and, bent over like a C, walked into the kitchen. When he picked up the phone, the voice on the other end was Paul Smith, just as he had expected. He insisted that Harry come to New York that very moment. "I'm not feeling very well," Harry explained.

"This is urgent. Very, very urgent."

"What are you doing?" Cecilia cried out, when she saw Harry come out of his room dressed.

"I have to go. It's very important," he told her, moving toward the door in a crouch.

By the time he was actually sitting, facing the agent in a quiet bar in the Bronx, the three pills which he had taken before leaving had worn off. He forced himself to pay attention to what Paul Smith was saying. To Harry's dismay, his every word, every sentence, was an attack. At times his voice rose in volume till he was shouting, as if he didn't care who was around. At other times he whispered so harshly, his voice became hoarse. And what was he saying? It all came down to the same thing: Harry was not doing—had not done—enough.

Harry was stupefied. He opened his mouth to object but then he remembered his reports on recruiting Si Shapiro and all the others. He recalled the little touches he'd given for verisimilitude, naming restaurants and bars, where they'd met, even giving details of the conversations. How could they know these reports were made up?

He ordered another Canadian Club, this time without a chaser. He shut his eyes; he felt the pain. He opened his eyes. He watched Paul Smith's mouth, his lips and tongue working so furiously. The onslaught

of words was like a blow on top of the blow he had already received
from the oven door. Once more he was being wedged in. He felt a stirring
of something that might have been anger. He drank the whiskey neat and
stood up, weaving a little on his feet. "Couldn't this have waited?"

"Wait? Wait? You talk about waiting?" Paul Smith yelled. "There's
no time for waiting any more. Why are you bent over like that?"

"I had a small accident," he said.

"What kind of accident?"

He tried to explain it to Paul Smith.

"This is the way capitalists treat their workers, endangering them,
not giving a damn if they're hurt."

"It was an accident," Harry insisted.

"There is no such thing as an accident." He paused after that pronouncement and then muttered something about worker's rights and the
need for protection against the employer. "You're not paying attention to
me," he whispered furiously, grabbing Harry's injured hand.

"My hand," Harry yelled. "It hurts."

"Pay attention to other people for a change. Stop being so concerned
with yourself. You talk of hurt. What is your hurt compared to what's
going on in the world? Don't you know what's happening in Czechoslovakia, what's happened in Spain?"

"In Spain?" Harry thought of Dave White. Had he been wounded?
Had he been killed?

"The capitalist countries are appeasing Hitler, hoping he'll attack
the Soviet Union—"

Through the spongy cloud of his own pain, he was aware of something like fear or even desperation in this man across from him. "What do
you want me to do?" Harry asked.

Paul Smith shook himself like a dog who has just come out of the
ocean. "We must do more. We must do more."

ONLY ONCE IN the days that followed did it occur to him that he could have said No to Paul Smith: No, I won't do more; No, I won't do anything. But by that time, his wounds having healed from the accident that wasn't really an accident, he was already doing more. Every three weeks he received a call assigning him a mission as a courier. He always did what was asked of him, even if it involved traveling overnight. North to Buffalo, south to Raleigh, north to Syracuse—wherever he was asked to go, Harry went without question. Nor did he ever submit an account of his expenses.

In Harry's daily life, in his family's daily life, things had improved financially. You could almost say that they had turned a corner. Not only did Pop have his old job back but Stan also had a job, part-time, and would soon be finishing high school and could take a job full-time. Harry himself received a raise of four dollars a week. He was going to pass it on to Mom but she insisted on his keeping it; he accepted reluctantly.

It wasn't that he didn't like money but he was so used to being on an edge financially, with the specter of poverty always at his back, the money seemed unfairly his, an overabundance. Dave had once said something about the Marxist doctrine of "To each according to his need." Harry didn't believe in that doctrine any more than he believed in any doctrine, but the extra money did make him feel bloated, as if he'd gulped down too much rich food.

When a technician in his department lamented that he needed five dollars to get by till payday, Harry found himself offering to help. Soon it became known at the company that he was a soft touch. All you had to do was ask him to lend you a few dollars; you didn't have to explain why you needed it. As for paying him back, he acted so embarrassed at taking the money that a number of borrowers just didn't repay him. Several times, when he was asked for money and he didn't have it, he went to the trouble of borrowing the money from someone else to make the loan. Once, after a complete stranger, a technician working in another part of the company, asked him for some money, Harry went to another friend and borrowed the money and even took a long ride on a streetcar out to the man's house to bring him the cash. It didn't occur to Harry to wonder if he could have asked the man to come to him.

He didn't have much time for wondering of any kind because he was so busy. He was not only working at the lab six days a week and going to school at night, and tutoring four students, but in addition to being a courier he was being asked to take on other missions. Once he was asked to follow a man suspected of being a Trotskyite. He was supposed to observe his behavior, see where he went, see who he met with, etc. etc. Harry did not like this assignment at all. Receiving and passing on information was one thing. Hiding and spying on another man, in order to rat on him, was something else entirely.

When he reported to Paul Smith that the suspected Trotskyite had eluded him, the Russian frowned. "I can't believe you lost him." Shaking his head in disgust, he added, "No more of those jobs for you." Though the Russian seemed to feel he was taking away a special benefit, Harry was much relieved. After that, Paul Smith piled on even more missions for Harry as a courier. To fulfill these duties Harry often had to be away from home at night on a weekend.

Of course, Cecilia did not know where he went or why on those nights but she began to suspect that he was involved in a secret love affair. Harry only laughed uneasily when she said something to him about this, which made her all the more suspicious. She reminded him that he was already twenty-five years old; it was time for him to be thinking about getting married and having his own home and his own children.

"I'm not ready yet," he told her, as she was arguing with him one evening in the kitchen.

"But you are ready for wild flings?"

In response he became stubbornly silent, his best and only refuge from her recriminations.

"You are, aren't you?" she insisted.

When he still did not answer, she went into the living-dining room. She plumped up the pillows of the new parlor set, a replacement for the one they'd had to return years ago. She smoothed the wrinkles of the upholstery, ferociously yet tenderly, as if she feared that this set too might be taken from her at any moment. Though things were better, she was not someone who would ever take anything for granted. Her actions implied that to do so could invite retribution.

Watching her from the kitchen, Harry sighed. He felt a certain guilt that he was not telling her the truth, but then he reassured himself by saying that in his own way he was only trying to protect her from knowing what it would be better for her not to know.

In June Harry graduated with honors from Drexel Institute. Although he did feel a sense of pride in his achievement, he also realized that to go forward, to really learn about his field—and he did have a passionate desire to learn—he would have to enroll in a college with a degree program in chemistry. Since Mom and Pop and Stan were no longer dependent on him, that is, since they could get by on the income from Pop and Stan, he could take two years off and go to college. He was encouraged in this by the family, particularly by Mom, who never ceased stressing the importance of education in life.

When Dr. Rink appeared in the lab one morning, Harry took the opportunity to speak to him. He told him that now that he had finished the technical degree, he was thinking of going to a university to get a higher degree. He asked if the company would keep his old job for him, so he'd have it on his return. Certainly, Dr. Rink said, he would save Harry's job. He was a valuable employee and he did not want to lose him. Moreover, he would be very glad to give him an excellent recommendation.

Harry was dazzled by the sudden enlargement of possibilities open to him in the world. After he got a bachelor's degree, he might even get a master's. Then he could be the head chemist in a lab, supervising experiments in his own research. Maybe by then he might even be married and have children and a home of his own. In the face of these heady prospects his heart raced; his breathing quickened and grew shallow. It seemed he did have a future. He felt something that might have been exhilaration, though it was tinged with fear, a fear that too much hope sometimes brings in its wake.

As he was trying to decide what he should do, an important and defining event occurred. Or rather, something didn't occur that he expected to occur: He did not hear from Paul Smith. At first, he speculated that it was due to a momentary lapse in communication. But as the days wore on and he still heard nothing, he reminded himself of a remark the Russian had tossed off a while ago. In the midst of giving him instructions about picking up a packet of information, he had muttered the words, "I could be recalled."

"What for?" Harry had asked.

"Don't you understand anything? Don't you understand what that means?" the Russian retorted, which was hardly a reply as far as Harry could tell.

The agent had shown up at their next meeting and at several meetings after that and he'd never once referred to what he'd said earlier. But now, as the days passed, and there was nothing but silence from his end, Harry decided that indeed Paul Smith must have been recalled. Harry didn't want to think about what that meant. But if Paul Smith was recalled, now maybe they—the Russians—were done with him. Without his having had to say No, I don't want to do any more, the situation had simply resolved itself. It had also resolved his uncertainty about what he should do.

He began by sending out letters to various prestigious schools, requesting applications for enrollment. When they came back, he filled them out and enclosed his transcript. Right away he got answers from Columbia and MIT, saying they wouldn't credit him with the work he'd done at Drexel. It was a blow to Harry but he waited patiently for the answers from the other schools. These too, it turned out, refused to give him credit for his previous work. They all said he had to start over again, from the beginning, something he could not afford to do.

Undeterred, he filled out applications to eleven colleges, working his way down from mid-size to small. Someone told him about Xavier, a Catholic university in Cincinnati that had a good program in chemistry.

Remembering that they had a good football team—hadn't they won an upset victory over Tulane?—Harry also applied there at the last minute. The eleven smaller schools turned him down. In September, just before the fall term began, he received an acceptance from Xavier, allowing him credit for all his previous work at Drexel.

At Xavier, Harry was happier than he'd ever been in his life. He was spending full time learning just what he wanted to learn in an atmosphere of kindness and serenity. He loved his scientific courses, working all hours, day and night in the lab, in order to perfect his technique and his understanding. He responded eagerly to the teaching of the fathers, to their seriousness of purpose, their selflessness, their sense of devotion to what was beyond themselves. He noted that they treated him no differently from the other students because he was a Jew.

He remembered the pressure that Dave had put on him, when he had tried to convince him of the rightness of the Communist cause so he too would become a Communist. (Where was Dave, now that the Spanish Civil War was over, and he had been on the losing side?) The Fathers made no attempt to convince him of the rightness of their beliefs, to convert him. Of course, he would never have converted. He would not betray his own history, dim and uncertain as it was. Still, he found comfort in being surrounded by those who believed so intensely. As an outsider, admiring them, he could contemplate their ritual with the safety and assurance that no demand would be put upon him. The mystery of the mass, which he witnessed on several occasions, intrigued him with its intertwining of the real and the not real. He himself always made a point of keeping the two separate.

Wandering into the church one day, he observed from a distance the discreet ritual of the confession. He wondered what it would be like to enter into that small dark box, to be one of two invisible presences, the penitent and the confessor, screened off from each other. Through that screen, in one direction, would flow the most intimate and dark secrets. And in return, in response, like a kind of sacred osmosis, would flow absolution and forgiveness.

Leaving the church unobserved, he concluded that apparently, if one was a believer, one could do wrong and afterward ask to be forgiven by

God. Harry's sense of the Jewish God was that total forgiveness, absolution in this world and the next through acknowledgment of one's sins, was not what one should expect from Him. From childhood on, Harry had the impression that Jehovah was a God who was tied to a life that had been, in another country, a God that had been carried over land and water and had become, if anything, harsher in the carrying.

When Cecilia spoke of God, which she did rarely, though she often spoke of the Law, her words had unexpected intentions and lapses. Because she was so fierce in her pronouncements, Harry had always thought of her God as fierce. One thing she made absolutely clear: you did not apply to God for help in this life. That was not part of the agreement with Him. There was only your obligation in this life, to obey the Law. And the reward for obeying was yet another duty to be obeyed. Whether there was or was not another life, you must live—this too, she made clear—as if there was this life and this life only.

Much to his surprise, he did not miss home. Of course, he wrote Mom dutifully and called home once a month, but his new life was so absorbing that he didn't have time to think about Philadelphia. Besides, he knew he would go back to his old job, to his old room, when the two years at Xavier were over.

In his living arrangement he had been very lucky. He had found a room in the house of Mrs. Bucknell, a widow, who charged him a minimum rate as he was a student. She gave him breakfast and dinner, and she was a good cook. In turn, Harry ran errands for her. She was kind, even motherly, to him, and Harry thought she was a fine looking woman and was glad to be in her house which was also fine looking. He grew fond of Mrs. Bucknell's bulldog Jerry, who had taken to sleeping at the foot of his bed, snoring like Stan.

He was grateful to discover that his own secret sexual life had gone into remission with his abandonment of his secret life out in the world. Here he felt a kinship with the fathers, who submitted so willingly to a vow of chastity and celibacy. In this growing sense of identification with them, in a strictly non-religious way, he began to believe in the possibility of his own moral purity.

The week before Thanksgiving, Mrs. Bucknell asked Harry if he was going home for the holiday. When he said No, she asked if he'd like to have Thanksgiving dinner with her. He was delighted to accept and looked forward with excitement to the whole day. He was going to sleep late and then in the afternoon go to the football game, Xavier against the University of Toledo, and then come back to the house and have a splendid dinner with Mrs. Bucknell, just the two of them.

Thanksgiving morning went just as he anticipated. He didn't wake until ten-thirty, but he wasn't going to feel guilty about that. He had been in the lab very late the night before. He thought about getting up, but instead he dozed, hardly even thinking, glad not to be thinking. Jerry, lying across the bed at his feet, made snuffling noises, as if he too were enjoying the holiday.

Half in and half out of sleep, he heard the phone ring. After a while there was a knock on his door and he came awake with a start. "Harry," Mrs. Bucknell said timidly, "I'm sorry to bother you. But there's a phone call for you. Some man is calling and he says it's very important. He has to talk to you this minute."

Harry got up out of bed, gently pushing Jerry aside, put on his bathrobe, and shuffled to the phone. His hand trembling, he lifted the receiver. "It is very important that I see you at once," came the words in a Russian accent.

"Now?"

"Now."

"But it's Thanksgiving."

"It does not concern me whether it is Thanksgiving or not Thanksgiving. I have traveled here today for the express purpose of meeting with you. I am calling from a phone booth at the Netherlands Plaza Hotel. There is a department store nearby called Shillito's. Do you know it?"

"Yes," Harry mumbled. "But surely it's going to be closed today."

"It does not matter whether it is closed or open. Meet me at the main entrance in ten minutes."

"But it will take me at least forty minutes to get there by bus, and the buses are on a holiday schedule—"

"Take a cab," the Russian barked and hung up.

To Mrs. Bucknell, who was working in the kitchen, Harry said sorrowfully, "It's an emergency. It's very important. I have to go out and I don't know when I'll be back."

"But you'll be back for dinner?"

"I'm not even sure of that."

"Oh, that's too bad. But I'll keep your dinner warm for you, so whenever you come home, it will be waiting for you."

In the cab going downtown Harry was miserable. He kept thinking, I am going to miss the football game, to say nothing of that nice Thanksgiving dinner. He got out of the cab a block from his destination, and walked through the slush to the main entrance of Shillito's. A big man with a harsh-looking face was standing in the doorway. Plug-ugly was the word that came to Harry.

Even before he could say "It's me, Harry," the man motioned to him not to speak but to follow him. The two of them walked, Harry several paces behind, for many blocks. The big man kept turning around to make sure that no one but Harry was following him. They came to a block lined with warehouses, with no one about. They're all home celebrating, or getting ready to celebrate, Harry thought glumly.

The man stopped and faced Harry squarely. "I am Fred," he said affably.

"Glad to meet you, Fred. My name is—"

"I know who you are," Fred cut him off.

Harry sighed and waited. He was ravenously hungry since he hadn't had any breakfast, and he longed for a cup of coffee and several jelly doughnuts.

"How is everything going?"

"Fine." Harry spoke of the excellent courses at Xavier, of the high academic standards.

Fred smiled and grunted.

Encouraged, Harry went on to speak of his admiration for the Fathers, of their kindness and thoughtfulness, of their devotion to their work. Fred kept smiling and grunting. To himself Harry said, This man Fred is really okay. It shows how wrong first impressions can be. I should have remembered what Paul Smith said about paying attention to other people. How could I have forgotten? This man too has a history. He too has suffered. "How is everything going for you?" he asked.

Frowning, Fred ignored his question, and announced that he was here today to discuss a special mission. "You are to go to Dayton today—"

"To Dayton? Today? That's a couple of hours away, isn't it? Actually, I was planning to go to the Toledo-Xavier game."

"You'll have to miss it," Fred said, not at all affably. "You are to go to the house of this man—" and here he took a piece of paper out of his pocket with a name written on it—"and you are to persuade him to provide technical information of interest to us. He is an employee at Wright Air Force Base." He whispered these last words though there was no one around to hear them.

"But—" Harry said. "I'm so busy at school, I'm not really—that is to say—I'm working so hard—the Fathers are wonderful teachers—I can't tell you how much I admire and respect them—I have a number of reports due—I can't take the time—"

"What do you think you're doing? Do you think you can play games with us?"

"I'm not playing games. I'm only trying to say that I feel my services in this particular matter might not be all that helpful. When you get right down to it," he ended lamely, "I'd rather not—"

"And how do you think it will be for you if we send a little anonymous note to the good Fathers you seem to be so fond of? How do you think they will feel about you when they learn that you are a spy for the Soviet Union, Mr. Rather-Not?"

Harry blanched. Could he go to Father Reilly, his wonderful chemistry professor and say to him he had something to confess? What would Father Reilly do? Would he assign him a certain number of Hail Marys and then grant him absolution? Not likely.

"I was only about to say that I'd rather not go today. Today," he repeated, "since it's Thanksgiving and all that. But seeing that you feel so strongly about it—"

SINCE THIS IS A true story, it is necessary to admit that when the time comes for Harry to confess, not to Father Reilly but to the FBI, there will be a curious branching in his account of going to Xavier. Two stories will appear.

The first, the one I have just reported, will tell that Paul Smith berated him, and then Harry did do more, and then he graduated from Drexel, and then Paul Smith was recalled, and then Harry applied to many schools and was turned down and finally went to Xavier, a decision made by default, as no other school would accept his credits from Drexel.

The second begins like the first: Paul Smith berated him, he did do more, he graduated from Drexel, he didn't hear from Paul Smith, he applied to Columbia and MIT, which would not accept his Drexel credits, he applied to smaller schools . . . But—here begins the divergence— he still hadn't gotten the final word from five of them one August morning, when he got a letter with some tickets to a prize fight, a signal telling him to appear at a specified corner in the Bronx at a specified hour, three days after the date of the fight.

Dutifully, he obeyed. He went to the Bronx, and met a new agent, this one called Steve, a small and surprisingly dapper man. Steve didn't say anything about Paul Smith. In fact, he remained resolutely silent during the entire taxi ride to downtown Manhattan. The cab driver was listening to the baseball game, a Yankee game; Harry listened too but he didn't like what he heard because naturally the Yankees were winning.

They got out on Sixth Avenue, under the El, and made their way east to a restaurant. After ordering an excellent meal, Steve launched into an appreciation for all that Harry had done, saying how grateful he and his superiors were for Harry's good work. It was like a balm to his spirit, after what Paul Smith had said. Steve assured Harry that he personally was looking forward to a very good working relationship with him.

What with the drinks before dinner and the wine with dinner, Harry became very talkative, telling Steve about his plans to go back to school to get his degree, even though, as he admitted, things were going to be very tough for him financially.

"This does not seem a wise move," Steve interrupted. "If you want a change, think about getting a job at the Navy Yard. That would be of great assistance to us."

"But I don't want a new job. I want to get a degree." Harry grew more and more expansive, saying that he hoped that with a degree he could get a really good job as a chief chemist, and, who knew, if he was lucky, someday he'd find the right girl and get married and have kids. He told of his disappointment that none of the big schools would give him credit for the work he'd done, but he was not giving up. He said he was applying to a number of smaller schools, which he proceeded to name, one by one.

At the mention of each small school Steve reacted with disdain, until Harry came to Xavier. "Ah, Xavier. That's in Cincinnati, isn't it?"

Harry assured him that it was.

"That's close to Dayton, isn't it?"

"Yes, but—," Harry said, puzzled by what could possibly be so important about Dayton.

Steve ordered dessert, a wonderful chocolate cake, and over coffee Steve said, "You know, you have been a great help to us and we in turn would like to be of help to you in getting your degree. If you go to Xavier, we will be willing to pay for your tuition, and we may, in addition, add a stipend for books and other expenses."

Harry opened his mouth but no words came out.

"So it's agreed on," said Steve, leaning forward and shaking Harry's hand. "One more thing," he added. "From our viewpoint it would be better that you remain single. A single man is free to travel here and there, without anyone inquiring into his habits. You understand what I mean?"

Yes, Harry nodded. It did occur to him that even single men some-times had people inquiring into their habits, but he didn't say anything about that to Steve.

Two stories, alike in every way, except one has a scene missing, a hole in it. But every scene has its ramifications and its consequences. Without that scene Harry simply waits and waits, not knowing what school he will go to, until Xavier is the one that finally chooses him. One would be forced to conclude that Fate guided him, that Fate was the issue here. In the second story the choice was encouraged by the Russian. Fate was granted a little assistance, even manipulated. One would have to conclude then that will was involved, someone's will, if not Harry's.

Obviously, both stories can't be right. Either he met Steve or he didn't. Either the Russians paid for Harry's tuition or they didn't. Which story is one to believe? Is one a lie or the other a lie? Or are both lies? But then why should one be surprised if Harry lied? After all, this is a story about a man who was a spy and a spy, by definition, lies.

Perhaps one should not be surprised, if Harry lied about anything, that he lied about money. Think about what money was to him: how its effect, through its absence, was so powerful in his life, how it dictated whether he and his family would go hungry, whether he could go to college or not. And yet, he acted as if he didn't care about money. Recall how he lent it, even gave it away the minute he was asked, sometimes even if he wasn't asked.

Undoubtedly, for Harry money was connected with many other feel-ings, urges, and possibly even desires. Perhaps, as psychologists have gen-eralized for others, it was connected for him with excretion, with feelings of taking in and giving out, with feelings about hiding and revealing, with the threat of sudden explosions, with the need to hold on, regardless. It could have been like a field of force to him, a locus for shame and shame-lessness, as well as for impulses of generosity.

Whatever the explanation, and explaining is after all, a rather hopeless endeavor in trying to tell the story of a man's life—or two lives—when the time comes to confess, Harry will tell two stories. What is curious is that for some reason, when Harry does tell, the second story will not replace the first. Rather, the first lingers on, side by side with its alternate version, as if uncontradicted, as if story itself can have two lives.

So—after this divergence—where were we? The two men were standing on a deserted street, lined with warehouses. Plug-ugly Fred had just threatened Harry with disclosing his secret activities to the Fathers and Harry had caved in.

Thereupon Fred gave him a whole host of instructions. It was to be a gradual campaign, not a one time effort. If possible, he was to win the confidence of the Wright employee, an aeronautical engineer, then bit by bit persuade him to cooperate. If that didn't work, stronger measures would have to be taken. To be precise, intimidation, threats.

Once more Fred went over the instructions for his first meeting. Harry was to say that Joe had sent him. Joe was a Russian student the engineer had tutored at MIT. It was through this connection that the engineer was deemed vulnerable.

"Is this clear?" Fred wanted to know.

"Yes," said Harry.

"You will, of course, report through the usual channels."

"Yes," said Harry.

They began to walk in the direction of the train station. Surreptitiously, Harry glanced at his watch and noted that the game was going to start in forty minutes. To Harry's surprise the Russian accompanied him all the way to the main entrance of the station, clapped him on the back, and wished him a safe journey.

"So long," said Harry, and went in to buy his ticket. He turned around and there was Fred, smiling, at the entrance. Harry smiled weakly and walked toward the ticket booth, taking his place on line. He turned once again. From this vantage point, Fred, if he was still there, was obscured by a pillar. If I can't see him, he can't see me, Harry decided, and went to the men's room. When he came out, he slipped from pillar to pillar, circling the vast room until he found an inconspicuous exit.

Outside, Fred was nowhere to be seen. Harry hailed a cab and jumped in. He told the driver to take him to the stadium. With luck, he would be on time for the starting of the game.

THE FIRST THING Harry did when he got off the train in Dayton on Saturday was to look up the engineer's address in the telephone book. Next he took the trolley car all the way to the end of the line. He knocked on the door of a modest bungalow and when it was opened by a sandy-haired man in glasses, he said, "I'm looking for Tom Cranak."

"That's me." The man stood there, making no gesture to invite Harry in.

"Joe gave me your name, Joe from MIT. I bring greetings from Joe."

Cranak frowned as if Harry had said something distasteful. He didn't say anything, neither How is Joe? or So what? Not knowing what else to do, Harry asked, "May I come in?" When the engineer still didn't answer, Harry took it upon himself to slip inside. Cranak didn't look at all pleased by his action, though he didn't try to stop him.

In the living room two large men were sitting on the couch, talking. At once Tom Cranak entered into conversation with them. He didn't introduce Harry or ask him to sit down. Eavesdropping—what else could he do?—he heard several different names being mentioned; this one was doing this, that one was doing that. Joe's name was not among them. After ten minutes, Harry got tired of standing and sat on a straight chair in the corner. The conversation was about people he didn't know and had no interest in. Actually, he didn't have that much interest in Tom Cranak either. If it were up to him, he would not be in Dayton at all. Where he would really like to be was in the lab, working, or in the library studying. But there was the matter of Fred's threat. Fred would surely follow through just as he had said, by sending an anonymous note to the Fathers, if Harry hadn't come here.

After a while the two hefty men, still not acknowledging his presence, got up and left. Cranak accompanied them to the door and then came back and stood in the center of the room, brooding. The silence extended, awkwardly. Harry felt it was his responsibility to make Cranak feel at ease. "Joe gave me your name," he offered. "Joe from MIT."

"So you said."

"I'm new to this area. It's lonely when you're all alone in a new place, so Joe suggested I look you up."

Cranak was looking at him as though he didn't believe a word he said. Harry had to admit to himself that it wasn't a very good story but it was the story that Fred had told him to use.

"Do you live here alone?" he inquired, taking a new tack.

"My mother and father and brother live with me," Cranak said begrudgingly.

"Just like me. That's the way I live."

"I thought you said you lived alone."

"I do, I do, but at home—when I am at home—I live with my mother and father and brother."

This coincidence in their situations elicited only more silence. Pointedly Cranak looked at his watch. "If you don't mind, I have things I have to do."

"Sure, sure, I understand. I know I just dropped in on you without any warning. Sorry to have disturbed you." As Harry went to the door, he feared that his words had been too mild for his assignment. He felt the need to muster up a little more assertiveness. "It's been great getting to know you, and I look forward to knowing you much better in the future. I'll call next time I'm in Dayton, if you don't mind."

When Cranak didn't say No, I don't mind, Harry knew that this assignment was definitely going to take much longer than he had hoped. On the other hand, he hadn't said, Yes, I do mind.

Three times, over the next few weeks, Harry traveled to Dayton. The first two times, he made the mistake of telephoning on his arrival at the train station to ask if the engineer was at home. But when he gave his name—or rather gave the name he had given Cranak, which was Raymond—the voice of a man, a voice that sounded like Cranak's, said he was out and he had no idea when he would be back. Harry figured that he was being put off, so the third time, instead of calling ahead, he simply went out to Cranak's house and rang the doorbell.

"What do you want?" the engineer asked sourly when he opened the door and saw Harry standing there.

"Just paying a friendly visit," said Harry.

"I'm very busy."

"This'll just take a minute." Once again Harry slipped past him. He looked at the couch—it was not occupied—and at the straight chair in the corner. He also noticed that the furniture was much less crowded than in the living room–dining room at home. "How are things?" he asked, trying to sound affable but not too affable.

"What kind of things?" came the surly response.

"Work. How's work?"

"Work is all right."

"I gather you work at Wright Field."

"How do you know that?"

"Joe told me."

"How does Joe know?"

"Oh, Joe would not want to lose touch. He sends his best regards." Cranak stared at him suspiciously. After a moment Harry said, "I was hoping we could go out and have a little chat. Perhaps you'll let me buy you a drink."

"I don't drink."

"It's just a manner of speaking. How about coffee?"

"Not now. I'm very busy." Cranak was almost snarling.

"I know how that is. Ah, well, maybe next time," Harry said in his most cheerful voice, as he went out the door.

Naturally Harry was reporting to Fred on his attempts to get Cranak to cooperate. He may have embellished his account a bit, but on the whole he presented a fairly accurate picture of what was going on: In short, despite a number of attempts, he was getting nowhere. At last he got word from Fred that he was to "use pressure, as was discussed."

Once more Harry went to Dayton. Once more he knocked at Cranak's door. Once more the engineer answered, a frown on his face. Once more he asked in a nasty tone of voice, "What do you want?"

"I have to see you about something important," Harry said severely. "I think it would be better if we spoke inside." He brushed past Cranak. As before, he didn't try to stop him. It was almost as if he was afraid to. Harry had never been in a situation in which someone was afraid of him and he found it very peculiar. He certainly couldn't say that he liked it. On the other hand, it was probably better than being afraid yourself.

"May I sit down?" Harry asked, taking off his hat. He thought it was best to be as polite as possible. Cranak kept standing, so Harry didn't sit down. He rummaged in his coat pocket and brought out several slips of paper which Fred had sent him. "I thought you might want to look at these," he said, as he handed them to the engineer.

Cranak turned pale. "What is this? What are you doing? Do you know what you're doing?" He swayed on his feet, as if he were about to faint. Harry put out his hand to steady him.

"Don't touch me," Cranak yelled, pulling away. "This is terrible, awful, what you're doing. These things don't mean anything. I tutored Joe. When he paid me, he said he needed receipts. So I gave him receipts. That's all these are, receipts for tutoring."

"Rather large sums for tutoring, wouldn't you say?"

"I tutored him a lot. He needed a lot of help because he was having so much trouble with the language. He was a student, and I tutored him. That's what these receipts are for."

"Receipts from a Russian? What would the security people at Wright think of that?" Harry asked. He noticed an odd echo of Fred's voice in his own words. He was forcing, just as he had been forced. He was threatening, just as he had been threatened. Cranak was blanching, just as he had blanched. The engineer fell onto the couch and put his head in his hands.

At that moment, an elderly man entered the room. "Is there something wrong?" He looked at Cranak; then he looked at Harry.

"Nothing's wrong."

Harry put on his hat. "I'll be going now but I'll be in touch. Nice to meet you," he said to the elderly man, as he left.

Harry let the engineer think about the receipts for two weeks before he returned to Dayton. At three o'clock on a Saturday afternoon he knocked on his door. Cranak opened it, took one look at Harry and slammed the door. He reappeared a moment later, wearing his coat and hat. "I don't want my family to hear any of this," he muttered.

As he hurried down the street, Harry strained to keep up with him. At the next corner, Cranak stopped and faced Harry. "I haven't done anything. I told you, I tutored Joe and that's all I did. What do you want from me?"

"We thought you might like to—that is we thought you might not be averse to—"

"Averse—averse—," he laughed bitterly. "I'm averse to anything you have to say to me."

"Given the circumstances, we thought you might not mind providing us with a little information on your work at Wright Field."

"Fuck you!" he shouted and began to run. It was not a very rapid run but Harry huffed and puffed, trying to keep up with him.

Three blocks further on, Cranak stopped and gestured wildly. "You see that house across the way? That is the house of an FBI man that I know. I am going into that house. If you want to come into that house with me, feel free to come along."

Ignoring the oncoming traffic, Cranak darted across the street and ran up the outside steps of the semi-detached house. Is he lying? Harry wondered. Or is he not lying? Is it really the house of an FBI man? Harry could not be sure. As the door opened and Cranak entered, Harry slipped away.

On the train back to Cincinnati, he composed his next report to Fred, trying to get the words just right: "In spite of continuous arduous work, including the application of heavy pressure, the subject has not been willing to cooperate."

At least I tried, Harry comforted himself. They can't say I didn't try.

From then on, Harry's studies at Xavier were uninterrupted. It was as if he was within a world inside of the world, sealed off from everything outside. Now and then he allowed himself to emerge into awareness of the outside world, for the World Series, or for a Xavier football game, or a boxing match with Joe Louis. Naturally, Harry rooted for Joe Louis.

Toward the end of his senior year he began to do independent research on thermal diffusion. When he was on the job in Philadelphia, he had had an intuition that this process could be used in the recovery of carbon dioxide from flue gases. But he had only been a lab assistant then, without the technical know-how to turn his intuition into actuality. On the basis of his present calculations, however, he was now convinced that, in contrast to the existent technique, which only recovered about 18% of the carbon dioxide from the flue gases, with thermal diffusion close to 80% would be recovered. Some day he would discuss his conclusions with Dr. Rink. With luck he might even be assigned his own project at the lab.

After his graduation in June—he was awarded his degree cum laude—Harry took the train to Philadelphia. He arrived at the Broad Street Station with thirteen cents in his pocket. Once outside he stopped and looked up and down the familiar streets. Even the familiar (perhaps especially the familiar) can harbor strangeness. But there was nothing strange in what he could see. He spent five cents to call home to say I'm here. Then he spent another five cents taking the trolley to Phillip Street. He arrived home with three cents.

ONCE HE WAS HOME, Harry was content. He did not feel any regret at having left Xavier, despite the good time he'd had there. It was enough for him to be with Mom and Pop and Stan, and to be working at Franklin Chemical in a better job than he'd had before he left. He fell into his old routine of working every day, including Saturday and Sunday, from early morning until late at night. When he got home, he'd eat the supper that Mom had left for him in the refrigerator, and fall gratefully into bed. Then, in the morning, he'd get up and repeat the cycle of his day, carried along in a benign synchronization of habit and satisfaction.

One evening, however, as he had worked without sleep for two nights running, he came home early enough to have dinner with the family. He looked forward to the old easy conversation of who did what during the day. But there was no conversation during the meal that night. Instead, everyone sat in silence as they listened to the news on the radio. When the commentator spoke of the Germans occupying Paris and setting up a puppet government, Mom clenched her hands and her whole body stiffened, as if what was happening so far away was happening within her, at that moment.

"Maybe we shouldn't listen to the news at dinner," Pop offered gently.

"I want to hear it," she answered sharply.

"But it gets you too upset."

"I have to know what's going on."

"It's not going to change anything, your listening. You can't do anything about it. You have to go on with your life."

"Do you see me stopping? Who else is doing the cooking? the cleaning? the shopping? What do you think I do all day long?"

"Okay, okay." Pop said. "We'll listen, if that's what you want."

When the broadcast was over, Pop sighed again. Now that the U.S. was sending supplies to the British, he suggested, Hitler would be defeated eventually.

"Eventually," Mom said bitterly. "And what will happen to the Jews in the meantime?"

"Someone will help."

"What someone? England? France? America?"

"Maybe Russia—," Stan piped up.

"Don't talk to me about Russia after what they did—signing that pact with Hitler. Russia!" she spat out the word, and walked out of the room, leaving the three of them, not looking at each other, not knowing what to say.

Sitting with the back of his chair pressed against the wall, unable to move until the others moved, Harry kept hearing the terrible accusation in the word Russia, as she had pronounced it. Of course he had heard about the non-aggression pact between Hitler and Stalin the previous August, but he hadn't given it much thought, focused as he had been on his studies and research at Xavier. But now he felt that something huge and monstrous was congealing in and around the very idea of Russia, making it nothing like the Russia—wasn't it Russia?—that he had flown over in his dream that night so long ago, after Dave had asked him if he would help.

At the thought of Dave he was overcome with remorse. How was it possible that he had not even thought of him during these last years? Was he back? He must be back.

On Sunday morning Harry went to Jersey City. When he got to Dave's door, he knocked with his old knock, one hard beat, a light one, then two hard ones. There was no answer. He's gone out, I should have called ahead of time, he told himself. He knocked again and heard a faint "Just a minute," then a shuffling sound.

The door opened: It was Dave but it wasn't Dave. That is, it wasn't the Dave he had once known, the big, hearty bear of a man he had been. This Dave was shrunken and twisted, one leg hanging uselessly at his side. He was wearing a torn maroon bathrobe that was so large for him it trailed on the floor.

Not knowing what to do, Harry put all his effort into looking at Dave and not running away, into not showing the horror he felt. "It's me, Harry," he said.

"I know it's you."

Harry would have liked to be able to say the same words to Dave but he couldn't. Instead, he just stood there. After a pause, Dave said, "You don't have to stand there. You can come in." He turned and half-dragged, half-propelled himself to where the Murphy bed was sticking out from the wall. Harry had never seen the Murphy bed pulled down before. The sheets and pillowcases were wrinkled and dirty as if they hadn't been changed for months. Dave maneuvered himself onto the bed with a great effort, and sank back against the pillows, breathing hard. Though it was hot in the room, he covered himself with an old tattered blanket. He pointed to a straight chair, piled with books. "Throw those on the floor."

Harry picked up the books and stacked them neatly beside the chair. He read the names Marx and Engels; he saw the name Koestler. He sat down. He looked at Dave and then he looked away, as if he could be endangered by looking, as if he could fall into—he didn't know what . . .

He forced himself to think about the times he'd been here before, how he and Dave had wine and spaghetti and talked for hours, good talk, hopeful talk. He told himself he must believe that those times could still go on, no matter what had happened between then and now. He must pretend—to Dave, to himself—that things were just as they had been.

"It's been a long time and since I didn't hear from you, I thought maybe you didn't want to see me, but then I thought how we used to talk and how you got me that job—seven years ago—"

"Only seven years? It seems much longer."

"That's because you've been away, and when you're away time seems to stretch out."

"But now I'm back. Or at least, what's left of me is back," Dave said and grinned. The grin made everything seem even more terrible, the way it twisted his face to the side. Harry tried desperately to think of something to say. He came up with "How's Rosa?"

"I haven't seen her." Dave lifted himself up to sitting, slowly and painfully, then got himself up off the bed.

"Can I help?" Harry asked, jumping up, but Dave brushed him aside and dragged himself across the room to a table in the corner, and picked up a whiskey bottle. He poured himself a drink and offered one to Harry.

"It's a little early for me."

"It's never too early for me. *Salud*," he said, lifting his glass and taking a drink. As he retraced his steps, Harry watched him, worrying that he might fall, seeing the agonizing slowness of his lifting a foot and putting it down and then twisting himself and dragging the other foot forward. He got himself back onto the bed, spilling a little of the whiskey on the sheets, but he didn't seem to notice.

"So what have you been doing with yourself, Harry?"

"I've been away, myself, for two years. I just got back." Harry told him about going to Xavier and getting his B.S., about the courses he took, about how he was able to get a better job when he came back, how it had all worked out. He talked about what he was doing at the lab. The old Dave would have wanted to know every detail but the new Dave merely grunted. Had he been boasting too much? He felt a terrible guilt that somehow it was his fault that here he was whole, and here Dave was, his body all broken. But he mustn't think that way. He must hold on to the fact that Dave was a man who had been a hero to him. He must let Dave know he had not forgotten that. "You must feel proud—"

"Proud?"

"That you did what you believed in. Even though the Party didn't want you to go, you went—"

"How do you know the Party didn't want me to go?"

"Bob told me. Bob Silver."

Dave grunted. "Things get around, don't they? People talk, talk, talk—"

"I guess," Harry said lamely.

"Ah, well, what difference does it make?" Dave finished his drink and got himself off the bed, and slowly worked his way across the room. He poured himself another drink, and just as slowly dragged himself back into bed.

"No, they didn't want me to go. They said I was more useful to them providing information on technical processes, or spying on Trotskyites. But I insisted. I told them I had to go to Spain." He finished the drink and held the empty glass in his hand, staring out into space.

"Do you want me to bring that bottle over?"

"No. I like it just where it is. I wouldn't want to make it too easy for myself, would I?"

"I guess not. I suppose the exercise is good for you."

Dave laughed, an almost loud laugh. "That's funny coming from you, Harry. Aren't you the man who hates to exercise?"

"Well, not exactly—I mean—I love sports but I was never any good at them."

"What was it you once told me? That in high school you kept trying out for the football squad and finally you made it to the second team. And at last, when they did call you in as a replacement, the first thing you did was break your collarbone. So that was the end of your football career, right?"

"That's right," Harry said, sheepishly.

After a long silence, Dave twisted himself around and reached toward the little table beside the bed for a pack of cigarettes.

"Can I help you?"

"I told you I don't need any help. I don't want any help." Putting the glass on the table, he pulled a cigarette from the pack and lit it with shaking hands. Then he twisted himself back and fell against the pillows. He sighed and closed his eyes. Gazing at him, Harry was fearful that he was going to fall asleep and maybe drop the lighted cigarette on the blanket and start a fire. He began talking, raising his voice, about how everyone had been so nice to him at Xavier, especially the Fathers.

"What—?" Dave suddenly opened his eyes. On his face was an expression of terror, as if he didn't know where he was. "What did you say?"

"I was just saying how nice the Fathers were to me at Xavier."

"Nice?" Dave looked at him, and his eyes seemed to clear. "So, Harry, are you thinking of converting?"

"No, of course not. I would never do that. I was just saying I admire their dedication."

"I will say that for them. They are dedicated."

Harry was stunned by the almost savage note in Dave's voice. How could he have forgotten that Dave was a lapsed Catholic? "I guess for you—you know all about—after all, you used to—"

Dave pulled himself up to sitting on the edge of the bed. "Ah yes, I was a choirboy, so I know all about their dedication. I know all about the answers they have to everything, in this world and the next. Do you remember how I used to talk to you about the opiate for the masses?"

"I remember."

"All those lectures I used to give you. What did you really think of them?" His voice had become cajoling and thicker at the same time. "Come on, Harry. You don't have to be polite with me. We're old friends. It's just the way it used to be between us, right?"

"Yes," Harry said heartily, longing that it would be so. "It's just the way it used to be."

"So what did you think? Did you believe what I told you?"

"That's a hard question to answer. It's not as though I'm really a believer in doctrines, or religion, or anything like that. I just wasn't born that way."

"You think that some people are born to believe and others are not?"

"I guess. I don't really know that much about believing."

"I always knew—" Dave pulled himself up to standing. "I always knew how innocent you were. But you know what? I was just as innocent as you were." He picked up the empty glass and dragged himself across the room to the table.

After he had poured his drink, he stood for a moment, swaying. "I used you, you know. Just the way I was used."

Harry didn't know what was happening to this conversation, where it was going, or where it was supposed to go. It wasn't logical. It wasn't making any sense. It was like another being had taken the old Dave's place, called himself the old Dave but wasn't, someone who was drinking and wasn't really coherent. Looking at the bent and crippled body making its way back to the bed, Harry could not help feeling that he had to defend the old Dave against this new Dave.

"I don't think you used me. I don't believe that. I can't believe that. You did what you thought was best at the time."

"You think so," Dave said.

"Yes. I believed in you."

"Ah. So you did believe after all?"

"Well, that kind of belief. In a person. You were a hero to me and you're still a hero. You always did what was right and brave and decent. It was right and brave and decent for you to go to Spain and get wounded in action—"

Dave trembled, spilling some of his drink on the bedclothes. "What if I was to tell you that I was not wounded in action, that before I saw any action at Jarama, I slipped and fell—"

"What difference would that make? You were willing to go and risk your life—"

"Or what if I was to tell you that I was running away when I fell? What would you say then? Would I be a hero then, when other men were fighting and dying—"

"I don't know why you're saying this to me."

"I'm not sure I know, either." Dave sighed. He closed his eyes again, and then opened them at once. He was staring straight ahead of him. He began telling in gasps, in spasms, as if he didn't want to tell but he had to tell. "All I know—for sure—I know for sure that when I came to I was at the bottom—at the bottom of something—a ravine—it was pitch black— I didn't know where I was—for a long time—I couldn't move—when it was daylight an old woman—an old peasant woman found me—she dragged me to her hut—she had nothing, almost nothing but she fed me some kind of broth—I don't know how long I was there, I was out of my head most of the time—I kept trying to remember what had happened before I fell—I couldn't figure it out—I didn't know—I thought maybe I'd been cut off from the others—I thought I remembered slipping and falling—I thought maybe I had been running and stopped to take a piss— I thought maybe I was trying to avoid the gunfire, and I dove at the ground, and the ground wasn't there—I thought maybe I'd just been run- ning away—I didn't know—I still don't know—there's no one alive to tell me . . ."

"But then, what—," Harry said.

Dave turned and looked at him, as if surprised to see him there. "Do you ever think about sacrifice, Harry, about self-sacrifice?"

"I can't say that I have."

"I kept thinking about it in that hut, about how I had wanted to sacrifice myself for the cause, how I had always thought it was the most thrilling thing in the world—but then when the moment came, the crucial moment—was it my own skin that mattered? I didn't know and I'll never know."

"But—"

"Do you know what that old woman did? Not only did she take care of me. She gave me a can of evaporated milk. She must have been saving it for years, and she gave it to me." Tears came to Dave's eyes. "She didn't ask me why I had fallen into the ravine. She didn't ask me if I was running away. She just gave it to me."

"You're still a hero—," Harry started to say, but Dave interrupted him, the words tumbling out faster, some of them being swallowed up in his hurry, something about the Anarchists having coming through the area and his being taken along by them to a place behind the lines. "But the civil government arrested all the Anarchists—they'd been on the same side but the government arrested them. I was arrested—I kept telling them over and over, I'm not an Anarchist. But they didn't believe me. I was thrown into jail, along with the others. Finally someone got me out and got me to a hospital. They put me in a full body cast. By this time I had osteomyelitis. That was the worst. The stink of my own body—of my own mind—"

He paused now, and Harry asked, "Are you saying you don't believe anymore in what you used to believe in?"

"I didn't say that." He took a drink, swallowing half of what was in the glass, and dragged himself to the edge of the bed. He shivered, and suddenly dropped the glass and its contents on the floor.

Harry jumped up and got down on his knees. With his handkerchief he tried to wipe up the spill on the floor. He handed the empty glass to Dave, who took it and seemed to be weighing it in his hand. Then he looked up and there was a kind of passion in his scarred face. "I still believe in love for my fellow man. I believe in justice and compassion. I believe in the rights of people everywhere for freedom, in the struggle of people everywhere against imperialist exploitation." Harry felt tears come to his own eyes. This was, after all, the old Dave.

But then he started saying something about "POUM" and "CNT" and "PSUC" and the Russians, about the fight between the factions on the Republican side. It was all disconnected and Harry couldn't figure out what he was talking about, only that it had something to do with the politics in Spain. Harry was remembering how in the old days Dave always said, "Everything is political." Dave's voice was getting lower and thicker, and his eyes were bleary and bloodshot. Yet he kept talking. One minute he was accusing, the next minute he was justifying. He seemed to be saying one thing, then he'd say its opposite. And in the next instant he was speaking about the old woman and the can of evaporated milk.

Suddenly he grasped at Harry's sleeve. "Sometimes I think this was all a punishment," he blurted out.

"What would you be punished for?"

"For thinking I knew all the answers. For being a coward. Was I going to take a piss when I fell into that ravine, was I running away, or did I just slip? I don't know." He let go of Harry's sleeve.

Standing up, looking down on Dave's bent head, Harry was bewildered. Who was this man I once knew? he wondered. Was he always this one I am seeing now? Or was he the both of them, this one and that one, even then?

Dave had grown silent, sitting on the edge of the bed, staring at the dirty floor. Harry's heart contracted with pity. "Are you hungry, Dave? Do you want something to eat?"

Dave just sat there, not answering.

"I can go out and get something to eat, some wine and some spaghetti."

"No, no, I don't want anything. I just want to sit here for a minute."

"You sure you don't want something? Do you need any money?"

"Are you so flush you're offering to lend me some?"

"I'd be glad to."

"I don't need any. I have everything I need here."

Harry felt a desperate urgency to help him, to do whatever he could to get him out of this terrible obsession, a kind of madness that propelled him from one thought to another without stopping—

"I think," Dave said, "it's time for you to go."

"Are you sure you don't want me to do something, anything?"

"I'm sure."

"If that's what you want. It's been great seeing you," he said as heartily as he could. "I can come back next week, at the same time."

Dave shrugged. "If you like."

But as Harry got to the door, he heard Dave call out, his voice cracking, "On second thought, Harry, do me a favor. Don't come back."

Harry walked to the bus stop in a daze. Listening to what Dave said, you could fall into something from which you would never get out, a place of such suffering . . .

Automatically, it was such habit with him he was not even aware of it, he began encapsulating what he had just seen and heard, isolating it, setting it off in some space within him, treating it as if it were a contaminant, separating it out from ordinary existence as an impurity. If you fell into suffering like that, you'd never even know what came before or after. It didn't allow for ordinary life. He needed ordinary life. He needed ordinary hope. He did not know why it was that hope for him depended on other people, on their hope, as if it were a flame he could warm himself by.

THERE CAME ANOTHER communication from Amtorg. A new agent was coming to Philadelphia, expressly to see Harry. He was to meet him the following Saturday afternoon at two at the art museum, not on the steps this time, but inside in a gallery.

Harry did as he was instructed. He waited for the Russian agent in the gallery of nineteenth and early twentieth century American art. After the usual recognition signals were exchanged, instead of immediately going elsewhere to talk about Harry's assignment, the new agent lingered in the gallery. He expressed great admiration for the paintings of Thomas Eakins. In fact, he stood for almost fifteen minutes looking at one of Eakins's works that showed an operation being performed. It seemed a particularly gloomy painting to Harry.

Finally they left the museum to go to a restaurant. On the way Harry noticed that this agent didn't keep looking behind him to check if someone was following them, the way the other agents always had. There was something else unusual about this new man. He wasn't "foreign" at all. He spoke with a barely perceptible accent. He used a lot of American slang. He wore his clothes the way American men wore their clothes. His hat was at just the right angle. He looked neither seedy nor overdressed. He said his name was Sam.

At the restaurant Sam began by asking about Xavier: Had Harry enjoyed being there? "Yes," Harry said. Did he find it difficult as a Jew to be a student at a Catholic university? "No," Harry said. Sam asked him about his course work, and Harry listed all the science sequences he had taken. Then he mentioned that he'd taken some required courses in English literature. Sam went on at some length about how he loved Dickens. Harry felt an immediate connection with this man that he'd never felt with any of the other agents. In fact, he even felt free to say something about Tom Cranak. "I'm afraid I didn't do too good a job with him."

Sam smiled benignly. "You can't win 'em all. But that's in the past. We have some new assignments for you that you'll find much more to your liking."

"Before I can go on," Harry said, "I have to get something straight." He took a deep breath and waited.

"Say what you have to say. Don't be afraid that I'm going to jump down your throat."

"It's about the Non-Aggression Pact, the Nazi-Soviet Pact. I don't understand why this—"

Sam laughed. "Is that all?"

"You're saying it's nothing that Stalin made a pact with Hitler? You're saying it's nothing that he just lets Hitler do what he wants to do? And not only that, he goes along with it?"

"Come on, Harry. This is politics we're talking about here. Do you think the Soviet Union is really going to work with the Nazis? Don't you see that the whole thing is only a delaying action? After the way the British appeased the Germans over the Sudetenland and over Czechoslovakia, don't you think that the Kremlin realized that there was going to be a war, and that they weren't ready? The Nazis had been arming for years. No matter that at every step of the way they were violating the Versailles Treaty. France and England let them get away with it. Did they ever even consider inviting the Soviet Union to the Munich discussions? No, they didn't. So what was the Soviet Union to do? We needed time to arm. You just wait and see. In a few months time, that pact is going to be dissolved. Hitler will attack the Soviet Union but by then we'll be prepared to resist him."

This friendly man was so forthright, so easygoing in his defenses of the Soviets, he convinced Harry at once. He was glad to be rid of his uneasy feelings about "Russia," that word which Mom had spat out so bitterly that it had tasted bad in his own mouth.

Once again Harry was back in his two lives. Work, mission, work, mission, work, mission. In his second life he was always either running or waiting: running on his short legs to catch a train to Syracuse, to New York, to fifty different places; waiting on street corners or in a flea-bitten movie theater playing a triple bill of B movies.

It seemed perfectly natural to him to be sent as a contact to meet technical people, who had processes they were willing to give information about, sometimes for a fee. It always irked Sam when he had to pay for the material they supplied. He thought informants should be willing to help out of idealism, out of belief in the Soviet Union. "Oh well," he'd say to Harry, "you can't expect many people to be as idealistic as you are, to believe in the Soviet Union as you do." Harry didn't bother to correct him, since he didn't have another answer as to why he was doing what he was doing.

He definitely took pleasure in being a courier. He felt buoyed up by the thought that he was a human bridge, a conduit for information, though he never knew what was done with what had passed over or through him. As the months went by, he discovered in himself a capacity for nearly exact recall of technical detail, when it was required. At such times no transfer of papers took place between the informant and himself. Harry would simply memorize what he was told, and then, in the safety of his home or the lab, he would write out his report, going over it for possible errors. He would then make a second clean copy, and transmit it personally to Sam. He tore up the first draft but he did keep odds and ends from his journeys: receipts of various kinds, stubs from movie tickets, train schedules to places he'd been to—things he didn't need now but that he might need someday, you never could tell. He threw them onto a pile of papers at the back of his closet.

In July 1941, the Nazis invaded the Soviet Union, just as Sam had predicted. "We have to work all the harder now," he said, and Harry did his utmost to obey. It was clear that anything that could be done to help the

Russians would be a direct blow against Hitler and the Nazis. His heart ached when he saw a photo in the paper of a small boy with his mother, both wearing Jewish stars on their sleeves, trying to run from a Storm Trooper. She was all in black and he was wearing short pants and you could see his little white legs. In his right hand was a tiny bundle, all that he possessed in the world.

By now, he, himself, was always hurrying as if he were being pursued. Even sitting in a movie theater, he wanted the images on the screen to come faster, the end to come sooner, the suspense to be ended.

On December seventh, the Japanese attacked Pearl Harbor and the U.S. was finally in the war. Shortly after, Harry was called up to report for induction. Early in the morning he arrived at the Armory with hundreds of other young men. They were shepherded into a group and marched through the street to a nearby center, where they were stripped of their clothes except for their shoes and socks. For hours they stood in line, waiting to be examined.

As the line moved slowly forward, Harry was overcome by a sense of shame about his body, about his paleness, about his paunch, about his short legs. He was naked, exposed, before all those others whom he didn't know, though they too were naked. Waiting his turn to be prodded and grabbed without ceremony by examiners who seemed totally indifferent to human concerns, Harry began to sweat at the thought that he was about to enter into a world without privacy, where all secrets would be disallowed.

He tried to anticipate what it would be like to have to kill or be killed. He was not capable of such imagining. He was no hero, that he knew. Yet he still wanted to be accepted, to fight with others against the Nazis. He recalled the newsreels of the bombing of English cities, the sirens, and the people running, and the air raid shelters; he recalled the pictures of the Germans advancing all over Europe, with their troops and their tanks. He felt a sickening dread at their inexorable conquests, at the way they were led on and on by a madman who proclaimed that the Aryans were a master race, and that he, their leader, was the embodiment of their will. It was horrible to think of the terrible forces set loose in the world by one man, as if there was a conjunction of history between outside events and this one man's individual life.

When it came his turn to go into the room for the final checkup, the doctor looked at his chart, then examined him, then prodded him again. "You know you have high blood pressure?" he said, "dangerously high." Harry murmured that he didn't know. Unfit for service, the doctor wrote on the paper. Harry dressed and left. Soon after, came the official notification in the mail. He was classified 4F.

He had been brought to an edge but he had not been granted the choice to go over it. Who is to say what his history would have been, had he been accepted by the Army? That is another of those might-have-beens, those parallel worlds, which have to be ignored when one is telling the true story of a life.

When Sam and Harry met in New York, it was usually in a museum. Before conducting business, Sam always spent a long time in front of the paintings and drawings. Once when they were at the Frick, he stood before a Rembrandt drawing for fifteen minutes. Harry shifted back and forth on his feet. "I don't know how can you look at it for so long," he remarked. Sam spoke of light and shadow, of edges and lines. "Look at this line here at the edge of the face. Do you see how astonishing it is?"

Harry couldn't see. To him the line was a line, going from here to there like every other line.

"But in this one you can see, you can feel the hand of Rembrandt breathing life into it."

Harry wondered if there wasn't something missing in him that he could not see this "life," no matter how hard he looked.

Later over a drink at the Ferris Wheel Bar on 57th Street, Sam revealed to Harry that he had always wanted to be an artist himself. It just hadn't been possible, not the way things were when he was younger, but he knew the time would come when life would be different, when everybody in the Soviet Union could choose to be what they wanted to be. "When this war is over, you come to Moscow and I will show you around myself. No more secrets. We'll be able to sit and have a drink and talk about everything, talk about life."

Clearly, Sam was a man with an artistic temperament who chafed at the restrictions of secrecy. Harry, on the other hand, found the restrictions oddly liberating. He couldn't have explained this to Sam, since he couldn't even explain it to himself.

One day Sam said to Harry, "You've been in this game a long time, maybe too long. Have you ever thought of that?"

Harry shrugged and said he hadn't.

"There is always the danger of a slip, no matter how careful you are."

Harry was grateful for Sam's concern but he did not feel endangered. He knew, in practical terms, that he was taking chances with every mission he went on, but by now he no longer felt it was foolhardy, or if it was foolhardy, it was the wise foolhardiness of an acrobat on a high wire, who had practiced and practiced until every motion was second nature.

After months of diligently carrying out his duties as a courier, Harry learned that he was being considered for a special assignment. "However," Sam said, "my superiors want me to assure them that you are ready for this demanding service."

Harry looked at him with surprise. "Of course, I'm ready. I'll be glad to do anything to help. I'm surprised you even ask."

"Ah," Sam smiled benignly, "that's what I thought. That's just what they'll want to hear." He went on to explain that the assignment was to work with a chemist who had developed a process for the manufacture of Buna-S, a synthetic rubber that would be very valuable for the Soviet Union. "He's been telling us this for some time, but he still hasn't delivered. You'll be exactly the right one to handle him. You're such a good listener."

"I am?"

"Sure you are. Haven't you noticed the way I talk to you? I don't talk to people this way, usually."

Harry was flattered by this remark of Sam's and said he would be delighted to accept the assignment to work with the chemist. He just hoped he could do a good job with him.

"If anyone can work with Sid Roth, you can," Sam said. "Oh, by the way," he added as they were parting, "people like Roth—in fact, most people—are more trusting of someone who is a family man. You should start constructing a story about a family of your own."

Harry didn't find it difficult at all to do what Sam suggested. He gave himself a big old house in Philadelphia. He gave himself a red-headed wife named Louisa. He gave himself two children, twins. He couldn't quite decide on their names or sexes.

Sid Roth was just as Sam had said he would be, always talking a good line, always giving excuses for why his Buna-S paper was not ready. Obviously he was a brilliant man. Harry soon learned—Sid told him— that he had graduated from college at eighteen and got his Ph.D. from Columbia when he was twenty-one. He was a short man, hardly any taller than Harry, but he was very muscular. When he'd start to talk about a technical problem, he would pace back and forth, his eyes shining, his hands tensed. He seemed to be brimming over with energy, leaping from one idea to another with elation. At such moments Harry was persuaded that Sid was capable of solving any technical problem he put his mind to.

Of course, the difficulty was that Sid's brilliance spilled over into many different directions at once. One minute he was talking about a vacuum technique to lay down a thin film of gold on plastic, and the next he was talking about a new idea he had for extrusion. Buna-S was only one of his many preoccupations.

During their first few meetings Sid talked and Harry listened and nodded.

One day Sid started telling him about his family. He had a wife, Lillian, and two children, and lived in Astoria. His mother-in-law Minnie lived with them, he said glumly. "She hates me and my wife is always taking her side." Harry volunteered the information that he lived in a big old house in Philadelphia with his red-headed wife and twins.

"That's nice," said Sid, and in a moment he was talking about some new idea he had for plastics that was sure to be a winner. Obviously, as far as Sid was concerned, it didn't matter whether Harry was single or married, but as long as he had started the fiction, he might as well keep up with it. In fact, he rather liked saying the words, "my wife," and "my kids."

This time, as every other time, Harry ended their meeting with a gentle reminder, a question about the progress of the report on Buna-S. Sid assured him that, Yes, he was getting around to it, he'd have it ready soon. But at the next meeting, nothing had changed; the report still wasn't ready. Sid had a new excuse about how he was so overloaded with work; he really wanted to sit down at his desk and just concentrate on writing the report, but—he threw up his hands—surely, Harry knew how it was.

After many weeks of these meetings, Harry finally had to admit to Sam that he wasn't making any headway with Sid.

"Nothing at all?" Sam asked sharply.

"Not really. I mean, I spend time with him, but it all comes to nothing."

Sam closed his eyes and bent his head. He tapped the fingers of his right hand against the fingers of his left. He looked gloomy, unhappy, not at all American.

But when he opened his eyes, he smiled that same old Sam smile. "I tell you what, Harry. Let's create a little drama here. Why don't you tell Sid that an important official from the Soviet Union has just arrived in this country specifically to meet with him to talk about Buna-S."

"What official?"

"Me. I'm going to play the official. Let's see if that will shake a little something out of him."

At his next meeting with Sid, Harry told him about the important Soviet official who wanted to meet him. Sid got very excited. "When does he want to see me?"

"Now. He's waiting at a bar around the corner."

When Harry and Sid entered the bar, there was Sam sitting at a table looking considerably more Russian than usual. After Harry introduced the two men, the three of them ordered drinks. In a heavy Russian accent, Sam praised Sid's work to the skies, emphasizing how important it was to the people of the Soviet Union, to its very survival, that information on Buna-S be available to them. Harry was very impressed with Sam's acting, it was so convincing. Sid kept nodding and grinning.

After they'd drunk a number of toasts, Sam got up and bowed, saying he regretted he must leave. Again he praised Sid and thanked him for taking the time to meet with him. As he left, he looked around cautiously and said, "Please wait five minutes before leaving."

Sid was so excited he could hardly contain himself. "That man was truly impressive. Do you think he's a general or something?"

"I couldn't say. Where are you going?"

I'm going to go right now to the lab and get this report done."

"Wait. Wait five minutes, the way he said."

"No, I can't wait," Sid said, as he hurried off. "I want to get this done by tomorrow."

Naturally the report was not done by tomorrow, nor by the next day, nor by the day after that. In desperation Harry booked a room at the Henry Hudson Hotel and told Sid what he had done. "We must finish this report. I will sit with you in the room all night, however long it takes. I'll ask questions and you answer. That way it will go faster."

Harry expected resistance from Sid, but to his surprise Sid immediately agreed to his suggestion. Harry asked him if he didn't want to call home and tell his wife he would be working all night. "It's not necessary," Sid said. "There's nothing unusual in my working all night. Besides, she has Minnie-the-Moocher to keep her company." Earlier Harry had considered adding a mother-in-law to his own little family, but now he decided that would complicate matters unduly.

They went up to the room and settled in for the night. It was a single room with a little table that they could use for a desk. The only light was from a small bedside lamp, which Harry moved to the table. Right away, Sid said he was hungry and thirsty. Harry sent down for chicken sandwiches and for some Canadian Club and soda. I will have to charge Amtorg for this, he decided. I am way beyond my budget and I have already borrowed against my salary this month.

They ate and they drank and then they started to work, with Harry asking the questions and Sid answering. Harry was finally beginning to feel he was getting somewhere, when suddenly Sid got up and started pacing back and forth in the small room. It had just come to him, he announced, that he should set up the Buna-S plant in Russia himself. Did Harry think the Russians would go for that? Harry said he didn't know what the Russians would or wouldn't go for.

Sid yawned. "God, I'm sleepy." He hadn't slept the night before and it was all catching up with him.

"Take a cold shower," Harry suggested. Sid went into the bathroom and emerged twenty minutes later in a cloud of steam. He fell on the bed and was asleep in an instant, snoring. No matter how much Harry tried to wake him up, it was hopeless. "Dead to the world," Harry said aloud, shaking his head in disbelief.

Every single night the following week, Harry went to New York to work with Sid to try to get the information on Buna-S. Every night it was touch and go whether he'd even get to see him. And every night, once he saw him, getting him to talk about Buna-S was like pulling teeth. In the early hours of the morning Harry would take the train to Philadelphia and that same evening he was on his way back to New York.

On Saturday night he had a meeting with Sam. Sam took one look at him and said, "Harry, what the hell has happened to you? You look like the walking dead."

Harry told him that he'd been to New York every night to work with Sid, so he'd had almost no sleep for five nights running. "That goddammed Roth!" Sam yelled. "He's just leading you on. There's probably nothing there."

"No, no," said Harry, "he's got something and I'll get it. I promise you, I'll get it. If not tomorrow, soon."

"You mean you're coming in here again tomorrow?"

"Well, I thought, since it's Sunday I could—"

"I forbid it! I absolutely forbid it! He's just jerking you around, that's what he's doing. Look at you. You look like something the cat wouldn't even drag in. You tell me you're always worried about your mother and how worried she is about Stan since he was drafted. What must your mother think about you when she sees you this way?"

"She hasn't seen me much," Harry mumbled.

"Harry, tell me, what good is a sick agent going to do me?"

"I'm not going to be sick," he insisted. "All right, all right," he sighed. "I won't come in tomorrow. I'll take a rest tomorrow. I may even spend the whole day sleeping."

"Good. That's settled. And tonight, what we're going to do is go and have some drinks and a good steak dinner and then I personally am going to put you on the train to Philadelphia. I'm even going to get you a seat in the parlor car so you can relax."

Once during dinner Harry started saying something about Buna-S but Sam held up his hand and stopped him. "We're not going to talk about that. We'll talk about anything else but not about that."

As the night wore on, Sam grew more and more ebullient. Soon he was declaiming poetry in Russian. "Pushkin," he said to Harry. "I would translate but you'd lose the flavor." Harry liked listening to the sound of the words. He liked the fact that he didn't understand the meaning. What with drink and the food and the dense rhythmical sounds, he sank into a pleasurable daze. At one point he thought of the names of the twins, Doris and Daniel, one girl, one boy.

After dinner, Sam insisted they have brandy. He sat back in his chair and looked at Harry for a moment. "So?" he asked, "Are you feeling better?"

"Much better."

"Very good. Tell me something, Harry. Why is it that in the U.S. nobody talks about life? In Russia, everybody talks about life. You probably think that because we're Communists we don't talk about such things."

"No, no, I wouldn't say—"

"We're Russians and Russians talk about life," Sam insisted. "What about you? What do you think about life?"

"I don't think about it all that much."

"How is it possible that you can not think about it?" There was the slightest edge of belligerence in Sam's voice.

"I don't have time to think about it."

Sam shook his head. "No matter how busy you are, you should think about life. Everyone should think about it." Then he began talking about life and death and the meaning of life. He went on and on about destiny and will, about fate and God and destiny. Now, in the Soviet Union, Sam added, it was true that they did not usually speak in these terms. "One speaks of the will of the people, of the will of the Party, of the complete expression of an individual life through sacrifice, through service to the Party. We do not speak of an individual life as such, but of lives lived together in brotherhood, in hope for a better future for suffering humanity."

Abruptly, he stood. "Let's go, it's time to go."

Outside, in the cold night air, he took long deep breaths. "On a night like this, one feels the pulse of the city beating like a great heart. One feels in one's own bloodstream the bloodstream of humanity every-where." He wavered slightly on his feet, but brushed aside Harry's steadying hand.

"Tonight on this wonderful night, for it is a wonderful night, I feel like singing. But of course, it would not be wise to call attention to one-self that way. It is sad not to be able to sing when one wants to. Singing," he added, putting an arm around Harry, "is the true expression of the Russian soul." He let out one sound, a muffled roar, as if he could not contain the impulse. Harry looked around. A number of people were pass-ing by on the street but no one seemed to have heard.

"Do you know that story by Turgenev called 'The Singers?'"

"No," said Harry.

"It's a wonderful, wonderful story. If you want to know Russia, you have to read that story. It's about a man walking with his dog, and he comes to a village that is on the edge of a ravine. He toils up a steep path to a small tavern, a pot-house I guess you'd call it. It's very hot—"

"Hot?" asked Harry. "How could it be hot? It's never hot in Russia."

"My God, man. In some places it gets very hot. Hotter than New York. Much hotter." He walked forward, weaving a little, then stopped. "In this story there is a contest between two men in the tavern, between two singers, to see who can sing best. The first man sings. He is a wonderful singer. The listeners are amazed at his voice, at how it rises, how it falls, how it reminds them of the course of their life on earth. He is done. Everybody present thinks, Now that one has won. But then the second man gets up. He waits a moment before he starts to sing. The listeners become silent. The moment his song begins, they are transfixed. It is like nothing on earth, it is the expression of the soul rising to heaven, being heard by heaven as well. A wonderful story—" He sighed. "But, after all, just a story."

Before Harry could say anything, Sam was whistling with his fin-gers in his mouth at a taxi coming down the street. "To Penn Station," he said to the cabbie.

Three months later, having squeezed all the necessary information on Buna-S from Sid, Harry handed the report over to Sam. "Good work," Sam said, clapping Harry on the back and embracing him. Since the night of the dinner, Harry had thought Sam had grown cooler to him but now, he saw, he had been mistaken. He was pleased at Sam's words. He was also pleased to be finished with Sid.

Once again he was back to being a courier, going from here to there, up and down the East Coast. Traveling was harder than ever, with the trains so crowded with military personnel. He had to wait a long time just for a chance to stand in the aisles. Harry took this as just one small sacrifice, compared to the great sacrifice so many others were making, including Stan, who was in the Army. In the crowded waiting rooms, he had the sense of everyone working for a common purpose, to win the war against Hitler. And indeed there was the feeling in the air that the tide had begun to turn. The German offensive in Russia had stalled. Harry had seen pictures of German bodies in the snow—pathetic white corpses, indistinguishable in a white landscape—but he would not allow himself to feel sorrow. He would think only of what the Germans had done to their victims.

On a Saturday night in February, Harry was waiting for Sam on the corner of Forty-Third and Lexington. For the first time in his experience with him, Sam was late. Harry paced back and forth, and then walked halfway down the block, keeping the corner in view. No Sam. Harry went back to the intersection. He was just about to leave—he would return for a fallback appointment—when suddenly Sam was there, apologizing profusely for being late.

They walked down to Forty-Second Street and mingled with the crowds. Taking Harry's arm, Sam announced that this meeting was a special occasion. In fact, its being special was the reason he was late. He had a surprise for Harry. He would not say what the surprise was until later. First, they were to go and have drinks and then a wonderful steak dinner.

Harry looked forward to continuing their conversation about life, about free will and destiny. After the drinks were served, he announced boldly, "I have been thinking about individual will and destiny."

"You have? That's nice. Well, let's not talk about that now, Harry. This is a celebration. Let's talk about poetry."

"I was thinking about Hitler," Harry persisted, "about how this one man has been the cause of so much evil in the world. If he had never lived, would the world—"

"You're wrong about that," Sam cut in, curtly. "It wasn't just Hitler. Hitler alone couldn't have done what he has done. He never could have come to power in the first place without the connivance of the capitalists, the owners of industries, and the Junkers and the Army. All of them were perfectly willing to betray the Weimar Republic, as long as Hitler promised to get rid of the Communists and let them strengthen their own power. They thought they'd end up getting the old Kaiser back, the old Germany. Then Hitler turned and betrayed them. No, no, Hitler couldn't have done it himself. You ought to know enough about politics to know that."

"I don't know much about politics," Harry mumbled.

"Come, come, old friend. Let's not argue, tonight of all nights. Tell me, what poet do you like?"

Harry did not read poetry but he felt he owed Sam an answer. He dredged his memory, going all the way back to high school days, for the name of a poet he'd had to read in English class. "Sandburg, Carl Sandburg," he said.

"Sandburg?" Sam said scornfully. "His work is so predictable. Surely there's somebody else whose work you know."

"Browning," said Harry quickly, remembering another poem from high school, "Browning's 'The Last Duchess.'"

"Ah, yes 'The Last Duchess.' A very interesting work." Sam pointed out that hidden in this one-sided dramatic dialogue about the painting of a woman was a whole series of events, including her murder by the speaker, the Duke. Once again, Harry was astonished by what Sam could see that he himself had never seen. "So," said Sam, after they had finished dinner, "it is now time for the special present for you. But not here. It's too public." They left the restaurant and went to look for a dark bar. As they walked through the crowded streets, unnoticed by any others, Harry kept wondering what the present could possibly be. Not money. He wouldn't take money. Sam knew that.

They found a very dark bar and went to a table in a corner. Sam took a newspaper out of his briefcase and put it on the table. Harry took this to be the signal for him to put his newspaper on the table beside it. Ordinarily, Sam would pick up Harry's newspaper, and Harry would pick up Sam's newspaper. Hidden within the pages of Sam's newspaper would be a special message with instructions. Harry pulled out his newspaper but Sam stopped him.

"Not tonight," he said. "Tonight, I have something to say to you." He paused and when he began to speak his voice trembled with emotion. "Don't think we are not aware of the sacrifices you have made to help us. We know how you have been willing to give up the possibility of a private life of your own. You are the kind of man who should be married and have children. But you have been willing to put all that aside to help the people of the Soviet Union, to help them achieve their destiny in the service of all mankind. In recognition of your contribution, a special honor is being conferred on you."

Harry flushed with pleasure but he was also embarrassed. What had he done to deserve such recognition? The report of Buna-S, once delivered, had never even been mentioned again. He himself had grave reservations about its usefulness. Of course, he knew he'd been a good courier but there was nothing momentous in that. And as for giving up the idea of his own family—well, how could he say—he had Doris and Dan and Louisa—Of course, they weren't—but then again they were.

"You have been awarded 'The Order of the Red Star,'" Sam whispered. "The official citation is here." He opened the newspaper just enough so that Harry could see a white paper with some printing in gold letters and at the very center a large red star. "Of course, I can't give it to you now for obvious reasons. It says, in Russian, that this award has been given to you for service to the Soviet Union."

It looked very official, indeed, even in the dimness of the dark bar. "For service," Sam repeated, his voice husky.

For service, Harry said to himself. The words touched him immeasurably.

"With this citation, when you come to the Soviet Union after the war, you will be able to ride free on the Moscow subway."

"Thanks, thanks a lot, I feel very—very—honored."

Sam folded the newspaper and put it back in his briefcase. "And now—" he stopped and ordered two brandies from the waiter. "There is a saying—perhaps you have heard it—that the reward for a great service is to be able to do one even greater. Tonight it is my privilege to tell you of that greater service, a service of such importance that you are to drop all other work for us and do only this."

The waiter brought the drinks and Sam lifted his glass to Harry. "To you," he said, tossing off the drink in one gulp. After a prolonged silence, he went on in a low voice. "A man is coming to New York, a scientist who will be doing work so important that it is crucial to the very survival of the Soviet Union."

Harry had the eerie sense that he had heard these same words before, or something closely approximating to them, and then he remembered Sam's speech to Sid when he was masquerading as a top Soviet official. But there was no suggestion of acting in Sam's manner now. His voice was deadly serious. "You will be this man's one and only contact. Whatever comes from him will come to us through you. As you must be continuously available to him, the suggestion has been made that you move to New York."

"But—"

"Didn't you tell me that for some time your company has been wanting you to transfer to their lab in Jamaica?"

"Yes but Mom didn't want me to—"

"Take the transfer, Harry. Come to New York. Get a room. It will make things easier in every way. For us, for you, for everybody."

Leave home, Harry said to himself. Leave just as he had left to go to Xavier. "I'll do it—soon," he said.

"Immediately, Harry," Sam insisted.

As they parted—it was to be the last time they would meet, though Harry did not know it—Sam said in his usual jovial tone, "See you around."

Several weeks later, having transferred to the lab in Jamaica, and settled into his basement apartment in Queens, Harry received instructions from his new superior, Y. He was to make his first contact with the scientist who had come to New York. Trembling with anticipation at the importance of what he was about to do, he took the subway to Brooklyn, got off and took a bus, and then took the bus back to the subway stop.

Standing across the street from where they were to meet was a tall thin man, his hair glinting in the light of the street lamp. He was carrying a tennis ball in one hand and a red book in the other. He was looking in the opposite direction, away from Harry. Will he turn and see me? he wondered.

The tall thin man turned.

T URNING, KLAUS SAW no one across the street, and turned back. An instant later, a man appeared before him, as if summoned up, a small man, a dark man, wearing a dark overcoat and a dark hat. In his right hand was a black glove, in his left a green-covered book. What an insignificant-looking man he was, pale, eyes so heavy-lidded he seemed half-asleep. But what did it matter who or what this man was, what he looked like? All that mattered was that contact be established.

"Nice weather." It was what he had been instructed to say.

"Too hot," the small man responded, as he was supposed to respond. It was a bitterly cold evening. But weather was not the issue.

Klaus led the way down the street, around the block, into an alley, out of an alley, down another block. Satisfied that they were not being followed, he walked toward the shadows of a residential street. The courier introduced himself as Raymond, though Klaus was sure from the man's hesitant smile when he said it that it was a cover name. He, himself, gave his real name. He saw no reason not to.

They discussed the ground rules for their future meetings. They would not go to a restaurant or a cafe. They would strictly limit the time they were together. They would never meet in the same place twice. If there was to be a transfer of technical material, it would take place just before they parted. At each meeting a time and place would be set for the next meeting. An alternate date and time would be designated, in case either one of them was unable to appear at the appointed time. Did the courier have any questions? If not—

Before parting, they agreed to meet the following Saturday at three in the afternoon, at the West Eighty-Fifth Street entrance to Central Park.

It snowed lightly on and off during the week but when Klaus entered the park on Saturday, the weather had turned crisp and clear. Standing against the iron fence that bordered a small playground just inside the entrance was the courier, pudgy and amorphous, easy to miss in a landscape where everything else was sharp-edged. Klaus proceeded along the white untrampled paths that led deeper into the park. When the courier fell into step beside him, he did not object. What could be suspicious about two men walking, openly, in the park?

Beneath their feet the snow was finely packed. The sun shone brilliantly upon the bare encrusted branches of the trees. Klaus walked on in silence. There was about the little man an air of expectancy but not of demand, as if he was used to waiting and waited willingly.

As they passed a wide white meadow, Klaus told the courier that the package he was about to give him contained copies of his notes relating to a gaseous diffusion plant being built for the production of fissionable uranium. His own work was concerned with the mathematical hydrodynamics of the flow of uranium hexafluoride through metal barriers. From the few questions the courier asked, it was clear that he had had some technical training. Klaus guessed that he was probably a chemist, a rather low-level chemist at that. One could not have a detailed scientific conversation with him. He didn't expect to be able to. Why should he? The man was a courier.

He led the way into a deep grove of evergreens, where the transfer was made. But afterward, instead of walking off at once, according to their agreement, he lingered. Perhaps it had something to do with the grove, the darkness of the evergreens against the surrounding white, the smell of the needles, the astonishing silence, which walled them off from the great city.

The little man also continued to stand and wait, holding onto a small black bag, in which he had placed the packet of papers. At the thought of his own notes in his own handwriting enclosed there, Klaus felt a rush of excitement. It was now out of his hands. There would be no going back. That was what mattered most of all. Others might cling to the need to temporize, but not he.

As for the courier, it was impossible to know what he needed or didn't need, as he waited like a stop-gap, a transition point, a way-station for others' intentions. So Klaus judged, even as he found himself remarking, almost companionably, to the courier that he was working in the Manhattan office of Kellex in a group of British physicists.

"Are you British?" the courier asked.

"No, I am German. I was born in Germany."

He had had no intention of saying anything about himself but in the silence more words were coming out. "I left Germany in 1933."

"Are you a Jew?"

"No, I am not a Jew."

Abruptly he turned and walked out of the grove. He was puzzled by what he was doing. To give voice to thoughts is to allow them power that they never have unvoiced. He stopped at a small lake, which was partially frozen over. The courier had caught up with him and was waiting with servile expectancy.

"My name was on the list of those who were enemies of the Nazis." As he uttered the words, Klaus felt as if pieces of himself were breaking off, floating like small ice floes in a sea of larger ones, while he watched from a distant shore.

"You risked your life—," Raymond began, but Klaus had already hurried away.

Walking to his apartment on the West Side, Klaus was overcome by a sense of shame. But what had he told, after all? It was nothing. Yet any telling is a betrayal of oneself. He had learned that long ago. Whether the telling is a lie or the truth does not matter. The lie of a lake frozen over; the truth of not being frozen enough.

He shut the door of his apartment behind him. He went to his desk. Now began that exquisite melding of thought and feeling, where he felt the thoughts, he thought the feelings in his brain, in his nerves, in his muscles. He fell into the pull of abstraction, its protection, its certainty, its gravity.

The next time they met, it was on the corner of Riverside Drive and 151st Street. When Klaus arrived, Raymond was already waiting. A fierce wind was blowing from the river and from the Palisades, tunneling between the apartment houses up the street to Broadway. The courier's coat collar was turned up; his shoulders were hunched against the cold. But his half-lidded eyes were alight, burning with something like anticipation. Klaus was determined that there would be no lingering this time. He set the time and place of the next meeting, as well as that of the fall-back meeting. The information was transferred. As he turned to leave, Klaus saw the fading of hope in the little man's eyes and anger flared within him. He wanted to say, What do you want from me? But he said nothing.

It was a cold, rainy day when Klaus entered the Metropolitan Museum for their next meeting, two weeks later. Inside the entry hall he turned left and made his way through long corridors to the Roman atrium. A pale blue light filtered down through the skylight onto the immense enclosed room. The shallow pool at the center glistened here and there at the darting of a goldfish. A miniature waterfall poured from the mouth of the lion at the front of the pool. Around the court, pieces of sculpture stood guard with blind eyes.

There were only two other occupants in the garden, two middle-aged women sitting on a stone bench, whispering, their heads bent together. At his entrance, they got up hurriedly, and left. He was glad to have the stillness to himself. Outside, out in the world, everything was noisy, jarring, in the process of change. Here in the silence, a moment of history had been captured and preserved. One could be in it, and yet one was out of it. In this atrium one could think of what a life in it might have been and yet be completely distanced from it. To Klaus, this was a comforting thought. To be freed from history—one's own and all others'—was in itself a wonderful form of abstraction.

He picked up a brochure from the stone bench where the two women had been sitting. He read that the earliest Roman house was only one room, a room without windows or chimney, that the house came to be called the atrium, from *ater*, black, because the walls were blackened by the smoke from the family hearth and altar—

From behind a pillar the courier appeared, in his black coat and black hat, carrying his little black bag. Unaccountably, irritation began to rise in Klaus. This is ridiculous, he told himself. I am meeting this man for the sole purpose of giving him information, which he will convey to others. He, himself is of no importance. Yet the irritation remained; he could not rid himself of it. Perhaps it had something to do with the way the courier looked, with the way he seemed to reduce everything to banality.

"You were expecting me, weren't you?"

"Yes, of course. Why do you ask?"

"You just seemed—"

"What?"

"I don't know—" Then, hurrying on, as if embarrassed, the courier said, "I've never been here before. It's nice. It almost makes you forget there's a war on."

I am not going to let this man provoke me into trivial and unnecessary responses, Klaus insisted to himself. I am going to give him what I came here to give him and then I'll leave. Looking around to make sure that they were not being observed, he handed the material to the courier, and turned to go.

But the courier blocked his way. "When do you think it will end?" he asked.

"End? Will what end?" Klaus asked, his voice strident.

"When do you think the war will end?"

"I am not a military expert."

"A place like this makes you think about life and death. It makes you think about how civilizations die. What was it Hitler said?—that the Third Reich would last a thousand years? But it won't, will it?"

"No."

The courier was silent, gaping, waiting for more, overeager and stolid at the same time. Klaus felt a wave of disgust at the little man, as if he were deliberately choosing to incite him. The disgust was of an acute physical nature so intense that he stepped back, away from the courier, and in his retreat stumbled against the stone bench.

"Are you all right?" the courier asked.

"I'm fine."

"Are you sure? You look—"

"I'm fine, I said." But he was not fine. In the presence of the courier, this atrium—this recreation of a garden out of a distant past—had begun to take on an almost menacing quality. "I appreciate your concern," he forced himself to say, formally, politely.

"Well, it's natural that I be concerned. After all, we are working together."

"Yes, we are working together," he admitted. He had not fully realized until this moment that in doing what he was doing he had entrusted his life into this man's hands. The thought was enough to shock him into self-control, into the liberation of detachment. He even felt free enough, as they parted, to ask if Raymond thought their Russian superiors would have any objection to his bringing his sister and her child from Boston to live with him in New York.

"I don't see why there should be any objection. I'll ask and let you know."

Because he was traveling for his work, Klaus missed his next appointment with the courier. When he appeared at their alternate meeting place in the Bronx, on the Grand Concourse at Fordham Road, in front of Alexander's Department Store, he saw the courier before the courier saw him. All one had to do was look at the little man's face to know exactly what he was feeling—anxiety that he, Klaus, might not appear. For a moment Klaus toyed with the thought of making him wait longer and watching his reactions. Why am I getting so caught up in this again? he reproached himself. He is a courier, here to receive information from me, which he will pass on to someone else. That is all.

By now the courier had seen him, and his face was flooded with relief. He hurried over to Klaus, who indicated that he had had to travel so he had not been able to make their earlier appointment.

"I understand. It's just one of those things." The little man smiled his half-lidded smile, which grated so on Klaus's nerves.

In silence they walked several blocks till they reached a dark street, almost deserted in the cold wet weather. Klaus reported on what he knew about the security precautions that had been put into place for the project he was assigned to. Though he was working on the calculations for the gaseous diffusion plant, he had never visited the site. He did not even know its exact location. "It is in the southeastern U.S., probably Georgia or Alabama."

There were also plans being developed, he added, for a plant using electromagnetic techniques for the separation of uranium isotopes. When Klaus had finished, he was seized by an extended fit of coughing that shook him so violently he gasped for breath.

"That's a terrible cough," the courier said. "Do you have a fever?"

"I don't know. I don't have the time to worry about it."

"You sound as though you're really sick. You ought to get out of this cold rain, and get something warm to eat. I know a restaurant right next to Alexander's that serves very good chicken soup. After you have that, I'll put you in a cab and you should go home and put a mustard plaster on your chest or maybe Vick's Vaporub. My mother always used to do that when we were kids."

Klaus was racked by another fit of coughing. When it was over, he managed to say, "I thought we agreed not to go to a restaurant together."

"That's true, but these are not the usual circumstances." Still coughing, Klaus found himself following the little man without further objection. As they approached the Grand Concourse, the courier added, "The soup at Rosenheim's is almost as good as my mother's chicken soup. You'll see. It'll really make you feel better."

And indeed, after the huge bowl of chicken soup, consumed under the watchful eye of the courier, Klaus did begin to feel better. He thanked the courier, trying not to be begrudging. He was aware that in his own mind he had been unduly harsh with him. The man is reliable, he does his job; that is the important thing, he told himself. "It has been helpful. I appreciate your being so considerate," he added.

"In this life we must help each other. When I was a boy, we were very poor, but even so it was made clear that we had an obligation to help others who were even less fortunate."

Once again Klaus felt revulsion—contempt—the beginning of rage. How did this little man always manage to drive him into a fury, just by saying things that were so innocuous? You should never have come here with him, he reproached himself. You ought to simply get up and go. But he could barely move. He felt an intense longing to put his head on the table and go to sleep. Befuddled by his cold, by his cough, by the chicken soup, he could feel himself slipping off an edge, unable to hold on—

"Once in school . . ." he heard the courier say, ". . . Mrs. Hess—that was the name of our English teacher—she was a blonde woman with a large bosom and very thin legs—she assigned a composition on what we did on our summer vacation." The words rose and fell and rose again: "My friends, Si Schaefer and Howie . . . and Bernie Siegel . . . and . . . Murray . . . we were sitting in . . ." The courier piled word upon word, which Klaus's numbed brain refused to absorb. "They said they couldn't write . . . they asked me if I would do it for them . . ."

Barely aware of the courier's voice, Klaus stared at the adjacent table, where a harried woman was holding a small child on her lap, trying to entice food into the child's mouth. The child shook his head and turned away. Again the mother tried to put the spoon in his mouth. This time the child hit at the spoon with his hand, and the food flew all over the mother's dress.

The courier was still going on and on. "I worked on their papers all evening. Mom told me to go to bed but I kept writing, using a flashlight under the blanket. I made up a different exciting story for each one—this one went to camp—that one went traveling with his family. I was done by two o'clock but by then I was so tired I couldn't start on my own so I set the alarm for six o'clock. When I woke up, I wrote my own paper, in a hurry."

"Come to the point!" Klaus muttered.

"Well, what happened was I handed in my paper and each of them handed in their papers which I'd written for them, and when the papers came back they all had A's and I had a C. Mrs. Hess had written a note on mine, which said, 'Surely you did more than this on your summer vacation.' She didn't believe me, but it was true. It was exactly what I had done."

"So you were angry?"

"Why should I be angry? Because they got A's and I got a C. No, I wasn't angry. I'd done it to help them out. That was what made me feel good, helping them out."

"What are you trying to say? That you're a saint?"

"No, no, I'm not saying that at all."

"Why are you telling me this?"

"I don't know. Maybe I just wanted you to know something about me, about the way I am, since we're working together. It's the most important thing to me, to help people. That's why I'm doing this." He gestured to the small black bag beneath the table. Then he turned his head and looked behind him to see if anyone was listening. "To help the Russian people," he whispered. "And you must want to too or you wouldn't be doing this."

Klaus forced himself to get up. "I think we should leave separately. Someone may have been following us."

"No, I don't think so. I always take special precautions. And I assume you do too," he added, with a hint of sharpness.

"Naturally." Klaus started to leave but then turned back. "It has occurred to me that it is possible that someone you know or someone I know may see us together, and they might wonder where we met. We should have a story ready for such an eventuality."

"We can say we met early this month at one of the concerts of the New York Philharmonic at Carnegie Hall. We can say that we had adjacent seats and talked together during the intermission. Is that okay with you?"

"It's all right."

"All we have to do is pick a date. I'll look up the back issues of the *Herald Tribune*, and find out what was on the program. Then I'll give you a list of the musical selections. So we'll both have the same story, in case anyone asks. But I don't think anyone is going to ask."

Their next meeting, two weeks later, was on the northwest corner of Fifty-Ninth Street and Lexington Avenue at the subway entrance. From there they walked east in the direction of the Queensboro Bridge. The courier had suggested that they walk across the bridge into Queens, but since the bridge was closed to foot traffic, instead they turned north on First Avenue to Sixty-Third Street, then walked west to Second Avenue, doubled back to First Avenue, and proceeded south. The courier was silent except when he suggested a change in direction. On Sixty-First Street, in the doorway of a closed shop, Klaus handed over a small packet. The courier accepted the packet without comment, and slipped it into his black bag. Then he pulled several three by five cards from his pocket. "Before you go, I have been told to ask you a few questions."

"What kind of questions?"

"Not personal questions. About the work. These were given to me and I'm supposed to ask you—" in the dim light he consulted one of the cards—"about the factory where they are making out the uranium isotopes—"

"A factory? Why do they call it a factory? And making out? What does that mean? Do these people know what they're talking about?"

"There's probably some problem in translation, that's what I think. I think they just want a little more information about—"

"I don't need anybody to tell me what information I should be giving, whether it's enough or not enough. I have already covered what material is available to me in my reports and I will continue to do so, without instructions from anyone. Is that understood?"

"I didn't mean to—I mean, I was just asking what I was told to ask."

"Then tell them," Klaus said sharply.

"I'll tell them. I will absolutely tell them just what you said. I'm sorry that you were offended."

Even before his next meeting with the courier, Klaus suspected that it would be the last time he would see him. In the past week there had been indications that he and the entire British Mission would soon be moved to a secret destination somewhere in the western part of the country.

When he arrived at the meeting place, in front of the Bell Cinema, just off the Eastern Parkway in Brooklyn, the courier was waiting, on time, as usual. The thought passed through Klaus's mind that the little man had no other existence than this, surfacing to receive information and pass it along to others, and then crawling back into his burrow, out of sight of the world.

Once again Klaus felt disgust welling up within him, but he brushed it aside. At least, if he did leave New York, he would be rid of the courier. Then he would not have to deal with these troubling responses, which were out of keeping with his usual way of being. For it was not like him to feel disgust for others—detachment from them, from their lives, yes, but not disgust.

The two men walked side by side through the streets until they found themselves in a neighborhood of single family dwellings. The weather had turned mild and the trees were in leaf. Now and then

Klaus smelled an odor reminiscent of his childhood. He thought he remembered that the odor came from a bush with a yellow flower, but he was not sure.

"About your sister," the courier said. "There will be no objection to her moving here."

"That's good," Klaus said and shrugged. Of course, it did not matter now since he was quite certain that he would be leaving New York soon. Nevertheless, he set a meeting place and time for three weeks later, and an alternate place and time for three weeks after that. As they walked beneath the trees, he made a few comments to the courier about the latest calculations on the gaseous diffusion process, focusing in particular on the diffusion membranes which would be made of sintered nickel powder. "Do you want to write this down?" he asked.

"I will remember. I have a very good memory for what you tell me."

"That must be useful." He stopped and pulled out of his briefcase a heavy manila envelope with his own handwritten notes and three reports, typed copies from the British Mission. "I had hoped to include several more typed reports but unfortunately they are not ready. Our secretary left and we have had some problems hiring a new one. The Hunter College Employment Office sent us a very qualified person and we were about to hire her but the personnel woman at Kellex said she wouldn't do. She was a Negro and the other secretaries would have objected."

"Because she was a Negro, she wouldn't let you hire her? That's terrible. Wasn't there anything you could do about it?"

"I could have protested but I did not want to draw attention to myself."

"It doesn't seem right."

"What seems right and what is right at any given moment are two different things. If it were another time and the circumstances were different, of course I would have objected. But the reality was that other factors had to be taken into consideration."

As he heard himself say these words to the courier, Klaus felt uneasy. But of course he was right to do what he did. It would have been wrong to draw attention to himself, when what he was doing was ultimately in the furtherance of a better world. It was more important than what happened in the life of one individual. And besides, he probably could not have affected the situation.

To the courier, who continued to gaze at him, almost sorrowfully, Klaus said, "We must do what we are told to do, what we have agreed to do. We have our place in the struggle for a better world. We have our duty. It is not for us to decide what is right. The end-point is what matters. If sometimes I disagree, I remind myself of that. It is the end-point that matters."

As he turned and walked away down the dark street, there came to him again the odor from his childhood. He peered into the garden he was passing, but he could see no yellow flower.

ARRY WATCHED AS Klaus disappeared into the darkness at the end of the street. Seeing him stop, he told himself, He is going to turn and look back. But Klaus did not turn. He simply went on.

As usual, after being with Klaus, Harry was in a state bordering on elation. But this time the edge was an uneasy one. When he told Klaus his sister could move to New York, Klaus seemed indifferent. Then why did he ask him to ask in the first place? Actually Harry had not asked Y if it was okay. He simply took it upon himself to say that it was. He felt it was a way of helping when he could help, but in the end it turned out that Klaus didn't even care.

Harry was also uneasy about that business with the young Negro woman. Perhaps what Klaus said was right in the abstract, that you had to think of the larger picture, but what about her, what was right for her? Klaus had justified his inaction by saying he did not want to draw attention to himself. Of course, Harry didn't have this problem, since no matter what he did, he did not draw attention to himself, so he could not imagine what he would have done under the circumstances.

He had been made uneasy, as well, by Klaus's words about a better world. Not that he didn't believe in working for a better world—of course, he did, everybody did, except for Hitler and monsters like that—but there was something unnerving about Klaus's intensity when he said what he said. It was like he was in a fever, a religious fever. His eyes were shining, his head was thrown back. It was this belief business, again. Harry thought of Dave but then decided that he would not think about Dave. It was all too confusing and also sad. He sighed and decided to get on with what he had to get on with, which was to take the subway to the next stop, where Y would be waiting for him to deliver the packet from Klaus.

Harry did not look forward to seeing Y. He found him fussy and overbearing, nothing like Sam. But then, Sam vanished without a trace, right after giving Harry the assignment to work with Klaus. Harry could not understand why Sam didn't tell him he was going. He felt that they were friends and he would have expected that Sam would have done that, at least.

Six weeks later Harry was once again standing and waiting, this time on the northwest corner of Fifth Avenue and Eighty-Fourth Street, just outside the entrance to Central Park. Klaus had not appeared at their scheduled meeting three weeks earlier, undoubtedly because he had been traveling. Today was the date of the fallback meeting. It was a warm Saturday and many people were strolling in and out of the park. Buses were discharging passengers right in front of Harry. He kept looking to see if Klaus was among them. More likely he would come on foot, from the direction of the park.

By now Harry was no longer upset about Klaus's words. A little time had passed, and he had, as always, found justification for his behavior. During their first meetings, it is true, Harry was hurt by Klaus's abruptness, by his frequent outbursts of irritation. The strangest things seemed to set him off, sometimes almost nothing at all. What did I do? Harry would ask himself, but he couldn't come up with an answer. Eventually, he convinced himself that the reason Klaus was behaving the way he was behaving was that he was a genius. Surely it was in the very nature of genius not to behave like an ordinary being, to behave inexplicably.

Watching one bus and then another and another stop and discharge its passengers, hoping to see Klaus and then not seeing him, Harry felt he was caught in a time warp, in which the same bus stopped over and over again, with the same disappointing outcome. He looked south along Fifth Avenue toward the Metropolitan Museum, searching for a tall figure with blondish-red hair. No Klaus.

As the minutes dragged on and became an hour, and then another hour, he became aware of an incipient panic. Could I have missed him somehow? he wondered. That's not possible. Could I have made a mistake about the time and the place? That also is not possible. Could Klaus, walking across the park to meet me, have been mugged? Such things do happen. Klaus with his tall but slight build would be an inviting prey.

Harry went to the park entrance and scanned the paths in the fading light. No Klaus.

When Harry met Y and told him about the two missed meetings, Y was very disturbed. He and Harry spent two hours speculating about whether Klaus was still in New York and for some reason had been prevented from keeping the appointment, or whether Klaus had left the city. "I will make inquiries," Y muttered. "Meet me Sunday morning in Washington Square, and I will have further instructions for you."

On Sunday there was Y on a bench in Washington Square, checking his wristwatch, looking around as if Harry was late, though it was only eight-fifty. The minute he spied Harry he rushed up to him and told him that he had obtained Klaus's address. "You must go there right now and see what you can find out."

Harry was only too glad to get this matter settled at once. There had been moments during the past week when he had visions of Klaus alone and ill, a stranger in a strange land. I must help him, he had resolved. So now, he rushed to the subway, took one train, transferred and doubled back—even at moments like this, especially at moments like this, it was necessary to be careful. At one of the station newsstands, he saw a copy of a recently published novel by Thomas Mann, *Joseph the Provider,* and purchased it. On the inside cover of the book he printed, "Klaus Fuchs, 128 West 77th Street, New York, N.Y."

Klaus's building was a four-story apartment house with a front entrance down a short flight of steps. Next to the doorway an old man was putting some rubbish in a garbage can. Assuming he was the janitor,

Harry hurried down the steps and asked if Klaus Fuchs was at home. The man seemed puzzled by his question and shook his head. Giving up on any help from him, Harry opened the door into the vestibule. Above one buzzer, apartment 1E, he saw the nameplate, Dr. K. Fuchs, and pressed it. There was no answer.

After several rings, Harry was in a sweat. He tried the door to the inside. It was unlocked. He walked down the hallway, till he found 1E. He knocked, once, twice, three times. There was no answer. A door across the way opened and an old woman peered out. Harry told her he was looking for Dr. Fuchs. Speaking in a heavy accent, she said that he no longer lived there.

"Do you know where he went?" Harry asked. In reply, she shook her head. Just then, the old man from outside came in and he and the old woman engaged in a conversation in some foreign language.

"I have a book that belongs to Dr. Fuchs. See," Harry opened *Jacob the Provider* and displayed the words he had printed on the inside cover to the old woman and then to the old man. "I want to return it to him," he said, slowly and deliberately. "I need to return it to him. Do you know how I can get in touch with him?" They both shook their heads. No, they didn't know where he was. "He said he was going somewhere on a boat," the old woman said.

"Maybe we should send a letter to him at the Seventy-Seventh Street address," Harry suggested to Y, when they met again. "Maybe he left a forwarding address."

"No," said Y, "that is not a good idea."

"What should I do then?"

"Wait."

"But—" Harry was desperate to do something, anything.

"Wait," repeated Y.

"I just thought of something. He has a sister in Boston. Maybe she knows where he is."

"I'll see what I can find out."

"Should I—"

"Wait."

Harry waited and waited.

At last a call came from Y. "I have it," he said in triumph. "I have the address of the sister in Boston."

And so it is that Harry will go to Boston, to Klaus's sister's house, will enter, no, will push his way in, will wait for Klaus, though Lottie insists he is not coming. When he leaves, it will be only to wait again. He will have lost the line of his life, the sense that he is being led from point to point.

Then it will be that he will take his own journey, a journey without a visible purpose, a journey in which he becomes visible to others. He will get off the train. He will wander in a strange town into an empty church. He will leave the church, he will leave the town, he will find a drunken man lying in the middle of the road.

When we left him, he was on the road, fleeing from a man in need. We have gone back, then forward, to catch up with him. A piece of a story has been told too early, out of sequence. The future has become a memory. It feels something like a twice-told tale.

Is it possible that by altering sequence one hopes to ferret out the secret life of a story? The secret life of a story? What is that? It is bewildering even to contemplate. It has something to do with watching and being watched, implacably. It has something to do with what hides within words, between words. It has something to do with the holes in stories, even, especially, in true stories.

J UST AS KLAUS expected, he has been transferred to New Mexico, to a highly secret installation. Before he left he was briefed on the importance of not revealing anything about his travel arrangements or his destination to anyone. He made no attempt to contact the courier. In his own way he is a stickler for obeying orders, particularly orders having to do with security. As for his sister, he told her only that he is probably being transferred out West somewhere and he may not be in touch with her for some time.

Since arriving in Los Alamos his every waking hour has been devoted to familiarizing himself with the technical problems of the group he is assigned to, T-1. Their responsibility is to develop the mathematical calculations for the yield and efficiency of two projected bombs, one using uranium-235 and the other plutonium.

Here, as opposed to his previous experience in New York, where everything was so tightly compartmentalized that his group knew nothing of the work of any other group, he and his colleagues are invited to all important seminars and colloquia. At these meetings no technical idea, no matter how fantastic seeming at first, is considered unworthy of consideration. But once voiced, it is subject to the most intense scrutiny, collectively and individually.

Of course, as this is an Army installation, one is always aware of security. There are the barbed wire fences, the guards at the gates, the continual validation and revalidation of one's pass. Some of the scientists, particularly those from Europe, complain about the fences. Klaus does not feel them to be confining. After all, they also act as protection, keeping others out.

As the weeks have gone by, he has made no attempt to contact the Russians. In any case, it would have been very difficult. Mail is censored. Phone calls are censored. These are the reasons he has given himself. Soon he finds that not doing can be as habitual as doing; not doing, too, has its own momentum. Besides, he needs no excuse. He is working at the lab fourteen hours a day, seven days a week.

He who has always been used to being separate from others, distanced by the rapidity and tenacity of his own mind, now finds himself one among many, and not the most brilliant at that. He is surrounded by men of great scientific capability, even genius. Everything at the lab has been arranged so one can focus on the problem at hand. Everything has been simplified. The sense of adherence to a cause, the energy of intent, the devotion to a single purpose, is palpable.

In this secret place, cut off from the rest of the world, he is living a communal life with others, one that is almost socialistic in its structure. No one is rich, no one is poor. Four hundred dollars a month is the maximum salary for a Ph.D. with years of experience. Two hundred dollars a month is the salary for a junior physicist who has just graduated with a B.S. No one lives in a mansion; no one lives in a slum. Each family is assigned housing, such as it is, according to the number of children. As a bachelor, he lives in a dormitory with the other bachelor scientists. He has been assigned to Room 17, Dormitory T-102, a small space but adequate for his needs. His rent is thirteen dollars a month, including utilities. He does not avail himself of the room service for an extra two dollars a month. He eats his meals at the cafeteria, where the food is abundant and cheap, if not particularly good. But that is of little matter to him.

Only gradually does Klaus come to realize that he is happier in Los Alamos than he has ever been before. Perhaps it has something to do with being on an isolated mesa more than seven thousand feet high, surrounded by a range of even higher peaks. At this altitude the air is thin but bracing. A brilliant sun dominates an everwidening sky. There is a purity in the landscape here, or so he judges. It is an odd word for him to use, even to himself. Some benign essence—yes, that's a better word—is entrenched here, affecting one's sense of time as well as of space. The past has receded; it is down in some deep valley, as if it were at the bottom of the sea.

The weather turns cool and one day the snow begins to fall. Klaus has not been skiing for years but now he allows himself to take a few hours from work to go skiing on the untouched slopes nearby. Since there are no lifts, once he comes down a hill there is an arduous climb to get back up again, but even that is exhilarating. Physically he feels better than he has in years.

He allows himself to indulge a small desire. He buys a car, a battered blue Buick from a technician who is leaving. He tells himself he can use it for going to Santa Fe—though he almost never goes to Santa Fe—or perhaps, in the spring, for trips exploring some of the Indian villages. Mostly, the car stays parked outside of the dormitory, sometimes mired in the mud. He tells Hellman, a physicist who lives in his dorm, that he is welcome to borrow it whenever he wants to. Hellman is married, but his wife, who is very ill with tuberculosis, is confined to a sanatorium in Albuquerque, and he tries to get there as often as he can.

Klaus spends more time with Hellman than with anyone else at Los Alamos, though Klaus certainly does not think of him as a close friend, but then he does not think of himself as close to anyone. He admires Hellman's brilliance. He is bemused by his outrageous behavior. Hellman has an absolute obsession about security; he hates the restrictions imposed by the Army, and often deliberately violates the rules in order to challenge the authorities. Once after a particularly long, drawn out session with a security official, he knocks on Klaus's door. "For God's sakes," he yells as he paces the floor, "the questions they ask me—they act as though I'm a spy. They're such idiots. A spy wouldn't act like me." He stops pacing. "A spy would act like you," he says, and laughs.

"Like me? What do you mean?"

"Oh, you know, buttoned up, never saying anything, except about work, unless someone asks you a question first, and even then—"

"Ah, yes, I see," Klaus says, and laughs but not loudly. "If you'll excuse me, I must leave."

"You're not coming to the cafeteria with me?"

"I have a dinner invitation tonight, and I'm afraid I'm already a little late."

His colleague's wives often invite Klaus to dinner parties. He is considered a perfect dinner guest, a single man of pleasant appearance, quiet but with excellent manners. The women have noticed how kind he is with the children, talking to them easily, as if they were adults. Now and then he goes to a Saturday night dance, where he is also a welcome figure. Surprisingly, he is a fine dancer, graceful in his movements, quick and light on his feet as he guides his partner with ease and fluidity. Several of the women have made tentative overtures to him sexually, but he acts in such a way as to make it appear the approach hasn't been made. The need for caution is as entrenched in him as ever.

In pursuance of what he is now pursuing—this project—he strives to make the maximum possible contribution. His colleagues admire him for his ability to grasp the essentials of a technical problem with great rapidity. His written reports, though not in his first language, are a model of conciseness and lucidity.

At times there will be discussions, particularly among the refugee scientists, about the war, about what's going to happen after the German surrender. For that now seems, if not imminent, inevitable. There are arguments about what the Russians will do, how much they'll try to take over in the postwar world, how much they can or should be trusted. Klaus never offers an opinion. He seems either uninterested or uninformed. He has accepted secrecy's effects; he has not tried to analyze its processes.

If he ever does think of the actions he has taken to help the Russians—he would never use the word "spy"—he thinks of himself as having shared information that needed to be shared. He has done what he had to do, to become the man he needed to be.

With the arrival of the New Year, there is a darkening of the mood at the laboratory as the scientists for the first time are forced to acknowledge the possibility of failure. They have not been able to solve the problem of how to prevent plutonium, which is subject to spontaneous fission, from pre-detonating in a plutonium bomb. After intense discussion, they have decided to focus on making the bomb an implosion device: an initial explosion must force the radioactive material inward toward a center before allowing the explosive force to travel outward. With his colleagues in T-1, Klaus has been assigned to an analysis of the use of high-explosive lenses to achieve this outcome.

Early one Sunday morning, Klaus is lying on his bed in his dormitory room, dozing on and off, unable to fall into sleep. He has been working for twenty-four hours without letup. The work has not been going well. He has reached a point where the more he goes over the equations on the page, the more resistant they become to solution. As he dozes, he can feel them circulating round and round in his brain, not at all pleasurably. At one moment, a mathematical conjunction occurs; in the next, everything falls apart. He is determined to get up in a few minutes and go back to the lab and start again, from the beginning.

There is a knock on the door and, shaking himself from his stupor, he gets up to answer. Standing in the hallway is Donald Furst, a theoretical physicist in his group, who apologizes for waking him.

"I wasn't sleeping," Klaus assures him, expecting that Furst wants to talk to him about the lens calculations. Instead, he announces that he has come to invite Klaus to join him and his wife on an expedition to explore Indian cliff dwellings. Klaus thanks him politely for the invitation, but says that he has to work.

"It might do you good to take a break."

"I don't think so," Klaus responds wearily, and is about to shut the door when Furst tells him how disappointed Linda will be. He mumbles something about her not having had an easy time of it lately, and that it would help to take her mind off what is bothering her if he would join them.

Why me? Klaus wonders but does not say. Yet once again, as with the courier—why is he thinking of the courier now?—he finds himself giving in, and going along without protest.

An hour later, they are driving in the Furst's Studebaker out of Los Alamos, past the sentry gates, down the curving road toward the flatland. It is a clear, surprisingly mild day for winter. Slumped in the back seat,

Klaus is lulled by the motion of the car. He tells himself that, after all, it may help his work, if he gets away for a few hours. Haven't there been times before when he looked at a problem so long he became blind to it, and then when he went away and came back, somehow in the interim it had solved itself?

His eyes half-closed, he overhears a conversation between Donald and Linda, or rather Linda is holding forth, while Donald only says, "M-m-m" or "Uh-huh," now and then. She is apparently upset about their living situation, and keeps asking why he hasn't objected, why he hasn't been able to get them a better unit. He shrugs and says that the assignments are given out according to certain rules, and he has no say in the matter. He's told her this before, he adds, his voice mild. "If you have children, you're allotted a larger unit, and if you don't—"

"You don't—" she says bitterly.

After a silence, she bursts out, "But you could at least do something about getting some of the things fixed. It gets so hot in there you have to throw open the windows so you don't suffocate, and then it gets too cold. What kind of an idiot would devise a heating system that you have no control over?"

"Look, I didn't design the heating system. The army designed it the way they did, and you've got no choice. You have to put up with it."

"What do you think, Klaus?" She has turned to look at him. "Do you think one should just put up with things, accept whatever they dole out to you and not object? After all, this isn't a police state."

He smiles and does not commit himself. Facing forward again, she launches into a litany of complaints: the faulty stoves, the laundry facilities that are often out of commission, her problems with the "Indian maids." Why does she need a maid? Klaus wonders. She isn't working and she doesn't have children. Why doesn't she do the housework herself? Shrugging off the irritation, he allows himself to fall a little more over the edge into half-sleep.

"You don't have to put up with any of this in the bachelor's dormitory, do you?"

He opens his eyes and sees Linda has again turned in her seat, arching her long neck, provocatively.

"Not really," he says, holding to the safety of non-responsiveness.

"But if you did, you would make a fuss, and eventually someone from the Army would come and fix it, wouldn't they?"

"I couldn't say what someone would or wouldn't do, since it hasn't happened."

She looks at him and shakes her head. "Men," she says, and turns back to facing front. Then she lapses into silence, and curls up on the front seat, childlike. He could almost feel sorry for her, but he reminds himself that at any moment, she will lash out again.

Even in his lassitude, Klaus has been keeping careful track of the route they are taking. He always needs to know where he has been so that, if necessary, he can retrace his movements exactly. He has noted the place where they turned off onto a side road. Now, as they start to ascend over an increasingly rutted roadbed, the car jolts and sputters. They climb slowly through a series of hairpin turns, and then descend into a narrow valley, walled in on two sides by overhanging cliffs.

"According to the map, we park here and walk in," Donald announces.

When he stops, Klaus gets out, and goes to the front to open the door for Linda. She is still sleeping, her head against the seat, her mouth partly open. He knocks gently on the window and she opens her eyes with a start. "What? What?" she says, in a panic, her eyes unfocused.

"We're here."

"Oh, oh, yes." She shakes herself, and in an instant the look of panic is replaced by a flirtatious smile.

"Thank you, sir," she says with exaggerated politeness, as Klaus opens the door for her. She steps out and stands for a moment, surveying the valley. As he watches, she opens her arms and throws back her head. "Free at last," she exults, whirling in a circle. She stops and laughs. "Don't you approve, Klaus? You think I'm being an exhibitionist?"

"No, I—"

"I'm certainly not one in Los Alamos. Who would even notice? Everyone's so busy, paying attention to their little secret—"

"Linda," Donald interrupts, "that's enough of that."

"Yes, master," Linda says and executes a mock bow. "Which way do we go?"

"That way." Donald points ahead of them to where the cliffs appear to converge.

"Okay, troops," she calls out. "Forward march!"

Linda is in the lead, moving swiftly. To Klaus, who follows directly behind her, she is a shadow that never solidifies, a woman in panic at one moment, a whirling dervish in the next, a woman out of control, self-indulgent, repellent in her display of self or in her pretensions of display, he can't tell which. As they climb through the crevices between massive rocks, he allows his mind, for one instant, to touch upon the lens problem. But it is like a sore spot, something not quite healed or congealed, and instead he focuses on the gritty surface of one rock, the red color of another, the worn tracings of incised markings on a third.

Suddenly they emerge into a vast clearing. On their right is a cliff riddled with many openings, caves, some just above ground level, others a bit higher. The highest caves of all are accessible only by long rope ladders, dangling from the cliff face. Looking at the ladders, he is excited at the possibility of climbing them. Though he does not consider himself an excellent athlete, he has always been good at climbing, allowing himself to go into a mindless state, in which what matters is where one will put one's right foot, how one will shift and put one's weight on the other foot, as one goes higher and higher . . .

They explore the lower caves first. In one of them they find broken pieces of brown and white pottery, and small black shards of obsidian. As they climb higher to the second level of caves, he notices that the Fursts keep repeating a strange ritual. Each time they come to a spot that requires hefting oneself up, Donald kneels down and Linda climbs on his back. He then hoists her up and she slithers onto the ledge on her stomach, like a snake.

On the wall of one cave, Klaus discovers faded markings, barely visible under the glare of his flashlight. "What do you think those are?" Linda asks, coming up to him.

"I have no idea. I am not familiar with American Indian mythology."

"Have you been to the Stone Lions?"

"No."

"Donald and I hiked in to see them last fall. It took four hours each way. We had to go up a mountain and down a mountain and up another mountain, and when we finally got to the Stone Lions, they looked like nothing—just two rocks. But then after a while, it begins to get to you that this is a sacred place. You don't know anything about it—why it's a sacred place, what it has to do with lions—how could they have known about lions, anyhow? You don't know and yet—"

"They're not part of your history, so I don't see that you could expect to understand them."

"I didn't say I understood them. I said I felt something about them."

"Sorry, my error." Klaus leaves the cave and looks up toward the top of the cliff face. He sees a large bird, a vulture of some sort, on a ledge before one of the highest caves. Donald follows Klaus's gaze. "Are you thinking of climbing one of those ladders?"

"You're not going to get me up there," Linda says. "You know how I hate heights. Let's just finish up down here."

"Maybe Klaus wants to—"

"But it's way past lunchtime," she wails, "and I've made a wonderful picnic."

"I'm perfectly happy to stop at this point," Klaus says politely. He looks up again. The vulture is still perched on the ledge, waiting.

When they return to the car, Linda asks for the keys, opens the trunk, and lifts out a large picnic basket. In a space sheltered from the occasional gusts of wind, she puts down a blanket and spreads the picnic before them. Even Klaus, who usually doesn't pay attention to food, is impressed. Where has she gotten the caviar? Donald asks. "That's my little secret," she says. "I'll never tell."

When they have finished eating, she insists that they finish the second bottle of wine. "No more for me," Donald says.

"What about you?" she turns to Klaus.

"No more for me, either, thank you."

"Spoilsports. I've got two spoilsports here instead of one. I guess it's up to me to finish it."

"Linda—"

"Donald, don't start that again."

In the warmth of the sun, Klaus begins to grow drowsy. He would like to take a short nap on the blanket, but he feels it would be impolite, so he forces himself to sit ramrod straight. Leaning back on her elbows, Linda looks at him speculatively. "Where were you born?" she asks.

He is unprepared for this new twist in her behavior. "In Germany."

"I know that, but where in Germany?"

"In Russelheim."

"Where is that?"

"Near Darmstadt."

"And where is that?"

"In the province of Hesse."

She laughs. "That doesn't tell me much."

"Maybe he'd rather not be interrogated," Donald says mildly.

"It's not as though I'm asking about government secrets." To Klaus she says, "You're not offended, are you?"

"No, of course not."

"Here in America, when we're friends with somebody, we talk about ourselves and about our past. It's just what we do."

"Ah, yes," he says.

She questions him further: Where did he go to school? When did he leave Germany? He tries to answer without revealing, politely, always politely. He is trying to hold himself intact. He has the sense that she is trying to provoke him. He will not be provoked.

Suddenly she yawns. "I'm so sleepy."

Klaus too can hardly keep his eyes open. It is probably the wine that is affecting him, as well as the many hours without sleep. Bit by bit he lets himself sink down onto the blanket. His eyes close and he feels the glare of the sun through his eyelids, white and hot and penetrating. In a stratum deep below the surface, he can sense a movement in his brain, in his nerves. It is like the lightest touch of the lightest breath of air. He must not disturb it. An answer is taking shape, like a memory being recaptured. It is a familiar feeling, having happened to him before. After long effort, a solution to a problem, sought and sought without success, finally prepares to reveal itself, though it still demands inattention on your part. Then, unexpectedly, it is there, clear in outline, obvious, a beneficent gift, a kind of grace, if you believe in grace. But one cannot force it. One must wait.

The next thing he knows there is a shadow between him and the sun. He opens his eyes to see Linda bending over him. It startles him to see her blue eyes so intent upon him, her blond hair falling forward. He has not looked at her before, not really seen her. Involuntarily he pulls back, his hands shooting up in front of his face.

"Good God!" she says. "Don't tell me I frighten you that much."

"No, no. I was just a little surprised."

"I'll bet you've been working. You had the same expression on your face that Donald sometimes gets. It's like a wall that he's hiding behind."

"That's enough of that," Donald rebukes her.

"I was just joking."

"I don't like your joking about it."

"How can you help joking when you're surrounded by so much silence?" Standing, she holds out her hand to Klaus. "Come on, let me help you up." She smiles coyly and arches her neck again. Klaus glances at Donald, who is busy, packing up the picnic. "Perhaps we should get back," he says, getting up, ignoring her hand.

"Get back? To Los Alamos? This early? Oh no, we invited you for the day. I've got another expedition all planned out for this afternoon, a surprise for you. This time," she adds, shaking the car keys in front of his face, "I'm going to drive."

"Linda, I think you better let me drive."

"I'm perfectly fine, Donald. Don't worry." To Klaus she says, "I've been driving since I was fifteen and I've never had an accident yet."

During the next few hours, they drive for miles in silence. From the rear seat Klaus stares out of the window. In the slanting late afternoon light the cliffs in the distance seem like fortifications of some ancient civilization. He hears Donald tell Linda that he thinks she should have turned off this road earlier, but she says she knows what she is doing. A half-hour later, she changes her mind, and makes a sharp U-turn, spinning the back wheels on the shoulder. By the time they have retraced their route and turned off to an even more narrow road, the sky has darkened. The clouds are threatening but no rain falls.

"Maybe we ought to get back to Los Alamos," Donald says.

"No, we can't go back, now that we've gotten this far. It's just a little further," she insists.

"I knew I'd find it," she says triumphantly, as she pulls up in front of an adobe church at the center of a small Indian village. She jumps out and leads them through a small courtyard, enclosing a group of graves, into the dark building. "Here's the nave and there's the sanctuary, just as it says in the guidebook. There's a clay pit in here somewhere that has a special clay with miraculous powers. See, there's a board with photographs and cards and even drivers' licenses of people who came here and were cured because of the clay—"

She hurries into a chamber to the left of the altar, where the walls are hung with crutches and bandages. "See. The people left these behind, when they were cured." She stoops down and points to a pit at the center of the chamber. "There's the clay, right there. You're supposed to put it on your skin. Some people even swallow it," she says, her voice rising with excitement.

"I've had enough," Donald says. "I'll wait for you outside."

"Why don't you want to see this? You ought to see this," she calls after him, but he does not come back.

She turns to Klaus. "It's been known to cure people of rheumatism and sore throats and paralysis and—" she laughs a half-laugh, "—all sorts of things." She scoops some clay from the pit and holds it in her hand. "It's even supposed to help you conceive a child."

She is looking down at her hand now, her mouth a little open. He can see her teeth white in the dimness.

"Of course, you have to believe in it or it won't work."

Slowly she rubs the clay on the side of her face. She reaches into the pit again and this time when she lifts her hand, she strokes the mud onto her forehead. No longer aware of his presence, she is rubbing the clay between her fingers, caressingly. She is taking her forefinger and putting it into her mouth and sucking on it. When she removes her finger, her whole mouth is blackened.

There is no moon; the countryside is dark except for the beams of their headlights on the unpaved road. Once they reach the main road, Donald drives rapidly back to Los Alamos. After they go through the sentry gates, Klaus says, "Will you drop me at the Tech area?"

"Don't you want to have some dinner?"

"I'm not hungry, thanks. I want to do a little work."

But in fact, after he gets out of the car, he goes to the dormitory. He throws himself upon his bed and lies there hour after hour, his face turned to the wall. He sleeps and dreams of an enormous wave making its way toward him over the mesas under a strangely dark sun. In terror he begins to run from it but he cannot move fast enough. He turns and sees others behind him being swallowed up in the rushing wave, which is no longer of water but of light.

The next morning it is as if a switch has been thrown in his brain, in his body. The darkness is gone. He gets up and goes to the lab. When he sits at his desk, the solution to his problem is at hand. That afternoon he requests permission to take a few days leave the following month to travel to Boston. He knows it will be granted as the authorities have recently eased the rules to allow residents to take short leaves. He writes to Lottie, telling her what day he will be arriving. He is ready to pass information to the courier.

I f they did see him—his fellow passengers on this train to Boston—
would they see that he is flooded with something that he can only call
excitement? He knows what it is to feel steady, keeping to the course,
even phlegmatic. But at this moment there is a speeding up in him, a sensation of being carried and of throwing himself forward at the same time.

It was only last night that Y contacted him and told him that he was
to come to Boston to meet Klaus at his sister's house. To think that he has
had less than twenty-four hours in which to take possession once again of
his secret life. It is true that he has tried to imagine this journey many
times these past months, but there has always been a stopping-place. He
gets on the train to Philadelphia, he gets off the train to Philadelphia as it
is pulling out of the station, he takes the train to Boston, he gets off, he
takes the bus, he gets off, he walks down the street, he goes up the path,
he knocks on the door, Lottie answers—but then behind her there is the
Sly one and the scene, along with hope, dissolves into thin air. But this
is not imagining: He is actually on his way, one moment taking him
inevitably to the next. As he is here on this train, now, so he will be in
Lottie's house—in a new now. Klaus will be there and since Klaus will
be there, the Sly one will not be. Of that Harry is sure.

It is raining outside, a bitter cold rain. He is sitting on his small
black bag in the aisle. Every seat is taken; he was lucky to get onto the
train at all. The smell of wet wool saturates the air. Through the steamed-

up windows, he can only see traces of the rain pelting down. He has been living in a dim, clouded state, not allowing himself to realize how painful it was to lose touch with Klaus. For the first time in his life he has had a clear purpose and then without warning he was purposeless. But now everything is back on track.

He shifts his weight on his bag and reminds himself that he must not exaggerate. He has not been entirely purposeless. After all, he did have and still has his other life, his life in the lab. He has kept up with his work there as painstakingly as ever. Nothing would deter him from that. He relies on something in him that might be called stolidity, an inertia in the best sense of the word. He simply proceeds with what must be done. But in this life, this secret life, all was awry. Thank God, that is over.

What will be the first words he and Klaus will say to each other? Klaus is so reserved, so outwardly cold, Harry hardly expects anything very emotional. Yet he believes that below that coldness is a deeply sensitive man. Harry feels they have become fast friends, brothers in a way. That was why his suddenly cutting off contact was such a blow. It was like a betrayal of that friendship. What a stupid fool you are to even think that way, he reproaches himself. Who knows what difficulties Klaus has had to face that prevented him from contacting you?

At times Harry has the feeling that Klaus is the kind of man who should be commanding others but that there is a refusal in him, almost a disdain, for power of any sort. It is connected with some sadness in him, some deep need. Harry can tell this because he has in him a special listening device for need. Need cries out to him, even when the other is silent and does not ask.

He needs me to listen to him, Harry knows. At times, I become so caught up in what he says—even if it is only a germ of a story—I am in it, inside it, in his telling. My heart bleeds for those sorrows he does not tell me. If I sometimes feel I cannot feel my own sorrows, I can feel his. It is almost as if I cannot live my own life but I can live his.

Naturally he realizes that it is nonsense to even think such a thing. Each one must live his own life. And yet, can't it be that in some totally forgotten and secret existence, before we were born, we were buried with other unformed beings, lying in strata, undifferentiated? Then and only then, when our time came, were we exposed, laid bare, brought to the surface to become discrete selves, each one the inheritor of a single life. But all the time—and why shouldn't this be so?—beneath and beyond our knowing, is the leftover past of our shared preexistence.

So he muses, sitting on his black bag on the train to Boston, traveling north, letting thoughts come and go. Don't go too far, he cautions himself. But actually he doesn't need cautioning. He can put on moderation, stolidity at any moment, just like an old overcoat.

On the street everything looks grey and bare—the trees, the houses, the dead lawns with their leftover snow, even the cars—but there is nothing grey in the prospect that lies ahead. It is already giving out gleams of color, suggesting that nothing will ever be muted and dull again. At 363 he turns sharply up the path and slips on an icy place in the walk. He composes himself and proceeds more slowly, with more dignity, as if someone were watching from a window. He knocks. The door opens. He is expecting Lottie to answer. But it is not Lottie; it is Klaus. Harry stands open-mouthed, his vision trembling at the shock. So it is when one has hoped for so long in vain and hope is finally granted. He cannot believe his eyes. But then in an instant, he believes. It is Klaus in a bathrobe. (Has he come too early? But it is not that early.) Klaus, thinner than Harry remembers him but still Klaus.

Yet in this rush, this vibration, he cannot help seeing that Klaus is startled, no, puzzled as he stares at him. Surely, he tells himself, he, above all people, knows it's me, Raymond, Harry, Raymond. That he is not memorable has been a source of pride to him in his secret life as well as a means of protection. But now the thought that he is not memorable to Klaus sends a chill through him. A coldness pierces Harry's heart, and he is reminded of a story he read as a child. Of course, it could not really have been his story—it was about a little Christian boy—but still he felt what that boy felt, when, looking at the Snow Queen, a sliver of ice penetrated his heart and corroded his mind.

"It's me, Raymond." To his own ears his voice is strained and taut.

"You look—different." After a moment, Klaus adds, "You have gained weight?"

"Oh, yeah," says Harry in relief. "A lot of weight. Almost twenty pounds since I saw you."

He does not say that in the time since Klaus has been out of touch, on many Saturday nights he has taken the subway to Pennsylvania Station, bought a ticket to Philadelphia, boarded the train and stayed on it, forcing himself to remain in his seat if he had a seat. He had told the people at the lab that he had to go to Philadelphia because the twins, Doris and Dan, were not well, but once he got there, he simply went home. Of course, Mom insisted on preparing his favorite foods and serving him huge portions. He ate and he ate as if he would never be filled up. Afterwards, he was disgusted with himself. Yet the next time, he ate just as voraciously, as if it was the last food left in the world. Now, with Klaus before him, so fine, so absolute in his thinness, Harry resolves to go on a diet.

Klaus shuts the door and directs him into the living room. "Please wait here. I will be right back."

Harry circles the room slowly, looking at the couch where Lottie held the baby, at the chair where Sly sat. They are as they were before, but now they are the furnishings of a hopeful present. He had been so anxious when he was here last time. He would like to have been able to reassure that one—himself—that it was all going to come out all right, which it has.

Crossing to the mantel, he examines the photos of Klaus and of Lottie, and of the baby. There is also a picture of an old man, white-haired, with a white beard. It is in a silver frame. Harry picks it up and scrutinizes it. The old man could be an Old Testament prophet, except that his face is kind and gentle. Hearing Klaus return, he puts the photo back on the mantel.

"Your father?" he asks, as Klaus comes in, dressed in a dark suit with a tie.

"Yes, my father."

Harry waits for him to go on but he is tight-lipped and turns away in irritation. I knew I shouldn't have asked him that, Harry reproaches himself. "I have two things for you," he offers, trying to make amends for his thoughtlessness. From his black bag he takes out a thick white envelope and a small package, gift-wrapped. He hands the envelope to Klaus.

"What is this?"

"It's fifteen hundred dollars. For your expenses."

"I have not asked for money. I don't want money." He hands the envelope back to Harry, as if it were something dirty, to be gotten rid of at once.

"Okay, I'll give it back and say you don't want it. I didn't mean to offend you. I was told to give it to you."

Klaus shakes his head. "It's all right." But Harry sees that it is not all right, that Klaus is still upset.

"I have something else for you," Harry says timidly, handing him the wrapped package. "It's a belated Christmas present, from me."

"A present? Thank you." He smiles a rare smile, disarming and disarmed. His face, his blue eyes, are no longer cold. He opens the package, which contains a fine leather wallet, which Harry has purchased at an extravagant price at a store on Fifth Avenue.

"I hope you like it. I hope you'll find it useful."

"It's very nice."

Harry flushes. "It's just that I wanted to express my—" He cannot find a word. Appreciation wouldn't be right; it sounds too distant, too formal.

"I appreciate it very much," Klaus says, folding the wrapping paper neatly and putting it and the wallet on the coffee table. "To get to the matter at hand, I have a number of things to tell you but I must be brief as my sister will be back shortly."

In a concise and well-organized fashion he proceeds to give Harry information on the project at Los Alamos: on the two projected versions for an atomic bomb, on the comparative critical mass of plutonium and uranium-235, on the problems with the predetonation of plutonium, on the hydrodynamics of implosion, on the experiments being done on high explosives for use as a compressive force in the plutonium bomb, on the principle of the lens system, on the difficulties of multi-point detonation.

"I have put this all down in greater detail in a written report which I will give to you when you leave," Klaus concludes as the front door opens and Lottie appears in the entryway with the child.

"This is an old friend who has stopped by," Klaus says.

She is turning to Harry, looking at him, not recognizing him.

"I was here once before," he reminds her.

"Were you? I'm afraid I don't—"

"Some months ago." He points to the child. "I remember he was crying. He had a cold and you had a visitor."

She bends down to take the child out of his snowsuit. Her dark hair falls over her face, so Harry cannot guess what she is thinking. When she stands, she says, "Ah yes, I remember now. You are the man with the twins."

"Twins?" Klaus looks at him with surprise. Harry merely shrugs.

"I'll put these groceries in the kitchen and then I'll make some coffee."

"We are going out right away," Klaus says.

"I'll just take a minute." She picks up the child and takes him into the living room, where a playpen stands in the corner. Do people put children this age in a playpen? Harry wonders. Would I have done it with Doris and Dan at this age?

Klaus follows her out of the room and Harry hears him talking to her in German. The child, who is standing with his hands on the rail of the playpen, stares at Harry suspiciously. "Mommy!" he cries.

Harry tries to smile ingratiatingly. "How are you today?"

"Mommy!" the child cries again. Just as he has on his earlier visit, Harry feels resentment stirring within him at the demands of this child, who seems to get his way in everything.

"Mommy!" the little boy whimpers and Harry, seeing that he is about to cry, feels shame at his own hardness.

"Here," he says, taking his keys out of his pocket, "do you want to play with these?" He goes over to the playpen and, holding them out to the child, jangles them. The little boy takes the keys, examines them, shakes them as if they were a rattle, and then throws them across the room.

"You threw my keys," Harry says in mock sorrow and the little boy laughs as Harry retrieves them from near the fireplace. He returns to the playpen and hands the child the keys again. The child looks at him, looks at the keys, and throws them across the room. Again Harry mourns, "My keys, you threw my keys," and again the child laughs.

Each time the sequence is repeated, the child laughs more uproariously and his throw becomes wilder. Finally he throws the keys in a low arc and they land under the sofa. "Oh, no," Harry says in an an exaggerated cry of despair. "Now, look what you did." The child laughs ecstatically as Harry gets down on his hands and knees and gropes under the couch.

"What are you doing?" Klaus asks, coming into the room.

"I'm looking for my keys. He—uh—" he gestures toward the child, "He's been throwing them."

"More, more," the child cries out, stretching his arm out for the keys.

"No more," Klaus says gently, lifting the boy out of the playpen.

"More, more," the child cries again, as Harry gets up and puts his keys in his pocket.

Lottie comes in with coffee. "You shouldn't get him so excited before his nap," she says to Klaus, taking the child from him. As she passes by Harry, carrying the little boy out of the room, he sees she is looking at him with beseeching eyes, as if to say, Don't tell, Please don't tell. Why would he tell? As for the child, he has forgotten all about the keys. His arms are around his mother's neck. His head is nestled on her shoulder.

At the bus stop Klaus stands and waits with Harry. Is this how it will end, Harry wonders, in silence, at a bus stop, on a street with puddles? A man who has joined them steps out into the street to see if the bus is coming. "Nothing," he says impatiently.

Abruptly Klaus turns and gestures to Harry to follow him.

After walking two blocks they turn into a park. Ahead of them are vague shapes of trees, suggestions of paths, dissolving in the mist. Harry is reminded of a scroll of a Japanese landscape that Sam once contemplated for what seemed like hours. He feels light, almost giddy, at the thought that the meeting which was about to come to an end has not ended.

Klaus stops and faces him. "I hope you will understand if I say something personal—," he hesitates—"about Lottie. She is not a very strong person. That is to say, her emotional state is not very good. It never has been. So it is very important to make sure that she is not involved in any way in our—"

"Of course not. Don't worry. She won't even remember me."

"She remembered about your twins."

"Oh, that. Oh, well. I was told it is better to be married than not married as far as other people are concerned. They trust a married man more. They think you're more—"

"I don't want to hear." Klaus turns and strides deeper into the park. Catching up with him, Harry steals a glance at his face, so closed, so imperturbable. He has been wrong to see coldness there. It is the face of

a man imprisoned in silence. Yet Harry can tell, there are words he needs
to speak, words he must speak. As they turn onto a narrow path, obscured
by mist on all sides, Klaus stops. Harry readies himself to fall into a state
of listening in which every word Klaus will say will strike deep into him,
deep into layers where sounds are more than sounds, where words carry
more than meaning.

"This place reminds me of Sherbrooke," Klaus is saying, the words
coming as if against resistance. "I was interned there—in Canada—in
the first year of the war—as an enemy alien . . ." Harry waits for him to
go on. "I and other German refugees—we were sent from England with
a group of German prisoners of war. Our identification papers had been
on board a troop ship, which was torpedoed. At first, they thought we
were all Nazis." He stares into the mist. "It was straightened out . . .
eventually . . ."

This time Harry does not wait. "It must have been difficult for you."

Klaus shrugs. "Difficult? I don't know. In some way the civilians
back in England had it much worse than we did. We didn't have to suffer
through the air raids. We had adequate food. The commanding officer
allowed us to organize a camp university. I was asked to give lectures in
physics. They were well attended . . ." His voice trails off. "I could understand the reasoning of the British authorities. They did not want to take a
chance in wartime."

A light rain begins to fall, the sound of the water on the evergreen
needles a rhythmic accompaniment to the words that start and stop and
start again. "What I did mind was being kept from my work. Now and
then one of my colleagues at the university would send me a technical
paper, but I had to do without books."

"You mean there were no books at all in the camp?"

"It had a small library. But nothing of interest to me. Primarily
mysteries—," he says curtly.

"Don't you like mysteries? I like to read mysteries myself. I like
the suspense."

"To me, suspense of that kind is sadistic."

"How do you mean sadistic?"

"When I read a mystery, I feel that someone is playing games with
my mind."

But a kind of pleasurable game, Harry is about to say, then thinks better of it. Up ahead what had looked like a crouching animal from a distance now reveals itself as nothing but a large shrub. After a long silence, Klaus says, "I have found it is better to expect the worst, to prepare for the worst. If one accepts that, then one can go on, without false hopes."

"I don't know," Harry says, not sure that he is following Klaus's logic. "Where there's life, there's hope," he asserts.

Klaus looks at him, and laughs oddly. "Do you believe that?"

"Well, yes . . ."

Klaus shakes his head. "My father—"

The rain is drumming harder now, on the needles, on the bark of the trees. The water is sloshing over Harry's shoes but he would risk a thousand colds to be able to hear what Klaus has to say. "Your father?"

"He believed that. But then he had to. He was a pastor. He lived his life believing and trying to convince others to believe. Like his father and his father before him—"

They are no longer alone. A woman has appeared among the trees. She is wearing a yellow slicker, and is leading on a leash a little black and white dog, also wearing a yellow slicker. The dog is pulling on the woman, trying to sniff at the underbrush. She is pulling on the dog, trying to make it obey. "Come!" she yells and drags him along. The dog is running beside her but his head keeps turning, looking back at the underbrush.

On the train, returning to New York, Harry is surrounded by many others but he feels separated out from all the rest. He alone knows of the contents of his little black bag, something that none of them can even suspect. Before he boarded the train, he peeked into the packet and saw the mathematical formulae in Klaus's tiny handwriting. His part in this now, his duty, is to complete the mission he has been assigned. He has obtained the papers. He must deliver them to Y.

He is to meet him in the men's room at the Earle Theater in the Bronx at midnight. Once he met Sam there. He misses Sam whenever he sees Y. Y has told him that Sam has left the U.S. Several times Y has said that Sam sends his warmest greetings.

Harry knows that Y will ask him when he is to see Klaus next. He will tell him that they have made an arrangement to meet in June.

Since Klaus will not be able to get to Boston for at least a year, Harry will have to go to New Mexico. They will meet in Santa Fe on the Castillo Street Bridge. It is strange for Harry to think of himself going west. He has never been further west than Dayton—he'd rather not think about Dayton. He tries to imagine desert, mountains, and more desert, but his imagination falters.

In Santa Fe will they talk again, as they have talked in Boston? To hear those utterances of Klaus's, fragmented and confusing as they were, was like receiving a special gift. Harry is sure that Klaus has not spoken those words to anyone else. They are the counterpart to their shared secrecy. What would he have gone on to say, if the woman and the dog had not appeared? He recalls how, as they walked beneath the trees, drops fell upon them from the wet branches. He could see them trembling on the dark limbs before they fell.

As he gets off the train in New York, he slips easily into being one of a crowd, unseen. He does not delude himself that he is a special kind of man. Klaus—now there is someone different. But he himself is ordinary, one of many. Yet by some strange chance he has been chosen for a destiny not at all ordinary. With Klaus he is caught up in the forces of history, at a critical juncture of life and matter.

Someday, he will dissolve back into the others, as a molecule of water into a great sea. He wants it to be that way.

Y HAS INSISTED THAT Harry use a roundabout route for this journey to Santa Fe. He wanted him to go first to San Francisco, then take a bus to Denver, then another bus to El Paso, and finally a bus to Santa Fe. I don't have the time, Harry told him. "I do have a job, you know. I'm needed at the lab."

"But you have to take precautions," Y said severely.

"Don't worry, I will," Harry said with some irritation. It wasn't as though he were some beginner at this trade. "I'm not going to be followed."

Harry could have taken the train through to Lamy, and then the bus to Santa Fe, but he figured that the Los Alamos employees would regularly go that way, and he didn't want to go on any route that anyone there used regularly. Instead he has taken the train from Chicago to Albuquerque, and from there he'll take the bus to Santa Fe.

Luckily he has managed to get an upper berth so he's been able to sleep at night. He finds it very comforting to sleep on a train. In the middle of the night when the train stops at some isolated station, you wake up and you don't know where you are, but that doesn't matter. You know you're in the middle of a journey whose end-point is fixed.

Tonight, awakened at a stop at an unknown junction, where sudden lights flare in the darkness, he thinks of his conversation with Klaus in the park in Boston. He remembers every word Klaus has said, hearing his

155

confidences as if for the first time. As he falls into sleep, lulled by the rocking of the train, he holds to the words as if they have become a keepsake, to be taken out and gone over, and then to be put away with the utmost care.

At the station in Albuquerque, stepping down from the train, he holds tightly to his little black bag. The intensity of the sun so early in the day stuns him. He has heard people talk about dry heat being better than wet. Give me wet heat any day, he thinks. In the humid Philadelphia summers he is like a hothouse plant, in his element. Here he feels the moisture being sapped from his body by the greedy and oppressive heat, just as if he were being dessicated.

Boarding the bus to Santa Fe, he takes a seat by an open window. The bus is stifling, but once they are on their way he can feel a breeze, if not a cool one. He stares at the landscape, hypnotized. One goes on and on and yet nothing changes: still the same desert, the same mountains. Feeling carsick, Harry forces himself to focus on the back of the seat in front of him, with its meaningless scratches and marks.

On solid ground, on his own two feet in Santa Fe, he feels much better. It is certainly a lot cooler than Albuquerque. As he has time to kill before his appointment with Klaus, he wanders through the dusty streets, looking at the adobe houses and adobe walls. As usual, no one is looking at him. He retraces his steps to the plaza and follows the covered walkway till he sees a sign pointing to a historical museum. Inside he moves from case to case, looking at photos of the early days of Santa Fe and at Indian artifacts, but he absorbs little of what he sees. His mind is on the time that must pass before he sets out for the meeting-place. At the desk he purchases a map of Santa Fe so he will not have to ask anyone for directions.

Shortly before the appointed hour, he makes his way to Castillo Street, passing by the old cathedral to the little bridge crossing over the Rio Santa Fe. How can they call it a river when it's hardly more than a thin stream between narrow banks? As for the bridge itself, its surface is like a continuation of a dirt road. Standing on it, looking over the edge, he sees that, shallow though the water is, it is perfectly clear.

At the sound of footsteps behind him, he turns. He is stunned to see

Klaus, though it is for him he has been waiting. He is different from before, more—shining—is that the word? Maybe it's only the effect of the sun. In this brilliant light his hair gleams red-gold. He is lean, sun-tanned, sturdier than Harry remembers him. But in his face there is still that tension between the open and the closed, between that which would hide secrets and that which would reveal them. No one else would see that, he tells himself, but me. It touches Harry so, tying him to Klaus in ways he has never been tied to anyone before.

The two men exchange a formal greeting. It almost makes Harry laugh to think that they can speak like any two ordinary people meeting on any street in the world. But there is nothing ordinary about this meeting on this bridge that is not really a bridge over this river that is not really a river. This place, this sun, this heat, all have a quality of disconnection from life as he has known it, secret or otherwise.

Klaus gestures to him to follow him to his car, parked a half block away. This *is* real, Harry tells himself as he gets in the battered blue Buick, so real that he feels that this is the only real thing that has ever happened to him. It is hidden from the world, and yet what will pass between them will have its effect upon the world.

Klaus is silent as he drives and yet Harry can feel an accumulating tension in him, betrayed by a vein pulsing just below his hairline, on the right side of his face. "Nice car," he says, his impulse as usual to try to make things easier, to defuse tension.

"I have problems with the carburetor."

"Can't you get a new one?"

"They are not being made."

"Ah. Because of the war." It's unfortunate he can't say more about carburetors. In fact, he knows little about cars, except, of course, for the principle of the internal combustion engine. He's never had a car; he's never even been in a position to aspire to owning one. He tries to think of other potential subjects. Maybe he should say something about the Phillies, who lost yet another heartbreaker last week. But Klaus probably wouldn't be interested in the Phillies.

If only he had taken other car trips before, he could bring up his earlier experiences, compare, contrast, whatever. But he has gone nowhere by car—only to Gettysburg, in imagination, a long time ago. (And that was for his pal Fred Mandel, not for himself.) Since he began his courier work, he has been to many places by train and by bus, but in retrospect each place has blended into the other—a generic place defined by movie houses and diners and street corners, so many street corners. In a curious way, he now realizes, he always felt that these places were not really places in the sense of being outside of himself. Of course, they were outside; they just felt inside. But this place is definitely outside. It is like the concept of outside carried to the highest power.

After driving through a long stretch of flat land, they have turned off onto narrower and bumpier roads, have gone up and up and down and down, and then up and up and down and down again. Surely it is not for safety's sake that Klaus is taking him to such an out of the way place to make the transfer. Harry is definitely feeling carsick from one sharp turn after another. He hopes he does not throw up; that would be embarrassing.

Suddenly they stop. Klaus opens his door and gets out; Harry opens his, taking his little black bag with him. "Leave it," Klaus says.

"But—"

"No one will take it." He locks the car and strides toward a pile of large rocks. Harry follows with trepidation, as Klaus climbs over and between the rocks with great ease, moving like a mountain goat, Harry supposes, though he has never actually seen a mountain goat. His breath coming in gasps, Harry stumbles and almost falls. He manages to negotiate the rocks, only to come out on a path blocked by brambles that keep catching on his rubberized raincoat. At last, to his relief, he emerges into a large open space, where he sees Klaus standing below a rope ladder suspended from a high cliff.

"Wait a minute!" Harry calls out, running up to him, as Klaus starts to ascend the ladder.

Klaus stops and looks down.

Harry wants to say, Why are we doing this? This is crazy. Why do we have to climb a ladder God knows how many stories high? But he fears that might end the possibility of any interchange forever.

Instead he says, "I haven't mentioned this, but I'm not all that wild about heights."

Klaus descends the ladder. "You go ahead of me."

"But what if I fall?"

"You're not going to fall," he says irritably. "I'll be behind you."

"Maybe I should just watch you while you go up there. I mean, is this trip really necessary?" He is making a joke, but the joke rings hollow even to him. Still he laughs to show he's only kidding. He puts his right foot on the ladder. It looks so small in the once-shiny black shoe, now scuffed with dust. He steps up one rung, and then the next. The ladder is not what you could call steady. Harry would retreat but Klaus is behind him, barring his way.

"Don't look down," Klaus says sharply.

But in fact, the higher Harry goes, the less he wants to look up. He feels the moisture on the palms of his hands. Will he be able to hold to the rungs? Under his black raincoat, he is sweating profusely. Even his hatband feels wet. The sensation of falling, as in a dream, is rushing through him, from his chest down through his stomach to his groin. In a dream, it ends with awaking. But this rushing, this dragging down within him, does not relent. Nevertheless, he keeps going upward, propelled by the realization that Klaus is just behind him, climbing steadily. A dark cloud comes over the sun; in an instant the air has turned cool. What heat there was in his body is draining out, as if the atmosphere were sucking it out of him. There is a gust of wind, followed by a much stronger gust that threatens his footing on the rung. This place, he thinks, never lets you alone. In the next moment he is assailed by an even more powerful gust and his hat is torn from his head. Instinctively, he reaches out to grab at it, and he feels everything swaying, himself, the ladder, the world. He wants to look down to see where his hat is, but he must not look down. As he clutches the rung above him with both hands, rain begins to fall, heavily. The water pours onto his bare head, over his face, obscuring his vision.

"Go up! Go up!" Klaus shouts.

Harry scurries up the remaining rungs, racing against gravity before it can find out he is there. He propels himself onto the rock ledge, and lies there exhausted, not even getting out of Klaus's way as he clambers over him. As Harry lifts his head, he sees Klaus entering the small cave before them. Clinging to the solidity of the ledge, Harry crawls into the cave. He waits in silence to hear why Klaus has brought him here.

Klaus is a confirmed believer in the power of thought over feeling—that is, in the power of his thought over his feeling. As a corollary to that belief, he takes pride in the logic of his actions, though, as he often acknowledges to himself, that logic must always incorporate the forces of external circumstances. But now, seated on the floor of the cave, feeling the roughness of the cave wall against his back, he does not know why he has come here, why he has brought the courier here. Of course, he knows how he got here; he can retrace his steps if necessary, from this road to that road, from this turn to that. But the thought processes that provoked a decision at each turning are maddeningly obscure, as if he's been drinking and a part of his consciousness has been banished, and he has willingly let it go. But he has not been drinking.

In his uneasiness, he goes back to the moment he met the courier on the bridge, no, to the moment just before that, when he saw him from the car. He had instantly recognized him from the back. Who else but the courier would be wearing a black fedora and a black raincoat and carrying a black bag on Castillo Street? It was as if the man was crying out to be noticed. If he is caught, then I too will be caught, came the thought.

And then, at the moment when he came face to face with the courier, when he saw the sallowness of his skin, the mole on his right cheek, the shadow of his beard, the small indentations in his forehead, from chicken pox or some other childhood disease, and saw, last but not least, that awestruck and reverential look on his face, there arose in Klaus a sense of such revulsion that he felt ill—revulsion not only at the man but at himself for having told the courier things he should never have told him. In retrospect, the telling had seemed both involuntary and willed. Yet who could have willed it, if not himself? Certainly not that little man, that powerless man, a man who was only obeying the orders of others, a man like a cipher . . .

Hearing a guttural sound, he opens his eyes and in the dimness sees the courier staring at him. "What did you say?" he asks.

"Do you think there are poisonous spiders or scorpions in here?"

"Perhaps."

"Can they kill you?"

"No, I do not think so," he says evenly. He is oddly reassured by the fear of the courier. It is as if there exists in the universe a principle of the conservation of fear, like the conservation of energy. A totality, once given, unchanging. If one—the courier—has more fear, the other—himself—has less. Outside the rain is falling so hard there is a curtain of water at the entrance of the cave, a veil between them and the world.

Harry stands and paces back and forth in the small space. His head, his neck, his shirt, his trousers, his socks, his shoes are sopping wet. His black raincoat has been no protection. I should have said no, he tells himself. I should have said, No, I won't come to Santa Fe, No, I won't climb that ladder. Probably I should have said no long before this, even as far back as when Dave first asked me. I should have said, No, I have my own life to live, my own simple safe life. Instead I said yes. My hat, he suddenly remembers.

"My hat," he says. "It blew off."

"We'll get it when we go down."

"We have to go down that ladder?"

"There's no other way down unless you want to jump."

"That's not funny."

"It wasn't intended to be funny," Klaus says and closes his eyes. He sits and waits, and in the silence he thinks that silence itself is like a cave into which you can crawl, in which you are protected, in which you are shut off from the outside world.

Staring at the other man huddled against the wall in the dimness, Harry realizes that Klaus is a total enigma to him. I thought he was noble but what do I really know about him? He could be a counterspy for all I know. All this stuff that he's given me could be false, misleading, a lie. How would I know? He could even have brought me up here deliberately, so I would fall. When you get right down to it, I know nothing about him, only the few facts that he told me. That he left Germany, that he escaped to England, that he was sent to the camp in Canada when the War started, that his father—something about his father's believing. Were these things even true? Maybe Klaus has been giving him a story, constructing a history, just like he himself had been told to do, just like what he's done, with Louisa and Doris and Dan.

With his back to the cave wall, Klaus smells an odor that is like that of the clay pit in the sanctuary. Is it from the air? from the dirt? from the wall? Inhaling it at every breath, he cannot resist it. It is creeping into every cell of his body, invading every vessel, every organ. He has been intact, but now that intactness has been penetrated. He has been running and running, and finally memory has caught up with him. Mind, which has always saved him, which has been his refuge, is now in the process of betraying him, inviting in all and any images, making him a repository of waste matter, of detritus from the past. Images are pouring into him like the rain pouring down at the entrance. There is no chain of events; one image drives out, replaces the next. In the house, his father's house, the walls have the solidity of stone, cold stone; when you touch them, you lean your forehead against them, you take on the hardness of stone. In the church, the old stone church, light is coming through the window, falling upon his father in the pulpit, revealing him as a man in God's image, God-like. In the church the light is behind him, he is in shadow, his being almost obscured, a frail man, a small man, a simple man, speaking of God's will as the image of God disintegrates. Pieces are flying out through every hole in Him, each piece breaking into several pieces, which in turn break into several pieces . . .

On Klaus's face Harry sees the look of a man in grave peril. But what kind of peril? How can he guess what goes on inside a man like this, a man of such brilliance? What it is like to be someone who lives most of the time in a theoretical world? When he leaves that world and comes into the everyday world, does he just lay all thoughts of that other world aside, and become like anybody else? Or are his brain and his being so deeply tied to that theoretical world that everything he does and feels is still affected by it, so he can't leave it behind, so he can never be cut off from it? And yet, Harry remembers, there was that look on his face when he spoke of his obligation to fight for a better world. He did fight against the Nazis, and he may have suffered tortures and beatings and humiliations worse than beatings, all unimaginable in my life.

Feeling a terrible shame that he has been so caught up in himself that he has given no thought to the other man's needs, he asks, "Are you all right?"

Even in the dimness Klaus can see the pity in the courier's face. "I'm all right," he says. "Why shouldn't I be?"

"It's just that you look—"

"What? What do I look? What concern is it of yours how I look?" Klaus explodes. The ludicrousness of being here in this situation with the courier, who is looking at him with that reverent obedience, that disgusting eagerness to diminish himself. He is like a shadow, beside him, behind him, all around him, suffocating him, draining him, yes, draining him. Something in this man, perhaps his very emptiness, is waiting to suck the secrets out of him. "Don't think—" he says and stops.

Harry is bewildered by Klaus's anger. "I wasn't—I don't—I only—" He reaches out his hand.

"You only what?"

"Nothing," Harry says, letting his hand drop.

As suddenly as it began, the rain has stopped. In an instant the sun is out, blindingly bright at the cave entrance. Klaus does not move. His eyes are closed. Harry gets up and goes out of the cave. Standing on the stone ledge, he looks across the valley to a series of mountains, massed one behind the other. In the midst of confusion, shame, fear, this landscape is the proof that behind one barrier is always another, even more impossible to climb, an immense height to fall from . . .

He peers over the cliff edge, first planting his feet firmly. My hat, my hat, I can't see it. He thinks of it falling from a great height and he falling with it. He is thinking of Dave, imagining his falling, which he has never let himself do before, imagining what happened when he slipped into that ravine, how his body was broken, how he survived—to become that man in that room—that room he has never gone back to. I should have gone back, though he told me not to. It is one of the things in my life I should have done that I did not do.

At a slight scraping sound—up here, the silence is so immense, the faintest sound reverberates—he turns and sees Klaus appear at the cave opening. He seems dazed, like someone who has been underground for years, and has suddenly been exposed to the light.

"Are you all right?" Harry asks again.

Klaus does not answer. Instead he moves along the ledge. "Here, over here," he calls out excitedly.

Cautiously Harry follows him, clinging to the cliff face. "What is it?"

"Look at it. Don't you see? It's an amazing petroglyph."

"All I see are some lines."

"Look at them, look at them."

"I'm looking and all I'm seeing is a large stick figure that any kid could draw."

No, it is not one figure, Klaus realizes, but a figure and behind it another figure, with rays shooting out of its head, sunlike, godlike, a record of a life, of lives lived in this place centuries ago. He feels a curious elation, as if secrecy, once acquiesced to, has the power to replicate itself endlessly, carving out niches where further secrets can be laid down and encapsulated.

Did he bring me all the way up here just to see this? This petroglyph? Harry wonders. Was it a test of some kind? How am I supposed to respond to a drawing on a rock?

Staring at the courier in his black garb, Klaus realizes that though he has feared that he has committed a totally senseless act coming here, one in which intention was separated out from the act, he has been wrong. After all, there was intention here. It has come to him that for all that he has felt revulsion at the sight of the courier, he knows now—he does not know how he knows but he knows—that no matter what happens, this man will not betray him. He has placed his life in my hands, just as I have placed mine in his.

Maybe this all would have been different, Harry thinks, if I had been braver, if I could have shown true bravery. If, for instance, Klaus would have slipped coming up that rope ladder, and if, when I heard him shout, even though I was terrified, if I could have forced myself to look down, and seeing him dangling by one hand, then if I could have leaned down and grabbed at his hand with my other hand, and held on . . . (And if someone was watching from a distance, would that person have been able to tell which one of them had slipped, which one was holding, which one was grasping, which one was fending off, been able to tell whether they were struggling with each other, or aiding each other, as the rope ladder whipped in the wind?)

Harry watches as Klaus makes his way to the ladder and prepares to descend.

"Wait a minute," he stops him. "I wanted to ask you, I have to ask you— The things you told me about yourself. They weren't a lie, were they?"

"No, they weren't a lie."

L ATER, MUCH LATER, when Harry is trying to tell all, when words are pouring from him, he will, of course, tell of his meeting in Santa Fe with Klaus. He will describe traveling there. He will speak of the Castillo Street Bridge. He will mention that they drove out of town and then carried out the transfer of the written material. He will discuss the information that was exchanged as they drove back to Santa Fe: Klaus's statement that the design for the plutonium bomb was now completed, that it would have a solid plutonium core, that the initiator would be made of polonium, that there would be a tamper to hold the bomb together for a few microseconds while the chain reaction began. He will say that in the papers Klaus handed over to him was a detailed drawing of the bomb with exact dimensions. He will also mention Klaus's opinion that the bomb would not be ready for use for another year, though there was to be a test in the desert the following month. But he will say nothing of the climb up the cliff face and what happened there.

"What else did you speak of at this meeting?" he will be asked.

"Nothing special," he will answer.

"You didn't talk about the fact that the war in Germany was over, that the Nazis had been defeated, that Hitler had killed himself? You didn't discuss the effect that might have on your continuing to spy?"

"No, we didn't speak of it."

166

"So you just went on?"

"Yes, we just went on," he will say.

Harry lingers for a moment at the Castillo Street Bridge, watching Klaus drive away on the dusty road until the car vanishes from sight. Then he reminds himself that he had better be on his way. There is a six o'clock bus to Albuquerque from Santa Fe and he doesn't want to miss it.

As he walks rapidly past the cathedral, he feels the weight of the packet in his black bag, the pages and pages of notes in Klaus' small intricate handwriting that he will turn over to Y. But he has accomplished only part of his mission. The further he gets from the Castillo Street Bridge, the more surely he returns to planning what lies before him. He is back, solidly, in his life as a courier, preparing to do the next thing and the next thing after that. Whatever has happened, has happened, he tells himself. He still has another mission—or rather the second part of this mission—to attend to.

At a meeting with Y in New York, just before he left, Y told him that after he met Klaus in Santa Fe he was to meet another contact in Albuquerque. Harry was surprised at this because he thought Klaus and Klaus alone was to be his assignment. Maybe he was assigned this mission because he was going to be in the vicinity. Maybe they didn't have anyone else available at the time. It was hard to know why, and he certainly wasn't going to ask Y why.

Immediately following his statement that there was to be a second part of his mission, Y handed Harry a page of typed instructions. Harry could not recall Y ever having given him written instructions before. It made him think that Y considered the meeting with this second man to be of particular importance. But how could any meeting be as important as the one he was to have with Klaus?

The instructions spelled out precisely where in Albuquerque he was to find this contact and what he was to do when he found him. He was to introduce himself, using an alias, as usual, and to say that Julius had sent him. Then he was to present the man with a torn half of a Jell-O box top. The man must then present him with the other matching half. If he didn't have the matching half, Harry was to abort the whole mission. If he did, Harry was to hand over five hundred dollars which Y had given him, but only after receiving the promised information.

At the bus station Harry realizes that he has not eaten all day. He goes to a little cafe next door and orders and devours a hamburger and then orders and devours another hamburger. After that he has two chocolate malteds. Surprisingly, he is not at all tired despite his recent physical exertion. The only thing bothering him at the moment is that he has a headache. He almost never has a headache. It is probably because of the altitude, he decides.

By the time he arrives in Albuquerque his headache is gone. He follows his instructions to the letter. He takes a local bus to the address Y has given him. As it turns out, it was silly for him to have taken the bus. It would have been only a five minute walk and he could have saved the ten cent fare. He gets off at the contact's street and walks around the block, then circles it again. When he returns to the house, a dilapidated two-story building with a screened-in front porch, he sees no sign of activity within. He knocks on the flimsy screen door, which has several holes in it that any flying insect could get through. He wonders if there are mosquitoes in Albuquerque. If there's one mosquito in the neighborhood, it'll single him out above everybody else. He'll itch for days afterward and the marks will stay on his skin for weeks.

An old man comes to the door and turns on the porch light. Harry asks for the man he's supposed to see. "He's out now, him and his wife. I don't know where they went but when they go out on Saturday nights they usually stay out real late. Come back in the morning. You're sure to find him here then. They always sleep late on Sundays. Just married a few months," he winks at Harry. "You ought to hear the noise they make."

"I'll be back at nine tomorrow," Harry says, irritated by the man's sly comments. He is further irritated that he will have to stay overnight in Albuquerque. Though he starts looking for a room right away, by twelve at night he hasn't found anything. Apparently there's an army base or several army bases nearby so the place is bursting at the seams. He wanders through the streets, crowded with servicemen and girls, wondering if he's going to have to settle for a park bench—if he can find a park. But he can't possibly consider sleeping out in the open, not with his black bag and its precious contents.

He plods from one hotel to another, from one rooming-house to the next, ending up at a motel at the very edge of town. But even here, when he asks for a room, the woman in the office shakes her head. She is a heavy woman, middle aged, wearing an array of Indian necklaces, and many Indian bracelets. Every time she moves, the jewelry makes a clinking sound.

"Nothing at all?" he says.

"We've been full up for days."

"Do you mind if I sit for a moment?"

"Be my guest." She points to a woven leather chair in the corner.

There are a number of torn straps in the seat so he eases himself down very carefully. He has suddenly been overwhelmed by fatigue. He cannot remember ever having been so tired on a mission. The woman at the desk is moving again, her jewelry clinking and clanking in an almost soporific rhythm. He sighs and leans his head gratefully against the seat-back. The next instant—is it the next instant?—his head, jerking at the neck, snaps him awake.

He has heard the words "Klaus is dead." Who said this? The words frighten him. The thought frightens him. Is he picking up some message in the atmosphere? He has read accounts in magazines of paranormal happenings, people knowing things before they should know them. No, it can't be, it can't be that Klaus is dead. They were just words in an instantaneous dream.

Getting up as carefully as he sat down, he passes a long hallway to his right, with a series of doors on either side. Like a cell block, the thought comes to him. "There is one more place you might try," the woman at the desk volunteers. "The Taylors, five blocks down, have turned their home into a temporary rooming house. Maybe they can put you up." As he shuts the door, he hears the sound of her jewelry jangling.

Outside, though there are no street lights, the moon is very bright and he has no trouble finding his way. The stars are out, millions of them, it seems, filling the sky. It gives him a cold chill to think of Klaus, up there beyond Santa Fe, high up in the mountains, like a distant star receding in the universe. No, he's not dead, he rebukes himself. That was just something weird in my brain. I'm so tired I'm not thinking right. But how would I know if he was dead? No one would tell me. No one even knows I know him.

At the Taylors, a woman who has dried-up, wrinkled skin, though she is not old—it must be the sun that does this to people—answers his ring. "No, I don't have a room," she says, "but I could put you up on a cot in the hall."

Grateful to be able to rest for a few hours, he takes off his black raincoat, which in this desert air has long since dried, and without undressing lies down on the iron cot. He places the black bag next to him, slipping his fingers through the handles. If someone should try to take it from him at night, he'll feel it. He lies there, ready to fall asleep, but the cot sags so badly at the center, his spine is in a V position. He turns on his side, clutching the bag in front of him. At the slightest motion he makes, the cot lets out a creaking complaint. For some reason Mrs. Taylor has put a screen of gauze around the cot. To give the illusion of privacy, he supposes. Certainly it's not because of mosquitoes. He hears no buzzing here. The only sound in the hallway is from someone in another cot, snoring gently.

Harry falls asleep and wakes up and falls asleep and wakes up, all night long. He keeps hearing the noise of sirens in the street. Either there are fires or accidents or the MPs are corralling soldiers who have had too much to drink and have been brawling.

In the morning, still dead tired after his on-again off-again sleep, he gets up and takes his turn in the bathroom. By nine o'clock he is knocking at the door of the house with the screened-in porch. The old man shuffles out in his carpet slippers and opens the door for him. He points upstairs. "They're there. Second floor to the left. No noise yet this morning."

The stairs are narrow and dark with a sudden turn two steps from the top. He makes the turn awkwardly and bangs his black bag against the wall. Despite three cups of coffee, he's still half asleep. When he knocks on the door, at first there is no answer. He has been through years of knocking on strange doors, some of which are answered, some of which aren't. He knocks again. He hears footsteps from inside. The door opens; standing before him is a young man wearing a pajama top and Army pants. Behind him, hanging on a hook, Harry can see an Army jacket, on the sleeves the stripes of a corporal, T-5, just like Stan. Harry is shocked to see that his contact is an Army man. This is the first time he has had to deal with someone in the Army and he feels very squeamish about it.

He follows his written orders. He says the words he is supposed to say. He hands the soldier the piece of the Jell-O box. The soldier starts to say something about information but Harry stops him. "You have the other piece?"

"Oh, yeah, it's here, somewhere." He goes over to a table strewn with papers and other things. He picks up a carton of cigarettes, then a wallet. "Doris, do you know what I did with that—that piece of a—"

"How would I know what you did with it?" The words come in a small voice from the young woman in bed in the corner. "Maybe it's in your jacket."

The soldier goes over to his coat and searches through the pockets. "No, it's not here."

Harry waits, not saying anything. He will say nothing until the soldier shows him the matching piece of the Jell-O box. From years of experience he knows that people hate silence. They don't know what to do with it. This too, Harry has learned over the years.

The soldier is again rummaging through the things on the table. "I couldn't have lost it. I know I had it right here. Are you sure you didn't see it?" he asks in a panicky voice as he turns to his wife.

"I never saw it."

"Maybe you threw it away while you were cleaning up."

"I wouldn't touch your papers." She gets out of bed, carefully wrapping the sheet around her. Even though she is covered, Harry can see she is a buxom young woman. She notices that Harry is looking at her and she blushes. "He forgets where he puts things sometimes. He's got too much on his mind."

"I know exactly where I put it. I put it right here, on this table," the soldier yells.

"We'll find it," she says to Harry. "We just need a little time. Could you come back in a little while? He won't be so nervous looking for it, if you're not watching him."

"I'll come back in two hours. Do you think you might find it by then?" He detects a note of sarcasm in his own voice that surprises and somehow pleases him.

"Oh yes, I'm sure he will. Probably the minute you leave it'll turn up."

As Harry shuts the door behind him, he can hear the two of them arguing. She is saying something about how can he have lost it, when it was so . . . He is telling her he has so much to do and so much on his mind and she's always bugging him about keeping things neat and clean, no wonder he . . . As he walks down the narrow stairs, maneuvering carefully around the sharp bend, Harry is grateful that he doesn't have a wife to berate him about how he does or doesn't keep his things in order.

Exactly two hours later he is back, knocking on the door of the screen porch. He has made good use of the time by going to the station and buying a ticket for the six o'clock train to Chicago. He couldn't get a train from Chicago to New York; not one seat was available for days. He'll have to work something out from Chicago when he gets there. He has to get to Brooklyn to deliver the information to Y. Then he has to get back to the lab.

Once again he is going up the steps, once again his black bag is banging against the wall when he gets to that sharp turn. That's part of what it is to be a courier, enduring, even welcoming repetitions. They serve as a warning that though things can seem the same, they may not be the same at all.

This time when he knocks on the door of the room, it opens at once. The soldier, completely dressed in his uniform, announces gleefully, "I found it," and hands him the torn piece of the Jell-O box. Harry matches it against his own torn piece. It fits exactly. The soldier's wife, dressed and made up, smiles nervously.

"You have something for me?" Harry says curtly.

"Yes, right here." The soldier hands him several pages, folded and wrinkled. On the first page is a crude sketch, almost like a kid's drawing. Harry looks at one of the other pages. At the sight of the words spilling across the page in large awkward characters, Harry thinks of Klaus's delicate, intricate handwriting, so neat, so contained, so precise, and wonders how these messy pages can possibly have any value at all. He folds the papers and puts them in his black bag, then takes out the envelope with the five hundred dollars and hands it to the soldier.

Holding the envelope in his hand, as if he doesn't know what to do with it, he stammers, "I hope—uh—that it's—uh—I could explain it if it needs to be—"

"I'm sure it will need no further explanation."

"I could ask around and see if other people are interested in providing information," the soldier offers.

"No, no, don't!" Harry is horrified at the idea of this naive soldier
rattling around Los Alamos, ruining all that has been so painstakingly
accomplished. "This is fine. We don't need anything more."

"In case you do, I'll give you an address in New York, of a relative.
He'll always know how to reach me."

"There's no need."

"But just in case, I ought to—"

"He says there's no need," the young woman says, and the soldier
subsides into silence.

Grateful for her intervention, and recalling that her name is Doris,
like the Doris of Doris and Dan, Harry asks her in a friendly tone, "How
do you like Albuquerque?"

"I don't know yet. I only came out here a few months ago. It's not
anything like Brooklyn. Everything's different. The weather and the people—"

"And the food," the soldier adds. "That's the hard part, the food.
There isn't a good delicatessen in the entire town."

"Well, it does have other things," Harry says. "The desert and the
mountains and—"

"It's too open. It makes me feel—" Doris gestures aimlessly.

"Do you know how many different kinds of salami you can find in
New York?" the soldier asks. "In my neighborhood delicatessen at home
I can get fifteen different kinds, each one better than the next, but all I can
find here is baloney or Spam—"

"He really misses his salami," the young woman says tenderly and
smiles at her husband as she puts her hand out to him; he takes her hand
just as if Harry was no longer there.

In the lobby of the Albuquerque Hilton Harry inquires about renting a
room, day rate. He doesn't want to wander around town with his black
bag until train time and he certainly can't risk leaving it anywhere. The
desk clerk says he can have a room until six. Harry tells him to buzz him
at four-thirty.

Sprawled out on the bed—no sagging springs here—he thinks with distaste of the soldier and his brashness. Imagine him thinking he could recruit in Los Alamos. It's like he's playing some game; he hasn't the slightest idea of how dangerous this work is. Harry makes it a point to keep the possibility of something going wrong, of being found out, at the edge of his consciousness. It's not right there in the forefront, but it's there. Only when he's with Klaus, for some reason, it's not there. But at all other times he's aware of it, at the back of his brain, keeping him on his toes mentally. But that idiot of a soldier seemed totally unaware, even foolhardy. Was he doing this for the money? For five hundred dollars? With Klaus, of course, there has never been any question of his receiving money. He is like I am, Harry knows. We do not do what we do for money.

The last thing he thinks of before he falls asleep is that moment after Klaus said he had not lied. It was a moment of silence, that he can think of with tenderness, in a world where tenderness hardly ever enters. So it was for Harry, and by his silence, so he knew it must have been for Klaus. It was spiritual, somehow, that silence, man to man, offered and accepted, a kind of believing.

At the train station in Chicago, he is back in the hurrying world of the city. Silence is over. Doing is what matters. Because he is pressured for time, he decides to travel by plane from Chicago but the only flight he can get goes to Washington, D.C. From Washington he takes the train to New York. Then he descends into the subway to go to Brooklyn, where he is to meet Y. The platform is crowded but Harry is used to the press of bodies all around him.

As the train comes into the station, everyone pushes and shoves to be first in the door. Harry lets himself be carried along by the crowd into the car. Since no seat is available, he stands holding onto a pole with his right hand, his left hand clutching the black bag. The doors shut; the train starts up. He smells the familiar subway odor of summer, heated metal and sweating bodies. Through the window he sees lights in the darkness flash by as the train roars through the tunnel.

They stop at a station. The doors open, even more people crowd in, the doors close. He checks his black bag. Just to be safe he moves it so it is lodged between him and the pole. He looks straight ahead. Now there are other hands on the pole beside his own, above his and below his, holding on while the train rocks back and forth gathering speed. He looks at the heavy man, his face moist in the heat, at the young woman in her flowered dress, her slip straps showing at the shoulder, at the old woman, wrinkled, but not from a desert sun. They are staring straight ahead, so still, their faces showing nothing but the boredom of waiting for their stop. Yet their knuckles, jutting out under the taut, almost transparent skin, reveal a tension beyond boredom, as if in this underground world the hidden cannot be or should not be obscured.

On Metropolitan Avenue, on the border between Brooklyn and Queens, he meets Y. He gives him the papers from Klaus and from the soldier. He tells Y he will meet Klaus again in September. Y nods, smiling.

"And what about the soldier? Will I have to see him again?"

"Forget him."

O N AWAKING KLAUS has remembered that today he is to meet the courier—one last time. He has given no thought to him since their meeting in June, as he has been so immersed in the project. First, there was the final preparation for the atom bomb test. Then came the test itself in the desert, just before dawn. Though they had made innumerable calculations, no one knew with certainty what the magnitude of the explosive force of the bomb would be. Like the others, he gave no credence to the possibility, raised once or twice, that the explosion could set off a world conflagration. There was no world conflagration. And yet, seeing what happened in the desert, being there, was like seeing the secret made visible, in an immense and terrible image.

After Alamogordo he joined with a number of scientists at the lab in a petition asking the government not to use the bomb, but to demonstrate it on a remote unpopulated Pacific island in the presence of Japanese observers. They were convinced that if the Japanese saw the blast, the light, the mushroom cloud, they would have no choice but to surrender. The authorities denied the petition.

The bomb was used, not once, but twice. The lab received preliminary reports of the number of people killed and injured, of people with their skin flayed, falling off in strips. He has seen one report of a man walking in Hiroshima after the blast, holding his eyeball in his hand.

Harry had waited with great anticipation for this day, but when it came he wasn't ready. He didn't have enough money to make the trip to Santa Fe, so he had to run around borrowing money from co-workers at the lab. Though he didn't realize it when he made the arrangement with Klaus, the day he had to leave was the Day of Atonement. Not that he is observant but nevertheless, if he had known, he might have chosen another day.

He had planned on going by plane, as he figured flying was cheaper than taking the train, if you took into consideration that on the plane you didn't have to pay for meals or lodging. But so many military people were traveling, many of them already discharged from the service, that not a seat was available on any flight. He ended up taking the train to Chicago and spending the night at the Palmer House before taking the morning train west. At the hotel he registered in his own name. About anything having to do with his contacts with Klaus, he has been, as usual, fatalistic.

So now, he can hardly believe it, once again, he is standing on the Castillo Street Bridge. The sun is very intense, and the river that was hardly a river before is now a trickle. Yet he feels that he is being carried along on another kind of a current. Whatever happens is going to happen. The minutes pass, five, ten, fifteen. He continues to wait patiently. But by the time an hour has gone by, and Klaus has not appeared, he is in agony. Klaus is too meticulous to have forgotten. Can he be ill? Has he had an accident? They have not set a fall-back appointment.

Looking in the direction from which Klaus came the last time, Harry almost succeeds in persuading his eyes that he sees his car coming. But there is nothing. Only quiet—a few houses—a dusty road.

Driving slowly, Klaus sees the courier, just where he is supposed to be. He is standing on the bridge, looking down over the stone railing. He is wearing the same black hat and the same black raincoat. The nearer Klaus gets to him, the more revulsion he feels, as if it were a force inversely proportional to the distance from him. How can this be happening all over again? he wonders. He thought all this was settled at the last meeting. But here it is, surfacing again, if anything more intense, more irrational than before.

Harry hears a car slow down, then stop. He turns. It is a big blue car, a Buick. A man is getting out. It is Klaus. Harry almost doesn't believe it, so bereft has he felt. He has held off the memory of that voice—was it his own?—that said the terrible words, "Klaus is dead." It *is* Klaus, his hair glinting in the sun, walking toward him with that graceful easy stride, dressed casually in tan slacks and a sports shirt and sneakers.

As he comes up to Harry, he says, "I must apologize for keeping you waiting but I was unavoidably delayed." He tells him about having come down the mountain with two men from the lab and taking them to a liquor store to purchase a number of cases of liquor for a big party at the lab tomorrow night. He tells of waiting while they bought the liquor, waiting while they put the liquor in the trunk of the car. And then, when he did manage to get away, he says, he had to drive very slowly because of the bottles in the trunk.

"Why do they buy liquor here?" the courier asks.

"You don't think you can get it in Los Alamos, do you?"

"How would I know?" Harry says mildly, determined not to take offense. "I've never been to Los Alamos."

After a short pause he asks tentatively, "Do you often have parties up there?"

"No, not often. This one is in celebration of the success of the project."

Imagining a world of good comradeship and laughter and sparkling talk, with Klaus at the center of all the others, Harry feels a twinge of jealousy. But at once he tells himself he has no right, no reason to be jealous. The life that he shares with Klaus is a secret life, not destined for overt celebrations. Those others—they not only don't share that secret life with him, they haven't the slightest suspicion that it exists.

Klaus turns and looks behind him along Castillo Street. "We shall drive to some place more secluded."

In the car Harry steals a glance at Klaus. His hands are grasping the wheel so tightly his knuckles are white.

Klaus is thinking that everything is in the process of ending, yet nothing has ended. When he arrived at the lab this morning, he discovered that a division technical meeting was in progress, but neither he nor anyone else in the British contingent had been invited to attend. It was further proof, if proof was needed, of the diversion of American from British interests, as if the two countries are no longer allies now that the war is over. Yet before he goes, he must finish a final report for the entire group.

He is thinking how this too is about to end. The papers he has with him are the final ones he will supply to the courier. Soon he will return to England. A new nuclear laboratory is being set up at Harwood, and he is sure to get one of the senior posts. He is in a hurry to get this meeting over with. But the further he drives along the road, the more he detects a residue of that last meeting in himself, something nagging and irresolute that cannot easily be brushed aside, something unfinished.

Looking through the windshield at the desert landscape, Harry settles into the continuous drone of the car in the wind. The side windows are open, letting in warm air with a cool undertone. They have been driving for miles, but still Klaus does not stop. He has said he was looking for some-place secluded. But everywhere around them, there's no one in sight. There's nothing but seclusion.

"We're not going where we were before, I hope," he says cautiously.

"No, no. Some other place."

"What place?"

Into Klaus's mind comes the image of the church with the clay pit. It would be interesting to take the courier there. No, he will not take him there. Why am I even thinking this? he wonders. All of what he has done with this man—like going up onto the cliff with him—was as if done by some other being, not himself. If action makes a human being who he is, and Klaus has always thought that this is so—with the courier he has not been who he thinks he is. He even provokes in Klaus, who in no way con-siders himself a savage man, vestiges of something like savagery.

Klaus turns off on a small dirt road and then, in what seems to be the midst of nowhere, he stops. Without a word he gets out of the car, and makes his way toward an area of free-standing brush. Harry too gets out, leaving his black bag behind. He follows the other man through the prickly dry weeds to a short path leading down into a dry wash screened from the road. Scattered here and there in the red dirt are rocks, large and small, as well as dry bushes.

Harry hurries to catch up with Klaus, who is moving silently and
rapidly along the wash. He does not feel the silence as oppressive or
threatening in any way. He will simply wait for the other man to speak.

Though Klaus is hurrying ahead, he feels that his mind is lagging behind.
It is as if he has lost contact with the direction and purpose of his own
thinking. He tells himself that if he'll just stop and pull himself together,
he'll be all right. He tells himself that it's just a matter of exhaustion, of
brain exhaustion. He tells himself that it was to be expected that he would
be exhausted, after all the weeks and months of working without letup.
He has worked so feverishly, as if he has been in combat, and a mortal
one at that, with the Nazis to insure that the Americans and British solve
the problem of manufacturing an atomic bomb first. Yet when the Germans surrendered in April, he kept on working just as feverishly as before.
The project had to be completed.

He goes forward several paces and stops. "There should have been
a demonstration of the bomb on some uninhabited island to show the
Japanese what we had made. Some of us petitioned the government to
do that but we were told it was out of our hands. We were told it was a
political decision."

"Everything is political," Harry sighs. Of all the things Harry might
have expected from Klaus, he certainly could not have expected this
regret. He rushes to exonerate him. "Look at all the people's lives it
saved. If there had been an invasion of Japan, many more people would
have been killed." Harry is thinking of Stan in the Pacific. What would
have happened to him? Now he is safe. "The main thing is it ended the
War. That's the main thing."

"Yes, it ended the War."

"The whole project was started in the first place because of the
Nazis, wasn't it? Can you imagine what would have happened if they'd
gotten the bomb first? It would have been the end of the world."

"I know that. You don't have to tell me that."

Klaus is once again moving rapidly, lightly, scurrying along, as if he were
being propelled forward by the wind but there is no wind. He cannot rid

himself of the feeling that some thoughts in him are hiding, and will not do his bidding, that some are cowering, as if they been impaired, wounded, shattered . . . All around him the landscape is still, agape, as if surprised by his silence.

Has he nothing to say in his defense? What is he being accused of? Why does he have to defend himself?

I have not always been silent, he reminds himself. As if delivering a report on his own history, he enumerates for himself how decision followed upon decision, action upon action, leading him inevitably, logically, to this place. When he was a student at the University, he was a vocal leader of those who protested against the Nazis. But after the Nazis came to power, he went underground and escaped to England. There he let silence take him over. It was not a sacrificial act on his part. He simply fell into the habit of speaking only when spoken to, of never volunteering anything.

As compensation and more than compensation, he had his work, his scientific life. Entering into his work was like entering into an enormous room. There was a mystery in that room that led you on and on to other rooms, closed off, safe. He was making progress in that room when history intervened again. He was interned; he was released from internment. His mentor, also a refugee from Nazi Germany, asked Klaus to work with him on a top secret project code-named Tube Alloys, to design and build an atomic bomb for use in the war against Hitler. So now there was a conjunction of the two sides of his life, the silenced political one and the active scientific one, both aimed at one goal, the defeat of the Nazis. He was immediately granted a top-secret security clearance and threw himself into the work on gaseous diffusion and isotope separation.

But in the summer of 1941, after Nazi Germany invaded the Soviet Union and Russia became an ally of England, he learned that the alliance did not include sharing of scientific secrets by the British with the Soviets. That fall, he contacted the Soviet Embassy in London, and volunteered to supply reports on his own work at Tube Alloys.

Here, on this red ground, in this dry arroyo, which is sometimes flooded with rushing water, remembering has become like hovering over a landscape. Accepting the effects of silence and of secrecy, he has not tried to analyze the processes by which the two are interwoven in him. He has believed, and still believes, in his right to choose not to be a prisoner of history.

Struggling to catch up with Klaus, Harry sees him stumble. But he recovers his footing quickly and forges ahead even more rapidly. A moment later he stops, a puzzled look on his face.

"Is something the matter?" Harry asks.

"Did you see that flash of light?"

"No, I didn't see any flash of light."

"Are you sure?"

"No, I didn't see anything. Maybe you've had too much sun. Maybe we better go back to the car."

"No, no," Klaus says, and shakes his head.

"At the end it was taken out of your hands. But you did what you thought was right."

"What are you talking about?"

"What we were just talking about. About working on the bomb. About what you said. You did what you thought was right," he adds lamely. Harry trembles at the thought that he is repeating the words he once said to Dave White in that room he never went back to, and should have gone back to.

Yes, he was right to work on the bomb. Yes, he was right to devote himself in secret to the Communist cause. There is no question in his mind that the only hope for the world is in the replacement of the capitalist system by one in which all exploitation of the individual will end, by an ideal society in which all would benefit equally, all would serve and be served alike. And there is no question that others will try to prevent it. He recalls how outraged he was when some of his colleagues had accused Stalin of persecuting innocent men, in what they called "show trials." They were guilty, those men, he wanted to say but did not say, guilty of betraying the revolution. They confessed to their guilt before the world.

How much further is he going? Harry wonders. My feet are beginning to hurt. I should have brought sneakers. I should have known from the last time that I should have brought along my sneakers. Why did he pick this place? How is this place different from any other place? I don't see any petroglyphs around here.

"What is going to happen now?" he asks.

Klaus begins to talk about what he is going to do when he leaves Los Alamos, how he will visit several other laboratories for short stays, and then return to England. That wasn't what Harry meant by what he was going to do now, but he lets it pass. Now he knows for sure that this will be the last time he will see Klaus. He is not surprised. After all, he expected it. Why then does he feel that he is being abandoned?

The flashes of light have begun again. Klaus has been expecting them, waiting for them. He has decided they are a small visual disturbance, something having to do with nerves, even perhaps with what he ate. He can sit back, detach himself, and observe them. They come slowly at first, now one—he waits—now another. But soon they are coming often and with such increased intensity, they are filling the entire field of his vision. He knows they are not outside. Outside, he says to himself, clinging to this final separation between outside and inside, but even as he says it there is a rapid turning, a frantic speedup in everything before him, the arroyo, the dry fields, the mountains beyond, looming, ready to fall. Two motions are converging in the landscape, one with everything turning clockwise, the other with everything turning counter-clockwise, both pouring into each other.

He no longer knows what is upright, what is horizontal. He drops onto the ground, onto all fours. Crouching like a dog, he thinks, like a dog.

"Let me help you." It is the courier, grasping his elbow.

"Don't touch me," Klaus shouts in revulsion, thrusting him away. He tries to get up but then sinks onto the ground, rises, then sinks again, then clings to the ground as if it were the only solidity.

The turning of the two motions is relentless, pulling Klaus into a whirlwind. He believed in whirlwinds when he was a child, when he believed in God. They were what God hid himself in. He has the sense of explosions within him and without him, of things falling apart. There is a sudden hardening in the air, as if sound itself were turning into matter, true sounds, false sounds, secrets told and hidden more in the telling.

"Let me help you," the courier says again.

This time Klaus does not stop him. He feels the courier struggling to lift him, half-dragging, half-lifting him. He is panting and groaning with the effort. He stops, then tries to drag him again. He is too heavy for me, Harry knows. He tries once more to lift him but this time he stumbles under the weight and the two men collapse in a heap. Harry's hat rolls away. He gets up and retrieves it and brushes the dirt and small rocks from it.

Though the sun is beating down relentlessly, Klaus is shivering. Seeing him, Harry remembers that terrible man trembling in his bed—things do come round and round again. The thought had come to him then that he could lie beside him, keep that man warm with his own body heat. But it is so hot here. He takes off his black raincoat and covers the other man with it. He looks like a crumpled heap, black against the red ground.

With the raincoat over him, Klaus is hot, he is cold, he cannot tell. He hates his own piteousness. He is being pressed down by the sun, by the air. Though his eyes are closed, the world is alternately converging and expanding, so rapidly he is in danger of being flung off of it. He forces himself to turn on his back. At the moment of turning he remembers, he allows himself to remember, but he has always remembered, how he turned his mother over—she was lying on the ground in the back garden—she was barely breathing—she had been silent for weeks, for months, before that moment, refusing to speak but now she spoke, the words coming out of a mouth blackened by the poison she had swallowed: "I am coming, Mother." She had taken her life, just as her own mother had. The dead had called to her, and she had listened . . .

When he opens his eyes, his entire field of vision is filled with jagged light. He tries to look for a pattern. There must be a pattern here, and if he can find the pattern, then—what will he do then? Will the pieces of his life, of thought, fit into place again? (And what if those men who had pleaded guilty were not guilty?) He struggles to pull himself up, to rise to the surface and breathe. Hiding behind a wave of light like water is yet another one, and another one after that.

Looking down at Klaus, watching him try to get up, Harry is appalled. His lips are pulled back in a grimace, his teeth bared like an animal's. He is saying something that sounds like German, though Harry doesn't know any German. What bony hands he has, Harry thinks. I never noticed his bony hands before.

Looking up, Klaus detects through the shimmering jagged lights an immense black shape standing between him and the sun, waiting for him to tell, commanding him to tell, needing him to tell.

Harry is frightened at what is happening here. He thinks there may be even worse to come. You take a step and then a little step, you let down your guard a little bit—what guard? does he even have a guard?—and you end up in some dry space, surrounded by more dry space, with a maniac groveling on the ground. How can I be thinking this? he accuses himself. This is Klaus, Klaus, a noble man, a genius, not a maniac. The man needs to be helped.

He leans over him to try to lift him. Even as he does this, he feels Klaus grab at him, snatching at his sleeve, as if it were life itself, holding so tightly that Harry fears it will tear at the shoulder seam, will split apart.

There is a point where seeing becomes too much, when it is better not to see. The other man's eyes, his face, are so close he has become indistinct. At this distance he is a stranger. He doesn't want to show that he is pulling away, but he needs to pull away. He longs for a world in which there is no suffering to bear, except his own.

Suddenly the flashes of light have stopped. You're prisoner of it, and suddenly it stops, it's over, thank God, you're free. He has been in darkness in this light. And now he is simply in the light. He looks at the courier and sees that he is no longer chained to the little man by the need to tell. There is no secret. It is the courier who needs secrets, who creates the need for secrets, who sucks the secrets out of you, truth or lies. He lets go of his sleeve.

On Klaus's face Harry sees a curious exhaustion and yet a relief. "Are you okay, Klaus?" he asks.

"I'm fine," Klaus says. He does not call him Raymond. He knows my name is not Raymond, Harry knows.

When they reach the car, Klaus hands Harry the packet of papers and gets into the driver's seat. "You want to say something about this?" Harry asks.

"I don't think that's necessary. It needs no explanation. Everything is self-evident."

"I was surprised when I read in the paper about the bomb being dropped. I remember you told me you thought it would be another year before they finished it," Harry says.

"I was wrong." And he goes on in a polite, clipped way, as if he and Harry were two people who had shared a ride on a train and were now parting. "In the future someday, if you come to England perhaps we can meet. I can show you London. Do you like the theatre? English theatre is very good."

"Yes, I like the theatre—" Harry stops. He knows that though things come round and round again, they will never come round to a future for them. At the end, for this is the end, he must say something, he must not lose this last chance to speak, to say something to make up for all his doubts about this man. "If it had been another time—" he mumbles. He does not know what he must say, yet he goes on. "If it hadn't been for the Nazis and the War—" He raises his arm toward the horizon; it seems to be rushing away, though he knows horizons don't do that. "Maybe there could have been . . ."

In the silence Klaus shakes his head wearily. "Could have been? We must not waste our time thinking of what could have been. It is necessary to think of what should be and of what must be for humanity and for the individual to be freed from coercion by the forces of society and of the past as well."

What past? Harry wonders.

Carrying his black bag, the material from Klaus securely inside, Harry walks toward the center of town. Everything is as it was, the houses, the deep blue of the sky, the dry redness of the earth. He moves slowly; he still has a half-hour before the next bus. As he approaches the town center, he becomes aware of noises—of voices, and of music. A crowd is gathering. The closer he gets to the center, the larger the crowd grows, and soon, when he is right on the main street, he is unable to move. A parade or a procession of some sort is blocking his way. People are lined up on each side of the street, watching, and he cannot see past them. Above their heads, he can detect some kind of religious statuary and banners being carried by.

He thinks, maybe I should find another way to the terminal. If I'm not careful I'll miss my bus. But perhaps the procession will be over soon. Several people in front of him leave and he moves up. There is a halt in the procession. At the end of the street three men are crawling on their knees. He watches them as they move past him, scraping their flesh against the rough surface of the road, their eyes shining as if they were seeing an ecstatic vision. What would it be to be so seized by belief that even your pain becomes part of that believing? He does not know. He thinks he will probably never know.

I T WAS FEBRUARY 1946, six months after the war's end. As always, Harry was working at the lab day after day. Yet he felt a strange inertia. Around him, out in the world, others were ready to go on, ready to change. He sensed in them a willed hope, a determination to start a new life. Everyone else was moving out of a dark age, turning away from what had been. Why shouldn't he? He didn't know why, but he couldn't.

After weeks and months with no word, he was still waiting to hear from Klaus, though he knew he would not hear. Something in him even waited to hear from Y, though he was glad to be left alone. He told himself his secret life was over, that he was just living one plain ordinary life. But the past, still going on in him, was like a second life. It was a story that had to be lived and lived again, how he first met Klaus in Brooklyn, how then came this meeting and that meeting, on and on to Santa Fe . . . It was a story without an ending that kept beginning.

One day in late February the weather, which had been unseasonably mild, turned wintry again. At night there was a heavy snowfall. The next morning he got to the lab late because the buses were delayed. People were clustered in small groups, talking. Because of the snow? They'd all seen snow before. One of the women was crying. Shortly he learned that the company had decided to close down the lab, and everybody, including him, would be jobless in two weeks.

Much to his surprise, he was not upset. In fact, he welcomed the respite being forced upon him. It wouldn't hurt to have a few days off, even without pay. He did worry about Mom and Pop. He wouldn't be able to send home half his salary, as he had been doing. Luckily, Stan would be home soon and he'd get a job and could make up for what Harry did not contribute.

Lil and Howie, the two assistants in the lab, came to him at the end of the week. They'd been out looking for work every day, without success. All the laboratories they'd been to were giving preference to returning veterans. What should they do? Harry worked with them on their resumes. He showed them how to capitalize on their experience, to present themselves in the best light, exaggerating a little, not much but just enough. He coached them on what to say when they went into the personnel offices, telling them they must not be discouraged. Soon, in fact, almost immediately, Lil and Howie did find jobs. They said they were grateful, and took him out to lunch, though he didn't hear from them after that. Not that he expected to.

At home, in his basement room, he laboriously wrote out his own resume, being careful not to enlarge his experience at any point, striving to be as exact as possible. What he had been able to do for Lil and Howie, he could not do for himself. It seemed wrong to puff himself up, as if different standards applied in his own case.

It all had to do with need, of course. Help me, help me, was the pull of the force upon him, actual, physical, demanding. He could not say No. As for himself, he had long ago gone through a process of renunciation, though he had no recollection of ever having renounced anything.

For days the cold snap continued, and Harry stayed in his room, since he no longer had a job to go to. New snow piled up against the slit of a window, high up in the wall, at street level. He couldn't even see people's feet as they passed by. He decided to read some poetry, Browning, whose work Sam had admired, and a little T. S. Eliot. He particularly liked the phrase "hollow men." He slept a lot. He did not dream, or at least he did not remember his dreams.

Mostly he waited, just as he had so often waited in his old secret life. There was so much to think of concerning his past with Klaus. At times it was like walking through a vast storehouse; he could pluck a meeting from here, a conversation from there, any one of which could evoke pity and wonder. At other times, it was like traversing a minefield, and he had to tread carefully or something, everything could blow up. He was amazed at the power of the past to override everything in the present. As for the future, well, he had never been certain that he had a future, in any case.

Lying in bed on his side, facing the blank wall, he began to dream a kind of waking dream. He was not an imaginative person, yet here he was imagining he was getting up, shutting the door behind him, and climbing the cement stairway to the street: It is a clear cold day, no sign of snow, the sun shining in that brittle comfortless way he remembers when he was a kid and had been indoors, sick, for a long time and was suddenly outside and everything looked different, wrong. It feels like he has been inside for so long he doesn't know what outside is, or maybe there is yet another outside beyond the one he is in. He is beginning to sweat, though it is cold. He thinks of going back to his basement room. Coward, he reproaches himself. He is at Penn Station. He is taking the train to Boston. He is on the bus to Lottie's house. He is going up the path. He is knocking on the door. Lottie is standing before him, her hair matted. She is wringing her hands, muttering something about being alone. She is hitting herself on the breast with her fist and weeping. He is in the living room; on the mantel he is seeing the photo of the man who looks like the Old Testament God. The child is huddled in a corner, the little boy with Klaus's eyes . . .

It was only a story he was making up, he could get outside of it any time he wanted to, so why was he weeping? It was as if imagining could be stretched and stretched, had no limits to the grief it could evoke.

He got up. He turned on the radio to the classical music station. He opened a can of baked beans and emptied it into his one pot. He put the pot on the hot plate. He waited for the pot to cool down and then ate the beans directly from the pot. He didn't feel like going out, into noise, among crowds. He went back to bed. He could feel that another waking dream was about to start. He had to be careful. When you're alone, new things come up in you, things that wouldn't come up when you were with others because then you had to pay attention to what was coming up in them.

He is getting on the train to Philadelphia, staying on the train to Philadelphia, getting off the train, taking a bus to the house he shared with Louisa and Doris and Dan. The door opens and Louisa is standing there, with red hair, but otherwise vague. You? she says, not at all vaguely. Yes, it's me, he says, I'm back. After all this time? she says sharply. I couldn't help it, he says. I had to do all these things. What things? she wants to know. He says he couldn't tell her even if he wanted to. They were secret things. It was better for her not to know. After all these years, she says, you come back and tell me you can't tell me what you've been doing and—now she's in a rage—you think you can walk back in, just like that. I know what you've been up to, she sneers. I know about all those other women. What other women? he says, dumbfounded. There weren't any other women. Don't try to kid me, she shouts. Doris and Dan—still six years old—peek out from behind Louisa. Their poor little faces . . . They shouldn't be hearing this, he cries out. You shouldn't be doing this, Louisa shouts, as she slams the door in his face. He goes out on the street. He hides behind a tree, watching. Doris and Dan come out, holding hands, on their way to school. He follows them. He stands outside the schoolyard as they go in. Through the steel fence, he sees their dear innocent faces . . .

He pushed the covers aside. He sat up on the bed, his legs dangling. He thought of what had been, of what might have been, of what would not be. He thought of the future others would have but that he would not have, did not, perhaps, deserve to have. As for the past, his past, in here, in this room, more and more it was taking on the quality of a vast emptiness. Stories can wear out, can be told too many times, so they lose their life, it seemed.

He forced himself to get up. He began to clean the room. He scrubbed every surface with soap and water. He changed the sheets. He wrapped the dirty linen in a pillowcase. He would take it to the laundry tomorrow. He opened the door to the outside; he felt he had to air the place out completely. He felt he had to air out his brain. When it got too cold for him, he shut the door.

He heard a scratching outside. The noise stopped, then began again. He thought of rats and tried to ignore it. Then he heard a meowing, a pitiful meowing, a siren song of need. He couldn't help himself; he got up and opened the door. A cat scampered in, a calico; wet, shivering, mangy, obviously a stray, desperate to eat. Harry fed it some sardines from a can. The only kind he had was with tomato sauce but the cat didn't seem to care. Afterwards, it lay on the cold floor, washing itself. Then it jumped up on his lap and lay there purring.

So, Harry mused, I have a cat. It was a gift, given to him to show that he was wrong to bring misery on himself, to feel sorry for himself, when he did have a tie to the outside just like everybody else. Since he now had something to come back home to, he could go out.

He put on his heavy coat and his galoshes. He walked to the subway. He got off at Sixty-Third Drive, Rego Park, and went to the Trylon Theater, where he had so often waited for Y. He went inside. No Y anywhere that he could see, certainly not in his usual seat, fifth row on the aisle. On the screen was *The Best Years of Our Lives*. Watching the return home from the war of those who had been away—Frederic March and Dana Andrews and a man whose arms had really been lost in a battle—it wasn't make believe—Harry wept. All around him he could hear the muffled sobs of others. To weep with them was a different kind of weeping, a safe weeping.

When the film was over, he filed out of the lobby with the others onto Queens Boulevard. "Harry!" he heard and turned. In the moment before turning came the thought, Klaus, but no, it couldn't be Klaus because Klaus didn't know him as Harry. And indeed, it was not Klaus. It was Sid Roth, with a woman Harry thought was his wife (though it turned out later it wasn't his wife but his secretary, Dorothy.)

"I can't believe it," Sid said. "You're just the man I've been looking for. I was going to call you tomorrow at your lab."

"I'm not working there anymore."

"Even better. Then you can start right away."

"At what?"

"Working for me."

Harry stared blankly.

"I'm setting up my own lab. I've got my own consulting company. Don't think I don't remember how you were after me about Buna-S— how you kept after me and after me. You wouldn't let go. That's just what I need, a man like you who won't give up."

"I've been thinking of moving back to Philadelphia."

"Philadelphia? Come on. I'm talking about the big time here. Now's the time when you have to have the courage to strike out on your own, to fill in the gaps, and, I can assure you, there are many gaps that are going to have to be filled. There's lots of money to be made out there, Harry. You have to be willing to take the risk, to be at the right place at the right time."

"Well—" said Harry doubtfully.

"Don't tell me you're not interested in money!"

"It's not that I'm not interested in money. It's just that I'm more interested in doing work that—"

"You'll be doing terrific things. Just wait till you hear the projects I have in mind. They're perfect for you. Harry, I need a chemist. I need a good chief chemist. I need you."

So this was destiny. Life did have a plan for him, unrecognizable though it was at first. A cat meows and you go out of the house to the Trylon Theatre, and suddenly everything has changed.

"Okay," Harry said.

So he was able to leave his new basement life behind him, just like that, in an instant. But then basement lives don't have that much to recommend them, especially when compared to life in a lab with real solid things, reagents and catalysts for the transformation of real compounds.

ADMITTEDLY, SID'S COMPANY was starting out small. The lab was a storefront lab, with shades at the window, and Harry, though chief chemist, was so far the only chemist. But when Sid talked about the future, you couldn't resist him, he was so persuasive. The man's a genius, Harry told himself, recalling that Sid had gotten a Ph.D. from Columbia when he was only twenty-one.

Sid certainly did have grand ideas, one after another, overarching ideas for the future. One that he was sure would be a winner was his proposal to set up a vitamin plant in Russia. "The Russians have a terrible diet; they don't get enough sunshine; they drink too much. Their people would really benefit from vitamins, particularly C, A, E, and the B vitamins," he announced to Harry. Their whole economy, their whole culture, would be better off, he insisted, though even he acknowledged that it might be a hard sell at the moment.

Harry's first project was in no way a grand one but still it had its interest, as every technical problem did, if you just put your mind to it. The problem concerned putting titles on book covers, in gold letters. Sid had taken on the project because Phil, who was renting the lab space to him, owned a company that did this kind of work. As Phil told Sid and Harry, the difficulty was that, after a while, the gold letters his company put on books were tarnishing and the customers were complaining. But Phil had a competitor in Jersey whose gold letters were not tarnishing.

Of course, it wasn't really gold that Phil (or his competitor) was using. It just looked like gold. It was actually brass, a brass powder that was floated in wax, that in turn was impregnated in paper Phil manufactured. When the paper was heated to the right temperature, it released the brass powder onto the book cover in the shape of the desired gold letters. Since Phil was convinced that his competitor was using a special wax that protected the brass from tarnishing, Sid told Harry to run tests on the other guy's wax to see if he could find out what it was made of.

Harry set to work in his usual methodical manner. In his testing he used hydrogen sulfide to speed up the tarnishing process, but try as he would he could not get the competitor's brass to tarnish. He did experiment after experiment over a period of weeks, trying to isolate the compound in the competitor's wax that protected the brass. Finally, he concluded that it wasn't the wax itself, but some chemical pretreatment of the brass that protected it. He was about to do further experiments to detect what that pretreatment was when he found out that some other guy, in Brooklyn, had just come up with a method of vacuum plating a very thin layer of gold leaf, using genuine gold instead of brass, so Phil's wax process as well as his competitor's had become obsolete.

Sid didn't get mad, he didn't get even the slightest bit upset when Harry told him this. He simply said, "You can't win 'em all." And immediately he told Harry of another great project he had lined up for him.

That Saturday Harry decided to go home to Philadelphia to see Mom and Pop. For some reason, he didn't know why, he told Sid that he was going home to see his wife Louisa and his twins, Doris and Dan. The words popped out of his mouth before he could stop them.

He took the subway to Penn Station as he had done so many times before. Under the East River he felt the pressure in his ears but there was no transition, only the memory of a transition, leaving him exactly the same. A heavy middle-aged woman across the aisle, with grey hair and very red lipstick, was looking at him. Was it simply chance that her eyes fell upon him? He got off at the stop for Penn Station and went through tunnels and up stairways. He went to the ticket booth and got a ticket to Philadelphia. He got on the train and did not get off the train.

At home Mom and Pop were so glad to see him he felt guilty about having been away for such a long time. He got Mom aside and handed her seventy-five dollars out of his salary of a hundred and twenty.

"Why are you giving me so much?" she asked him.

"I got a raise and I don't need the extra money. I work all the time anyhow, so what'll I spend it on? You and Pop can use it."

"It's not necessary, Harry. Pop's working and Stan's got his job at Norfolk and is sending home a little money every week so we're getting along okay. In fact," and here she smiled, "I have a surprise for you. You know that money you've been sending me every month? I've been putting as much of it away as I could. And now, look," she showed him a savings passbook. "Look how much there is."

Harry could hardly believe it. There was four thousand dollars in the account. "It's for you when you get married," she added, "to buy a house."

"I'm not getting married—at least for now. I don't need the money. You use it. You shouldn't have deprived yourself." When he saw how offended she was, he did not persist, but then he had an idea. "You know what we could do with the money? We could buy a house for us, for the whole family."

"We don't need to move. It's okay here."

"It's too crowded, Mom, it's always been too crowded."

"But what if we move and there's a Depression again and we can't make the payments?"

"There's not going to be a Depression," he said.

Back in Queens, Harry started on his next project, the development of a technique to manufacture transparent plastic. Of course DuPont had the patents sewed up on Lucite, but the problem with Lucite was that it could only be manufactured in rods or in sheets. Sid's idea was to make a molding compound, which would allow you to form the plastic material in any shape. After some discussion, he and Harry decided to start with methyl methacrylate, a monomer, and use benzoyl peroxide as a catalyst to get the monomer to polymerize. Their intention was to produce an emulsion suspended in water, which could then be dried into the molding compound.

Harry's first experiments were very promising. In fact, at one point,

Sid got so excited at what Harry was doing, and Harry was so pleased at Sid's excitement, that they both danced a jig around the lab. "Keep at it," Sid said, and slapped him on the back.

"I've got to go to Philadelphia so I can't work this weekend. My wife—my children—remember, I told you, we're moving."

"Oh, yeah," said Sid. "Well, then, get to it first thing next week."

Harry rushed home to Philadelphia with the sense of change in the air, good change that he himself had initiated. In the house boxes were piled up, taking up almost every bit of floor space. Pop was bustling about, whistling, but Mom, who was packing up the kitchen, seemed strangely quiet. Harry thought maybe it was hard for her to leave the place where she had been living for so many years. He looked around the kitchen, at the small sink, at the old refrigerator that made so much noise. "Won't it be great to have a nice new kitchen?"

"Yes, it will be very nice," she said, but he could see her heart wasn't in it.

"What's the matter? Don't you like the new house?"

"Yes, sure, I like the new house." She sat at the kitchen table, her head bent. After a while, she looked up. There were tears in her eyes. "I keep thinking about all the people—"

"What people?" he asked, in a panic.

"The people who died in the camps. I can't get it out of my mind how much they suffered. If I'd stayed—" she shook her head. When she began again, she erupted fiercely. "But I didn't stay. So why am I the one who's getting a new house, with a new kitchen, and a dining room? Is that right?"

Harry tried to calm her. "What's right? There is no right in things like this. It isn't as though you could have done anything if you'd been there . . . Once Hitler took power . . . Maybe some people tried but—"

"I don't know," she said vaguely, and he realized she was not paying any attention to what he was saying. In the glare of the harsh overhead light he noticed, for the first time, how wrinkled her face had become. One moment she had looked the way she always had, and in the next moment, suddenly, she looked old. "You ought to take a rest, Mom."

"How can I take a rest? They're coming in the morning with the van. Everything has to be done today." Suddenly, reverting to her normal stern self, she got up. "What you can do is clean out that closet of yours.

It's a terrible mess. I'm not going to go near it. I know you don't want me to touch your papers and your books. So you go in and throw away what you don't want and pack up the rest."

"I'll do it right now. Don't get upset."

But in fact, faced with the closet, he was the one who became upset. All those books and papers from his years at Drexel and his years at Xavier, piled in a heap, along with papers he had kept from all those years of being a courier—not reports, he never kept those—there was so much. Everything was jumbled together and he hardly knew where to start. He should throw it all out, but no, he couldn't do that. He'd go through it and see what he wanted to keep some other time. For now, he decided, he'd just pack it all up in boxes and the stuff could be taken to the new house and put in a closet there.

Just as everything was going so well with the polymerization of the methyl methacrylate, Harry ran into a problem. At first, when he had noticed a faint cloudiness in the plastic derived from the molding compound, he had figured it was because of contamination. But even with repeated trials, no matter how carefully everything was cleaned, no matter how pure the chemicals, the plastic that emerged from the molding compound was never clear.

He went to Sid and told him about it.

"What do you think it is?" Sid asked him, "a contaminant?"

"No, I'm sure it's not. I think it's residual water."

"Can you—" Sid said. And he suggested a number of things Harry could try. "I've already tried them and nothing helped," Harry said. "There's nothing we can do that I can see, no way of getting rid of those minute amounts of water. The process itself is flawed."

"Well, we tried. You have to be willing to make a lot of mistakes in this business. That's the way it goes. But when the breakthrough comes—" Sid got up from his desk and paced around the room gesticulating, so caught up in his hope for the future that no one, least of all Harry, could resist it. He simply watched in admiration at all the energy being generated before his eyes.

"I had this sensational idea last night, in the shower." Sid announced, and proceeded to describe a method for synthesizing organic compounds. "It will be very simple to do, very cheap. I know it's going to work."

Harry went back to his bench and put aside everything he'd been doing on methyl methacrylate. He got so involved in preparing for the new project that he worked straight through the night. In the morning he remembered the cat. He rushed home and fed it and let it out, even though it was cold, it was now December, he hoped it wouldn't freeze. Before rushing back to the lab, he looked in the mail box. It was habit; he never got anything but the utility bill and now and then an advertisement. But this time—and it was the wrong time of the month for the utility bill—there was something that looked like a letter. He could see it through the holes in the little metal door. He went back in and got his mail key and came back to open the box. It was probably only a Christmas advertisement. But it wasn't an advertisement. It was a note from Y, with some tickets enclosed, the signal for setting up a meeting.

The next Sunday night Harry met Y at the men's room in the Earle Theater in the Bronx. They walked around the corner to a bar. Y ordered Scotch and Harry ordered the same. Harry waited to hear what Y had to say. Y was not someone who indulged in small talk. He'd get right to the heart of the matter, and what would that be now? I'm not going to do any more, Harry said to himself, no matter what he says.

"You're looking good," Y said. "Have you lost some weight?"

"A little. I go up and down."

"I know what you mean," Y nodded sagely. "The problem is our way of life is too sedentary. We need to get out more, out into the air, exercising, walking."

"I don't have the time," Harry said. "I'm too busy."

Y ordered another Scotch, for him and for Harry. "I called you at the old lab. I was surprised to hear it's gone out of business."

"They closed it down."

"So where are you now? What are you doing now?"

"I've got a great job as a chief chemist in a small lab. We're doing some very exciting things there."

"Anything we might be interested in?"

"No, I don't think so." And then he added, knowing that what he was going to say would probably unsettle Y a little. "It's Roth's lab."

"Roth?"

"Yes, you remember, Sid Roth, the Buna-S man I—"

"You are working for Roth?"

"Yeah."

"I can't believe this. I can't believe what you're saying to me. You know this is against all our rules to become associated with anyone who was involved—"

"But," Harry said, "I didn't think it would matter that much to you. It isn't as though I'm involved right now—"

"Oh, my God," Y said, turning deathly pale.

"Are you all right?" Harry leaned over the table solicitously, putting out his arm to steady Y.

Y pushed his hand away and got up, unsteadily. He opened his wallet and put some money on the table, far too much money for the drinks. "Do you realize what you've done? You've ruined everything," Y said and rushed off, holding his head in his hands.

"Wait!" Harry called out after him, "You left too much money," but Y kept on running, his head in his hands.

ON A SATURDAY NIGHT in June 1947, Harry got off the subway at Thirty-Fourth Street/Penn Station, went to the ticket window, bought a ticket to Philadelphia, and boarded the train to Philadelphia. He was going home to the new house, to where Mom was dying. It was after midnight when he arrived. Pop was dozing in a chair in the living room. How old he's getting, Harry thought, seeing his head dropped forward, hearing the rhythmic sounds of his snoring. Pop's head snapped backward and he awoke. "Oh, it's you," he said and smiled.

"How is Mom doing?" Harry asked.

"About the same. She sleeps most of the time." His head shook up and down, side to side. Slowly he pulled himself up out of the chair. "Are you hungry?"

"I could eat. I'll help myself."

"Sit. I've got something all ready."

Shortly Pop came out of the kitchen carrying a plate with a dried up piece of chicken and two boiled potatoes and one carrot. The chicken was stringy and had lost all its flavor but still Harry devoured it.

"Is it okay?"

"It's good, Pop," he assured him. "When is Stan coming home?"

"He's coming tomorrow."

"That should make Mom happy."

"I don't know. I think she doesn't want him to see her suffering. You know how she is about Stan."

Entering the bedroom, Harry was stunned to see such a frail mound under the covers. It didn't seem possible that she could have shrunk so much in such a short time. Three months ago, she was still well enough to do the housework, though in the evening, when her work was done, she would sit and stare silently, for hours at a time. He would have liked to have said something to her but he didn't know what to say. Besides, he was afraid of provoking an outburst, she looked so angry even in her silence, so he said nothing. But two weeks ago, on his last visit home, Pop took him aside and told him Mom had been to a specialist, and the outlook was grave. Since last weekend, she had been in bed all the time.

As he stared at her, she opened her eyes and looked at him. At first, she seemed not to know who he was. "It's me, Mom. It's me, Harry."

"I know who you are. You don't have to tell me." She grimaced from what must have been pain.

"Can I get you something?"

He waited for more words from her but there was no word, no sign, as she slipped into sleep. In the kitchen Pop was cleaning up, using a dishtowel to wipe off the countertop. Once Mom would have had a fit, if she had seen him do that. Pop turned and shook his head. "Last week, every time I went in there, she would get angry and yell. I don't know what she was so angry about. I'm trying to do the best I can. I've always tried to do the best I can. Now she doesn't yell any more and it's worse than when she yelled." Tears rolled down his face and he dried his eyes with the dishtowel. "Do you think she's having a lot of pain?"

"I can't tell."

"She never would say what she was feeling inside." Bending down, to put the dishtowel on a hook in the cabinet under the sink, he stumbled.

Harry rushed to steady him. "Pop, what's the matter?"

"I'm so tired."

"You ought go to bed."

"I have to stay up in case she needs something."

"I'll stay with her tonight. You go to bed."

He was dragging someone over a narrow path in a desert place when he was startled awake by a noise. In the light of the small milk glass lamp on the bedside table, he saw that Mom was struggling to sit up. He moved her pillows up higher against the headboard, then tried to raise her so she could lean against them. As he lifted her—for all her frailty, she was surprisingly heavy—he smelled an unfamiliar odor, something cloying and thickening.

"Don't let me fall!" she cried out.

"I won't, I won't."

She looked around the room, staring at one object, then at another. She closed her eyes. Even looking, she seemed to be saying, is too hard for me.

"It's time for your medicine." He offered her the pills and a glass of water.

"I don't want them. They make me dopey. I keep falling asleep, but I shouldn't be sleeping. I have to—I have to—"

"You have to what?"

"I have to get to the house."

"What house? The house on Phillip Street? You don't have to go back there. You live here. You don't live anywhere but here."

"Here? Just here? You're lying," she said, and closed her eyes. He didn't know what to say. He felt a terrible guilt because he had lied to her so many times, for so many years.

"You're shivering, Harry." She had opened her eyes and the expression on her face was the one he had always known, her dark eyes as sure as they had ever been, commanding. "Go put on your bathrobe. You're going to catch a cold if you're not careful."

He went to his room and put his bathrobe on over his pajamas. He looked longingly at his bed, but he made himself go back into her room.

"Your father's going to need help," she said when he came in.

"I'll help him, I promise, don't worry. Try to get some sleep."

"Soon I'll have nothing else to do but sleep."

"Don't talk like that. Look at you. You're sitting up. You're getting better. You know what you used to say: Hope is just around the corner."

"Did I say that?"

"Yes, you did."

"When did I say that?"

"When we were kids."

"What did I know?" She looked around the room again and shook her head. "My life is a corridor."

"I don't know what you mean."

"At one end is this house. At the other end is the other house. I go between. I live between. Between two houses. This house and—"

"The house on Phillip Street?"

"How many times do I have to tell you? You're not listening, you're not paying attention. The house, back there." She gestured with her hand. "The top floor isn't finished. The hides are hanging there, drying. They smell—that terrible smell of the skins of dead animals—of dead animals . . ." She said something he couldn't understand, she kept saying it over and over.

"Don't talk, Mom. Try to rest."

She grew silent. Her breathing became softer. She slept.

Her grey hair, pulled back from her face, looked damp. He saw that her features had grown coarser: Her nose had grown broader, her ears larger. Or were they the same as they had always been? He had never looked at her before, really looked at her the way he was looking now, trying to memorize her, to hold her in place . . .

She opened her eyes and looked at him. Now she was the one who was shivering. "Are you cold?" She did not answer. He got up and got a blanket from his bed and put it over her other covers.

"It is cold. At night when I have to get up and go to the bathroom, I have to go outside in the cold and the dark. To the outhouse. To that terrible smell."

"There's no outhouse here, Mom."

Without any warning there it was before him, in his mother's room, as she lay dying, the smell and the sight of that man in the outhouse. He was afraid he might vomit. "Do you want the bedpan? I can get you the bedpan."

"There's no outhouse here? You're sure?"

"I'm sure. Do you want the bedpan?"

"No." She frowned, and closed her eyes.

"When did you come?" she asked.

"I came tonight. Stan is coming tomorrow."

"Stan is soft." She opened her eyes. "He can't bear to see me like this but you can. Stan is soft but you are hard."

Don't, he wanted to say, don't say that.

When next she woke, she was mumbling something about a tunnel, about a trapdoor in the floor, and a rug covering the trapdoor that led to the tunnel that led to another tunnel that people could go into, where they could hide.

"I have to hide . . . so they won't find me . . . I have to . . ."

"It's all right. You don't have to—"

"But what if they—"

"No one's after you. No one is looking for you."

"But I—" She looked around the room, puzzled. "It is cold, isn't it?"

"Yes, it's very cold."

"Such deep snow. Will we ever get out of it?"

"We'll get out of it," he said, and he thought he had quieted her, and she would sleep. But she did not sleep.

"They're not going into the tunnel," she said. "They're not going into the tunnel." Repeating the words seemed to incite her to a frenzy. "I have to tell them they're coming after them, I have to warn them they're going to be killed." Now she was gasping. "My father—"

"Your father?"

"He said I had to stay. He said I was selfish because I wouldn't stay. At first I stayed. But then I couldn't stay. I was the only girl in our town to graduate from high school. I wanted to go to on, I should have been able to go on to the University but they wouldn't let me. Because I was a Jew. If I converted—But I didn't convert. I wouldn't do that. Because I—I—"

"Because you believed," he said, feeling embarrassed, feeling ashamed, having prompted her out of his own disbelief.

She became quiet. He thought she was asleep. But all of a sudden she was talking again, saying something he could not make out. He leaned close. He was so close to her, he could feel her breath on him. "My grandmother has coins on her eyes. They put coins on the eyelids of dead people to keep them closed. She can't see me but I can see her."

He watched as her right hand clutched at the air. It reached out and clawed. Then it stopped. Then it reached out again, a hand alive yet mechanical. He seized it, holding it in his own, trying to stop the pitiful urgency.

She spoke once more, clearly. "I wanted to go, I had to go. There was nothing for me there but to be a tailor's helper, and I hated sewing. Was I wrong?"

MOM DIED THE next night. Stan was with her. He came out of the bedroom and told Harry and Pop, and then went back in again. Harry would not go in with him. He could not bear to see her dead.

At the funeral Pop broke down completely. So did Stan. Harry sat unmoved, responding only once during the entire service with irritation when the rabbi spoke of Mom's good character. Certainly she had a good character. But the rabbi hadn't known her. How could he say?

Several neighborhood women came to the service, as well as Myrtle, a distant cousin who lived in Trenton. She hadn't been to see Mom in years but now she came and wept. Maybe she came in order to weep. They all wept, except for him. He felt like a monster. He had wept before for others, he had been so easily touched by their sorrows, by their stories. But he could not weep for her. The being in that closed coffin was his mother, he kept telling himself, and yet it was not his mother. All he could think of was the decaying of the organic chemical constituents of a body; he could even enumerate them. He felt by this knowledge he was relinquishing any possibility of forgiveness.

Stan insisted that they get rid of Mom's clothes right away. He said it would be better for Pop. He took her things out of the closet and out of the bureau and packed them up in boxes. He said he'd talked to Myrtle and she'd suggested taking the clothes to some refugee organization. Looking at the boxes with her hats and coats, and her dresses, and shoes and stockings—many of the things from long ago—she never threw anything out—Harry wondered, Why did she think Stan is soft and I am hard? It's the other way around.

But then he remembered that time when he was a boy and found out several of his friends were taking music lessons. Couldn't he have them? he asked Mom. He kept at her even as she said No. Pop would have been willing but Mom said No. But I want to have them, I have to have them, he kept saying to her. It was the idea of the music, the idea of himself playing before others. She said No, they had to use the money for other things. He began to yell at her, saying the other mothers were good mothers, they wanted their children to have what they wanted but not her. She was always talking about hope but now when he hoped for this, she was the one who stopped him. Afterward, he'd never asked for anything else, he'd felt such shame at what he'd said.

On the train back to New York, gazing out the window, he kept hearing her say the words she said the last time he was with her. He kept looking at her, then looking away. He did not know how to get from the one he always thought she was to the one who lay in the bed in front of him, telling. Had she always been in hiding, while he had thought only himself hidden, in a terrible kind of pride?

She had said one must help others and yet he had not been able to help her, he had only been able to listen and do nothing. He felt within himself an upheaval so profound, so raw, growing thicker, need piling upon need, her need, his need, he didn't know which. She was so powerful and so pitiful at the same time. And when she was dead, he would not look at her lifeless body. He could not grasp the immensity of what had happened. She had become the immensity.

There was her telling and then there was her death, the two somehow connected—death and telling. He thought of a rug over a trap door that led to a tunnel that went into another tunnel and into another tunnel after that.

At Penn Station, he descended into the subway. He told himself that when he was on the train going under the East River, when he felt the change of pressure in his ears, then his thinking would return to ordinary thinking. He would go back to work. He would do what he always did. He must go on, no matter what. Someone behind him bumped into him, someone shoved past him saying something about idiots. He turned around and made his way back up the stairway, against the tide of those rushing to descend.

Outside, on the surface, light rain was falling. He started walking east. His black hat and his black coat protected him; his shiny black shoes would get wet but he didn't care. The little black bag he was carrying contained no secrets. He kept walking, convinced that if he just kept on he would be all right. All right was enough; he didn't ask for more. He looked up at the sky and rain fell upon his face. He recalled looking up when he was on the cliff ladder. Surrounding him now were high buildings, not to be scaled.

By the time he arrived at the East River, the rain was falling in sheets into the dark water—disappearing, invisibly, water into water. He had come somewhere near here on the first night he brought the material from the lab for Paul Smith. Things were coming round again and in an instant there would be another repeating, his mother here, there, everywhere, now and before now, going back through time.

He is standing outside the house, he is entering the house. He goes through the living room–dining room where all the furniture is together in one room. Mom is in the kitchen. He does not want to tell her he has lost his job. He tells her and then there are the weeks of looking for work and weeks of coming home and her turning away when she sees he has had no success. The furniture has to go back. Still she keeps hoping; her hope is what spurs him on. Yet at the end, didn't she say she had no hope?

Abruptly he turned and walked west and then north. He took refuge from the driving rain in the doorway of a bar near Times Square. A woman came out of the bar, bleached blond, heavily made up. He stood aside to let her pass, squeezing himself into the narrow doorway, but some damage had already been done to him. In the moment before she passed he had seen in her eyes a look of disgust or contempt. He went into the bar. He ordered a Canadian Club and another and another. He downed them swiftly without looking to the right or to the left.

He went out again and walked through the rain, which was finally slacking off. He walked beneath the elevated, hearing the trains above him. He had seen disgust in that woman's eyes. But what could she possibly know about him? Nothing. Yet he could tell she was judging him as a being that should crawl on the earth. But she, his mother, who is everywhere above—in the light of that lamppost, in the air, in the sky, in the stars that are not out—she must not know of that judgment.

Though it was not yet morning, he went to the lab. He could not bear the thought of being alone in a dark and moldy basement room. He was grateful that he could concentrate on what he needed to concentrate on, that he could shut out what needed to be shut out.

At six o'clock that evening, Bob Millman, one of the lab assistants, came to Harry's bench, and stood there watching him. "Is there something you need?" Harry asked.

"No." Bob stopped and looked uncomfortable. "I just—Are you all right, Harry?"

"I'm all right. I have a lot of things to catch up with, I don't have time—"

"Sorry, I didn't mean to—"

"My mother—," Harry said to his retreating back. "My mother died." As he said the words, her death sounded not more but less real.

Bob turned. He said he was very sorry, he asked if there was anything he could do. Harry shook his head.

"Maybe you ought to take some time off."

"I'm way behind. I have a lot of work I have to catch up with."

"You're going to stay and work here tonight, alone?"

Harry shrugged.

"What about dinner? Why don't you at least come over for dinner tonight? Then you can come back here. I know my mom would be glad to have you."

"Tonight? I don't know."

"Come on, Harry, it won't hurt you to take a little time off and have a decent meal. You look as though you need it."

"I can't come right now." He pointed to the beakers on his bench.

"So come later, when you can take a break."

"I'll come in about an hour. Please don't say anything about my— what I said. I don't want—"

"I won't. Here's the address."

As Harry entered the outer vestibule of Bob's building, he realized a man was following him. He stopped and turned to face him. The man went right by and opened the inner door with a key. Harry went in after him and turned left to 1A. He stood opposite the door, with his back against the wall, waiting for his heart to stop racing. The door to 1A opened and a young woman came out. The door closed behind her. He saw her look at him; she kept looking at him; he looked away. He heard her open the vestibule door. He heard the door shut behind her.

He rang the doorbell to 1A and, after a moment, the eyehole in the door opened.

"It's me—Harry!" he cried out anxiously.

Bob opened the door and said, "Do you think I wasn't expecting you?"

"I know you were expecting me but I thought maybe—" He trailed off. "I don't want to intrude."

"You're not intruding."

"I wouldn't want to impose," he said, though he was desperate to impose himself on someone, on anyone.

"You're not imposing, Harry. For God's sakes, stop apologizing. Let me have your coat and go sit down in the living room," he pointed down the hallway, "while I tell Mom you're here."

He walked down the long hallway, passing a massive breakfront. On top of each end of the breakfront was placed a narrow lamp, about two feet high, in the shape of a candle. Why make a lamp look like a candle? he wondered. Light is light, but a lamp is a lamp, a candle is a candle. Entering the living room, he saw against the opposite wall an upright piano. He saw a couch with a cover on it, a couple of upholstered chairs, a big console radio, a small television set, some photos on the wall. He felt he was taking inventory in a world where he had no other reason for being.

He heard Bob ask, "Can I get you a drink? We've got vodka."

"That's fine," Harry said, though he didn't care for vodka.

"I'm glad you came," Bob said, returning and handing him his drink. "It's not good to be alone at a time like this."

"No," said Harry, "it isn't."

After a long silence, Bob asked him how his kids were.

"My kids are all right."

"I know you said they get sick a lot."

"They're all right now."

Bob fell silent again. Seeing him look so uncomfortable, Harry asked him if he was still planning to go to graduate school.

"I'm applying at Columbia, for the Ph.D. program."

"In chemistry?"

"No, in nuclear physics. That's the place to be these days."

In the small dining room, almost completely filled by a massive, dark wood dining set, Harry edged into his chair, careful not to scrape it against the wall. Bob's mother was a tiny, birdlike lady, with short white hair. His father, if he had a father, was nowhere to be seen. Mrs. Millman kept jumping up from the table and going into the adjacent small kitchen, bringing in more pot roast, more noodles, more cooked vegetables, all of which Harry managed to devour voraciously.

As they sat over coffee and angel food cake, Mrs. Millman, asked Harry if he had a family. Harry blushed and looked into his plate.

"I told you, Mom," Bob said, "he's got twins."

"How nice. Two boys? Two girls?"

"A boy and a girl." He could feel his voice trembling as he spoke so he changed the subject. "That's a nice picture," he said, pointing to a photo on the wall.

"It was taken in Russia, many years ago. It's of my sister Molke and me."

"I didn't know they had cameras in Russia then."

"Oh, yes, we had a photographer in our little town." And then Mrs. Millman sighed. "She died soon after it was taken. She was so young when she died. She would be old now, but I think of her as a young girl. It's so strange—"

"Where's your family from, Harry?" Bob intervened.

"From Russia."

"Where in Russia?"

"I don't know, Mrs. Millman. They never said."

"Some people don't like to talk about the old country. They just want to forget it. To be American. I could never forget it, even if I wanted to. I remember so many things. The way the river froze over in winter . . . even horses and carriages could go on it . . . and in the spring . . ."

He would not listen. He had done enough listening. Instead he crawled within his own need, a space like a cave, not warm, not pleasant or pleasing but harsh and dark, forcing him, once he had entered into it, to go even further, as if need, his need, had a will of its own. He said to himself, Stop doing this, but the space was carving itself out before him, pulling him in, deeper and deeper.

"My father—," Bob's mother was saying.

Inside, in this cave he was entering—being forced to enter—everything was equally trivial and equally awesome. He knew about trivial but what did he, Harry, have to do with what was awesome?

He was at home, at his own door. His hand trembled in the lock. Once he was inside, he threw himself on the bed. He thought of the blood vessels within her decaying body, vessels like corridors collapsed, the blood no longer flowing through the artery and veins, through the branching vessels. In him was the same branching—his body had come out of her body—but now it was succumbing to a pressure, causing a swelling, like an aneurism in the vessels, a shoving out of the walls, preparing for an explosion, a melding, a mixing, of all things together.

There welled up in him a desire so intense, it was a vapor coming off of him. He knew he was a monster to feel this now. But he could not stop himself. Couldn't he seal her off, seal her eyes off so she would not see him lend himself, his body to this imagining, which now had the fierceness of a resolve?

He brought himself to climax and then again to climax, and again. Deep in the corridor of his mind was the sense that he was committing sacrilege. Afterwards, in a clarity born of satiated desire, there arose in him an awareness of a murkiness at the depth of his being, something deeply hidden, so covered over it antedated his own history.

The crying of the cat awoke him at dawn. He stumbled out of bed and let it in. Then he fed it. It gobbled the pellets up, eating so fast, it almost gagged. He filled its plate again. When it had licked the plate clean, it washed itself and jumped on his lap. Feeling it purr, he began to rock back and forth, weeping.

HARRY WAS IN THE middle of cleaning test tubes with hydrochloric acid the way he usually did, without gloves (he'd pour the acid into the testube, and shake the testube vigorously, with his palm against the open end—if you washed your hand right afterward it didn't burn your skin) when Sid asked him to come into his office in ten minutes. It occurred to Harry that he probably wanted to talk about money. In the last four months, since early summer, since Mom died, the lab had been having financial difficulties. For six weeks no salaries had been paid at all. Several of the employees at the lab had complained bitterly, but not Harry. Sid swore that things were just about to turn a corner, and Harry believed him.

Sid was slumped at his desk, his head bent, when Harry came in. He looked depleted, as if his energy and vitality had been sucked out of him. Harry couldn't help but attribute Sid's appearance to the effect Dorothy was having on him. Was it any wonder, considering that Sid owed his allegiance to his wife and the two kids, but here he was carrying on with Dorothy right in the open, in front of everybody? Harry hated it when he saw Sid's door shut and he knew she was closeted in there with him. How could he be so weak?

Sid looked up, then he looked down again. "There's something I have to talk to you about," he mumbled.

Seeing him so downcast, Harry couldn't help but take pity on him.

"If it's about my salary, it's okay. I can hold out for a couple more weeks."

"That's good of you, Harry. Like I told you, I'm expecting a big inflow of cash any day." He grinned but the grin slipped into a grimace. Uncharacteristically, he fell silent. He got up slowly and closed the door. "I—we've got a problem."

"A new one? Not the one I've been working on? But I've been getting such good results—"

"I'm not talking about the lab." Sid sank into his chair.

"They've contacted me."

Harry felt his heart thud, then skip a beat. "The Russians?"

"No, not the Russians," Sid said with irritation. "The FBI."

"What for? What do they want from you?"

"You know about Helen Bennett—"

"I don't know who Helen Bennett is."

"You must have heard about her. Her name's in all the papers."

"I don't have time to follow the news."

"It's in all the headlines," Sid snapped. "She's the one who claims she was in a Russian spy ring during the War and is now telling everything she knows. The FBI called me in because she said I was one of those who gave information to the Russians. I told them, sure, I gave them information, but it was totally legal. I was just trying to sell some blueprints I had for shafts and vats for making chemicals. And I did a little work for them on Buna-S, nothing special."

Nothing special is right, Harry thought but did not say.

"For God's sake, they were our allies in the War, weren't they? It wasn't as if I did anything against the U.S. It was all my own work anyhow, and there was nothing secret about it."

"You knew her, this Helen Bennett?"

"Yes, I knew her. She's the one who put me in touch with Amtorg."

"Oh," said Harry.

"Is that all you can say? Oh?"

"I don't see what you have to worry about," Harry tried to calm him. "It isn't as though the information on Buna-S was classified. A lot of the stuff came right out of technical journals. I know. Remember, I was there with you when you worked it out."

"I know that and you know that. But do they know that? The way things are now, with everyone rushing to rat on everybody else, ready to testify before this committee and that committee, I could lose the lab—I could lose everything."

"That's not going to happen," Harry reassured him. "You've already admitted you gave them the material on Buna-S—"

"Yes, I admitted it."

"So you don't have anything to worry about."

"That's easy for you to say." And then, in an aggrieved tone of voice, as if all of this was Harry's fault, he added, "I told them about you."

"You told them about me?"

Sid nodded.

"What did you tell them about me?"

"All I said was that you and I both knew Bennett, and she was the one who arranged for us to meet."

"But I never even met Bennett."

"I was trying to think of something to say, to show them I was coop- erative. I knew you'd back me up."

So Y was right, Harry said to himself. I never should have come to work for Sid. All on my own I was invisible. No one remembered me, there was no way for anyone to trace me.

"You will back me up, won't you, Harry?"

Hearing the pleading in Sid's voice, Harry sighed. "Yes, I'll say I knew her."

"Then maybe they'll leave us alone."

Harry knew from the Russians that once a questioner got going he did not just stop. "Prepare yourself. They could want more."

"Like what?"

"They can ask you who else you know who was involved."

"I didn't know anybody else. I'll tell them that."

"They can ask you if you were a member of the Party."

"Oh well, I did belong to the Young Communist League when I was in college but I never had time after that. I was just an ordinary guy, try- ing to make a living, trying to support a family. I'll tell them about my wife and kids. And you can tell them about your wife and kids."

"I can't do that."

"Why not?"

"I'm not married."

"You're not married? You mean you're living with a woman, and you had children with her without being married? No kidding? I have to admit I'm surprised. It's the last thing I would have expected from you."

"No, Sid, you don't understand. I'm not married. I don't have a wife. I don't have children."

"I don't get it. What are you saying to me?"

"They don't—they don't exist."

"You mean you made them up?"

Harry nodded.

"Why would you make them up?"

"It was a cover story. They figured married men would be regarded as more reliable—"

"They? They who?"

"The Russians."

"My God, you lied to me. You've been lying to me all along, since the moment you came here and even before then. I don't know if you're lying right now."

For an instant Harry was worried that Sid was going to run out the door, holding onto his head, just like Y. To steady himself, to steady Sid, he said, "I never lied to you about anything but that—the marriage and the kids. I never lied about the work."

But Sid wasn't listening. "What am I going to do now? Maybe I should go to the FBI and throw myself on their mercy."

"Don't do that," Harry said sharply.

"Who are you to tell me what to do after you've gotten me into so much trouble?"

"If we stick together and tell the same story, it will all blow over."

"Like Hell, it'll all blow over. Oh, no," he shouted, "I'm going to tell them every goddam thing."

The door opened and Dorothy came in. "What's going on?"

Sid just shook his head, not saying a word.

Dorothy looked at Harry. "He's upset," he said.

"I can see that." She turned to Sid. "What's the matter?"

"Nothing."

"I don't believe you. Tell me."

He told her, slowly, haltingly, about Buna-S.

"You goddammed fool," she said, when he had finished. "What kind of game did you think you were playing?"

"I'm going to throw myself on their mercy," Sid announced.

"On the mercy of the FBI?" Dorothy said. "You must be kidding."

"What else can I do?"

"I told you before," Harry interrupted. "We can get out of this if we both stick to the same story."

"You and your stories!" Sid shouted.

"Wait a minute. Do you think you can figure something out?" Dorothy asked Harry.

"Yes, I can."

"Let me talk to Sid for a minute."

Harry went back to his bench, thinking how odd it was that Dorothy, the temptress, was intervening on his side. A few minutes later, she came out and called Harry back into the office. She said that Sid had agreed to what Harry suggested. He would go along with whatever story he came up with, if it was plausible.

"But don't put in anything about your wife, whatever you do," Sid cautioned.

"I won't."

"Why shouldn't he tell them about his wife?" Dorothy asked.

"I'll tell you later."

As he was about to leave, Sid stopped him. "I'm sorry I gave them your name, Harry. It just slipped out."

"It's all right. I know how it is."

He went back to his workbench and sat on his stool, and looked at the test tubes and beakers and funnels and flasks and filters, all clean, all ready, lined up, waiting for the next run. As he sat there, he was already reworking the Buna-S episode. If they did ask him about his personal life, he would have to dispense with Doris and Dan and Louisa altogether, though that would be like a betrayal, somehow. Nevertheless, he would do what he had to do, to save Sid, to save the lab.

On Friday when he got to work, he went into Sid's office and started to say something about their story. Sid held his index finger up to his lips. He shook his head in warning. "This place could be bugged," he wrote on a sheet of paper, which he showed to Harry and immediately tore up into many pieces. "How would you like to come to my place in the Poconos tomorrow?"

At first Harry didn't want to go. He felt he would much rather be at work, where his mind was completely occupied.

"You've been working too hard," Sid said. "It would do you good to take a rest."

"I'm okay."

"I insist." Sid opened and closed his hands like a master of ceremonies inciting applause.

Finally, Harry gave in.

Early Saturday morning Sid picked him up at home. "Good God, can't you do better than this?" Sid asked, looking around the dark and moldy room.

"It's okay," Harry said. "I only sleep here."

"But still—"

They drove north in Sid's new red Studebaker. Harry started to say something about the story but Sid said, "Let's leave it till later. Let's just enjoy the ride. It's such a terrific day." The further away they got from the city, the more the leaves were turning red and gold. Sid kept pointing out this tree and that tree, how beautiful the colors were. Harry nodded but to him they were only one more sign of decay.

Set in the middle of a wood, with a stream nearby, Sid's house was old but in good repair. Ruth was in the kitchen preparing lunch when they arrived. The food was good—lentil soup and bread and cheese and fruit and cake—and there were large amounts of it. As Harry was eating, he thought again about that camp for undernourished kids he went to when he was ten. It was a memory he cherished, one he liked to go over and over for its simple demonstration of cause and effect. He hadn't really been undernourished. It was just that he wasn't that much interested in eating. But after the two weeks at the camp, he'd come back with a hearty appetite. In fact, he would eat anything and everything. He remembered how much it had pleased Mom when he ate.

After lunch he didn't quite know what to do with himself. Sid was busy chopping wood and Ruth was cleaning up. Harry thought about going for a walk, to explore the countryside, but it was too quiet for him. It allowed too many other sounds in, sounds it was better to keep out. The two kids, Ernie and Trudy, asked him to play Monopoly with them. In the middle of the game, as he was putting houses on The Boardwalk and Park Place—his color was blue—he was reminded of all those hours he and Stan used to play on summer mornings while Mom went out to do the shopping, and then she'd come back and give them lunch, cold borscht if it was very hot, and liverwurst sandwiches.

When the game was over, Sid asked Harry to go down to the high school with him to play handball. Harry told him he wasn't any good at handball but Sid said it didn't matter. They'd at least get a little workout. Harry had to admire the way Sid slammed the ball, putting as much energy into the game as he did into everything else. It was odd, the way he had recovered his energy since that session they'd had at the office, as if he was once again sure that everything would turn out all right. Harry was not so sure. He had a story, but still he was not sure.

"Put your heart into it," Sid yelled. Harry tried on the next shot and managed a soft lob to the wall, which Sid promptly killed.

After Ruth and the children went to sleep, Sid and Harry stayed up talking in the living room. As it had grown chilly, Sid started a fire in the fireplace. Now, finally, with the house silent except for the crackling of the logs, Harry went over the story they would tell: they had met at a meeting of the American Chemical Society in 1941 and become friends; Sid invited Harry to dinner at his house several times; in the course of their conversations they talked about the war, and about how many people were dying in Russia as a result of the Nazi invasion; they both wished they could help; Sid had met Helen Bennett and then Harry had met Helen Bennett. She had sent Sid to Amtorg where he volunteered his services. A man he thought was a clerk said the Soviet Union would be grateful for any technical information he could offer; Sid and Harry had put together a report on Buna-S out of unclassified material, most of it Sid's own work.

Harry went over and over the story inserting detail of time and place. He suggested that when Sid spoke to the FBI, he make a little slip now and then, and then go back and correct himself, so that it wouldn't seem too rehearsed. By three o'clock Sid's eyes were glazed. His head lolled against the high back of the armchair; his mouth opened; he was asleep. Harry was still wide awake. Looking into the last embers of the fire, smelling the wood burning, he thought of olden days, of people in a wilderness sitting around a fire, telling stories that could make the heart glad or make the heart ache—true stories or imagined stories.

When he was called in by the FBI for an interview, Harry could tell right away what the two G-men thought of him. He was nothing but a schnook, a fumbling little guy, stammering from fear, rather forgetful, completely forgettable. They dismissed him as if he wasn't worth the trouble. As for Sid, when he was called back by the FBI, he was able to stick to his story, Harry's story, and it was accepted. Nevertheless, they were told, they would both be required to testify before the grand jury.

Sid reacted by falling into a state of excitement, almost euphoria, as if he were involved in a game and was completely focused on winning, on beating his opponent. Harry was not excited; if anything, he felt dread. He had never been out in public, in front of others, being interrogated. He did not know how he would come off. He tried to rehearse it in his own mind: they are looking at him; they are seeing him, they are turning away, they are not remembering him; is that how it will go?

When the day came, momentum took over. He got out of bed and dressed; he went down to the courthouse. He sat outside the courtroom on a bench, waiting his turn. Sid came out and gave him a thumbs up sign. Harry went in the door. He was conscious of a searing light, the eyes of others upon him.

He fell into a state of numbness, holding to a single sequence, a single thread of story, a story to be told that would not be deflected by inquiry, that was strong as the strongest wire, that would in and of itself lead him on, when he was before others. At one point he was asked about Igor Gouzenko. Puzzled, he said he didn't know who Igor Gouzenko was. How could he not know? It was in all the papers for months that a cipher clerk in the Soviet Embassy in Ottawa had defected, with files, with lists of a spy ring. He didn't know anything about him, Harry repeated, which was true.

Later, when it was all over—neither Sid nor he was indicted—the whole episode in retrospect didn't seem quite real. It didn't seem imagined either. But it was as if someone else, another person, had taken over and testified, a person who believed what he said, and who was in turn believed. Who was that person in the courtroom, giving his testimony? It didn't feel like him, but who else could it have been but him?

During all the time he had spied, he had never thought about himself as lying. But this had been lying, pure and simple. He was grateful, after all, that Mom was dead, that she didn't have to know about this, that she couldn't see him doing this.

WEEKS DRAGGED ON into months into more than a year; by this time Sid owed Harry four thousand dollars. Finally, Harry had to admit to himself there was no chance he'd ever get what he was owed. Nevertheless, he might have gone on working at the lab, if he hadn't had the feeling that Sid was still uncomfortable having him around, after that grand jury business. All in all, he decided, it would be best to go home, especially as Pop had not been feeling well lately.

When he told Sid he was leaving, Sid was noncommittal. "Do whatever is best for you, Harry."

The day he was to leave, he packed up his few clothes and books. He wished he could take the cat with him but he couldn't because Pop was allergic to cats. He'd asked around at the lab and Bob had agreed to give it a home.

When he bent down to pick up the cat, it looked at him with wild eyes, as if it knew what he was going to do, and jumped out of his grasp. After chasing it for twenty minutes, he had nothing to show for his efforts but scratches on the back of his hands. Finally, he looked in the refrigerator and found some raw hamburger, which he wrapped around a pill of phenobarbital. Coaxing the cat to come to him with the meat, he grabbed it and pushed the pill-enclosed meat down its throat. After a while it seemed dazed, and he managed to get it into the box he had ready. Holding the box against his chest, he went out into the cold grey day, flagged a taxi, and told the driver to take him to the lab. Even drugged, the cat meowed piteously the whole way.

"What's it's name?" Bob asked, when Harry came in carrying the box, with the cat still meowing.

"It doesn't have a name. It's a nice cat, though." He placed the box on a bench and lifted the lid. The moment the box was open, the cat catapulted into the air, twisted, and dropped onto the floor ready for flight. Unfortunately, someone had left the door to the alley open, and the cat streaked right out. By the time Harry and Bob got to the alley, the cat was nowhere to be seen. Harry ran up and down the cold streets, calling "Cat!" He was heartsick. Poor cat, he thought. It was filled with terror, not wanting to leave what it knew.

Once in Philadelphia, Harry felt he had never left. He was sharing the house with Pop and Stan, who had gotten a job at the Philadelphia Naval Yard and had moved back in, as well. Pop, who had cut back to working part-time, did all the cleaning and cooking. They decided to buy a TV set. Day by day, they were settling into a comfortable routine. Of course, they could never forget that Mom was gone. But the image of her as she lay so ill and frail in her bed had given way to their memory of her from earlier times in the house on Phillip Street, her presence strong and vital, urging them on.

Almost immediately Harry found a job at the General Hospital, setting up and running a lab for the Heart Station. He was immensely grateful to be working with compassionate, dedicated doctors, who devoted themselves to the sick and suffering. He felt as if he had begun a new life of doing good, in which everything was above board, in the light, open to view, unencumbered by what had been.

If, now and then, though on increasingly rare occasions, he awoke in the middle of the night with a slight sense of regret that he no longer had a secret life, he told himself that was nonsense. What really mattered was that he was finally on the verge of having a life like anyone else, with a good job and doing good and soon maybe, or so he daydreamed, though it was night, he would meet a girl and get married and have children.

One morning in early spring, entering the animal lab to check on the supply of reagents, he discovered a new technician at work. She was a sturdy young woman with bright blue eyes and a snub nose, and short curly hair. The minute he saw her smile he knew she was the girl for him. It was as though Fate itself was smiling on him. Then happiness wasn't, after all, a reward for suffering. Life piled happiness upon hope, just as it piled misery upon despair. If it wasn't fair, at least it was well balanced.

His approach to Joan was wary as well as deliberate. At first he dropped by the animal lab twice a week, just to pass the time of day. Then he started going to the cafeteria, having lunch away from his workbench, which he'd never done before, hanging around, until she came in on her lunch break. What was more natural than that they should eat together, not every day, of course, but maybe once or twice a week? It was necessary not to be pushy, even if it took weeks or months for the right moment to present itself.

One day they were sitting in the cafeteria talking about movies and she mentioned that she was sorry she hadn't seen Laurence Olivier's *Henry V.* Everyone had raved about it so. He said he hadn't seen it either, but he had noticed it was playing at the local art house. He wondered if she'd like to see it with him. She smiled; she said yes. He could hardly believe his luck.

Before their first date he worried about how he was supposed to behave. What would he talk about? How would he keep the conversation going? Sitting beside her in the movie, he kept swallowing convulsively. On the screen, in gorgeous color, were beautiful women, chivalrous men, prancing horses. He kept turning and looking at her, watching her as she watched, wanting to see through her eyes.

After the movie he took her to her apartment door. He thanked her for the evening and then left, precipitously. He did not take the bus but walked home, though it was a cold night. Hurrying through the dark streets, he warmed himself with thoughts of Joan's openness, her willingness to say whatever came to her mind. There was no pretense in her; she never tried to impress you. She was not seductive; she was not a Dorothy. When he'd called for her, she'd said that this was the first time she'd been out in almost a year. Most other girls would have been ashamed to admit such a thing. They'd have been afraid of being judged unpopular. But she said it, simply and openly.

As for him, he was not yet ready to speak out about his own feelings. He told himself that he was right to go slow. He shouldn't take anything for granted. He must take only incremental steps, no matter how eager he was to go faster. It was necessary to be cautious about desire, which, uncontrolled, could turn "I want" into "I *must* have," thereby costing him everything.

It was a Sunday afternoon in late summer. There wasn't a cloud in the sky as they strolled along the banks of the upper Wissahickon. Joan was saying she loved being near water of any kind, whether a lake or a stream or the ocean. He nodded agreement. Gazing across to the opposite bank, he found himself remembering a painting he had seen in the museum, the first time he met Sam, a painting of men rowing their sculls on the river. Down he pushed the painting; down he pushed anything associated with seeing it. The only seeing he wanted was what he was seeing with her, walking where other couples were walking.

As she stooped to examine a flower growing along the path, he noticed a small whorl at the crown of her head revealing the naked scalp beneath. It thrilled and frightened him a little, this exposure. He crouched down beside her. "I was thinking, it's nice to take these walks."

"I've never seen a flower like this, have you?"

"I mean," he blundered on, "it's nice for me and I hope it's nice for you."

"Of course, it's nice for me." She got up and laughed. "I wouldn't come if it wasn't, would I?"

He looked at her looking down at him. With the sun shining behind her, it seemed as if there was a corona around her head, while at the same time he was prevented from seeing her face clearly. "I was thinking—," the words came, "—that is, I was wondering, if possibly—I wondered if you would be willing to consider thinking about—possibly considering a marriage proposal—"

He heard her sharp intake of breath. He saw her pull away from him, a little. He thought of that woman in the doorway in New York that night after Mom's death, of the look of contempt on her face. "Have I ruined everything by asking?" he stammered as he stood up. "I didn't mean to—"

"It never occurred to me, Harry. I thought we were just good friends."

"We are good friends," he pleaded, "but I want us to be more than friends."

She put her hand on his arm. "Harry, we don't even know each other."

"I don't know what you mean. I feel that I know you very well."

"You're wrong. We see each other at the lab and we go to the movies or for a walk, but what do we really know about each other?"

"There's not that much about me to know. I'm just what you see. I—"

"I believe," Joan said firmly, "that before people can even begin to think about marriage, they have to spend a lot of time together. They have to get to know each other in close circumstances."

"But couldn't we do that? I'm willing."

At Joan's suggestion, they arranged to go to the Jersey shore the weekend after Labor Day. She said they could stay in a bungalow owned by her aunt. However, late Friday afternoon, just before they were to leave, Harry was told that one of the doctors was ill and he was needed to assist the next day with an important procedure. When he told Joan about his dilemma, she didn't make a fuss, she didn't yell or reproach him. She simply said she'd go to the shore as planned, and he could come when he was done at work.

It was almost seven on Saturday evening by the time he arrived at the little bungalow, one of many in a row. When he knocked on the screen door, there was no answer. He called her name and knocked again, peering through the mesh into the unlighted room. Maybe she's gone, he thought. Maybe she got tired of waiting. Why are you thinking this? he berated himself. That's not being hopeful.

At that moment she appeared. "I was in the bathroom," she said and laughed. She opened the screen door. "Isn't this nice?" she asked. "Very nice," he said, and indeed it was, with its upholstered chair, and a formica table and metal chairs with red plastic seats. His heart leaped when he saw the door open to the small bedroom.

"Come on, put your things down," she said, taking his little black bag from him. "Let's go for a walk on the beach before we have supper." He was going to say, Wait until I put on my sneakers, but he didn't want to make her wait. So what if he ruined his black shoes in the wet sand? He'd get another pair.

They walked along the water's edge until the light faded. The darkness enveloped them, softly, thickly. The stars came out, piercingly sharp in the night sky. Then the moon rose and Harry told himself, This is a good omen: A new moon in the old moon's arms. He looked at the silver light on the dark moving waves. Everything was mysterious and at the same time open to view. It was like being in a dream of an ideal world, a world he had never even allowed himself to imagine. He watched Joan take off her sandals, and run in and out of the water like a wraith in the moonlight.

As they walked back to the bungalow, he looked into the windows of other bungalows. He could see men and women, sitting, talking, eating, drinking. In one room he saw a child. In front of each bungalow was a tiny fenced off yard. He remembered the ad in the *Life* magazine of the woman in the house with the white picket fence and a child and a dog, and he recalled his feeling that *Life*'s kind of life was not true life. But he had been wrong. Here he was, with Joan. He took her hand in his and held it tightly.

After dinner, a tuna casserole with noodles and cream of mushroom soup, a green salad and apple pie, all perfect, all delicious, he volunteered to help her with the dishes. She wouldn't let him. "You've been working all day. You look tired, Harry."

"I'm not tired, honest."

Still she made him sit in the upholstered chair while she finished cleaning up. Seeing some books on a wooden shelf built into the wall, he got up and picked out *The Outline of History* by H. G. Wells. He looked at the pictures of the dinosaurs, and thought about the ancient lumbering bodies that led to their own obsolescence. He put the book back and sat down again. He prepared himself to be honest, open, not secret.

She came out of the kitchen, taking off her apron, and he jumped up and said, "Here, you take this chair. It's the most comfortable."

"No, I like straight chairs," she said, sitting opposite him smoothing her dress, looking suddenly prim. That primness seemed sweet to him. After a while, she said, "Well, Harry," and he swallowed hard. There was that rush of saliva again, just as there had been at the movie with her. He tried to make his swallowing inconspicuous. He was back again to something like secrecy. He grew stern with himself, forcing himself to focus on her, on what was about to happen. He reminded himself that this was a test about him, about his capacity to be open. What was she going to ask and what was he going to answer?

She did not ask but instead she began to tell about her childhood in a small town in Pennsylvania. Her father had died when she was six, and her mother had to go to work to support her and her four brothers. She described the street where they had lived, on the edge of town. He saw it clearly, all the houses in a row, each house somewhat higher than the one below it, so the houses formed a series of giant steps.

In back of the houses, beyond the back fences, there was a sharp drop into a ravine, and all the children were warned not to go past the fences, which were rickety to begin with. Sometimes she stared through the fence, wondering what was at the bottom of the ravine, but she had not gone beyond the fence though her brothers and some of the more daring boys had. One of the boys—not one of her brothers—fell and was hurt badly. One day, when she was twelve, she suddenly decided she would climb down into the ravine, too. She loved to climb, she was a good climber—

Suddenly Harry yawned.

"Are you bored?"

"No, no. I'm just terribly tired. I never get tired like this. I don't know why I'm so tired." Yet this was not exactly true. He'd been tired for years and he'd always worked through the fatigue, pushing himself on, refusing to listen to the demands of his body. But this fatigue was something else, so profound his body was refusing the injunction to stay awake. I must listen, he insisted to himself, but his eyes began to close.

"Harry, if you're that tired, you better go to sleep," she said with a certain asperity.

"No, I don't want to." He could feel his lids growing heavier and heavier, his breathing more and more shallow.

"There's no law that says you have to stay up tonight."

"I want to hear more about you. I want to know what happened when you—"

"You can wait till tomorrow. We have all day tomorrow."

"Maybe I will rest right here, just for a little bit." It wasn't the answer he should have given, but he had run out of knowing what he should do. He was getting close to an agony of not knowing, and yet he was so fatigued even agony had no impact upon him. He opened his eyes and saw his little black bag just beside the front door. Inside it were his pajamas and his toothbrush and sneakers, nothing else.

"No, don't do that. Come into bed with me." She took him by the hand, and he followed her, feeling numbed and docile.

But once he was in bed with her something took over that had nothing to do with docility. He was feeling her skin against his skin. Was this what she called "close circumstances?" Was this getting to know her? In actuality, he found her more a stranger at this moment than he ever had. This closeness was too immediate, too raw, with no mitigating continuity. On the walk in the moonlight she had been a wraith. Now she was no wraith. She was touching him, making his penis grow harder, leading him into place to the opening within herself as her legs opened wider and wider.

Something switched in his brain, in his head, in his skin, in his genitals. He was dividing into two, one outside, one inside, the outside one watching as body prepared to get through, to plunge inside her, the inside one feeling the moisture, detecting a preliminary beating in the walls about to surround him, drawing him in. The light was on and he was seeing her breasts small and round, the nipples hard, the pubic hair lighter than he would have thought, almost red. He turned off the light, seeking darkness, a buffer.

He could feel himself surrendering to a long hidden brutality, a disregard for anything but his own need. Then he heard her gasping. Split as he was, he longed for sex with himself, by himself, where need of the other was never an issue, where he was, by definition the other.

He thought of Louisa with the red hair. Though he had made her up, she had staying powers beyond what he had intended; she had a permanent place, a permanent mission in his life, to appear at will, mocking. And now she was contributing to this that was going on, this entering, this rocking, as if she was a shadow figure, a hidden figure shaping his actions, his thoughts—though he had made her up.

There came over him a stillness like death, rising from the abyss between himself and his own exertions. He groaned and pulled himself out of her, off of her. He sat up on the edge of the bed and put his head in his hands.

"What is it?" she asked. "What's the matter?"

"Nothing. It's nothing." I am nothing, he thought, driving himself further downward.

"Can't I help?"

"No. No. I can't—," he gasped.

He begged her forgiveness. He said it was all his own fault. He blamed himself. He said it was an old story, his lack of ardor.

I T WAS A LATE Sunday morning toward the end of September, and Harry was in his pajamas at the kitchen table, eating breakfast and reading the paper. He had worked at the lab until two in the morning, and was taking a few hours off before going back for an all-night session. After he read the sports pages, he turned to the comics. Looking at *L'il Abner*, he laughed out loud.

He was a little relieved at being able to laugh, as if he'd escaped punishment for his own shortcomings. It had only been two weeks since the "episode" with Joan in the bungalow, but it had already been covered over—by events and schedules, by daily living. In fact, in retrospect, he felt it had started to be over even as it was happening, as if it had been corrected by his own foreseeing. Desire had always been allied with the secret, and now the episode was secreting itself. In his memory of it there was no rawness, only a small tender spot, which he was careful to go around. Somewhere along the way—was this a journey? a justification?—he did tell himself that at the crucial moment what had stopped him was the sudden and urgent knowledge that to be fair to her, to have been able to go on with her, he would have had to tell her about himself and his past. He had not been able to bring himself to do that.

Now that he'd finished with the comics, he searched through the papers for the front section, but couldn't find it. Pop must have taken it. Walking in his bare feet over the cold linoleum floor, he passed through the dining room with its hardwood floors, into the living room. There it was, in Pop's big chair, folded up. Harry picked it up, and turned to the front page. In large black letters the headline said: RUSSIANS EXPLODE ATOM BOMB. Beneath the headline was the text of the news release: "President Truman announced . . . it was reported that . . ."

As if in a delayed fallout of memory, he heard the shrieking of the sirens as he lay in that bed in that hallway that night in Santa Fe, clutching his little black bag that held the packet of papers in Klaus's minute handwriting. He had carried that packet east and had placed it in Y's hands. He had never thought of what would happen to the pages after that, how from Y it would be transmitted to Russian scientists, how they would pore over the formulas and the calculations, how they would use the information for the construction of their own bomb.

He remembered Klaus's talking about the bombings of the Japanese cities, which had left so many dead and maimed. He had wanted, he said, a test, on some uninhabited island, to convince the Japanese to surrender. You are not responsible for the use of what you did, Harry had said to him. At the thought of his own words, he tried to apply them to himself. What he had done he did for the best of reasons, to help others, those others in that cold country, not to hurt anybody. But even as he assured himself that he was only the messenger, the smallest being in this whole chain of events, he thought about the bomb, of its origin in the smallest bits of matter, of its eruption into the immensity of the mushroom cloud, with its terrible release of radiation, which was neither small nor large, but invisible, and deadly.

He folded the paper. He went upstairs in his bare feet and got dressed. He came down and went out into the backyard, where Pop was weeding. "I'm going to the lab," he said. Pop shook his head. "You could use a little rest, Harry. You look tired."

"I'm not tired."

It was a late Sunday morning in October. Once again Harry had worked late the night before. Once again he was having breakfast and reading the paper, first the sports page and then the comics. He was about to look at *L'il Abner*, when there was a loud knock on the door. "I'm coming, I'm coming," he called, hurrying to answer. He was worried that the noise would awaken Pop who had had a bad cold for several days and was sleeping upstairs.

The moment Harry opened the door, he knew who the visitor was, though he had never met him. The man's first words were polite, and heavily accented. "A few questions. I have a few questions for you."

Harry had the impulse to shut the door in the Russian's face, to start the day all over again. But he knew that if he didn't answer his questions now, the man would come back again, might even, God forbid, show up at the lab. He asked the visitor in. The man introduced himself as Peters. Of course, Harry knew his name wasn't Peters but he shook his hand and said, "I'm glad to meet you, Mr. Peters." There was a long silence. Harry led him into the living room. The Russian seated himself in a straight chair. Ah, but now, why now, was he thinking of Joan sitting in the chair opposite him, primly? He asked Peters if he would like some coffee. Peters declined. Harry apologized for being in his pajamas so late in the day, saying he had worked late at the lab, though the truth was that whenever Harry was at home, he preferred being in his pajamas.

The first questions were rudimentary. Where was he working now? When did he leave Roth's lab? He gave answers that were simple and factual. Next, Peters asked him what he had testified to before the grand jury in 1947. Harry reported what he had said about his first encounter with Sid. They had struck up a conversation at a Chemical Society meeting, and had found they had mutual interests. Sid had given him a lift home and on the way they had listened to the Louis-Nova heavyweight fight on the radio. Louis had won by a K.O. There were subsequent meetings, equally innocuous, involving discussions of previously published technical material, or unclassified work that Sid was doing. Repeating his own testimony was like watching himself on the stand, seeing that the jury was believing what he was saying, which in turn served to affirm his own belief in his telling. Of this, of course, he said nothing to the Russian, who merely sat there and nodded.

When it was over—it was a surprisingly short interview—Peters thanked him and said they would be in touch again. Harry didn't think it was a proper time to ask why, or to say, I'm not planning to work with you anymore. He let the Russian out and went upstairs. Pop was still sleeping, snoring loudly. When Harry was dressed, he tiptoed out of his room, careful not to make noise. For an instant, on the landing, he felt a surge of fear, or was it excitement? He couldn't tell which. As he descended the stairs, he reproached himself: he was finished with all that, for good.

A book came in the mail, an outdated chemistry text, the usual signal for him to look in the *Times* classified section for a meeting time and date. He found the ad: The time was late Saturday night of the following week. The place was a corner in the Bronx.

He arrived at the meeting place early, paced nervously back and forth, and then walked around the block. No, no one was following him. He watched as one walker, then another passed him by, moving from the light of the street lamp into darkness. What could the Russians want from him? Now that they were no longer allies of the U.S. but rather the enemy behind the Iron Curtain, he was determined there was nothing he would do for them.

Suddenly Peters was before him, motioning to Harry to follow him. Harry noticed an oddness in the way sounds were reverberating in the street. Everything, even footsteps, seemed to have a distinct echo. For some reason he was reminded of a stage set.

As Peters entered a small park, Harry caught up with him. In the dimness he could see that the leaves had already withered; many littered the ground. Walking side by side with the Russian, he thought of parks he had been to, of the desert, of hidden and open spaces. "You should ready yourself for the possibility of having to leave the country," the Russian said in a low voice.

"What are you saying?" Harry cried out.

"Keep your voice down. I am saying that the possibility may soon arise that you will have to leave the country."

"And go where?"

"To the Soviet Union, naturally."

Harry gasped at the thought of going to a country which heretofore had only existed in his mind as a place of ice and snow, with forests and immense spaces of frozen earth, an empty place where voices had once so tellingly cried out to him.

"But—," he said, "but—"

The Russian went on in great detail about an itinerary, telling him

that he would travel first to Mexico City, where he would go to a particular square, and meet an agent, who would provide him with a ticket to
get to Stockholm, where he would go to a particular statue and there meet
an agent who would—

Harry was not listening. He would never leave Pop and Stan. "I
can't—," he started to say but the agent was oblivious.

"Just as you have always been told, we will do what we can to help
you but we will not endanger any of our own people in trying to rescue
you." Harry searched his memory, going back to Y, to Sam, to Paul Smith.
Had any of them ever said this to him? Possibly.

Now that he was doubting his own memory, questions came to him
clumped, in spasms. Where was Klaus now? And Dave, what had happened to him? Poor twisted Dave. And Joan? Thank God, he had acted the
way he did. However shameful his performance was with her, it had
saved her from him, from having to share a life with him in which everything was at risk. But if she had loved him enough, wouldn't she have
stayed at his side, no matter what? Wouldn't she have forgiven him?

Harry yawned loudly.

"You do not seem to be taking this very seriously," the Russian
muttered.

"Oh, yes, indeed, I am taking it very seriously. It's just that I'm
tired, very tired." And indeed an almost deadly somnolence had taken him
over.

The Russian shrugged and said, "We will be in touch." Watching
him as he turned and abruptly exited from the park, Harry noticed the
curious duck-like quality of his walk. Surely that was a bad thing for a
man on a secret mission to do, to make himself so conspicuous. Who
could help looking at a heavy man who walked like a lumbering duck?
Harry yawned again and wondered about the judgment of the Russians.
Did they know what they were doing?

By now it was well past midnight and he had to wait a long time
in the station for the downtown local. In the almost empty car, he sank
onto the long seat. His body rocked back and forth with the motion of the
train as it roared through the tunnel. He felt like a prisoner of momentum.
At Times Square he changed trains and bought the early edition of the
Sunday *Daily News*. Turning to the Sports section, he read about
yesterday's game between the New York Yankees and the San Francisco

Forty-Niners. The Yankees had won in an upset. The victory, the sportswriter noted, was largely due to the Yankee defensive linemen, especially Arnie Weinmeister who kept breaking through the Forty-Niner line and stopping Frankie Albert.

How could I ever leave the U.S.? Harry asked himself.

At home he promptly fell into his daily life, getting up in the morning, going to the lab, working late, coming home and eating the supper Pop prepared for him, now and then watching television with Stan and Pop. It was a curious kind of falling, neither active nor passive, but rather halfway in between—as if he had simultaneously jumped and been thrown.

After what he had been through and considering the possibility of what he could have to go through in the future, one would think he would have been anxious, maybe even in a frenzy. But he was not. Some might say that was because he was simply of a phlegmatic temperament. But surely we have gone way past temperament as a guide to interpreting behavior. No, with Harry, it seems to have been something else: that he had an almost inexhaustible supply of protective devices. He was—how did I not notice this before, watching from the outside, thinking I was watching from the inside?—a master at allocating life. He was capable of transforming anything that happened to him, no matter how bizarre or unpleasant, no matter how painful or sad, no matter how mysterious or wonderful, into the mundane. In a remarkable act of leveling, he made everything equivalent. Perhaps he even experienced it chemically: that is to say, whatever happened to him ended up having the same valence. Everything dissolved in solution. Nothing precipitated out. If so, it was an amazing act of chemical juggling, in which he calmly but resolutely traduced his own history.

In early February he was asked to participate in an important new animal experiment. One of the surgeons at the Heart Station was performing a series of operations on dogs, in some cases replacing heart valves with artificial valves, in others replacing the main vessels to the heart with vessels from another part of its body. Eventually, it was hoped, such procedures could be adapted to human beings. Harry was grateful to be part of something that had such promise to directly benefit others, but there was one problem with this new assignment. He would have to encounter Joan frequently as she was a technician in that animal lab. Up to now, he had simply avoided her. As it happened, when they did meet, she made no mention of what had taken place between them.

One day he came upon her looking sadly into the cage where one of the experimental animals was lying. "That dog has such beautiful eyes," she said to Harry. "Did you notice?"

"No, I didn't." In fact, he made it a point not to look into any of the dogs' eyes.

She said something about its eyes being a little like his. At first he was offended, thinking she was making fun of him. But when he looked at her, he saw she wasn't laughing.

That night he stayed even longer than usual, as the animal he was monitoring had begun to fail. He could have gone home for a few hours between observations, but he was afraid that the dog was not going to last the night. And indeed it did not; he was there to record its last gasps. Only when it was dead did he venture to look in the dog's eyes. After that, he didn't go home. He went back to his own lab and started working on another procedure.

When morning came, he went out to the local eatery and had bacon and eggs and toast and jam and coffee. Walking to the lab, he stopped at the corner smoke shop for cigarettes. He was putting the money on the counter when he noticed a stack of newspapers at his elbow. On the front page was a picture of a man with a long oval face and a high forehead, above it a headline, BRITISH ATOM SPY ARRESTED.

Harry stepped back, away from the counter. It was as if the photo of Klaus had been thrust forward out of the page, too close to see. He looked at it again, from a greater distance. Then he picked up the pack of cigarettes, and slowly made his way to the lab. Methodically, deliberately, he set to work, though he felt panic gnawing at his edges.

Would Klaus betray him? That was the crucial question. He tried to summon up an objective picture of Klaus, not the one staring out of the front page, but the man he had known. What kind of a man was he? Noble, brilliant, of course, proud, wounded in some deep way, irritable but basically friendly, a man with a dark vision of the world. He recalled the conversation with Klaus in the park in Boston, when Klaus had been telling him about the camp where he had been interned, and when he had asked Klaus if he read mystery stories, and Klaus had been so fierce in his response, saying how much he hated suspense because things always turned out even worse than you expected. (And yet, he was also the man who was so fervent in his belief in communism, he expected it to bring about a kind of heaven here on earth.)

Now it was he, Harry, who was in suspense—not reading about it, but living it. The newspaper said Klaus had confessed. It must be so, if the paper said it, but still Harry could not visualize this proud man confessing. And if he confessed about himself, would he confess about Harry? Had he already betrayed him?

Each day he waited, as the minutes dragged by into hours, for a visit from the FBI. At the sound of every door opening, at every turn in the hallway, he expected to see one, no two of them—they always came in pairs, he knew, in their suits and their fedoras. He could visualize them approaching, but that was as far as he got.

How is it, he wondered, that he had never really thought of the possibility of being caught? Was it an inevitability all along, and maybe something in him knew it but didn't want to know it? Deep within him there were innumerable little bundles that up to this moment he'd always managed to tie up safely, and put on a shelf somewhere, way back, out of reach. But the ties were loosening and all the little bundles were shifting about, ready to disgorge their contents.

He sent a message to the Russians, asking for a meeting the following Saturday at ten at night in the men's room of the Trylon Theater. How would they help, now that he'd refused their offer to leave the country? He didn't know. He just wanted to talk, he had to talk to someone. On Saturday he took the train to New York, and then the subway to Queens. He felt the change of pressure as he went under the East River. At Sixty-Third Drive, Rego Park, he got out and headed up Queens Boulevard toward the theater. His time calculations were off and he had arrived early. He purchased a ticket and went in, noticing that *Unfaithfully Yours* had already started. He had never heard of the movie.

Always before, when he sat in an audience staring up at a screen, he had been caught up in the lives being depicted, as if they were his own. But he wasn't falling into this movie at all. He recognized the actor Rex

Harrison, who was playing an orchestra conductor, and the actress Linda
Darnell, dark-haired, dark-eyed, who was playing his wife. He gathered
that the orchestra conductor suspected his wife of infidelity. That was
about as much as he could take in of the plot. He went to the men's room.
No one was there. He waited. Finally, some white-haired guy limped in,
peed, sighed with relief, and hurried out again. He hadn't even looked at
Harry. Still, yet, invisible.

Harry went back to his seat. Rex Harrison was conducting the
orchestra and simultaneously plotting revenge against his wife and her
lover. No matter what they do to you, Harry warned himself, you must
never tell. He would not be a "squealer," no matter what punishment
they threatened him with. He could see himself imprisoned in a fortress
on an isolated island, no one to speak to, years going by, scratching the
passing of each day on the moldy stone wall with a spoon. Four vertical
scratches and then the fifth, crossing the four off.

He got up again. It was a good thing that he had chosen an aisle seat,
so that he did not disturb anyone else. He went to the men's room. This
time he had to pee. He washed his hands, taking a long time, running the
water, using the soap, running the water again, and yet more soap and
more water. No one came in. It was now well after ten. His contact would
not be coming. The rule was that you were there on time or you weren't
there at all.

He went out into the lobby, where the usher was chatting with the
girl at the popcorn and candy stand. Unnoticed, he waited. Ten minutes
later he went back into the men's room. Of course, he knew the Russian
couldn't be there because he had been watching the door the whole time.
Still, he looked into the stalls. No one was there. He washed his hands
again with water, with soap, with water, with soap, with water. He could
have been washing blood off his hands for all the energy he was using.
He went back into the movie. Rex Harrison was alone in his apartment,
trying to make a recording machine work. It was part of his plot to record
his wife and her lover in the act. But every time he put a disc in, the
machine threw it to the side. Around Harry everyone was laughing. He,
too, could not help laughing. When Linda Darnell joined Rex Harrison, it
turned out that she had not been unfaithful.

At the end of the movie, he got up and left the warm darkness of the
theater. Outside, passersby were bundled up against the cold. He kept

looking for someone with three pencils in the breast pocket of his coat, two with erasers up, one with the point up. No one. They have dumped me, he thought. Suddenly the suspicion came to him that Rex Harrison had accepted Linda Darnell's story too easily. Maybe she had been unfaithful, after all.

On the following Friday night—no sign of the FBI men yet—he went to Jersey City, impelled by the need to go back to the beginning, where all of this had started. He knew that the Dave he would find would not be the old Dave. He could not forget the intervening Dave, the one who had been injured, who railed at himself, and the world, and even, part of the time, at his own belief, though he said he still believed. Nevertheless, Harry hoped, against hope, that he would find the old Dave, good as new.

He knocked at Dave's door, wondering, Which one will it be? The door opened; it was neither. It was a woman, middle-aged, with glasses. Behind her, he saw an apartment that looked completely different from Dave's. Had he come to the wrong door? Or could it be that Dave was living with this woman, that she was taking care of him?

"Is Dave White here?" he asked.

"No," she said, doubtfully. "I think you have the wrong apartment."

"He doesn't live here?"

"No."

Harry groaned.

"Are you all right?" she asked.

"He used to live here," he said desperately.

"I don't know. I've been here for five years. Maybe you should ask the janitor."

As the door closed, he thought of the day he went looking for Klaus at his old address, and had asked the janitor, who was putting out the garbage, if he knew where he was. My life is nothing but looking for someone who has gone; my life is a corridor, he said to himself.

Descending into the basement, he noticed how warm it was in the passageways, as if all the heat from the boiler were being diffused down here. He passed the laundry room, and looked inside. No one was there. He came to a door, marked "Super," and knocked. A burly man in an undershirt opened the door. In the background, the TV was on. When

Harry asked about Dave, the man told him Dave had died, nine years ago, or maybe it was eight. He was smoking in bed and fell asleep, and a fire had started. By the time they got to him . . .

Outside in the cold, windy street he turned and looked back up at the windows that once had been Dave's windows. Inside that apartment, the first time he came, Dave had helped him, had saved him and his family. And then after that, they had had such good times there, except for that last time, when Dave had been so strange, bent and twisted, mocking, yet still believing. I should have gone back, he told himself, even though he told me not to come back. He kept thinking about Dave falling asleep with a cigarette in his hand, and the fire starting unnoticed, smoldering, then the first visible signs, a little smoke, still unnoticed as Dave slept, then the blankets suddenly bursting into flame. Did he wake up then, with the fire around him, the whole room on fire, the heat of the flames shattering the windows? Did he wake up? But even if he woke up, he could not jump up and run outside.

The street was deserted except for a single pedestrian in the distance, vanishing like a ghost into the darkness. Slowly, deliberately, Harry forced himself to go forward, though at every moment he feared being propelled backward. The fierce wind was trying to snatch his hat away, tearing at his coat.

No, my life is not a corridor, he corrected himself. Hers was, mine isn't. Mine is more like a collection of pieces splitting off, flying apart, further and further away from each other, or would be if I did not struggle to hold them together. Bracing himself, he leaned into the wind, went three steps forward, one step sideways.

At last, he was at the bus stop. He waited a long time for the bus to come, and finally took shelter in a doorway nearby. He kept on waiting. He looked down at his feet. In his shiny new black shoes his toes felt frozen.

H E WAS WORKING at his bench, one mid-morning in early May. Three months had gone by since that day he had seen Klaus's photo in the paper. I am going to be safe, the thought surfaced. As if in immediate retribution—can thoughts alone invoke vengeance?—two men entered the lab. They were wearing dark suits and dark fedoras; each was carrying a brief case. Somehow Harry would have expected triumph or glee on their faces, but there was no expression at all.

The taller one said, "We are from the FBI. We have a few questions for you." The shorter one asked if there was someplace where they could speak privately.

Harry led them into the office of Dr. Grant, who was at the moment operating on a dog and would not be back until the late afternoon. Seeing only one chair in the office, Harry excused himself and went out and got another chair, and brought it in.

"What about you?" the taller man asked.

"I don't mind standing, if it won't take too long."

"It'll take a while," the shorter man said.

"In that case," said Harry, "I will get another chair."

When the three of them were seated, the two FBI men on one side of the desk, and Harry on the other, the tall man, who said his name was Frank Gifford, took out some papers. The other, who said his name was Thomas Sutter, took out a yellow pad. They said they wanted to go over his 1947 grand jury testimony with him.

Once again, just as he had done with Peters, Harry repeated what he had said. He was surprised that he was not nervous. His voice was low and steady. He did not hurry. He even felt he was droning on. The two men seemed satisfied. They kept nodding as if he had answered an examination question correctly. After his lengthy answer, with Sutter taking copious notes on his yellow pad, there was silence.

Gifford asked him about his work at the lab. Harry spoke eagerly about the Heart Station, praising its work, saying he was glad to be part of it. He talked about the hopes the doctors had, that what they were doing would change people's lives for the better. Gifford nodded.

"Have you ever been to Santa Fe?" Sutter asked.

"No, I've never been to Santa Fe. That's in New Mexico, isn't it? No, I've never been out west, though I'd like to someday. I'm not much of a traveler. I work long hours and when I'm not working, I'm at home. In my spare time, though of course I don't have much spare time, I like to follow sports." Enthusiastically he added, "I'm very hopeful about the Phillies this season, after all those years of their being in the basement, especially those five consecutive last-place finishes from 1938 to 1942, when they averaged one hundred and seven losses per season, ending up between forty-three and sixty-two and a half games out of first."

Gifford nodded, saying it did look like the Whiz Kids might win the pennant this year.

"I'm sure they would have won the pennant last year except for that terrible thing that happened, when that fan shot Eddie Waitkus. How could anybody do anything like that?"

"People do weird things," Gifford said.

"Thank God Waitkus is back again playing this season. He's the best first baseman in the business."

Sutter, who had been quiet during this exchange, asked Harry to go over the grand jury testimony one more time. Harry told it again, changing a few words here and there, to make sure it didn't sound as if he had it down by rote.

Why had he left Roth's lab? Sutter wanted to know.

"He didn't pay me for months."

"You worked for him for months without pay?"

"Well, he kept saying he'd pay me, so I thought he'd pay me. But he never did pay me. He still owes me four thousand dollars."

"You're a pretty easygoing guy, aren't you, Harry?" Gifford said. "Four thousand dollars is a lot of money."

"I wouldn't say I was exactly easygoing, but I do believe people when they say something. I feel you have to give them a chance. And frankly, I don't care that much about money." It was true what he was saying. He didn't care all that much about money and he did trust people would do the right thing. He even thought these FBI men wanted to do the right thing.

"You're sure you've never been to Santa Fe?"

At these words, pronounced in a decidedly threatening tone by Sutter, Harry sighed loudly and slumped in his chair.

"What's the matter, Harry?" Gifford asked. "Are you having second thoughts about your memory?"

"No, no. It's just that I must be tired. I was working until three this morning, and I guess it's finally getting to me. Couldn't we talk later," he pleaded, "or my experiment is going to be ruined."

Gifford motioned to Sutter and stood up. "I'll tell you what, Harry, we'll leave you now but we'll be back this evening at seven."

"Seven will be fine."

"You can use the time to think about your memory," Sutter said, "about what you might have forgotten."

"I can't think of anything I've forgotten."

After they left, he put the two chairs back where he'd gotten them. He thought about Klaus. Had Klaus gone through an interrogation like this? He wondered if he really had confessed the way the papers said he had. He couldn't imagine Klaus confessing to men like Gifford and Sutter, who were nice enough, particularly Gifford, but they certainly weren't first-class brains like Klaus.

When Gifford and Sutter returned at seven, once again they went into Dr. Grant's office. Once again they sat as before, the two FBI men on one side of the desk, Harry on the other. Harry thought that Gifford might say something about today's game at Shibe Park but it was Sutter who began the discussion with a question. Where was Harry on February 28, 1944? Harry took some time answering, as if he were probing his memory and couldn't come up with anything. "I must have been working at Franklin Chemical's lab in Queens," he said, though in fact, he knew exactly what he had done on that date. That was the first day he had met Klaus. Obviously, they knew someone had met Klaus. Klaus must have told them that in his confession. But they didn't know who the someone was.

Why did he leave Franklin Chemical in 1946? Sutter wanted to know.

"I was laid off."

"And how did you get the job at Roth's?"

Harry told them about meeting Sid outside a movie theater. He told them what movie he had seen. He said that Sid had offered him a job. He didn't mention the cat's arrival that day.

The questioning went on for three more hours, about this day and that day and another day in February 1945. One of the days was the day he had gone to Boston to meet Klaus. Again he said that he had been working at Franklin Chemical. He knew there would be no record of his having been away. He answered quietly, politely, stolidly. Finally, Sutter got up. "That's enough for today. We want to see you tomorrow. Come down to the Federal Building tomorrow morning at nine."

"But what about my work? I have to take a bunch of readings in the morning. Can't I come later?"

Sutter looked at Gifford. "How about one o'clock in the afternoon?" Gifford said.

By the time Harry got home it was almost midnight. Pop was snoozing in his chair. Stan was already asleep. It was so peaceful and quiet in the house. All Harry wanted was for things to stay the way they were. Tomorrow evening early, he'd come straight home. They could watch Dave Garroway. They all liked Dave Garroway. They could just sit in the living room and watch and laugh. It seemed like a humble request to Harry to ask for this and nothing else, just for this life at home to go on a little bit longer. Stan had been talking about screening in the back porch. They could talk about that too. Stan had wanted to show him his plans for the porch but he'd been too busy to look at them. Never again would he be too busy for him or for Pop.

He fell into bed, aching for sleep, but he did not sleep. At some point, he reminded himself, before tomorrow he would have to get ready for their questions, think through what they might ask him, prepare a story that would satisfy them. He knew what they wanted him to say, but he would not let himself get mired down in the story they wanted, the story they needed. He must allow himself only to think of the story he would tell. He must give telling details, and he must believe every detail he told. He must so persuade himself to believe his own story, that they would believe him. What did it mean about belief, he wondered, if it could come and go, be used or discarded as needed?

At one he appeared at the Federal Building, puffing a little as he had run the last couple of blocks because he was late. He went up in the elevator to the fourth floor and was ushered in by a secretary to an empty room, where he waited and waited for what seemed like hours. I could have been working this whole time, he thought mournfully.

Gifford and Sutter finally came in at two-thirty. They did not apologize for keeping him waiting, not that he expected them to. Sutter sat at the desk, took out his yellow pad, and stared at him. Gifford stood next to a straight chair, his foot on the seat, leaning forward. He looked relaxed and friendly. He offered Harry a cigarette, which he accepted gratefully.

"Let's go over some of the things from yesterday," Sutter said. So there Harry was again, going over the same dates he'd been asked about before. He kept saying, "I must have been working that day just as I did every day. Couldn't you check the records at Franklin?" They didn't answer him, didn't say whether they would or wouldn't.

Had he ever been to Boston? Gleason wanted to know.

"No," he said.

"Not even to see the Red Sox play?" Gifford grinned.

"I wouldn't go around the block to see them," Harry said.

Gifford laughed, then went over to Sutter and whispered something to him. "Would you have any objection to our taking some pictures of you, Harry?"

"No, of course not. Whatever you want."

Gifford went out and Harry was left alone with Sutter, who occasionally looked up from his yellow pad and stared at Harry, as if he'd just seen him for the first time. Shortly, Gifford came back in with a man who was carrying a tripod and an eight millimeter camera and a standing light.

"Oh," Harry said, "moving pictures."

"Do you mind?" Gifford asked.

"No, I don't mind. I just thought you were going to take something like a passport picture."

They were all silent while the man set up his equipment. When he turned on the light, it was too bright for Harry's eyes, so he kept closing them.

"Keep your eyes open," Sutter said.

Harry tried but his eyes kept tearing.

"I said, Keep your eyes open."

"I can't help it, the light's so bright."

"Get up and walk around," said Sutter.

Harry stood up. "You want me to just walk?"

"Just walk like you usually do, back and forth, in a circle, I don't care."

Strange that what he usually did seemed suddenly so hard to recapture. It occurred to Harry that he might try to walk like a duck, the way Peters did, but it wasn't that easy to make your body do something it didn't want to do. So he shuffled back and forth, feeling very foolish, as if he were on display. He held to the thought that Klaus had not betrayed him. Otherwise they wouldn't be going through this picture taking.

"Have you ever been a member of the Communist Party?" Sutter asked.

Harry was so taken by surprise he laughed. He was remembering how Dave tried and tried to persuade him to join. "No," he said, "Of course not. I was never interested in their crackpot ideas about revolution."

"So you don't believe in revolution?"

"I'm a scientific man, trained in the scientific method. How could I possibly believe in violence or in revolution?"

Yet he remembered too—he must stop this remembering—that Klaus, who was a much more highly educated scientist than he, had joined the Party in Germany. But that was different. Things were different in Germany. "I'm not interested in politics," he added, "with a few exceptions."

"Like what?"

"Well, for instance, I believe everyone should be treated equally. I don't think there should be things like the Jim Crow laws in the South against black people."

"So are you a crusader?"

Harry stiffened at Sutter's nasty tone. "No, but maybe I should have done something. But I was always too busy with my work . . ."

"Tell us about your childhood, Harry," Gifford interrupted.

"I had a normal childhood."

"Normal in what way?"

"A happy childhood," Harry said stubbornly. "We were very poor but that didn't matter. We were very close."

"Where did your parents come from?" Gifford asked.

"Russia."

"Where in Russia?" Sutter interposed.

"They never said."

"I thought you said you were very close."

"We were," he insisted. "They just didn't talk about the past."

"Are they Communists?"

"Of course not."

"But they were sympathetic to the Russians?"

"Not really. In fact, my mother never forgave them for the pact that Stalin signed with Hitler. My mother is dead. She died two years ago." At the mention of her death came thoughts about telling, about death and telling. You better stop this kind of remembering, he cautioned himself.

After a silence, Gifford asked, "Where did you go to school?"

He told them the names of his grammar school and his junior high school. Then he remembered Mrs. Hess and the composition "What I Did On My Summer Vacation," and what she had written on his paper: "Surely you did more than this." That too had been about belief. He'd told the absolute truth and yet she hadn't believed him.

He told Gifford and Sutter about the compositions he'd done for the other boys. He told about his own composition in exact detail. He remembered almost every word he'd written. "I put down just what I did on my summer vacation," he said. He had described an average day: He got up at seven, had breakfast—Wheaties and banana and milk—which his mother served him and his brother Stan. While she went out to go to the butcher's and the vegetable man, he washed the dishes and Stan dried. They each made their beds, then they played Monopoly. When his mother came home, he went out and played stickball in the street with his friends. He came home and he had lunch, vegetable soup which his mother made—or, if it was very hot, cold borscht. He played Monopoly again with Stan. He read a lot. He was particularly thrilled by stories of lads with great courage, who surmounted all odds. He went out later in the afternoon, to one friend or another's. His father came home at six. They had dinner. They listened to music sometimes. His father had a victrola which had been given to him by his employer, the Victor Record Machine Company. For one day he had a job as a delivery boy for the corner candy store. On Saturday afternoons, he and his friends went to the movies. He liked the serials with their cliffhangers every week— especially Buck Rogers. He told how they all turned in their compositions to Mrs. Hess and three days later she returned them, saying how good the papers were, particularly four of them, and how pleased she was that they had taken the assignment so seriously. His four friends were the ones who had gotten the A's. His paper was marked C. "And she wrote, 'Surely you did more than this.' But that's just what I did," Harry said to the two FBI men.

"Why are you telling us this?" Sutter asked irritably.

"I don't know. You asked me about my schooling and I just thought—"

"Why did you do good papers for them and not for yourself?" Gifford asked.

"It wasn't that I was doing a bad paper for myself," Harry said uneasily. "I don't know—"

"Why did you do papers for them at all?" Sutter asked.

"Because they needed help."

"And if someone asks you for help," Sutter snarled, "you can't say No?"

"No, that wasn't it."

"What was it then?"

"I don't know but it wasn't that." Yet he saw how Sutter was looking at him, with contempt in his eyes, knowing what he was thinking: that to do what he had done for the other boys was a sign of weakness, of weak will. But it wasn't that, or at least, it wasn't just that.

Once again they returned to what he had done on a day in 1944. The questioning went on for hours, over and over the same questions, and then a sudden shift to yet another series of questions and these too were asked over and over again. He felt they were hammering at him with their words, even Gifford, who had become testy by now. Yet he trusted his own devices. He knew he could outlast them. There was always some niche he could take shelter in, some point he could cling to on the rounded surface of his own telling.

At ten o'clock, they told him he could go home. Instead of going home, he went back to the lab. He made a series of observations on the new subject, a large dog of indeterminate breed, and entered the data on the log sheet. He did not think of what he had been doing at the Widener Building today or what he would have to do again at one o'clock tomorrow. He focused totally on the dog's condition, its heart rate, its blood pressure, its laborious breathing. It was as if once again he had two lives, separate and distinct.

At two he went home. He let himself in quietly. Pop and Stan were asleep. Pop had left some chicken for him in the refrigerator. He ate that, standing up. Then he had a glass of milk. Here he had a third life, a life of relief and comfort and warmth, to keep him intact, to give him strength to go on, to keep things apart that must of necessity be kept apart. He slept dreamlessly. Even his dreams were cooperating, lying low.

On Saturday and Sunday the questioning continued as before. With the eyes of Sutter and Gleason upon him, it came to him that for the first time he was finding out something about heroism, though he would never have thought that heroism could be thought of as simply resisting. For he was resisting, not only his two questioners but also something within himself, a formless but urgent need—to disclose. He grasped at his own unimportance, as insurance against this odd and wayward impulse.

On Sunday night, as he packed his briefcase, Gifford turned to Harry and asked if he had any objection to their "looking things over" at his house.

"Of course not," said Harry. "The only thing is I don't want you to come when Pop and Stan are at home. They'd think something was wrong, they'd be upset. Pop has a heart condition and Stan is nervous. He's a very gentle person but he's nervous. He was in the Pacific for three years."

"We'll come when they aren't home."

"They won't be home tomorrow morning. They'll be at work," Harry volunteered.

"We'll come at ten," Gifford said.

That night he went to the lab and stayed late. The dog was not doing well at all. His breathing had become even more labored and his vital signs were not good. He would probably die within the next day or so. At three Harry went home and fell into bed at once, not even bothering to eat.

Pop was surprised to see him up at seven. "Why so early, Harry? I heard you come in real late last night. You should get more sleep than you're getting."

"I'm fine, Pop. I'll make it up by sleeping more tonight."

"You can't make up for it. Sleep doesn't work that way." Harry sighed. Then he added, "I'm fine. I'm going to be fine."

After Pop left, Harry wandered around the house. What would they be looking for here? There was nothing to see. He went into his room. Nothing there but ordinary things. He went to his bedroom closet. Oh, God, the thing was full, crammed to the top with books and papers. He looked through some of the papers. Old notes from Drexel, a few receipts, innocuous but still— He tore them up and flushed them down the toilet. He went back to the closet and looked at all the stuff. It seemed to have expanded, to still be expanding. It was too much stuff. He shut the door.

He sat at the kitchen table and had breakfast, Wheaties and milk and coffee. He looked at yesterday's paper. He read the sports pages. The Phillies had won again. He read Li'l Abner. The doorbell rang. It was only nine o'clock.

"Are we early?" Gifford asked when Harry opened the front door.

"That's okay. Pop and Stan are gone already. Sorry that I'm still in my pajamas."

"It's all right, Harry. You don't have to stand on ceremony with us."

He showed them around the house, downstairs and then upstairs. He showed them Pop's room and Stan's room and his room. They looked in his dresser drawers; they didn't find anything but underwear and socks. Gifford opened the closet door.

"Fibber McGee's closet," he said.

"That's what Mom always said. She liked that program. She used to listen to it every day and she would—"

"I'll start at the top," Sutter interrupted.

He stood by and watched as the two men pulled out and examined each book and each piece of paper. By noon they had sifted through only a small part of what was stacked inside. Harry wondered if they weren't getting hungry; he was. He was getting ready to offer them something to eat when he heard a very low sound from Sutter, something between a gasp and a growl.

"What's this label?" Sutter said sharply, pointing at the inside cover of a book. "It says it's from a book store in Syracuse. Have you been to Syracuse?"

"No," Harry said, "I've never been to Syracuse."

"So how come you have this book with this label?"

In fact, Harry had been to Syracuse. He had carried out a number of assignments there and once, having to wait for his contact, he had wandered into a bookstore and bought this very book. "I remember now," he said. "I got that book at a second hand store here in Philadelphia. But it already had that label in it."

Sutter eyed him suspiciously and shrugged. "Let's break now for lunch," Gifford suggested.

"I can make you some sandwiches. I've got peanut butter and jelly or tuna fish, or I can heat up a can of Campbell's Cream of Mushroom soup."

"No, thanks. We'll go out. Are you ready?" he said to Sutter.

"In a minute."

As he said these words, a whole stack of books fell on the floor, and a paper fell out of one of the books. "What's this?" Sutter said, picking it up. It was a map of Santa Fe. "I thought you never were in Santa Fe."

"Give me a minute to think," Harry said, sinking into a chair. In fact, he had the sense that he was not thinking at all. It was like that other time in his life, when he had to give Dave an answer. He had the same feeling he'd had then of waiting to decide something that had already been decided.

The two men were waiting, their eyes upon him. He closed his eyes. There was a further slowing down, within him, almost a stopping. It came to him that he had run out of avoidances.

He opened his eyes. He saw the flowered wallpaper, faded. He saw the men in front of the closet, looking at him. He saw the door open to the hallway. He was about to meet suffering, his own and the suffering he would cause others because of what he had done.

"I am the man who received the information from Klaus Fuchs," he said, standing up.

THE TWO MEN stared at him in silence—a long, drawn out silence, it seemed to Harry. Finally Gifford told him to get dressed, that they were going to take him downtown. Harry went upstairs to his room. He put on his good black suit. He put on his coat, though it was warm outside. He took his black fedora. He packed his little black bag with underwear and socks and a few shirts and his toilet articles.

"What's that?" Sutter asked, when he came downstairs.

Harry opened the bag and showed him what was inside.

"Where you're going, you're not going to need that."

"Just in case—"

"Let him take it," Gifford said.

At the Widener Building he was put in a room with three chairs and a desk. On top of the desk was a reel-to-reel tape recorder. After a while a young woman came in with a sandwich wrapped in wax paper and a Coke. The sandwich was ham on rye. After another hour Gifford and Sutter came in. "How are you doing, Harry?" Gifford asked.

"Up and down," he mumbled.

Sutter turned on the tape recorder and the two men sat at the desk across from Harry. Two against one, he thought, but then he corrected himself. This wasn't, after all, a contest. It was an ending he should have foreseen but never had. Or maybe he had foreseen it and kept it from himself, going on blindly, never even acknowledging the idea of ending, as if life didn't have endings in it.

The questions came, one upon the other, but now the answers were different answers. Words spilled out of him, dates, places, missions. Every half hour or so he had to stop so Sutter could change the reel. Harry chafed at the interruptions, as everything in him was now keyed to the forward motion of telling, to letting it all spill out. Well, not all, exactly. He would not implicate anybody but himself. He knew that the two FBI men, particularly Sutter, would immediately rush to judgment, labeling anyone he named as criminal. But that wasn't how he thought of the men he had worked with. He would not rat on any of them. He would adhere to the code of the streets from his childhood. He would speak only of his own actions. That would be enough. That would be a lot.

After questioning him all afternoon, and well into the night, they put him in a cell to sleep. They woke him up early the next morning and the questioning began again. There was so much that he remembered, the words poured out of him in a never-ending stream. He kept waiting for a sense of relief, but relief did not come.

"Can I call the Heart Station?" he asked. "I've got to let them know I won't be there today." He was allowed to call but he was only allowed to say he would not be in because of personal circumstances. He was not allowed to elaborate. He didn't know what he would have said, anyhow.

When night came, he asked if he could call home. He was often away for one night, he explained, but two nights without letting Pop and Stan know would really make them worry and he didn't want them to worry. They allowed him to call home. Stan answered and Harry said he wouldn't be home tonight.

"Again? You're working too hard, Harry. You're going to make yourself sick."

"No, I'm not." After a pause, he said, "Actually, I'm not at work."

"You're not at the lab? Where are you?"

When Harry didn't answer right away, Stan became agitated. "Are you sick or something? You sound funny."

"I'm not sick. I'm at the Widener Building, the Federal Building," he blurted out.

"At the Federal Building? What are you doing there?"

"It's a long story. I can't tell you now."

"There's something wrong, Harry, I can tell. I'm going to come down right now and see what's going on."

"Wait a minute." He turned to Gifford. "Can I see my brother? Can he come down here? I'm trying to tell you everything I know. I'm trying to be cooperative. Can you do this one thing for me, let me see my brother? I can't tell him over the phone."

When Stan arrived an hour later, and saw Harry sitting in the room with a guard, he blanched. "What is all this?"

Harry told him that he was being detained for questioning.

"Why? They can't do that. You didn't do anything wrong. Did you tell them they made a mistake?"

"It's not a mistake." Harry sighed. "I was a courier, a spy for the Russians."

"What kind of crazy story is this?"

"It's not a story. It's the truth. I was a courier for the Russians."

"When?"

"For a long time."

"Before the War?"

"Before the War. During the War."

"How could you have been such a jerk?" Stan cried out.

Harry shook his head. "Don't tell Pop, will you?"

"I have to tell Pop. What am I going to say to him? How will I explain that you're not coming home?" He fell into a chair. "I can't believe this, any of it, that you did this—my big brother, my smart brother . . ."

Seeing the tears in Stan's eyes, Harry was appalled by the horror of what he had done. And yet, he had to say this to himself, it had not seemed a horror to him before. It had simply been what he had done, unseen by others.

Pop came to see him, looking so old, so pale, so frail. "Don't worry," he said to Harry, his voice shaky, "We'll get you a lawyer. We're trying to get a second mortgage on the house."

"No, Pop, I won't let you do that," Harry said. "I am going to plead guilty. I don't need a lawyer. I'm going to accept my punishment, whatever they give me." That Pop should be the one who tried to comfort him, that he loved him and forgave him, caused Harry to feel even greater anguish at the shame he had brought upon him and Stan. Once again there came the thought that he was grateful Mom was no longer alive, that she didn't have to see this. If Mom were alive, would she have forgiven him? He remembered the sternness of her judgments, her insistence on following the Law absolutely.

He was benumbed by the thought of the Law. What Law? The Law that was about to punish him for his transgressions? The Law of courts and prosecutors and judges? Was that, too, absolute? He made a feeble joke to himself about looking for the absolute—the absolute alcohol—a joke that had been bandied about in the chem lab at Xavier. He didn't think it was funny anymore.

In the morning he awoke from a sound sleep to discover that he had decided to tell about others, as well as about himself. Once again, he was merely acquiescing to a decision that had been made beforehand. He proceeded to sift through the past as if he were on an archaeological dig, making grids in his mind to make sure he did not miss the smallest shard. One night, in his cell, as he was going over in his mind his visit to Albuquerque, he came across the image of the soldier's jacket hanging upon a peg in a room.

When he saw Gifford and Sutter next, he told them that he had remembered another contact, a soldier who had been stationed at Los Alamos. "What was his name?" Sutter asked.

"I can't remember what he said his name was. I'm sure it wasn't his real name. That wouldn't have been the way things were done." Then he told of having received the piece of paper with the crude drawing of a lens mold from the soldier, which he passed on to Y, who had said once it was very valuable and then the next time had said it didn't matter at all. A Jell-O box, yes, he remembered a Jell-O box, with the torn halves that had to be matched, and the phrase, "I come from—" but he could not for the life of him remember the name of the man he was supposed to come from. Joseph? James? Jesse?

Though he was a player in a drama, he did not feel himself dramatic. He was aware of no keen struggle; he was simply following a course in which he was giving information as precisely as possible. Fact followed fact. Before led to after. He wanted, he needed to get it right. He exhibited no self-pity, no self-recrimination, no rage, no rancor. He did not ask for a deal in return for information. The two FBI men listened and recorded, accepting what he said, as if they had no doubt about his honesty.

Now officialdom took over, and he was caught up in an inexorable progression of legal events, beginning with the arraignment. As he did not have legal counsel, Judge McGranery appointed John Hamilton, a lawyer highly respected in the community. "You should be grateful to have such a fine man represent you," the judge pointed out.

"I am, I am," Harry said.

A few days later Hamilton, accompanied by his assistant, Augustus Ballard, came to see Harry in jail. That these men, obviously from a world of wealth and privilege, a world that Harry had never had any contact with, spoke to him so kindly, knowing he had done what he had done, almost made Harry weep. Hamilton advised him that though he had indicated he was going to plead guilty, he must know that the only evidence against him was circumstantial. He wanted to discuss with Harry alternative possibilities for his defense.

Harry stopped him: "I want to plead guilty. I will plead guilty."

In that case, Hamilton announced, it would be his primary responsibility to do what he could to lighten the sentence. He would need to go over everything in detail with Harry, not only his life as a spy but also his family life, his childhood, his schooling, his work experience, and anything else he could remember in search of mitigating factors. He would also want the names of people who would be character references.

"I don't know," Harry said, shaking his head. "I don't feel right about asking anyone to talk about my character, when I deceived them so. I don't want to put anybody on the spot." Nevertheless, under Hamilton's proddings, he did give him several names, after being assured that none of them would be asked to testify on his behalf.

So the days of telling began all over again, though this time for a new audience, Hamilton and Ballard. Hearing himself say words he had said before to the FBI, he sensed the inherent danger in repetition. His words sounded like a refrain, a memory of what he had already remembered. He must not think that way, he told himself. He must only think of what had happened, as if it were happening again, in the present.

He had thought he was done with the FBI but they had not finished with him. After Harry had told Gifford and Sutter about the GI in Los Alamos, the FBI had tracked down three soldiers who were possible candidates, and after procuring photos of the three, they placed them before Harry. Harry was able to identify the man immediately. He was heavier than he had been, but his features were the same as the man he had seen in that room in that house in Albuquerque. At that moment Harry remembered the name of the man he was supposed to say had sent him with the torn half of the Jell-O box. It was Julius.

He was taken from the jail cell to court in chains. As he stepped out of the car, though he was surrounded by federal agents, the news photographers caught sight of him, and rushed over to take his picture. Blinded by the glare of the flashbulbs, he cast his eyes down. Then he heard screams and looked up. A crowd was pressing forward, people he'd never seen before. He was thrust out into them. He saw in the faces around him a flicker of something like disappointment. He heard a sigh, as if they had been waiting to see something huge, and before them was only an ordinary being. But then, they seemed to correct themselves, surging forward with renewed intensity, crying out. Once, in a silence in the darkness, he had heard another kind of cry, a calling out for help. Now he heard the word "Traitor," he heard the words, "Give the dirty Jew the death sentence." He felt spit upon his face.

Even as he listened in the wood-paneled chamber to the preparatory phrases, uttered in the driest of tones, he could still hear the screaming outside. The charge was presented by the prosecutor. A guilty plea was entered. He was allowed to present his written statement to the judge, detailing his offenses.

Back in his cell again, he kept seeing those faces in the crowd and hearing their cries. Their hatred and rage against him was beyond anything he had imagined. They wanted him dead. Yet he had never intended to harm them. He took up his pen. He opened his notebook to a blank page. In 1933, he explained, when he began his spying, so many people were poor, so many people were downtrodden, hopeless and without jobs, and discrimination was rampant, particularly against the Negroes. He had not believed that the country could change. That was his true failure, a failure of belief, he wrote.

Look at how different things are now, he went on. Look at the enormous number of people employed, look at how Social Security has guaranteed that old people won't starve, look at unemployment insurance and how it protects people if they lose their jobs. And look at all the houses being built that people with even low incomes can afford. Or take the question of discrimination: Who would have believed sixteen years ago that excellent ball players like Jackie Robinson, Larry Doby, Sam Jethroe, Roy Campanella, Don Newcombe, and Hank Thompson would have been accepted as players by the major leagues?

That night, awakening from confused dreams, he heard footsteps dying away in the corridor outside of his cell. There had been a time when he prided himself on his invisibility, even flaunted it. Now he wanted, he needed to be seen. In the darkness he got up from his cot and searched for his pen and his notebook. He turned to what he guessed was an empty page. If he had been allowed to have a flashlight, he could at least have seen what he was doing. He hoped he would be able to read his scribbling tomorrow. Whatever he had done, he wrote, he had never wanted another life elsewhere, only this life here. There was a wonderful free spirit in the U.S. that existed in no other place in the world. He gave examples of those things he cherished in American life, even some things that, he admitted, could be regarded as unimportant and even foolish. First there was his love of the sports in the U.S., of baseball and football and basketball. He named some of the great sports heroes he worshipped, Lefty Grove and Babe Ruth and Joe DiMaggio and Dizzy Dean. He listed entertainers he admired, starting out with Bing Crosby. He wrote of the pleasure he had taken in movies like *The Best Years of Our Lives*, and of his delight in comic strips such as *Steve Canyon*, and *Pogo*, and *L'il Abner*. Many of these things might seem of no great matter, he added, but as in the love of a man for a woman small things can come to stand for the large.

Staring in the dark at the words he had just written, he felt suddenly uneasy. What did he know of love between a man and a woman? The only episode of love for a woman in his life ended in disaster. His only marriage was imagined, on order.

He put the notebook and pen on the floor beside the cot, and lay on his back again. When he was writing the words, they had seemed so right. Now they seemed all wrong as if he had started writing for himself, but had ended writing a composition for another. The trouble was that he had accepted what he thought were his own thoughts, too easily. It was true that he had not believed enough and yet in another way he had always been too credulous. For example, when he had doubts about working with the Russians after Stalin signed the pact with Hitler, he had spoken to Sam. He had allowed himself to be persuaded, too easily, that Stalin's actions were justified. And now, what was he doing, but justifying himself and what he did, all too easily? He had not probed far enough. There was still more to be forced up, forced out of himself by more digging. He would unearth his every flaw, his every failure, judging himself as mercilessly as any court.

He turned on his side. He leaned down and picked up the notebook and the pen. He wrote that he had done what he had done because at his core was a being, hard, sharp, demanding, and willful.

He put the notebook and pen down. He turned on his back, stunned by the words he had written. He stared up into the dark ceiling. That being, at his core, was already verging on extinction. To try to recapture him was like trying to retrieve a memory of a dream after you wake up, you almost have it, it's almost there, but it's already slipping away, you try to grab at it, but it vanishes even as you pursue it further and further in . . .

B y FIVE MINUTES TO TEN on the morning of December 7, 1950, every seat in the courtroom was filled. Members of the public had waited in line for hours to be present at the sentencing of the man who had committed what FBI Director J. Edgar Hoover had called "The Crime of the Century."

The defendant was brought in, and the spectators turned to stare at him. They were familiar with the photograph, published in every newspaper, showing this small dark man handcuffed and head bowed. In the flesh, surrounded by others, he looked even smaller, his eyes and his full lips soft, his face so pale as to lack any depth or intensity. Seated in his chair at the defense table, he seemed to be receding.

When the door to the Judge's corridor opened, the Marshal called out, "All Rise!" Judge James P. McGranery, bulky in his black robe, entered and took his place on the raised bench. Seated once again, the onlookers watched and waited impatiently as the Judge leafed through some papers before him.

At a signal from the Judge, the Clerk announced: "United States of America versus Harry Gold. Is Harry Gold present?"

Defense attorney John D. M. Hamilton responded, "Ready."

"You may proceed," said the Judge.

Gerald A. Gleeson, the United States Attorney for the Eastern District of Pennsylvania, gave a brief statement, summarizing the facts from the viewpoint of the government.

When he concluded, John D. M. Hamilton rose to speak. Tall, white-haired and patrician, Hamilton addressed the Court in a formal, measured tone. On the table before him was a thick document, which he referred to now and then.

"May it please Your Honor, when Your Honor first approached me with the thought of representing the defendant in this case I was not at all unconscious of the work that would be entailed, and the offense which was charged violated every sense of obligation and duty of citizenship, as I saw it. At the same time I knew that I would undertake the defense, not only because the Constitution of the United States requires that every defendant shall have legal representation but centuries before that Constitution was written, the profession to which we belong had undertaken an obligation to society that no man, no matter what his status in life, no matter how grievous the charge with which he is confronted, should go without the benefit of counsel. That obligation on the part of the members of the bar has become a tradition. In my opinion it is one of the worthier traditions, not only of the bar, but of the processes of democracy as I understand it. That is the reason I stand at the bar of this Court today. I know the sentiments which I have expressed are also those of Mr. Ballard who has given unstintingly of his time to the work at hand.

"In approaching a case of this sort an attorney for the defendant must weigh his obligations from several angles. There is, of course, the obligation to the defendant to see that he is correctly advised, and Mr. Ballard and I have sought to do that in every way we know how. Fortunately, even at the time that Your Honor asked me to participate in this case, the defendant had made up his mind to plead guilty, so that we did not have the very serious decision to make as to whether or not that plea would be entered.

"There was, too, the question of the obligation to the Government in what might be exposed, and that has been seriously considered. Nothing will be said here today that will in any way impede the Government in the trials which are to be held or in its continuing investigations.

"As to the Court, I believe my duty can best be fulfilled by a revelation of all the pertinent facts. I shall do this dispassionately and without embellishment or exaggeration—and without any dramatics. In short, I come here to explain a crime and not to excuse one. I come here to state a case and not to plead one."

In his discussion of Harry Gold's relationships with the agents of the Soviet Union, Hamilton announced, he would go beyond the charges of the indictment, which were restricted to the Fuchs affair. "This sordid picture will be brought out in the full light of day in the thought it may illustrate how easily a man may become mired down in the intrigues of those who would seek the destruction of this country upon the basis of a false idealism.

"In an ordinary case, and particularly in a case where capital punishment may be the judgment of the Court, it is customary to bring before the court witnesses who may testify either as to character or to ameliorating circumstances. However, because of circumstances of this case and particularly because of the enormous publicity relating to it, I am assured in my own mind that if I were to call witnesses in this hearing they might well be subjected to ridicule or scorn. There are people who, through intolerance, or ignorance, or even viciousness, would someday point out these witnesses as men and women who attempted to aid a Communist agent. I will not therefore reveal the names of those who have had the courage in the interests of justice and fair play to give me facts or character statements. I ask Your Honor to be allowed to introduce what the witnesses would say of the character of the defendant, as if they were in this courtroom today."

"You can be assured, Mr. Hamilton," the Judge responded, "that you may conduct your side of this case as you see it, in the manner that you have arranged in your mind."

"Thank you, Your Honor. We are confronted here, not with a question of guilt—that is admitted. We are confronted with a question of motive, and of intent, and if I could find motive in greed, or avarice, or any of the baser qualities of men, this would be an easy case. If Harry Gold had received money as compensation for the work he did, this would be an easy case. But Harry Gold received no money from the Soviet Unioin other than a very partial and small reimbursement for expenses. So I cannot dispose of the case that easily.

"Factually, I think that Harry Gold's story started a good many years ago, in 1880, to be precise, when his mother, Cecilia Omanski, was born in a small village in the Ukraine of Russia, the sixteenth of seventeen children, to a poor Jewish carpenter. She was not only born into that family, but she was born in those Czarist days into poverty and persecution. She grew up a precocious child to whom the acquisition of knowledge and always more knowledge was an ever-recurring goal. One of the very few Jewish students who was permitted to enter the Kiev gymnasium, she graduated with honors, but further education was denied her because of her religion.

"There was one condition upon which she might have had the education she desired. If she would accept conversion to the Russian Orthodox Church the gates of higher education would be open, but Cecilia Omanski could not and would not abandon the religion of her fathers. She found work as a tailor's helper, and briefly joined with a group of others seeking to free the common people of Russia from Czarist rule. Apparently, at one time, she was interrogated and beaten by the secret police.

"Whether Cecilia Omanski tired of the struggle or found new ambitions, I do not know. In any event, shortly after the turn of the century, she went to Paris to study for a career as a dental technician. After a year or two her funds ran out and she was forced to give up her studies, seeking employment where she could find it. That opportunity came as a laborer in a tobacco factory in Bern, Switzerland.

"Samuel Gold, the father of the defendant, was also born near Kiev. The life into which he was born was—aside from common race and religion—as different from Cecilia Omanski's as is day from night. His father was a merchant of well-to-do circumstances. Samuel Gold must have known and felt social and political persecution, but he was not obliged to face poverty or the struggle for an education. If the schools were not open to him, that was of little real consequence, for his father provided tutors to make up any such deficiencies. There is little of the detail of his life in Russia that is relevant here. He served in the Russian army for several years and then his father bought his release from further service, which was a common practice in the conscripted armies of Europe. After his discharge from service he continued his studies and developed a marked aptitude for mathematics. This was such that in time his father entered him as a student in the Polytechnic Institute of Zurich, Switzerland.

"I must return now to one last phase of Samuel Gold's life in Russia. As he came into manhood the full force of the teachings of a great Russian were being felt not only there but throughout the world. It was during the last decade of the nineteenth century that Leo Tolstoy, son of a noble and wealthy family, forswore all material things, and in so doing developed a system of thought which emphasized simplicity of life, faith, love, the common brotherhood of man, and above all the dignity of human labor. None among the followers of Tolstoy took his teachings more seriously than Samuel Gold. In Switzerland, freed from the supervision and discipline of his father, Samuel Gold abandoned the career which had been laid out for him. Even though he knew that his course would mean a disruption of his family ties, he chose the way of Tolstoy and, refusing to enter the Polytechnic Institute, sought the life of those who labor with their hands. In time it came about that Cecilia Omanski and Samuel Gold met, and were married, and, in Bern on December 12, 1910, their first child was born—the man who stands before Your Honor for sentence.

"Upon their arrival in the U.S. in 1914 the Golds went first to Arkansas for a few weeks, then to Chicago for a month or so, and then moved to Philadelphia, where they settled permanently. I would say their surroundings were not all that anybody could wish for, but the Golds made the most of it. During these years the father did the best he could to get work, but his income was often sporadic. When he did work, the most he earned was eighteen dollars a week, on which the family barely managed to make ends meet.

"As far as I can determine, the Gold family, a father and mother and two sons, was a closely knit one. It was a family that was continually beset by the struggle for existence, but despite that there was not a single neighbor who was in need or in trouble who went unheeded by the Golds. I believe the mother was the dominating personality in the home. She must have been a very proud person, for she refused to take charity of any kind. She had a saying, 'If we have no money, we don't eat,' and there were a good many times when the Golds did not eat.

"I am not trying to picture to Your Honor a life of persecution because I do not think that is a fact. Rather Harry Gold, who was rather sickly—puny, is what his associates say—took to a rather monastic life in that he withdrew from a lot of the activities you would find in other boys. He became a prodigious reader, and during his school days, which started at Sharwood, he undertook to help others in doing their work, not only in their daily studies but in assigned school tasks, such as writing compositions and essays. This willingness to help others became, and I think I shall demonstrate it to Your Honor, a dominating characteristic of Harry Gold's later life.

"The facts which I have given to Your Honor are homely facts, but I think they are material. A minute ago I said I was not trying to paint a picture of persecution, and no more am I trying to paint a picture of a life of frustration, because, as far as I can understand the defendant, he has no feeling or sense of bitterness towards any persons or towards society as a whole. I have related these facts to demonstrate that in the earliest years of Harry Gold's life he was thrown into intimate contact with poverty and discouragement, and it is perfectly logical and a sequitur of his life that in time there would be engendered in him a sympathy for people in poverty, and for those who had suffered discouragement and were in want."

Returning to the defendant's history, Hamilton noted that he graduated from high school third in a class of one hundred and sixty. "However, because of the family circumstances, he was unable to pursue that education in science which he so desired. Instead he helped supplement the family income by taking a job gluing small parts to ship models, working six days a week from seven A.M. to five-thirty P.M. for ten dollars a week.

"In January 1929 he was hired at Franklin Chemical, nominally as a laboratory assistant, but in actuality his duties were mainly janitorial. Each week a portion of the money that the defendant earned was put in a fund for his education by his mother, and by September 1930, there was sufficient money for him to take leave from his job and matriculate at the University of Pennsylvania. However, as the Depression deepened, his father lost his job, and the family was left without any income. At this point the defendant voluntarily withdrew from the university and went back to his job at the chemical company. He was at this point the sole support of his family.

"Now, if Your Honor please, I want to digress from the chronology of Harry Gold's life to direct Your Honor's attention to certain facts which appear and reappear so consistently in his life that I think they may be considered as definite characteristics of the man himself.

"I have previously mentioned that the defendant as early as his grammar school days helped others in their studies and this practice continued throughout his life. In high school he spent long hours tutoring other boys in math and science. While working at Franklin Chemical, he tutored many fellow employees who were taking technical courses and had difficulty with assignments. Nor would he accept money for this tutoring. Harry Gold was doing this on days when he was working from eight in the morning until eight at night. He was still doing it later in his career when, working twelve hours a day, he took courses at Drexel Institute and was obliged to prepare his own work in the little time that was left to him.

"As further evidence of his character, I want to read to Your Honor from an astounding statement signed by five eminent medical researchers at the Heart Station, where he was working at the time of his arrest: 'Mr. Gold never measured time by hours, but by the tasks to be done. The time he gave not only exceeded all normal standards, but also exceeded the time which might be expected of a conscientious research worker. He was ready and willing to do anything asked of him, irrespective of the inconvenience or the length of time required. If an experiment required that it be started at three o'clock in the morning, he was there and remained there until it was completed. During the transit strike in Philadelphia in 1949, he proposed that he sleep at the clinic in order that he might be available, and this he did.'

"There is a further aspect of this man's character which is mentioned again and again by those who knew him: his willingness to help others in need of money, when he himself had little. I am not talking of an occasional instance. I am talking of what went on time after time, day in and day out. He has been described by one of his immediate associates as being the most generous person he has ever known, by still another as a gentle person who would give you the shirt off his back.

"I want to refer again to the joint statement I mentioned a minute ago: 'In his relationships with the personnel of the Heart Station and with the hospital generally, he was as unselfish as he was in carrying on his work. He was solicitous to the point of fault. He loaned money not only to those with whom he was associated, but to employees who were strangers to him. Upon one occasion at least in making such a loan he was asked by one of his associates if he had any assurance the money would ever be returned to him and his reply was that it was unimportant whether he got it back or not. Under no circumstance would he ever remind anyone of their indebtedness to him and it was almost embarrassing to return borrowed money to him because of his reticence in accepting it.'

"If what I have said here to Your Honor of the kindnesses of Harry Gold to his fellow men, as manifested upon so many occasions, makes it seem that I am gilding the lily, then I want to add a statement of my own: I say to Your Honor, after forty years of association with men—and I am testifying now—Harry Gold is the most extraordinarily selfless person I have ever met in my life."

When Hamilton paused, there was a murmur in the courtroom, whispered asides from the observers: *What's he trying to do, make him out to be a saint? The man was an easy touch, that's what he was. Is that any reason to let him off easy?*

Imperturbably Hamilton leafed through the document on the table before him and went on. "In the fall of 1932 Harry Gold, the sole support of his family, lost his job. For weeks he continued to search for work as the family's situation became desperate. At this most hopeless moment, through the sudden and unexpected assistance of a friend of a friend, a chemist in Jersey City, the defendant found work in a laboratory there. I think Your Honor will have to appreciate, because it is very necessary that you should, the gratitude that Harry Gold felt toward his benefactor, Dave White.

"Over the following weeks, the two men became close friends and spent many hours together. In time White began to tell a story to Harry Gold, the gist of which was that there was a great number of people in the country who were out of work and suffering, and that the capitalistic system had failed to meet the problems of the masses of people the world over—I am summarizing—Your Honor will know that—and that the only way of life which could deal with the distress of the masses was communism. I speak of communism as an ideology at this point and not as a political party.

"In time White admitted that he was a Communist and he tried to get Harry Gold to go to Party meetings. In fact, the defendant went to two of them and he found them about the drabbest affairs he had ever been to in his life. In any event, he never joined the Communist Party.

"Finally, in 1933, as times began to look better, Harry Gold heard that he could go back to work at Franklin Chemical, and he did go back, as an assistant chemist. The friendship with White continued, and White made several visits to Philadelphia over time. Then came the day when the chemist visited the defendant and asked him to provide technical information to the Russians, specifically copies of blueprints of machin-

ery, operating records, and laboratory reports from the company where he
was employed.

"Now, if Your Honor please, the profession to which we belong does
not explore the human mind with any scientific precision, but we live in
a world of commonplace reactions. And I submit to Your Honor that at
that moment Gold's answer was inevitable. What else would one expect
of a boy whose mother's hopes for an education had been dashed in
Czarist Russia, who as a young woman had joined with others to fight
against injustice and persecution, and whose philosophy of life was based
on the injunction that one must help one's fellow men? What else would
one expect of a boy whose father had adopted the beliefs of Tolstoy as to
the brotherhood of man? What else would one expect of a boy who at
twenty-three had suffered more discouragements and more disillusion-
ments that the average American boy knows in a lifetime. I repeat to Your
Honor that when one weighs the factors involved realistically and not
upon theories it was inevitable Harry Gold should accede to the proposal
made by his friend and benefactor—and he did just that. Just as inevitably
he had charted the course which brings him to this bar today."

Once again there was a stirring in the courtroom. Now some of the
spectators seemed angry. It showed in the stiffness of their leaning forward, in the tension of their jawbones, in a barely audible sound, a quick
indrawn breath, a sharp exhalation like contempt. *Inevitable means that
man didn't have a choice. But he had a choice. He didn't need to do what
he did.*

After turning over several pages in the document before him,
Hamilton proceeded with his statement. He spoke in detail of the industrial secrets the defendant had obtained for the Russians; he described the
defendant's meeting with Russian agents at odd hours and at out of the
way places. "The Soviet practice was to abruptly replace one agent with
another. They came and went like evil wraiths, dissolving into the fog and
mist of intrigue as suddenly and as inexplicably as they had appeared.

"One agent gave the defendant the assignment of recruiting others
to work with the Soviets. He made one sorry attempt at recruiting and
then went into a process or procedure that would be amusing if it were
not, in my opinion, tragic. Harry Gold began feeding his Soviet agent
fictitious names, any number of them; he furnished a list of names and

addresses purporting to be those upon whom he was working. This conduct on his part only spells out one thing to me. Although the defendant had not passed one piece of information that had to do with the national defense, he was already so involved and so fearful of these people that he did not dare cross their wishes.

"In any event, he kept on supplying fictitious names, and during this period, he also furnished plans, specifications, and procedures for obtaining carbon dioxide from flue gases. That too is simply an industrial process, for carbon dioxide has no more sinister use, if Your Honor please, than the preparation of refrigerants and the operation of such things as soda fountains.

"Now I come to 1938. Having graduated from Drexel with a diploma in chemical engineering, in the spring of 1938, when he judged that his family was no longer dependent on his salary to make ends meet, the defendant applied to a number of colleges. He notified his Soviet contact of his intentions, and the agent at first objected. Then suddenly, he encouraged him, when he discovered that he was considering applying to Xavier University. The defendant applied to Xavier and he was accepted.

"The period of Harry Gold's stay at Xavier was probably the happiest period of his life. The Fathers and instructors of the university were sympathetic with a man who had struggled as Gold had for an education. For instance, when it was apparent that he was deficient in mathematics, one of his instructors arranged for a regular period in calculus at six o'clock in the morning so that this deficiency might be overcome. At Xavier he could work to his heart's content with men rooted in the sciences, who like himself knew no hours and who gave him encouragement at every step of the way."

In his own investigation, Hamilton said, he had received six replies from the faculty of Xavier about the defendant. "Not a single letter contained an adverse criticism as to the defendant's record as a student or as to his general character. It is necessary, I think, to refer to some of these letters, in fairness to the defendant, though I do not want to be laborious.

"One letter from a member of the administrative staff who was a student with Gold reads: 'I was acquainted with Harry Gold when I was in attendance at Xavier University. Xavier at that time was a school of less than six-hundred students and it is not difficult to recall an individual. I remember Mr. Gold as an intelligent person who seemed eager to learn and as a result applied himself to his school work more than the average student . . ."

"A second letter contains this statement: 'I was in frequent contact with Gold when he was on this campus. Among undergraduate students, there are some who impress one by their quiet conduct and seriousness of purpose. Harry Gold was one of those . . .

"And finally, an instructor wrote: 'It seems to me that through the years the memory of him has stayed with me in an exceptional way. In fact I should say that he is one of the half-dozen men who have most impressed me in twenty-one years of teaching. He was brilliant. He thought carefully and intelligently. He had, because he was older than the students we were accustomed to dealing with, a maturity that of itself was most welcome. He also possessed a suavity of manner which marked him as far above the average man . . .'"

"In the course of Mr. Gleeson's talk, Your Honor, he mentioned that during the time Mr. Gold was at Xavier, he sought to recruit a man who was employed in the aeronautical research laboratories of the United States at Dayton, Ohio. I object to that term. The man involved had already had some associations with the Soviet Union."

Hamilton related how the defendant was summoned by a Soviet agent to a meeting on Thanksgiving Day, 1938, and told that unless he did what he was told in connection with the man in Dayton, a letter would be sent to the Fathers of Xavier informing them that he was a Soviet agent.

"Mr. Gold has told me in numerous conferences that this was the only time he was ever threatened, and that from that time on, whatever happened after the fall of '38, he was a free agent. I do not suppose that it is the province of an attorney to disagree with a client, but I doubt that he was a free agent, realistically speaking. Your Honor and I know that there are many people in this world who are under the complete domination of others, but who through a desire to maintain their independence, deny that domination or do not realize it. It is my opinion that from that time on Harry Gold was in the position of the victim who has paid his first bit of blackmail.

"In any event, Harry Gold graduated magna cum laude from Xavier University with a degree in Chemical Engineering. Immediately afterward, he returned to Philadelphia where he was once again employed by

Franklin Chemical, but in a more responsible job. Following a hiatus, he was again contacted by the Russians."

After a detailed summary of the defendant's subsequent assignments, including his work with Sid Roth on Buna-S, Hamilton came to a stopping-point. "May I ask Your Honor's pleasure as to the recess?"

"Surely. Did you have any preference as to the time, Mr. Hamilton?"

"No, I am quite prepared to go on."

As there was no objection from the United States Attorney, Hamilton continued. "In early February, 1944, the defendant met Klaus Fuchs for the first time."

Now, thought the spectators, *we are coming to the core of the matter. Now it will be said straight out what the true offense was: Our secret—the secret that belonged only to us—the secret weapon that ended the war—has been stolen from us. It has been revealed by this man to the Russians, and, because of him, we are now in jeopardy.* They felt an urgent need to get to the judgment, as if the judgment would serve as protection as well as revenge.

Yet there was still more to be said before the judgment could be pronounced. Hamilton told of the subsequent meetings with Fuchs in New York. He told of Klaus Fuchs not showing up at a meeting in July, and of not keeping the alternative engagement, and of the defendant's going to see Klaus Fuch's sister and leaving an envelope for Klaus Fuchs with her. He told of the defendant's meeting with Klaus Fuchs in Boston in winter, and of his two crucial meetings with him in Santa Fe, in June 1945 and in September 1945.

"Your Honor will recall that between the June meeting and this night in September the Alamagordo test had been made on July 16th and also bombs had been dropped at Hiroshima and Nagasaki. Information was passed on both occasions." At this point Hamilton stopped and reminded the Court that he was limited in what he could say about the information, as there were national security issues involved.

"In the weeks which followed his arrest, the defendant has given every possible assistance to the government in unraveling the whole sordid picture of which he was but a small part. No doubt there are those who will cynically observe he has done this to save his own neck. I can only answer this in conclusion by stating that I do not agree. On this score the court should be informed there has not been the slightest attempt at bargaining by any of the parties involved. I believe that the defendant's confessions have come from a man who seeks to make such amends as are within his power to make. I think it is just as simple as that and nothing more.

"Through the defendant's efforts and cooperation, new channels have been opened up which will permit those charged with the national security to better carry out their tasks. By reason of his testimony, men and women who would undermine our security have been put under surveillance or subjected to arrest and indictment.

"As to the question of sentencing, it seems to me Your Honor cannot possibly arrive at a proper sentence in this case unless the part played by the defendant in the machinations of the Soviet agents is factually defined and brought into perspective. The prosecution has made him out to be the chief Soviet spy, but that is not so. The defendant was but a messenger boy and not an indispensable one at that, and no amount of cloak and dagger atmosphere can change his role."

Hamilton quoted from the language of the indictment: "Harry Gold and his confederates conspired to transmit information relating to the national defense 'with intent and reason to believe that it would be used to the advantage of a foreign nation, to wit, the Union of Soviet Socialist Republics.' I must reiterate that there is not even an implication in the indictment of any intent to injure the United States, and I give it as my judgment that had there been such a charge the government would have been met with a failure of proof.

"Fairness to the defendant alone would require an exploration of the atmosphere which existed in this country during the period of Harry Gold's relationship with the agents of Soviet Russia. During the period of Harry Gold's earlier activities from 1935 to 1939, many Americans looked to Russia as the one active force which stood in opposition to Nazism. A substantial majority of our people had the friendliest of feelings and sympathy for Soviet Russia. Undoubtedly that feeling suffered a setback when Russia entered into an alliance with Germany in August 1939, and also when it invaded Finland three months later. But any who had doubts as to their Russian sympathies by reason of these events were not obliged to entertain these doubts for any great length of time, for in June 1941 Russia and Germany were at war, and once again the pro-Russian sentiment was running at full tide in the United States. In the struggle to defeat Nazism and its counterparts the world over, Soviet

Russia was not only an ally but it was the subject of sympathy and admiration wherever free people congregated.

"Today public opinion has changed. Russia is now considered a ruthless enemy in every sense other than that of open warfare. The human mind—prone to wipe out the past in its contemplation of the present—forgets that five short years ago Russia was a respected ally. None of us can be unaffected by the tide of recent events, but I know also that this matter cannot be approached with judicial reason unless the passions and indignations of today are momentarily put behind us. I submit that reason and justice require the gravity of Harry Gold's offenses and the motive in which they were carried out shall not be weighed in the temper of these times but as they would have been weighed had he come before Your Honor for sentence at the time they were committed.

"The determination of the sentence to be imposed is entirely within Your Honor's discretion. But in the exercise of that discretion it is customary for a sentencing judge to give consideration to certain factors. In the entire legal history of the United States no man has ever suffered capital punishment for even high treason at the bar of a civil tribunal." He noted that none of the sentences that had been meted out to Fuchs and others involved in the conspiracy had been more than fifteen years.

"From what has gone before, my client is assured that the final pronouncement of this court will be marked with every consideration of law and justice. Your Honor may remember I said in my opening that I was here to state a case and not to plead one; thus in what has been said there has been no plea for mercy. I conceive that if as written in the Psalms mercy and truth are met together, so must mercy meet with justice and become a part of it. If then we find mercy in justice—knowing justice will be done—Harry Gold will find mercy in the judgment of this court as should be his due."

After a recess, Gleeson rose to make a brief statement for the government. "The whole history of this man," he said, "down to and including 1945, is a history of contempt for lawfully constituted authority.

"There was one great opportunity to change his mode of thinking and his attitude toward the authority of his Government and the authority of his superiors. He was accepted in the fall of 1938 into Xavier

University. Now, yes, it may be true that in those years from 1933 to 1938, when he was nibbling at communism, so to speak, and nibbling at communistic ideas, and breaking bread with people who were intent on advancing the interest of a foreign government and a foreign ideology, yes, it may be true that in those years he was an impressionable young man, and having come from a background that Mr. Hamilton has described, his heart went out to the suffering masses. All of that may be true, but comes the fall of 1938, he goes into Xavier University. The fact that he belongs to a different faith from the authorities of that university does not stop him from enjoying its privileges. The university is part of a great worldwide institution that has met the challenge of communism, and has never receded for one moment from that position. Here was a chance for soul searching, here was a chance for this man to do some meditation, here was a chance for this man to get himself straightened out mentally and spiritually, here was a chance for him to throw off the influence of all those shadowy, tawdry, melodramatic figures who came in and out of the night of his life in the years before the fall of 1938. Here was his opportunity to set himself straight. And what did he do? While in the very hallowed walls of the university itself he is yielding, yielding to an influence to make a contact at Wright Field in Dayton. Whether the contact was successful or unsuccessful is not important, but whether or not this man tried to make that contact is.

"Now it is true, and it has been very, very ably said by his counsel that he has cooperated with the Government, that he has given us information that perhaps otherwise we would not have been able to get, and therefore he is entitled to the consideration of this Court, no doubt about that. I have no hesitancy in saying to Your Honor that that is a properly expressed view, but let me say this to Your Honor, the question is not what some court in England did in the Klaus Fuchs case. Each case must stand on its own feet in this or any other court.

"Now the Attorney General of the United States had before him the relative importance of this man in the whole scheme of things, and he has made a considered recommendation, and when I say 'considered,' I mean he has considered all of the aspects. And I say to this Court, the recommendation of the Attorney General of the United States with respect to the punishment of this man is that he suffer imprisonment for a period of twenty-five years."

Judge McGranery then thanked Mr. Gleeson for his cooperation with the Court. "I am, of course, very happy to have the recommendation of the Department of Justice. I would like to say that all Americans have a proper pride in the Federal Bureau of Investigation. The skillful and intelligent conduct of the matter now before the Court adds luster to the record of the FBI, long recognized for its fidelity, bravery, integrity, and its advanced techniques of inquiry.

"I think it is very important for me to say that a view has gone abroad that this case was first exposed by Fuchs. That is not true. This matter was uncovered by the FBI, and Fuchs, as I understand it, had never cooperated in any way, shape or form with the FBI until after the arrest of Harry Gold. Am I correct in that?"

In response, FBI Agent T. Scott Miller, Jr., who had previously been sworn in, confirmed that the identification of Harry Gold's picture by Fuchs was not made until after Gold signed a confession.

"May I ask you," said Judge McGranery, "to convey to Director Hoover the commendation of the court for a tremendous task well done. I do feel now that I would like to reflect and will reflect on the summary and recommendations made. I want to dispose of the matter quickly, and with your indulgence I will do it Saturday morning at eleven o'clock. I will pass formal sentence at that time."

On Saturday at eleven, when the Court reconvened, the Judge asked the defendant if he cared to make a statement.

"If Your Honor please—," the defendant said.

"You may move to the bar of the Court, if you will."

The spectators saw a small man, an insignificant-looking man, a forgettable man, move forward. They were already in the process of forgetting him.

He spoke of his gratitude to Mr. Hamilton and to Mr. Ballard. He said that he had been given the most scrupulously fair trial and treatment that could have been desired, by the Court and by all of the investigative agencies. He stated that the most tormenting of all his thoughts concerned "the fact that those who meant so much to me have been most besmirched by my deeds. I refer here to this country, to my family and friends, to my former classmates at Xavier University and to the Jesuits there, and to the people at the Heart Station of the Philadelphia General Hospital. There is a puny inadequacy about any words telling how deep and horrible is my remorse."

When the judgment was pronounced, it was not the death penalty, nor was it the sentence of twenty-five years requested by the prosecution: It was thirty years. The *New York Times* reported that "The defendant heard the penalty without any sign of emotion."

Shortly afterward he was moved from Philadelphia to the Tombs Prison in New York, to await the espionage trial of Julius and Ethel Rosenberg, David Greenglass, and Morton Sobell.

In March 1951 he was taken to the federal courthouse in Foley Square in lower Manhattan to be a witness for the prosecution. When he took his place on the witness stand, he was questioned about his espionage activities for the Soviet Union. Speaking, according to *Time*, "as precisely and matter-of-factly as a high-school teacher explaining a problem in geometry," he supplied the details of his work for the Soviet Union from the spring of 1935 until his arrest in May 1950. He gave evidence about his visit to Albuquerque in June 1945 to the apartment of the soldier David Greenglass and his wife. He spoke of the five hundred dollars he paid to Greenglass in return for the handwritten sheets about the lens mold. He recalled bringing "greetings from Julius." When he completed his testimony, Emanuel Bloch, the attorney for the Rosenbergs, arose and said he would not cross-examine the witness.

In his final summation for the defense, Bloch insisted that what Gold said had not connected his clients directly to Soviet espionage. He justified his decision not to cross-examine Gold with these words to the jury: "I didn't ask him one question because there is no doubt in my mind that he impressed you as he impressed everybody that he was telling the absolute truth."

After his testimony was concluded, he was transferred to the federal penitentiary at Lewisburg. There he was assigned to work in the hospital laboratory. In addition to training prisoners as medical technicians, he was deeply involved in research work, including a glucose tolerance study for the U.S. Public Health Service and a study on jaundice. In 1966 he was paroled and he returned to Philadelphia to live with his brother and his father, now blind and confined to bed. Almost immediately he was employed as Chief Biochemist at the John F. Kennedy Memorial Hospital, where he was also put in charge of training medical technicians.

By 1972, his heart condition having seriously deteriorated, he was hospitalized. Open heart surgery was recommended as the only procedure which could prolong his life. He died on the operating table on August 26.

At his death the students in the medical technician program established the Harry Gold Memorial Fund in appreciation of his selfless and untiring devotion to their needs.

LEE COUNTY LIBRARY
107 Hawkins Ave.
Sanford, NC 27330